PUFFIN BOOKS

WEREWORLD

RAGE OF LIONS

Praise for *Wereworld: Rise of the Wolf*:

'. . . excellent new series' – *SFX*

'. . . superior to *Eragon*, and pure fun' – *The Times*

'The most exciting fantasy story I have read for years,
Wereworld had me enthralled from the first page until the
very last, leaving me hungry for the next instalment'
– *bookzone4boys.blogspot.com*

'Incredibly highly recommended – dramatic escapes,
incredible rescues, huge battles, terrible betrayals, human
sacrifices, and all of it feels perfect!' – *thebookbag.co.uk*

'A fantastic blend of action-adventure, with a great sprinkling
of horror-magic stirred in' – *mrripleysenchantedbooks.blogspot.com*

'*Wereworld* is a brilliant adventure story that keeps
you utterly hooked. I can't wait for the next one!'
– *wondrousreads.com*

Shortlisted for the 2011 Waterstone's Children's Book Prize

The designer of *Bob the Builder*, creator of *Frankenstein's Cat* and *Raa Raa the Noisy Lion*, and the author/illustrator of numerous children's books, Curtis Jobling lives with his family in Cheshire, England. Although perhaps best known for his work in TV and picture books, Curtis's other love has always been horror and fantasy for an older audience. *Wereworld: Rise of the Wolf* was shortlisted for the 2011 Waterstone's Children's Book Prize.

www.curtisjobling.com

Explore Wereworld if you dare at
www.wereworldbooks.com

Books by Curtis Jobling
The Wereworld series *(in reading order)*

Rise of the Wolf

Rage of Lions

WEREWORLD

RAGE OF LIONS

CURTIS JOBLING

PUFFIN

For Mark and Karen, my brother and twin:
it's always about the siblings

PUFFIN BOOKS

Published by the Penguin Group
Penguin Books Ltd, 80 Strand, London WC2R ORL, England
Penguin Group (USA) Inc., 375 Hudson Street, New York, New York 10014, USA
Penguin Group (Canada), 90 Eglinton Avenue East, Suite 700, Toronto, Ontario, Canada M4P 2Y3
(a division of Pearson Penguin Canada Inc.)
Penguin Ireland, 25 St Stephen's Green, Dublin 2, Ireland (a division of Penguin Books Ltd)
Penguin Group (Australia), 250 Camberwell Road, Camberwell, Victoria 3124, Australia
(a division of Pearson Australia Group Pty Ltd)
Penguin Books India Pvt Ltd, 11 Community Centre, Panchsheel Park, New Delhi – 110 017, India
Penguin Group (NZ), 67 Apollo Drive, Rosedale, Auckland 0632, New Zealand
(a division of Pearson New Zealand Ltd)
Penguin Books (South Africa) (Pty) Ltd, 24 Sturdee Avenue, Rosebank, Johannesburg 2196, South Africa

Penguin Books Ltd, Registered Offices: 80 Strand, London WC2R ORL, England

puffinbooks.com

First published 2011
001 – 10 9 8 7 6 5 4 3 2 1

Text and images copyright © Curtis Jobling, 2011
All rights reserved

The moral right of the author/illustrator has been asserted

Set in 11.5/15.5 pt Bembo Book MT Std
Typeset by Palimpsest Book Production Limited, Falkirk, Stirlingshire
Printed in Great Britain by Clays Ltd, St Ives plc

Except in the United States of America, this book is sold subject to the condition that it shall not, by way of trade
or otherwise, be lent, re-sold, hired out, or otherwise circulated without the publisher's prior consent in any form
of binding or cover other than that in which it is published and without a similar condition including this condition
being imposed on the subsequent purchaser

British Library Cataloguing in Publication Data
A CIP catalogue record for this book is available from the British Library

ISBN: 978–0141–33340–3

www.greenpenguin.co.uk

Acknowledgements

Prior to the publication of *Wereworld: Rise of the Wolf*, I was utterly unaware of the huge online community of reviewers and book-bloggers who shared their love of reading with one another across the Internet. As the first novel was released, its success in no small parts was aided by the support of these bloggers, as they championed *Wereworld* from the start. I'm no doubt going to forget a few of you guys, but it simply wouldn't be right to see *Rage of Lions* on the shelves of bookshops without mentioning you at the beginning. Apologies if I miss anyone!

Thanks to Dave Brendon, Liz Hyder, Bonnie Sparks, Carly Bennett, Liz, Mark and Sarah (*My Favourite Books*), Vincent (*Mr Ripley's Enchanted Books*), Darren (*The Book Zone*), Jenny (*Wondrous Reads*), Sya (*Mountains of Instead*), Matt Imrie (*Teen Librarian*), Emma (*Asamum Booktopia*), Melissa (*Spellbound by Books*), Robert (*The Bookbag/YA Yeah Yeah*), Sophie (*So Little Time for Books*), Cheryl (*Madhouse Family Reviews*), lovely Lucy (*Scribble City Central*), Danielle (*Alpha Reader*), horror Holly (*Spinechills*), Caroline (*Portrait of a Woman*), Claire (*Cem's Book Hideout*), Becky (*The Bookette*), Michelle (*Clover Hill Book Reviews*), Alisa (*Cry Havoc Reviews*), *The Slowest Bookworm*, *Mostly Reading YA*, *Nayu's Reading Corner*, *Gripped into Books*, *Girls Without a Bookshelf*, *Books of Amber*, *The Book Rabbit*, *Empire of Books*, *Books for Keeps* and all the gang at *Spinebreakers*.

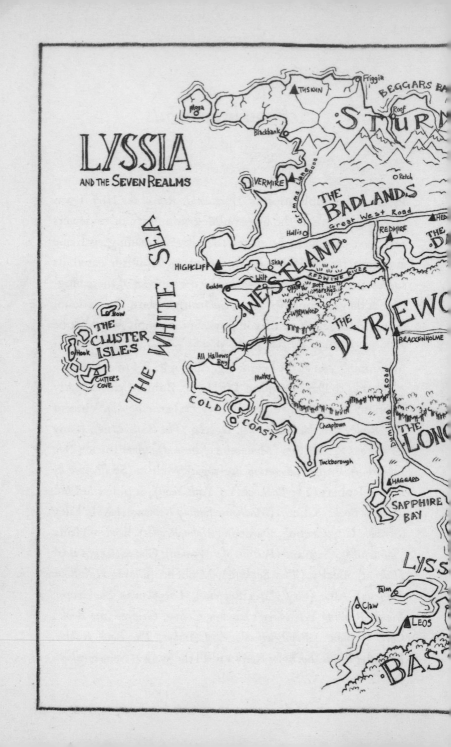

Contents

Prologue: Outrider

As the bells of Brenn's Temple rang out, the young man rose
from his chair and looked out over the Tall Quarter of the
city of Highcliff. From his lofty vantage point he might have
seen all of Westland's capital sprawling out before him, but
for the dark clouds that filled the night sky. The moon was
obscured, just as they'd predicted. The third chime that marked
the hour was his signal to go. Picking up his backpack from
the foot of his bed he checked it over once more. A thin bedroll
was stowed in the bottom. Reaching a hand into the folds of
material he felt around, his fingertips searching until they
connected with the hard edge of the scroll case. Content, he
removed his hand, patted the bedroll down and strapped the
pack tightly shut.

He double-checked his weapon belt once more, tugging
the buckle tight and shifting his scabbard around his left hip.

The sword hilt and pommel, wrapped in dirty cloth, disappeared into the dark recesses of his cloak as he hefted the backpack over his shoulders. Stepping up to the window he deftly lifted the latch before swinging it out. Cool night air rolled in, the smell of the sea riding on the wind up from the Low Quarter. The streets were empty, although those avenues closer to Highcliff Keep glittered with torchlight. The encampment of military tents surrounding the castle effectively cordoned it off from the rest of the city under the watchful eye of Lord Bergan and his allies. The man glanced down – two floors below the creaking wooden sign of The Halfway House inn swung to and fro in the breeze. If he were to slip it would be a swift plummet to the cobbles four storeys down and doubtless death.

The man reached up over his head and took a firm grip on the guttering. Turning his back to the street he stood on the window ledge before hauling himself up to the roof. A dozen buildings separated him from the stables, with a handful of alleys and treacherous drops added for good measure. He set off, staying low and hugging the shadows. Up one slope and skidding down the next, each of his steps threatened to dislodge a shingle and send it crashing to the cobbles. Guards had patrolled the streets every evening since the uprising, ensuring the curfew was maintained and nobody but the military was out after dark. As he approached a gap in the rooftops he didn't slow to look down – if he had he might have had second thoughts. Instead he flung himself across the gap, landing with as much grace as his frantic heart allowed.

On only one occasion did he see any of the City Watch,

but worse luck it was on the street corner nearest the stable block. At such a late hour they were quite relaxed, chatting as they walked the quieter avenues of the Tall Quarter. According to the Lord Protector, the curfew was simply a precaution in case hostilities recommenced. It was a good way for the allies' men to keep their attention focused on the deposed King Leopold the Lion now beseiged in Highcliff Keep without the distractions that the daytime brought. There was nothing for them to fear at their backs and consequently the further one moved away from the centre of the city, the slacker security became. Four weeks of relative inactivity since the uprising had led the Lord Protector's men to think that the battle was won. Nevertheless, the gates remained locked through the night, while by day they were heavily manned. Rumour had it that the guards had arrested at least thirty of the Lionguard who had tried to slip away from the city in the crowds, and that they now languished in the cells of Traitors' House, awaiting trial.

The young man watched as the soldiers moved on. He counted thirty breaths before trusting his life to the rusty drainpipe that snaked down to the street below. Dropping the last few feet he ducked back into the shadows, glancing up and down the street to make sure nobody was about. The stables backed on to Hammergate, one of the smallest entrances into Highcliff, traditionally used by the wealthier merchants who wanted to avoid the congested Mucklegate and Kingsgate. It cost a few bronze more to enter Highcliff via Hammergate, and consequently many of the townhouses in the Tall Quarter were home to Westland's most successful citizens. The man looked at the stables, lips dry with anticipation. There was bound to be a good horse or two to choose from in there.

Having scouted Hammergate thoroughly over the last two days he knew exactly what to expect here. Indeed he'd chanced coming out over the rooftops the previous night to see what the numbers were like. Two soldiers manned the gate after dark, and they'd remained in their guardhouse for most of this time, stepping out only once to speak with their colleagues as they passed on patrol. The stable block was right beside the gate, making access directly from it and out of Hammergate relatively simple. If the gate was open. If . . .

Scampering across the street, the man hit the shadows on the opposite side, on the corner of the stable block that was hidden from the guardhouse. He glanced round the corner. Low voices and laughter could be heard from behind the glowing window of the guardhouse. Bending low once more he slipped round the corner and up to the gate. It was pitch-black in the gate alcove, but he could just make out the wooden beam that held the gate shut. Taking hold of it he lifted it from its moorings and slid it back into the wall until one of the gates was free. He held his breath all the while, heart thundering as he listened for the guards, but their easy banter continued unabated. He eased the left hand gate forward and it swung smoothly on its hinges to a point that was wide enough for him, and a horse, to get through.

Backing away, the young man disappeared into the stable block. Stalls lined the walls on either side, the gentle sounds of horses moving lightly in their sleep emanating from each of them. He looked quickly into the stalls as he passed, left and right, trying to find a likely candidate. Halfway down the corridor he did a double take – there was a chestnut brown thoroughbred, the kind favoured by the cavalry. Stabled up here it no doubt belonged to a merchant's courier. The decision was too easy.

Lifting the latch he slipped inside. The horse started at the stranger's presence. He stepped up and smoothed his hands over the animal's neck and back, quickly putting it at ease.

'Good girl,' he whispered, bringing his face round to hers and blowing on her nose. She seemed lively, which would also be good. It had been so long since he'd worked with a horse that he found himself smiling. He reached in front and began to untether her from a stone ring that held her close to the wall. As he was distracted he didn't notice the rising glow of lamplight behind him.

'Who are you?'

He turned quickly, but it was too late to hide. An old man stood in the doorway, a hooded lantern held up so he could better see the intruder.

'I'm Goodman Wake's courier,' he said, thinking quickly. He squinted into the light, unable to fully make out the old man's features. 'Just come to check on my horse.'

'Never heard of no Goodman Wake, and I'm sure as houses that ain't your mare.' He stepped closer, moving the lantern forward. 'You know there's a curfew on, don't you, boy?'

There was no time for games. He moved quickly, instinctively. Reaching into his cloak, he withdrew his sword and the stable-hand staggered backwards. The old man swung the lantern defensively and the metal casing caught on the swaddled pommel, tearing free the material that covered it. As the cloth fluttered to the ground there was no mistaking the Lionshead that shone in the lantern light, golden and roaring. The old man opened his mouth to cry out and the attacker moved fast, swinging the sword round and bashing him across the temple with the pommel. A ragged gash appeared across his brow as he tumbled to the ground.

The young man had to work fast. He snatched down a saddle and threw it over the horse's back, hastily tightening the girth.

'Sorry,' he said to the prone stable-hand as he stepped over him, the horse following and doing likewise.

Once out of the stall he hauled himself up into the saddle with ease.

'Stop him!' cried the old man, recovering his wits enough to see what was happening. 'Thief!'

The young horseman needed no more prompting. He kicked the horse's flanks, causing it to rear up before charging for the stable doors. He burst out into the street to find the soldiers out of their guardhouse and standing in his way, fully to attention, their halberds raised before them.

'Halt!'

Beyond them he could see the open gate, freedom so tantalizingly close. To be stopped now, so near to escape – he grimaced, turning the horse and batting back the halberds with his Lionshead blade. He could hear the sound of more guards running now as they charged down the street to their comrades' aid.

'Halt, I said,' repeated the soldier. 'In the name of the Wolf!'

That was the spur the rider needed. With another hard kick he urged his mount forward, charging the guards; roaring, wild. They looked terrified, wavering momentarily as the madman rushed them. A moment was all he needed. He swung the sword furiously, slashing down on his right side and knocking the halberd from one guard's hands, before kicking out to the left and connecting with the second soldier's head. In a flash he was between them, past them and hurtling through Hammergate.

The guards didn't give chase. The man was just another coward who had served the Lion, desperate to get away from the Lord Protector's justice. They'd caught more than their fair share on the gates – so what if this one got away? They watched him disappear into the darkness, the sound of hoof-beats fading, before eventually closing the gate.

They would forever remain oblivious to the importance of his mission.

PART I

The Wolf's Council

I

The Lord Protector

Duke Bergan's boots pounded up the spiral steps of Traitors' House, eager to reach the top. He hated stairs, especially the stone variety. They always reminded him that he wasn't back in his beloved Brackenholme. Yes, there were steps there, but they were few and far between. The Bearlord's Hall sat high within the branches of one of the five Great Trees that marked the woodland city as one of the most marvellous throughout the Seven Realms. A series of strong wicker cages winched visitors skywards to bring them to the Hall of the Werebear, three hundred feet high in the boughs of the Great Oak. It was said that these trees were the ancient mothers of all of Lyssia's trees, a legend that Bergan had no trouble believing.

Homesickness he could handle, but the daily drudge of climbing up and down the stairways of Traitors' House was taking it out of him. If the Lion hadn't locked himself away within Highcliff Keep he'd have no need to go through this ritual. With no courtroom he and the Wolf's Council had been left with no option but to procure the old tower with its unfortunate name. Traitors' House had started life as a garrison tower and jail many years ago and, though dwarfed by Highcliff Keep, was still imposing alongside any other structure in the city. In the last few decades its sole purpose had been as a prison, home to thieves, pickpockets and the brave but foolish idealists who dared speak up against the king's rule. While the cells beneath the old white stone tower still contained a great many miscreants, once Bergan had assumed the role of Lord Protector he'd quickly set about reprieving as many political prisoners as he could. If they were enemies of the Lion they were usually friends of the Bear.

The world had changed dramatically since King Leopold, the Werelion, had been overthrown. Many lesser Werelords had been present at the aborted wedding of Leopold's son, Prince Lucas, to the Werefox Lady Gretchen. They now supported Duke Bergan and his allies, Manfred and Mikkel, the Stags of the Barebones. All were united in their support of Drew Ferran, the boy who had arrived out of nowhere, having grown up as a human, knowing nothing of his heritage as last in the line of Werewolves and rightful king of Westland. The boy was still raw, looking like he might run at the first opportunity, and it was taking all the Wolf's Council's diplomacy and knowledge to ease him into his role as heir to the throne. He wasn't just coming to terms with being the future king; he'd discovered he was a therianthrope, a werecreature like all the nobles of Lyssia. It was hard to tell what scared the boy more.

As Bergan finally reached the top, the staircase opened on to a stone landing before a heavy wooden door. A soldier stood on either side, loyal survivors of Wergar's old Wolfguard. They wore newly fashioned tabards that bore the Wolfshead, silver on a field of black, a reassuringly familiar sight to the old duke. He couldn't help but think back to the old campaigns he'd fought in alongside Wergar and the scrapes the two had got into. The boy, Drew, was a very different character from his father.

Wergar, driven and headstrong, had been predictable and stubborn whereas Drew was more thoughtful and considerate, wiser than his years. If he'd been raised in the Court of High-cliff by his birth parents, Bergan had no doubt that he'd have been the double of his father. As it was, Drew had been raised by a farming family on the Cold Coast. His adoptive father had been in the old Wolfguard, so the boy had been schooled from an early age with a sword, something most peasants never experienced. The mother had been a maid to Queen Amelie, pouring love and kindness into the boy. Those very human values had forged him into a unique Werelord – one who could touch the hearts and minds of the common man as well as his fellow therianthropes. Bergan was confident that one day Drew would make a great king.

The guards opened the door for the Bearlord, holding it wide as he entered the Wolf's Council Chamber. Bergan had made the building his home, while other members of the

Wolf's Council stayed in larger residences around Highcliff. Drew and his mother, Queen Amelie, were living with Duke Manfred, the Werestag, and his family. Manfred owned a handsome estate in the wealthiest part of Highcliff – for the most part Buck House had been unoccupied for the last fifteen years, as the Lord of Stormdale did not enjoy the warmest of relationships with King Leopold. With the Lion dethroned Manfred had quickly gone about airing the old mansion and staffing it with servants. Affording Drew privacy while he was schooled, it was the perfect home for the young Werewolf until they managed to oust the Lion from his stony bolthole in Highcliff Keep. But the Lion wasn't coming quietly.

'What kept you?' asked Earl Mikkel, Lord of Highwater and younger brother of Manfred. The Werestag was standing over a round table in the centre of the council chamber, leafing through reams of documents. At his shoulder stood Hector, the young Boarlord and heir to the seat of Redmire. He held a writing slate, attached to which was a scroll. A quill scribbled away as he took notes on the business of the day. Hector was the youngest member of the Wolf's Council. His early years in the Lion's Court as an apprentice magister had equipped him with enough knowledge of the Seven Realms to make him invaluable as they tried to rebuild old alliances within the scattered and fractured realms. Admittedly, he'd been under the tutelage of the vile Wererat Vankaskan, Leopold's inquisitor, whose own take on magistry had included the practising of the outlawed dark arts. It was a relief to Bergan that Hector had come through the other side of his apprenticeship having dodged these old magicks, concentrating instead on healing and medicine craft.

'More pardons to hear,' grumbled the Bearlord, striding up to the table and pouring himself a goblet of water. He gulped it down.

'Thirsty work those stairs, aren't they?'

Bergan turned at the voice, looking towards an open window. Count Vega sat on the sill, back against the stone frame as he chomped on the remainder of an apple. Left with just the core in his hand he smacked his lips before tossing it out of the window. He smiled brightly, showing rows of pristine white teeth, a reminder of the Sharklord's bestial nature.

'Nice to see you've risen from your pit, Vega,' said the Bearlord, dismissing the Wereshark and turning back to the table. The count made no attempt to join the others, instead relaxing where he sat and looking out over Highcliff.

'If you've nothing for me to attend to I see no reason in rising before noon, Bergan. Or is it simply that you don't trust me to do anything? I believe I'm still part of this little gang, am I not?'

Hector glanced up at the Bearlord whose face reddened.

'Count Vega,' said Mikkel, his tone polite but forced. 'You've been invited to attend every meeting of the council since it was formed a month ago. Of the daily meetings we've had in that short time I can count on one hand the number you've attended. Surely you can appreciate that some of us might be slightly irritated by that fact?'

'Oh, I do. But as the Wolf's sea marshal . . .'

'*Acting* Sea Marshal,' corrected Bergan gruffly.

'As the Wolf's sea marshal,' continued Vega, pointedly, 'land problems are of little importance to my field of governance. It would be a waste of my attention to have me reviewing the arguments of bickering farmers and market stallholders. No, I'm happy to delegate my vote – just add my name to yours, however you choose to go. You chaps seem to know what you're doing.'

Bergan snarled, his patience with the Sharklord worn thin. He punched a fist into the table, causing them all to jump. Hector stared in shock as the fist grew, knuckles crunching against one another as it began to transform into a paw. Bergan's shoulders expanded, the Bearlord's muscles swelling beneath his cloak. His face darkened, ruddy features shifting to a swarthier brown flesh, his teeth now shining from within his beard, sharp and white.

'You think to mock me, Shark? You forget yourself and who you speak to!'

He took a step towards Vega, batting away Mikkel's attempts to restrain him. Hector watched, helpless. Vega's transformation was swift and measured, the Sharklord welcoming the monster within. His torso rippled beneath his white shirt, chest ready to tear free, while his hands and fingers greyed over, sharp and deadly. Vega's mouth widened, revealing his own set of terrible teeth, as he faced the enraged Bearlord. His eyes blinked, black as the night.

'My Lords,' gasped Hector as the two partly changed therians faced one another. Even the Staglord had begun to change, readying himself to leap between the two Werelords if need be. The atmosphere was broken when the door swung open once more as Lord Broghan entered the room.

'Father?' he said, his voice thick with concern at the sight of the two ready for battle. Bergan turned suddenly, instantly distracted by his son. He breathed hard, panting, as he reined the beast in, Vega doing likewise. The two Werelords looked warily at one another as their features returned to normality.

'Is everything all right?' asked the young Bearlord. 'Have I interrupted something?'

'Everything is fine,' said Bergan, drawing his glare away from Vega to stride over and embrace his son. The Sharklord sat down again on the window sill, his composure returned.

'It's good to see you, Father.'

'And you, son,' replied Bergan, clapping his back. 'Happy hunting?'

Broghan quickly shook hands with Mikkel and Hector and threw a cursory nod towards Vega. The Wereshark waved lazily, bored with them, before turning his attention back to the view. The four Werelords pulled up chairs to sit down at the table.

'Not exactly,' said the young Bearlord. 'We caught a couple of the Lion's men down at the harbour, trying to hire a ship, but still no sign of the prince.'

Bergan ground his teeth. There had been a number of sightings of Prince Lucas since the siege began, too many to be mistaken identities. The council had given Broghan the task of investigating, his men chasing every lead that arose, interviewing citizens and rounding up the Lionsguard stragglers who were still in hiding.

'Do you think he's still here?' asked Mikkel.

'It's a week since he was last sighted,' said Bergan. 'Perhaps he's out of the city by now?'

'Well there've been any number of opportunities to leave,' said Broghan. 'Curfew or not, Highcliff still has to run just like any city. People need to work and trade – this is one of the busiest ports in Lyssia – and blind spots are bound to occur. We can have guards on the gates and docks every day and night, but the occasional deserter, like the one the other week, will get through. The net will only catch so many.'

'I only hope the occasional ones don't include Leopold's boy,' growled Bergan. 'He's worth too much to us. If he is out here and isn't hiding in the keep with his father, then he might be just the bargaining tool we need to end this siege. If I know anything about Leopold, I know he adores his son more than anything in the Seven Realms. He's spoiled that child throughout his life, granting his every desire – if we could get our hands on him today we'd have Leopold by tonight.'

'Speaking of Lucas's every desire,' said Mikkel. 'What are we going to do about Gretchen?'

Duke Bergan sighed and scratched his beard: back to the Werefox problem. She was the most eligible woman in Lyssia, months away from taking her family seat of Hedgemoor, one of the wealthiest of the old Werelord houses. Earl Gaston, the Werefox's late father, had traded widely across the Seven Realms, building a vast fortune that had funded many of the Wolf's – and the Lion's – campaigns. Gretchen stood to inherit this fortune, and there were many who suspected that Leopold had murdered Gaston in order to hasten his son's marriage to the girl.

Gretchen was staying with Bergan in Traitors' House, widely considered the safest place for her, but he wasn't entirely happy about the situation, and for two very good reasons.

'You know my feelings, Mikkel. I'm fond of the girl – we all are – but Highcliff isn't a safe place for her, not as long as this siege continues. I'd be happier knowing that she was far from the walls of this city. Furthermore her presence still acts as a distraction to Drew.'

Broghan and Mikkel nodded in agreement while Hector remained silent.

'For Sosha's sake,' said Vega from the window. 'Let them have their fun. They're only young once.'

Bergan shook his head, dismissing him.

'A feckless, misspent youth may not have done you much harm, Vega, but that's no way to raise the future monarch. He needs guidance now more than ever. Like it or not, the attention Lady Gretchen has paid to Drew can't be helpful. He should be listening to his tutors, like myself and Manfred. Instead he's mooning after the girl like a lovesick pup. No, we need to step in and end this now.'

'They may well be fond of one another,' agreed Broghan. 'But there's a time and place for courtship, and this is neither.'

Bergan noticed Hector raise a hand tentatively, still unused to speaking at the Wolf's Council.

'Say your piece, lad. There's no need to be shy – you're among equals now: brothers together. What's on your mind?'

'I just wanted to say –' Hector cleared his throat with a cough. Bergan had noticed that the young Boarlord had a habit of gripping his left hand in his right when anxious, massaging the palm with his thumb. He collected his nerves as all eyes settled on him. 'It's worth mentioning that strictly speaking Lady Gretchen is still betrothed to Prince Lucas. Working for Vankaskan for the last five years, I got to know the prince. Not as a friend, more as a spectator – I've seen his anger first hand.'

He dropped his head, shame weighing heavy on him.

'I've been on the receiving end of his beatings and witnessed his tantrums. I know what fires his passion. Gretchen fires his passion.'

The men all considered this silently for a moment. Finally Bergan clapped his hands together.

'Then it's decided. If Lucas *is* still on the loose and there's some truth in these sightings, we can't take any chances. We'll send her away, somewhere safe. Perhaps Hedgemoor – get her used to being back home and taking her responsibilities to her people seriously. It'd be good for the girl. Plus she'd be surrounded by her own people there – her father was about as loved as any ruler across the Dalelands, and there's a lot of goodwill waiting for her there.'

'We need to keep her there until we break Leopold,' added Mikkel. 'Once this business with the Lion and his cronies is dealt with we can think about the future. If Lady Gretchen and Drew are destined to be together, time will tell, but there's no call for haste in this matter. What will be, will be.'

'Wise words, Staglord,' said Vega, getting down from the

window sill and stretching. 'Now, if you've no more need of me today, there's a game of bones with my name on it in the Robber's Arms.'

'Do you really think it's appropriate, Vega, to gamble with commoners in the city's drinking dens? That's hardly the behaviour one would expect from a Werelord, even one with a past as chequered as yours.' Bergan shook his head.

'I know what I'm doing. You forget, Bergan, these people in the taverns – sailors, dockers and mercenaries – they're *my* people. If you want an ear to the ground picking up information fresh from the gutter, be it a threat to the Wolf or a prince in hiding, then – no disrespect to the splendid work of Broghan – I'm your man.'

The Wereshark winked at the young Bearlord. Broghan smiled back.

'Each to his own, Vega. I'll stick to my methods: following leads, knocking on doors, chasing tip-offs. You continue with yours: throwing bones and downing brandy. They seem to suit you.'

Vega bowed elaborately before the Wolf's Council and walked to the door, waving over his shoulder dismissively.

'Happy hunting, as they say.'

And with that, he was gone.

'Dear Brenn!' muttered Mikkel, shaking his head and relaxing now the count had departed 'Remind me again why he's on this council? I've not seen him do an honest day's work since the siege began.'

'He has his uses,' sighed Bergan, nodding in agreement. 'Can he be trusted? I don't know. But he stepped up when we needed him. He was one more Werelord who stood up against Leopold on the scaffold, so he's earned the right to call himself a member of the council. To the untrained eye his actions look suspiciously like those of a booze-ridden gambler. But what do I know?'

The others all burst into laughter. The atmosphere brightened with the absence of the count, as they settled back to business.

'Has my daughter returned yet?' asked Bergan.

'No, and she's overdue,' replied Broghan, lips drawn tight.

Bergan couldn't hold back a low growl. Lady Whitley was proving a handful. He'd tried sending her back to Brackenholme on numerous occasions since the siege had begun, but she'd dodged and sidestepped at every turn. Lady Rainier, her mother, patiently awaited the return of her family; the least Bergan could do was return their daughter to her. There was also the matter of Whitley's scoutmaster, Hogan, waiting for her, ready to continue lessons upon her return. Instead of following her father's requests she'd managed to go out with all sorts of military patrols as a scout, fully trained or not.

'Whose command is she under? Which patrol?'

'Father,' said Broghan calmly. 'Try not to worry, she's due back any day. She scouts for the army along Grimm's Lane to the north. Since the Lion was unseated there's been unrest in the rat city of Vermire. If any conflict occurs she'll be far from it, I assure you: Harker is in command. Furthermore as long as she's out there working alongside them, doing the job of a scout, then she's still training. One cannot beat field experience.'

Bergan grumbled under his breath.

'I worry. I cannot help it. She's my daughter for Brenn's sake. I couldn't forgive myself if anything were to happen to her. It pleases me to know that Captain Harker watches over her, but still; make sure you have her assigned under your direct command upon her return. Keep her close, son.'

Broghan nodded, keenly aware of how his father felt about Whitley.

'Hector,' continued the Bearlord. 'Have we had any word back from our more distant lords and ladies?'

One of the first actions of the Wolf's Council had been to send word to every corner of Lyssia. Tradition dictated that if a new monarch took the throne, each reigning Werelord was to be consulted. A majority decision was enough to ensure the next step – coronation.

'Not as many as we'd hoped, my lord,' replied the young Boar. He unrolled a large map on the table, taking the goblets and decanter of water to weigh down each corner. His stubby fingers pointed out each of the Seven Realms. 'The lesser Werelords who were present at the failed marriage of Lucas and Gretchen are with us, but the major lords of Lyssia have yet to respond. Nothing from Sturmland or the Longridings; the only approval from the Barebones is obviously that of Stormdale. And no word from Omir, but then that could be expected.'

'I can't speak for the other lords of the Barebones,' added Mikkel. 'But perhaps if I returned home and left Manfred here I might be able to bring our neighbours into line. This could be just the business to thaw our relations with the Crows of

Riven. My brother can remain here by your side, Bergan, strengthening your hand should the need arise.'

'That seems like a sound idea,' said the Bearlord. 'Although I have to say I'm disturbed not to have heard word back from those other realms. The least they could have done was send acknowledgement, even if they don't approve of Drew's claim.'

He'd known all along that they would have a struggle in persuading other Werelords to show their allegiance to a new king, especially one whose lineage could be thrown into question. Detractors were already saying that Drew was the illegitimate son of Wergar and shouldn't be allowed near the throne. Regardless of the support the young Wolf had experienced in Westland it was going to be tough to persuade those further afield to bow to his blade.

'Sturmland I hoped might have sent word by now. I know my cousin Henrik and I haven't seen eye to eye in recent years, but something as momentous as a new king should have awoken the White Bear. Perhaps he's asleep on his horde of gems and fancies keeping it to himself now the Lion is dethroned.

'The Longridings is curious; Duke Lorimer, the Horselord, used to be a staunch ally of Wergar's. Why go silent now when the Wolf's heir has made himself known? And Brand and Ewan – their silence disturbs me. We need to send a diplomatic party down there as soon as is possible.

'And Omir? That's a different beast altogether. It's not one of the Seven Realms and Leopold never brokered an alliance with them. Who would argue against King Faisal? The Lion always wanted obedience from the Jackal but never got it – niggling skirmishes have continued for years. Faisal wouldn't swear fealty to the Catlord, but perhaps he can find common ground with a fellow canine? Maybe with a Wolf on the throne all of Lyssia can finally be reunited – if we secured Omir then the rest would follow suit.'

'It may not be as easy as that,' said Mikkel. 'Rumour reached the Barebones that there is civil war in Omir. Faisal may be king of the Desert Realm, but he faces stiff competition from his neighbours. Lord Canan and his Doglords grow in strength and number, their forces holding all the land to the north of the Silver River. With Lady Hayfa holding the lands to the south, Faisal is surrounded by those who want his city, his throne and his crown. If the rumours are to be believed, I suspect he'll be too busy with his domestic affairs to worry about what happens on this side of the Barebones.'

'Regardless,' said Bergan. 'We need to inform him and the other abstaining Werelords of the situation; an alliance with us could only help Faisal's cause in Omir.'

Bergan turned to his son.

'We'll send more messengers and I'll handwrite the scrolls myself this time; one each to Faisal in Azra, Lorimer in Cape Gala and Henrik in Icegarden. I'll remind them of how the balance lies, how close we are to a prosperous new future if we can unite together behind Drew. Old differences can be put to one side, so there's a fresh start for all.'

He smiled, confident. He could be very persuasive when he put his mind to it, and his mind was set.

'Talking of our future king, where is he?' said Broghan.

'Still with my brother at Buck House, enjoying his morning drills,' Mikkel answered.

'Working him hard?' said the Bearlord. Earl Mikkel shrugged.

'No harder than my father worked us. He has fine natural ability, but he's raw. A diamond in the rough if you will. He has the makings of as great a warrior as Wergar, but he needs guidance. What did my father say? *Mastery of the blade and the beast.*'

'In which case, he's in very capable hands.'

The Lords of Stormdale had traditionally trained many of Lyssia's Werelords – the Werestags were well known for their passive nature until enraged, but also their wisdom and patience: considered in court, ferocious in battle. As teachers of many of the Seven Realms' rulers the Stags were held in high esteem.

'Well, there's just the unpleasant business of revealing our plans to Lady Gretchen then,' sighed Bergan. Telling her she was to return to her homeland was an unpalatable task for even the hardiest Werelord. Despite her young age, Gretchen was formidable, quick to anger. She'd got her way down the years, spoiled unsurprisingly by Earl Gaston of Hedgemoor as his only child. As the betrothed of Lucas her confidence had blossomed to such a degree that there were very few people she wouldn't stand up to, bar Queen Amelie or perhaps Bergan. With that knowledge at the back of his mind, the decision of who should tell the Werefox was easy for Bergan.

'Hector,' he said, and the Boarlord jumped. Bergan laughed. 'Don't worry, lad, I'm not going to land this on you. No, I'd like you to go to Drew at Buck House. If he's still training then there's a fine chance that Gretchen is in close vicinity. Can you ask her to make her way back to Traitors' House? Tell her it's urgent Wolf's Council business. I'll deliver the news to her when she arrives. We'll get her packed and ready to leave before first light tomorrow. A quiet affair, we'll draw no attention. Broghan, prepare some of your best men – five branches should do it.'

'Five branches: thirty of Brackenholme's best men,' nodded Broghan. The branch system of the Dyrewood created a brotherhood among the soldiers. These small teams – five men and one captain – were as close as family.

The men shook hands as the Wolf's Council was adjourned until the next day. Bergan followed Hector to the door, handing the Boarlord his red cloak that bore the crest of Redmire.

'Your father would be proud of you, lad. Your actions, your aid, your wits – they've been invaluable since the Lion was defeated. I may not say it often, Hector, but I'm glad Drew can call you his friend. You've been good for each other.'

Hector smiled shyly, his chest filling out as the warm words washed over him.

'I know I was soft before I met Drew,' said Hector, keeping his voice low and out of earshot of the others. 'But he's toughened me up. I've discovered my backbone; I just need to make sure I don't misplace it again!'

Bergan chortled.

'Don't underestimate the influence you've had on him, Hector,' said Bergan, wagging a big forefinger. 'These things run both ways. Drew has entered a new world, and he'd have

been lost without you by his side. You're the compass that's
kept him going straight as an arrow.'

'My lord.' The magister bowed briefly before stepping out
into the corridor and heading down the monstrous staircase.
Duke Bergan watched him go, grateful that the Wolf's Council and Drew had such a friend in the young Boarlord.

2

The Blade and the Beast

'Back on your feet,' barked Duke Manfred, towering over the fallen youth, cold steel in hand. Drew squinted up at him, sweat pooling in the corners of each eye. He wiped a forearm across his face, clearing his vision and catching his breath. The Staglord had the sun at his back, casting his whole frame into silhouette and making the already tall man even more imposing. Drew could see that the Werelord was breathing heavily, but he was far from spent. Unlike Drew. He spat on the ground, bloody spittle rolling in the dry dirt. His entire body ached, pushed to the point of exhaustion. The sword lay at the feet of the duke, just out of reach. Manfred kicked it across to him.

'I said on your feet.'

Drew picked up the blunt sword and used it as a crutch to haul himself upright once more. Manfred was relentless, keeping Drew on his toes at all times. From sunrise each day no moment was wasted. Days at Buck House were full for Drew – combat was just a small part of it. Therian races, Lyssian geography, etiquette: the Staglord's lessons were all encompassing. Manfred had taken special care to school Drew in controlling his lycanthropy. The late Baron Huth, Hector's father, had taught Drew some meditations and mantras during his brief stay in Redmire, but the old Boarlord had only scratched the surface. Manfred went much deeper, encouraging Drew to explore every facet of the Wolf. His lycanthropy mastery was the only lesson that was held out of sight of spectators, deep within the wine cellars of Buck House. Here, it was quiet, cool and dark, the perfect place to channel the beast undisturbed.

Drew rose to his full height, weighing the training sword in his right hand as he gathered his senses. His left hand rested at his hip, clenched into a fist. The stump where his little finger used to be still ached, a constant reminder of his battle with Vanmorten, the Wererat, that life as a Werelord could be deadly. Manfred smiled. Drew grimaced, annoyed that the Werelord was showing little sign of stress. The heat of the mid-morning sun only compounded Drew's weariness. He'd long ago ditched his shirt and now stood in nothing but his leather breeches. Manfred, in comparison, remained fully clothed, his long grey cloak thrown back off his shoulder. Drew was also painfully aware of the audience watching from the balcony of the mansion; Lady Gretchen and her ladies-in-waiting, keen to see the future king showing off his fencing talents. What they actually saw, to Drew's dismay, was a healthy young man failing to measure up to a venerable old Werelord.

'One more round, Drew, and you may take water.'

Duke Manfred's close aide, Magister Kohl, stood nearby under the shade of a fig tree, a jug of water at his feet. Drew glanced at the old man who reached a hand down to pat the jug's rim. A cousin of Manfred, Kohl was a Stag whom Drew had seen plenty of in the last month, but he was in no mood for the magister's gentle taunts. He was harmless but quick-witted, reminding Drew of Hector in many ways.

Drew readied himself, pumping life into his legs as he rocked on his heels. He watched Manfred intently, deciding on whether his next move would provoke delight or dismay. He no longer cared — he'd spent the last two hours being knocked around the courtyard by the Stag: by fair means or foul he wanted to win at least one bout with the old duke.

He paced to his left, drawing Manfred into following. The Werestag's steps seemed relaxed, but Drew realized that was just experience showing. Every move Manfred made was considered and deliberate. Drew kept moving, circling so that behind him stood the mansion and balcony. And the sun.

Manfred squinted. No amount of training allowed a man to stare wide-eyed into the sun. Drew flung his left hand forward.

The dirt in his clenched fist erupted from his hand, flying fast into the Staglord's face. Manfred staggered back, blinded by the cloud of dust. It was Drew's turn to grin now. He even allowed himself a quick glance over his shoulder at the onlookers. Gretchen was frowning in disapproval. Drew wouldn't allow this to concern him – anyone who had survived a scrap in Tuckborough wouldn't argue with these tactics, and Drew and his brother Trent had experienced their share of them. A fight was a fight.

Kohl stepped forward, about to shout his objections, so Drew moved fast and lunged at the stricken Werelord, his foot landing in the dirt as he thrust the blunt blade forward. To his dismay the combat didn't play out as he'd planned.

Instinctively Manfred moved to his left as the sword flew past him. Drew, unbalanced, stumbled and Manfred swept his right leg round in a fluid motion, connecting with Drew's shins and sending him flying. The young Wolf landed spread-eagled on the floor, his face full of dirt once more, the air escaping his lungs. He didn't have time to recover, feeling a hand clasp him by the shoulder and spin him on to his back. Manfred landed on him, his knees pinning the youth to the ground as he bucked beneath. The Werestag's hand shot out, grabbing Drew by the throat and holding him still. Drew stopped struggling, looking up at the Staglord as he straddled him. His eyes were still closed, blinded by the dirt flung into them.

'A most ungracious stunt to pull on his lordship,' said Kohl, rushing forward and shaking his head furiously. 'There are rules, young man: rules to fencing, rules to duelling. That was . . . unlawful!'

Manfred raised a hand, laughing, waving Kohl away with a smile.

'Oh hush, Kohl. The boy was acting just as I did. Instinct.

Survival. Two sides of the same coin. His instincts told him to improvise.'

Manfred released his grip on Drew's throat, allowing him to breathe in deeply. The duke rubbed the dirt from his eyes as his sight returned.

'Well done, Drew. Taught an old Stag a trick there. Just remember, though.' He pointed to his eyes. 'Sight isn't the only sense one depends on in battle.' He gripped the lobe of his ear and waggled it. 'You hear me?'

Manfred got up and held his hand down to Drew. Face crimson with a mixture of shame and embarrassment, Drew took it as Manfred hauled him to his feet.

'Let's see about having that drink now, eh?'

Magister Kohl, disgruntled but mindful of his liege's words, filled two wooden cups with water. Drew took one and gulped it down. Having polished off its contents, he held his cup out once again.

'Please, magister,' he said, bowing his head respectfully. 'Another drink?'

Sighing but forgiving, Kohl refilled the vessel, winking at Drew once his temper faded. The old sage couldn't stay angry for long. Drew smiled. He'd probably pull the same trick again given half the chance. Next time, though, he wouldn't let his opponent hear him coming. Manfred was watching him from beneath bushy grey eyebrows. As Kohl left them beneath the tree, Manfred spoke quietly.

'Your trick with the dirt; Magister Kohl's reaction isn't unusual. As unpalatable as it is during a fencing match, I'm under no illusion that in the heat of battle such rules don't exist. This morning was *not* the heat of battle. Know this, Drew – there's a time and a place for underhandedness. Let that be an end to it.'

That was as far as the punishment went with the Lord of Stormdale; carefully chosen words to remind Drew who he was. He took a moment to reflect. Manfred could have reprimanded him in front of Kohl, but instead picked a moment when they were alone: a measure of his manners and good grace. Drew wasn't the farm boy from the Cold Coast any more, picking fights and scuffling at Tuckborough market. He and Trent had learned to fight dirty there, the two brothers pitched against gangs of local boys. Drew often found himself thinking about Trent, the boy who'd grown up as his twin, wondering what had become of him; he hoped he was safe. Drew had to remember to act differently now. He was constantly being watched and judged.

'I feel such pressure,' sighed Drew, rubbing the back of his neck. 'From the council, my friends – even the people of Highcliff.' They were out there, beyond the gates. Expectations were still high, a month after the uprising. They knew he was here, behind the walls of Buck House. Each day a crowd gathered; many wanted to meet the future king, while most just wanted a glimpse of him.

'Don't be downhearted, Drew. You've made fantastic progress. I can't imagine what you've had to deal with since you discovered your heritage and powers. You're unpredictable, though, so much of what you know is either self-taught or fashioned by how the Ferrans raised you. You'll always keep us on our toes, I suspect. A positive thing, I might add!'

Their conversation was interrupted when a guard appeared at the edge of the courtyard.

'Your Grace, Lord Hector is here and seeks word with you urgently.'

Drew instantly brightened at the news.

'You'd better not keep him waiting, then,' said Manfred.

It was comforting for Drew to know that one he trusted so implicitly was at his shoulder. The shy Boarlord had taken a shine to Queen Amelie's lady-in-waiting, Bethwyn, but had yet to pluck up the courage to say a single word to her. Drew suspected half of Hector's visits revolved around the magister wanting to bump into the poor girl. Clearly this one did not.

As Manfred strode away Drew stepped out of the shade and walked towards the edge of the courtyard. The estate was built upon the hillside, meaning the house and gardens sat on terraces. The westernmost edge of the courtyard jutted out from the hillside. Servants' quarters were built below it and a low stone parapet marked its length. From this vantage point Drew could see the harbour and the various ships that made up the merchant and military fleet of Westland. Making out the black masts of the *Maelstrom,* he wondered if Count Vega was on board. Drew was fond of the Pirate Prince, the Sharklord having gone from being a two-faced traitor to a member of the Wolf's Council. Once Drew's captor, he was now his saviour, having rescued the boy from a watery grave when he'd fallen unconscious into the harbour.

He felt hands clasp round his face suddenly from behind, covering his eyes. He was about to struggle free when a familiar voice sounded in his ear.

'My king?' she whispered. The tension he'd felt at the possible ambush gave way to a new and familiar feeling of anxiety.

'Don't call me that,' he grinned awkwardly. 'I'm far from ready to claim that title.'

Gretchen removed her hands, giving him a playful shove in his back.

'It won't be long now, Drew, you'd better get used to it,' she teased.

A mischievous smile darted across her face, red hair tumbling around her perfect features. She wore a pale cream dress, embroidered with tiny crimson flowers round the sleeves and throat. Drew could feel his mouth drying and his stomach knotting. He could talk to most people readily. But not Gretchen, at least not lately. Gretchen, who he'd got to know so well on their travels from Redmire and their adventures through the Wyrmwood. Gretchen, in whose presence he should have been relaxed.

Behind, Gretchen's ladies-in-waiting stood in a huddle, giggling. Drew wondered what she saw in the girls; they seemed juvenile to him, children who swooned and twittered at the slightest drama.

'There's no hurry,' Drew finally replied, resting his eyes on the city again. 'Bergan can remain Lord Protector for as long as he likes. The people are happy with the Wolf's Council, they don't need some farm boy from the Cold Coast messing things up.'

'You're doing yourself a great disservice, Drew. The people of Westland love you; they want you to lead them.'

The idea that the Werefox knew what the people of Lyssia

wanted made Drew smile. She was a great many things – feisty, strong-willed and short-tempered – but voice of the people? He shook his head.

'How can you say that, Gretchen? What do you honestly know of what the people want?'

'You think I'm the same spoiled girl you met in Redmire? People change, Drew. Just take a look at yourself.'

'I'm still just a simple country boy.'

Gretchen laughed.

'There is *nothing* simple about you, Drew. You're only fooling yourself. I was there, remember, on the *Maelstrom*, heard the crowd chanting your name. You're the future, Drew. You're their king.'

He couldn't get away from it, try as he might. Everywhere he turned, his destiny awaited him. All roads led to the throne. His secret plans to disappear from Highcliff were fading with each passing day. He still harboured hopes of returning to the Cold Coast, but who was he fooling? That chance had gone.

Gretchen linked her arm through Drew's, grasping his left hand between both of hers. He felt a shiver, his nerves jangling. Where was Kohl's jug of water when he needed it?

'The Lord Protector is a temporary title, Drew, until you're ready to take your place on the throne,' she said, breathing the sea air in as she followed his gaze. 'He's popular with the peasants, but they expect the Wolf to rule by winter, mark my words.'

Drew prickled.

'Don't say that.'

'Say what?'

'Peasants.'

'That's what they are, isn't it?'

'They're people, Gretchen. I was one of your peasants not so long ago, remember?'

If Drew had hoped for an apology from the Werefox, he didn't get one. Instead she laughed. Her voice was harder when she next spoke.

'Oh don't be so sensitive, Drew of the Dyrewood. You were never really a peasant, you're the son of the old king for Brenn's sake. Everyone has their purpose, Drew. Everyone should know their place.'

'We have different visions, Gretchen. Under Leopold the people were oppressed. There was no way for the lowest classes to improve their lives, no routes out of their social station.'

'That's revolutionary talk, Drew.'

'I disagree,' he said, turning to her. His nerves had calmed, replaced by a feeling of indignation. 'It would mean a happier and more prosperous society; do you not want the best for the people of Lyssia?'

Gretchen glowered, any laughter in her voice gone.

'Is this the new Drew, then? I suppose you know everything there is to know now? Setting the world to rights after a few weeks as a Werelord? I think I preferred the old Drew, the naive farm boy from the seashore.'

The principles of right and wrong had been planted in his head from an early age by Mack Ferran, the man who had raised him as his own. Drew shook his head, knowing full well he wouldn't get through to Gretchen. If he carried on she'd only patronize him and get more annoyed. Thankfully, the arrival of Hector from across the courtyard allowed them to change the subject.

'Hector,' Drew called, running over to slap him on the back. Gretchen followed, speeding over for the reunion of the three friends.

'What brings you out of Traitors' House, councillor?' asked Gretchen, changing the target of her teasing words, the playfulness returned. 'It's so good of you to grace us with your presence.'

Indeed, Hector looked every inch the Werelord. He wore a smart brown cloak over his well-tailored city clothes, a brass clasp in the form of a charging boar fastening it round his shoulder. Against his chest Drew recognized the steel grey medallion that every member of his council wore, bearing the profile of a wolf's head.

The Wereboar laughed, blushing at the same time.

'Well, it's good to get out of there and see what the rest of the world is up to. It's hard work this governing. We're left with the task of keeping people happy while some fool who is supposed to be king puts his feet up.' He looked Drew up and down. 'Aren't you going to put some clothes on in the presence of a Wolf's Councillor? There's a lady present, you know!'

Drew was suddenly aware of how exposed he was. Wearing leather breeches and little else he was woefully underdressed when one considered that he was with two important nobles, regardless of the fact they were his best friends.

'Relax, Hector,' sniffed Gretchen. 'It's nothing we haven't seen before.'

She pulled a face when she looked at Drew's back, tracing a finger over a series of scars. He shivered at her touch.

'What?'

'Your wounds – I thought they'd all healed.'

Drew had endured all manner of injury when he had arrived in Highcliff the previous month. Beaten by King Leopold and his men, fighting the Lionguard, duelling the Wererat Vanmorten and falling from the castle ramparts into the sea. Every inch of his body had been battered or broken, but his therianthropic healing, unique to Werelords, had allowed him to mend at an accelerated rate. The only scars that still ached were those on his back.

'I'm stuck with those ones, it appears.'

Hector took a look also, and nodded.

'The whip? It was studded with silver, wasn't it?'

Drew blanched, thinking about the sting of the deadly metal against his skin. He'd taken beatings and broken limbs, had even recovered from his father Mack Ferran wrongly running him through with the Wolfshead Blade, but nothing burned the flesh of a Werelord like the touch of silver. It had been outlawed for many years throughout Lyssia, but King Leopold had seen no problem in arming his men with the forbidden metal. The swords of the Lionguard were laced with the precious poison.

'It's no way to treat their king,' said Gretchen.

'*Future* king,' corrected Hector.

'If we ever see the day,' chimed Gretchen.

'You know,' Drew said, smiling. 'Impertinent as you both are, I'm blessed to have two such noble friends.'

His words were heartfelt and the Fox and Boar looked at him with fresh eyes.

'What a lovely thing to say,' said Hector.

'He wants something,' whispered Gretchen, giving Hector a sly elbow in the ribs.

'I mean it,' went on Drew. He paused for a moment, searching for the right words. 'I know I don't say it very often, but meeting the two of you brought me back from the brink. I was in a dark place when I lived in the Dyrewood and when I was first captured by Bergan. It looked for a while like I had no future. I found one when I found you.'

He could feel a tear in his eye and, before it could fall and betray him he grabbed the two of them quickly for a sweaty hug. They returned it, heartily.

'Are you just using us to dry yourself on?' asked Gretchen, puncturing the moment. Hector and Drew laughed.

'How is the Queen Mother?' asked Hector.

It had been a curious month for Drew as he'd got to know Queen Amelie, his birth mother. Her moods swung from celebration at having Drew in her life, to sorrow at the loss of her other son, Lucas. She'd spent fifteen years mourning the death of Wergar and all her children in a fire. She'd discovered that her youngest child, Willem, had survived, but she also had to come to terms with the fact that the man she took as her next husband, Leopold, was behind their deaths. Willem was the name Drew had been born to, but it felt alien to him when she said it. Which name would he be expected to use when he took the throne?

'She rests,' said Drew. 'I expect we'll see her this afternoon. Mornings aren't good for her.'

'What do you mean?'

'You must have heard him,' said Gretchen, shivering.

'Oh,' said Hector with sudden realization.

Each evening since the joint armies of Brackenholme and Stormdale had taken the city, Leopold had appeared upon the battlements of Highcliff Keep, roaring his fury into the sky; the rage of the Lion, Bergan called it. The sound was blood-curdling, this nightly ritual reminding everyone for miles around who still held the crown of Westland. Those soldiers in the encampments that circled the ancient castle had witnessed the screaming rants and curses that accompanied these roars. Leopold roared for vengeance against those who had stolen his throne. Bergan and Manfred had to calm their troops' nerves and boost morale every night. After each roaring bout, Amelie inevitably had a fitful night's sleep. Mornings were when she could finally rest.

'Thank you, Hector,' smiled Drew. 'I'll let her know you asked after her.'

Duke Manfred and Magister Kohl appeared once more, stepping up to the trio and breaking up the reunion.

'Are you refreshed?' asked Drew. 'I'm ready for the next round, Your Grace. This time I'll keep it clean, you have my word.'

Manfred shook his head.

'As it happens, Drew, our classes will have to be curtailed. You can remain here and catch up with Hector. Kohl and I are to escort Lady Gretchen to Traitors' House. Apparently there is some news regarding Hedgemoor that needs relaying to her, and Duke Bergan requests her presence at the earliest opportunity. My lady?'

'Oh,' said Gretchen with surprise. 'A moment, while I get my cloak.' She went over to her ladies-in-waiting, one of whom carried her long red hooded cloak. As they fastened it around her shoulders, the four men spoke quietly.

'This was the message you brought here from Bergan?' Drew asked Hector.

'Indeed,' he replied. 'There's some concern about Gretchen's safety in the city.'

'A simple precaution, Hector, no?' whispered Manfred.

The Boarlord nodded.

'Indeed. We think the safest place for her is back in Hedgemoor.'

'Has this got something to do with the agents of Leopold still loose in the city?' asked Drew, eyeing Gretchen as she finished readying herself for the brief walk to Traitors' House.

'That's the bones of it,' said Kohl. 'Duke Manfred and I shall take her. Hector, I appreciate that you don't want to be implicated in this – we all know how fiery the lady can be. Let us old fools face her wrath on your behalf,' he said, winking. Hector breathed a sigh of relief, nodding enthusiastically as Gretchen rejoined them.

'Gentlemen,' she smiled and, taking the Staglord's arm, turned to leave.

'Until later,' Drew called before bending down to pick up the blunt steels from the floor. He handed one to Hector.

'Now then, Hector,' he said as the Boarlord handled the length of steel. 'On my word, come at me.'

Drew struck a heroic pose, ready for combat. Hector laughed.

As the gates to Buck House opened, the guards pushed the onlookers back. Gretchen counted at least thirty there, all waiting to catch sight of the Wolf. Ordinarily the appearance of Gretchen might have driven a crowd into wild excitement, and she couldn't help but feel a little jealous of the love these people had for Drew. She'd lived her whole life in the public eye, yet they clamoured for the youth who was new to this life of royalty. Leopold never knew this kind of adulation. A great deal of goodwill was Drew's for the taking.

Manfred and Kohl held people back as they led Gretchen through the throng. Within moments they were walking up the cobbled Lofty Lane, a quiet back street that would take them directly to Traitors' House. She was intrigued to hear what news awaited her from Hedgemoor. It had been too long since she'd been home and she missed it. But her place was now here, in Highcliff. Gretchen had been groomed to take her place in the king's court as queen. Though she'd once had her heart set on Lucas, Drew had won her affections in the short time she'd known him, not that she'd admit such a thing to him.

Buildings reached across the street from either side, threatening to touch one another in places. Washing lines hung over the road, creating a fluttering canvas of sheets and garments. It was quiet, peaceful.

'Do you know what the news is from Hedgemoor?' she asked Manfred, who kept pace at her side.

The duke shook his head.

'I'm afraid not my dear. I'm sure your Uncle Bergan will be fully informed. He asks that we don't tarry.'

The Bearlord was indeed considered an uncle by Gretchen. Her distant cousin, Lady Rainier, had married into the Bear clan many years ago, and was mother to both Whitley and Broghan. Such marriages between Werelords were not unusual, with the male usually dictating which therianthrope would rise from the union. She was fully aware she was the last in the line of the Werefoxes of Hedgemoor, although some Foxes lived in the eastern Dalelands.

A noise ahead made them look up as a handcart rolled out of an alleyway. The old man who pulled it was bent double, stooped, a dirty hooded cloak fastened about his shoulders. They stopped as he tried to manoeuvre it into the street, but he was having trouble steering it out of the alley. Manfred, ever helpful, stepped forward to aid him.

'Let me assist you,' he said, taking hold of one of the guide poles as the old man stepped back. Gretchen could make out the black ringlets of oily hair that hung down from within his hood. There was something familiar about that hair.

A noise behind her made her turn, but too late. Another man, dressed in similar garb stepped out of a shadowed doorway immediately behind Kohl. The magister didn't have a moment to react, his advanced years having slowed his reflexes. Swiftly and smoothly the man whipped out a short but sharp blade, drawing it across Kohl's throat and slicing it in a fluid motion. Kohl tumbled to the cobbles, his lifeblood gushing from his open neck.

Gretchen screamed.

Duke Manfred turned, his hand immediately reaching for the longsword at his hip. The sword was only half out of its scabbard when he froze, a look of agony flashing over his face. His mouth contorted into a deathly grimace, a cry failing to escape his lips. Like a ragdoll he slowly slumped forward to his knees in the street, the old man behind standing over him. In his hand the beggar held a wicked serrated blade, stained dark with the Staglord's blood. His hood fell back. She'd been right to recognize the ringlets. The Ratlord Vankaskan grinned at her with demonic delight.

Her scream was cut short when the man who had murdered Kohl threw a gloved hand over her mouth. His hot breath whispered in her ear as he dragged her into the alleyway, the Ratlord close to heel.

'I have missed you, my bride,' snarled Prince Lucas.

3

Dwellers in the Dark

Drew sprinted up the lane, feet pounding the cobblestones. He was in no doubt that had been Gretchen's scream. Behind him came Hector and three guards from Buck House, closely followed by the crowd from the gate. He wasn't supposed to go anywhere without an escort, but with his bodyguards a hundred yards back down the street, he had little choice. He could hear the cries of Hector, following as fast as he could.

'Drew! Be careful! This might be a trap!'

He was right, of course. It could well be a trap to lure him out into the open, but Drew couldn't care less. He wasn't about to let Gretchen get used as bait. Drew could feel the blood coursing through his body, his fingertips on fire as dark claws began to emerge. If they wanted the Wolf they'd get the Wolf.

Ahead a crowd had gathered about an abandoned handcart in the middle of Lofty Lane. The onlookers stared in horror at the bodies in the street, obscuring their identities from Drew. As he closed in he felt his legs turning leaden, and fought back the desire to vomit. Blood streamed through the cobbles like red rivers between black mountains. *Please, Brenn, don't let it be her.*

Barging the people aside he looked from one body to another: Duke Manfred and dear Magister Kohl. Manfred was slumped on the ground, face down, a great savage wound in his back. Whoever had slain Kohl had almost removed the old man's head from his neck, so deep was the cut.

There was no sign of Gretchen.

'You,' said Drew, grabbing the nearest man, an innkeeper judging by the ale-stained apron that was stretched tight over his portly stomach. 'What happened here?'

The man's face was ashen, and for a moment he struggled to respond. Drew shook him stiffly and his jowls wobbled.

'I was one of the first ones here. Found 'em like this. Poor souls.'

'Was there a woman here? A girl with red hair?'

Drew looked at them all desperately, but they each shook their heads. He crouched, reaching under the body of Manfred and withdrawing the Staglord's longsword from its sheath. Hector, the guards and the larger crowd gathered about them now as Drew rose to his full height once more. The mob was shouting now, some screaming as they saw the bodies. The guards recoiled, their liege lying dead before them. Hector blanched, his hand instinctively moving over his mouth.

'Did *anyone* see what happened?' shouted Drew over the noise.

An old woman stepped warily forward out of the crowd.

'Two men,' she gasped, eyes darting about the crowd. 'They done this. Killed them dead in daylight as I live and breathe.' She made a hasty sign of Brenn, kissing her thumb and touching her forehead.

'Did you see the girl?' asked Drew, shifting the sword in his sweating grasp.

'That way,' she said, pointing to a shady alleyway opposite. 'Took her down there they did!'

Drew nodded his thanks, then turned and began to push through the crowd towards the gap between the buildings. It was only the width of the handcart, and seemed to snake off into darkness. He felt a hand snatch at his elbow, holding him fast.

'Drew, please,' begged Hector. 'Wait a moment until the City Watch get here!' The guards from Buck House were trying to keep the crowd away from the murder scene.

'I can't, Hector! We're wasting time!'

He unpeeled Hector's fingers and set off into the alley. Hector briefly paused before following, leaving the guards to fight the panic and the crowd.

The passage was cramped and uncomfortable, buildings looming overhead and blocking out the sun. Occasionally the odd shaft of daylight broke the gloom, but for the most part it was like twilight. Drew looked around as he ran, searching for where the killers had taken Gretchen. Were they regular footpads, opportunist thieves? It was well known that Lofty Lane was a street that quickly went from riches to rags in the space of a hundred yards. No street was entirely safe in Highcliff, but to attack someone in broad daylight was relatively unheard of.

The alley was coming to a dead end. Drew crashed into a wall, his hands feverishly feeling about in the half-light. *Had they climbed out of here?* His hands slid over the mossy bricks, finding no purchase. *No, not climbed; where have they gone?*

'Perhaps the old woman was mistaken?' gasped Hector behind, slightly out of breath. 'She'd just witnessed two murders; who can say if she was thinking straight?'

Drew jostled Hector out of the way as he turned back.

'Good idea,' said Hector. 'Let's head back and get more men. Spread out. We'll find them.' Hector started to follow Drew and almost fell over him.

Drew had dropped to his knees, longsword on the floor as he looked around. He tried to steady his heart rate, blanking out all sounds: Hector's chattering, the shouts of the crowd at the entrance to the alleyway, doors slamming, dogs barking. He tapped into the Wolf, thinking about Gretchen; her voice, her movement, her smells. Red roses. Rose petals. Perfume. Her scent was strong, stirring emotions deep within. He turned his head, picking up a trace. He breathed in long and slow, catching hold of it. Then followed it.

Hector watched in wonder as Drew scrambled along the filthy floor, half naked and in a world of his own. The Boarlord looked back up the alley expectantly, hoping that a guard might appear to relieve them. Drew rose to his feet, reaching out and gripping a splintered crate with his free hand. A filthy cloth, stained with something vile and covered in flies, was draped across it. Hector grimaced. Giving it a yank, Drew pulled it to one side.

A jagged hole in the ground revealed itself, broken earth marking it as an old sewer entrance.

'This way,' said Drew, smiling, his expression slightly manic as he stepped into the hole.

'Shouldn't we wait?' asked the wide-eyed Hector.

Drew didn't bother answering, lowering himself quickly into the hole. His feet found rusted ladder rungs as he clambered down. Gretchen's scent was quickly overwhelmed by the stench of the sewer. Overhead he saw Hector climbing in, feet slipping as he followed. Twenty steps down and the vertical shaft opened up into a large chamber. He dropped the remaining distance, landing with a thump on muddy earth.

He was in a main sewer that no doubt ran all the way down from the Tall Quarter of the city. Curving brickwork held up the rock above, beams of rotten timber and twisted lengths of metal adding strength and support to the tunnel's structure. A river of feculence gurgled past, and a walkway clung to the wall along its length. The darkness was broken in places by pale daylight that arced down from grille openings in the streets above. This might have provided the only illumination, but for the faint glow of a fire round the bend. Drew moved quickly as he navigated his way along the ledge towards the concealed flames.

The tunnel curved ahead of him, the brickwork catching more and more light from the fire beyond. Drew heard something splash in the foul water. He squinted, watching the rippling brown surface as he edged along. A rat, almost a foot long, scurried ahead of his feet, away from the intruder. Another splash nearby: something landing in the water or moving through it perhaps?

'Drew!' called Hector.

Drew rolled his eyes – any element of surprise they'd had had just been lost. If there was someone round the bend by the fire, they'd be ready now. He gripped the sword, knuckles white.

The narrow path widened, eventually opening into what appeared to be a sewer junction, where four tunnels met. A large, roughly paved area provided firmer footing along one wall, as wooden walkways criss-crossed the dark rivers, connecting each tunnel to the other. A low-burning fire had been lit on the stony platform, its embers glowing as its flames died. Behind, Drew could hear the huffing and puffing of Hector as his friend struggled to keep up, cursing occasionally. Drew rushed up to the fire.

Rotting vegetable remnants and chewed bones were scattered across the flagstones. The platform was perhaps ten paces across, providing a modest – if cramped and filthy – living area. Torn pieces of paper littered the floor, too many to search through at that moment. Drew counted at least ten dirty blankets. Had that number of men been here? He looked up and about: three more tunnels headed in different directions. *Which one to take? Where had they gone?*

The sound of booted footsteps coming down one of the tunnels caught Drew by surprise. They came fast, making no effort to hide their passage. Drew had to think quickly. He took his longsword and, laying it flat on the flags he pushed the remains of the fire into the water. The embers hissed and spat as they hit the gurgling sewage, plunging him into greater darkness. Directly above the tunnel junction was a drain-cover grille that let the sun's rays cast dim blocks of daylight over the area. Drew shuffled towards the intersecting wooden walkways and stayed low to the ground, his longsword trailing behind him.

'Burn the papers,' said one voice, deep and gravelly. 'You should have done that before we set off, fool!'

'I thought you'd done it, captain' replied another, lighter voice. 'Let's get a move on. Place gives me the creeps, what with his pets still down here. Want to catch up with the others. Lucky he didn't slit us for this.'

'Damn sight darker than when we left,' said the gruff voice. 'That's all we need, the fire to have gone out. How do we burn these papers without a fire?'

'That woman had better be worth this. If the Bear's men find us we'll be for the gallows.'

The two men emerged from the tunnel opposite the one Drew had entered by. One was larger than the other, broad shouldered and hulking. The other was of a slighter build, a head shorter than his companion and half as wide. They were both clad in dirty black cloaks, providing them with near total camouflage in the sewers. But Drew was waiting for them, searching for their movement in the shadows. He didn't want them dead – they had taken Gretchen. For that reason alone he kept the beast in check, kept the Wolf locked away. He knew what he was capable of, what strength he possessed when he was transformed. There would be no reasoning with these men if he faced them as the Werewolf – it would be kill or be killed, and that wouldn't do. He needed these men alive, to question them. They were almost upon him before he jumped up from where he crouched.

Drew's fist flew straight into the chin of the smaller man, sending him crashing back on his heels, colliding with his companion who tottered into the guide rail that ran the length of the walkway. The rail splintered, cracking in two, as the big man struggled to steady himself. The wooden bridge rocked, unstable under the weight of the three combatants. Drew could feel the boards and planks groaning beneath him. He grabbed the smaller man by his cloak and tugged him back towards him, striking his face with his sword pommel. The crunching sound of his nose breaking was followed swiftly by a scream as Drew hurled him on to the stone platform and faced the big man alone.

More splashes caught Drew's attention. *What was that? Was there someone in the water?* A quick look over his shoulder through the dim light showed him the smaller man slumped on the ground, semi-conscious, as Hector appeared round the corner. He returned his attention to the bigger man who had now regained his balance.

The man whipped a broadsword out from inside his cloak, launching himself towards Drew in a savage attack. Drew brought his longsword up, parrying three vicious blows in quick succession. Each time the thug raised his blade high over his head and threw all his weight behind the blow. Drew's arms hummed with each clash of ringing steel as he was driven back.

Drew allowed him to advance, drawing him on to the stone platform. The man followed, pressing home what he thought was his advantage. They passed the man's companion who was slowly stumbling to his feet, his face dark with blood. Behind him Drew could make out Hector crashing about, trying to steer clear of the melee. In the dim light he could also see a shape clambering out of the water and on to the platform's edge. He had to speed this fight to its end. He backed further towards the wall.

'Who's your friend?' spat the man. 'I'll kill him next.'

Drew let him talk, staring up at the ceiling as the man advanced. Sparks flew as the broadsword hit the low roof, the blade flying from the man's grasp and clattering to the floor. Drew sprang forward, his sword slashing down across the man's right leg. He went down hard, crunching into the ground with a wail of agony. Drew hurdled over the hamstrung villain, now out of action. He could see the smaller man staggering across the walkway.

'Drew!' screamed Hector.

'He can't harm you now,' shouted Drew, closing on the smaller rogue.

'Not him,' yelled Hector. 'That!'

Drew looked back, his eyes slowly adjusting to the gloom. The large shape that had hauled itself out of the water was advancing towards Hector. It was around four feet long, hump-backed and stayed low to the ground. He could make out dark black hair covering it and a long tail trailed behind.

'Protect yourself, Hector. I'll be with you as soon as I can.'

The smaller of the two black-cloaked men had unsheathed his own weapon now, a longsword, which he brought down repeatedly on the wooden bridge. Boards splintered as the sword hammered, the man backing away all the while, cutting off the route Drew might follow. The walkway was collapsing, tumbling into the brown, brackish water. More shapes moved within the sewage as the rotten timbers showered down, black creatures like the beast on the platform. Drew ran and leapt off the edge of the crumbling walkway towards him.

The man was ready, bringing his sword around to deflect Drew and send him hurtling past. Drew's momentum brought him crashing into the wall on the opposite bank of the platform, lights flashing before his eyes as he struggled to avoid falling into the river.

'Sorin!' shouted the big brute, clutching his leg. 'Don't leave me, you swine!' But the cry fell on deaf ears. The smaller man was already moving, running while Drew was stunned. Drew caught sight of the fleeing Sorin being swallowed by the darkness, the sound of his footsteps soon fading.

Drew straightened himself, ready to follow him before he got too far away. Hector's scream stopped him dead. He looked across the tunnel.

Three black shapes were now on the stone platform, two more of the creatures having joined the one that had advanced on the Boarlord. Hector had drawn his dagger, a jewel encrusted but impractical thing that he'd bought from a visiting eastern trader. Semi precious stones studded the handle, and he could feel each of those cheap jewels digging into his sweaty palm. Two of the creatures broke off, their heads low to the ground, and advanced on the big man where he lay bleeding. They snapped at one another, snarling and squealing as they closed in.

'Get back, you monsters!' screamed the man, clutching his injured leg with one hand while kicking out with the other. One of the creatures bit the boot of the wounded leg, tugging hard at it. The man yelled as its teeth bit down into his foot. Drew wavered, caught between chasing Sorin and aiding his friend. Another shout from Hector helped him make up his mind.

The walkway was in fragments so Drew had to stand and jump towards the platform from the opposite bank. He bent his knees and launched himself, diving forward through the darkness as far as he could. He hit sewage a few yards short of the flagged landing, the awful brown waters erupting around him. He struggled to surface, his sword lost with the impact. His legs struggled through the sewage, slurry churning up as he kicked for the surface. He gasped for air, choking as he dragged himself through the awful water, limbs colliding with foul floating objects. He felt something brush his leg as he got to the bank, where metal rungs rose up the platform wall. Pulling himself up he felt another movement beneath the surface as claws raked his legs. They dug in, gaining purchase and trying to drag him back under. Screaming with fury Drew continued to rise, the claws tearing furrows into his thigh as he dragged himself clear.

Drew rolled on to the platform as one of the beasts surfaced in the sewage where he'd been seconds earlier. Large incisors like splintered yellow bones gnashed as it tried to follow him. Spluttering, Drew struggled to his feet. At the back of the alcove he could see Hector losing his battle with the beast on top of him, long tail whipping about as its jaws snapped at his face. Drew leapt over, his hands grabbing the beast's back and throwing it off his friend. The animal bounced along the flags before rolling and coming up on to its feet once more.

'Are you all right?' asked Drew, as Hector backed against the wall. His friend's face was scratched and bleeding, but the wounds looked superficial. The gaudy dagger was still in his hand, slick with dark blood.

'I am now,' his friend smiled bravely. 'Behind you!'

Drew turned quickly, guarding the stricken young magister and meeting the beast head on as it charged. It caught him in the chest with its full weight, sending him crashing to the ground. Up close he was left in no doubt about what he faced.

The rat was the size of a mastiff, the kind northmen used to hunt bears and wolves. Its rheumy pink eyes glistened, and it seemed maddened as it bit and clawed. Drew held it round the throat, keeping its jaws from his face as it snarled and spat. The rat's forelimbs clawed at his arms, tearing the flesh and causing him to cry out in pain. The beast brought its rear limbs up towards Drew's belly, kicking and raking at his exposed stomach. His hopes of capturing either of the men alive were fading fast, especially with the odds stacked against him as they were. No, thought Drew. This wasn't a fair fight at all.

The Wolf needed no prompting. As his body was battered by the rat he let the beast in, his eyes fluttering as his body began to change. His arms remained locked, holding the rat at bay, but he felt the limbs bulging and contorting, his hands elongating into claws. The rat began to find the youth's stomach impregnable, as his torso was transformed into the muscular body of the Werewolf. Drew could feel the bones beneath his skin growing and morphing, his jaws cracking and dislocating as they became a canine muzzle. The pain wasn't nearly as great as it used to be. Manfred's lessons had taught him not just to channel his lycanthropy but to speed it along painlessly. In moments he was transformed.

The rat had continued to fight and attack, seemingly oblivious to the shape-shifting until it was too late. It began to struggle to break free, Drew no longer holding it back by the throat but squeezing it. It yelped as Drew roared, tightening his fists. The rat's squeal was cut short as Drew closed its throat in his grasp, shaking it until the light went out of its eyes.

Tossing it aside, Drew found he was now facing two more of the beasts. The one that had attacked him in the sewer river was now on the platform, shaking the slurry from its coat as a dog might dry itself. One of the rats that had advanced on the injured thug had turned its attention to Drew, intrigued by the arrival of the Werewolf. Both were larger than the rat that had attacked Hector. Once more he could hear splashing in the sewage – more of the monsters?

This was the work of Vankaskan, without a shadow of doubt. These were the pets the two villains had mentioned, the Wererat's guard dogs. He could see that the silhouette of the big man on the floor had stopped struggling. A rat sat on top of his body, gnawing and tearing at him, its face obscured by shadow as it buried its head in his chest. Smaller rats gathered, scuttling out of the shadows to see what scraps they could get. The other two giant rats hissed at one another, poised to leap at Drew. He had to stay alert, give them his full attention. Things could get messy very quickly.

'Hector,' he growled. 'Get out. Quick.'

'What are you doing?' asked Hector, starting to edge towards the pathway out of the sewer.

'Holding them back,' barked Drew. Hector was great at many things, but shape-shifting wasn't one of them. As long as he remained in the sewer he was in mortal danger. 'Buying you time. Go!'

One of the rats leapt. Drew backhanded it with his forearm, cracking it across the face. It bounced into the wall as its brother darted in, jaws snapping round Drew's ankle. He clawed at it, its oily fur slipping through his grasp. It wriggled one way and the other, twisting Drew around and almost dragging him to the ground. He felt a powerful blow to his back as the other rat landed on him, its jaws clamping on to his shoulder blade. He let out a howl of pain, raising one hand to try to grab the beast. With one on his back and one tearing at his leg, Drew was outnumbered and losing the fight.

Hector was gone, retreating swiftly along the tunnel ledge towards the ladders. Another shape surfaced from the water. Drew had to finish this before he was overwhelmed. Rushing backwards he drove his shoulders into the wall, grinding back against the brickwork, trapping the rat behind him. It released its jaws from his neck and shoulders, wailing as its bones shattered with the impact. When he felt its head fall limp he staggered forward, reaching down to the one on his leg. As it tried to manoeuvre away from his grasp, he brought his free knee down, pinning it in one place. He moved his hands fast, grabbing it by its jaws and prising them apart. Its jaws full of filthy teeth, sharp as daggers, slashed from side to side, but Drew was stronger. With a mighty heave he pulled his arms in opposite directions, breaking the jaws of the rat and it dropped, lifeless.

He could hear shouting now from where he'd entered. Torchlight began to flicker along the tunnel walls. Drew could hear men calling his name; the City Watch were coming. Hearing the commotion the rats began to disperse. The giant rat in the water went under once more, disappearing from view. One monster remained, crouching over the dead man's body, snarling, guarding its prize. Drew advanced a couple of steps, towering over it and growling back. The rat backed off, recognizing a deadly opponent. Shuffling over the platform it splashed into the sewer, its tail scything through the water behind it as it swam away.

'My lord,' came the cries as the men neared, the clanging of swords and armour echoing down the tunnel. An exhausted Drew dropped to his knees beside the disfigured body of the dead kidnapper, letting the Wolf slip away and the young man come back to the fore. By the time the soldiers had begun to gather round him he was back to his normal self, albeit torn and tattered. He stared at the dead man, his face lit by torchlight, recognizing the black beard streaked with grey.

'Brutus.'

Captain Brutus had been a member of the Lionguard, one of King Leopold's most trusted soldiers. It was Brutus who had stormed into Redmire, slaughtering Hector's father. The captain had also taken great delight in torturing Drew when he'd first arrived in Highcliff; the scars on his back from the silver whip were testament to that.

Drew leafed through the few remaining pieces of paper, the majority of them were lost forever in the water. There was nothing here. Then remembering the City Watch he pointed ahead.

'That way,' he managed, chest heaving. 'Make haste: they can't have gone far.'

The men set off, struggling along, the broken walkways slowing their progress dramatically. One soldier remained with Drew, helping him to his feet. Drew couldn't get the vision of the murdered Manfred and Kohl out of his head. He'd been the duke's shadow for the last four weeks, Manfred constantly at his side throughout each day, as a teacher and a friend.

'Oh Manfred, my dear friend,' he said to himself mournfully. 'Please don't let Gretchen face your fate.'

'The duke?' said the soldier. 'I'm sorry, my lord, but you mentioned the Staglord?'

'Yes. He lies dead and there was nothing I could do.'

'My lord, that's not the case,' said the soldier. 'Duke Manfred lives!'

4

The Staglord's Vengeance

Earl Mikkel's fist pounded the table, almost splitting the top in two. Drew remained silent, watching as the Wolf's Council dissected the day's events.

'I'm going after them!' Mikkel shouted furiously. 'I'll gore that Rat in two!'

Drew could see the Staglord's features twisting as he tried to keep the beast in check. The beginnings of his antlers had emerged from his hairline, brown spikes transforming him into a horned demon. His face was drawn, veins pulsing and eyes bulging as his broad nose snorted with disgust.

'Please, Mikkel, calm yourself,' implored Duke Bergan.

'We should be searching for them!'

'The scouts *are* searching for them, but the sewers are a labyrinth. They could be anywhere, within or outside the city. At least three of those old sewers come out in Highcliff. We'll have them blocked up by tomorrow, ensuring they're impassable.'

Count Vega, serious for once, nodded in approval.

'No sign of them in the harbour,' said the Sealord. 'My agents are aware who they're looking for. There hasn't been a sniff of a sighting.'

'I should be helping,' grumbled Mikkel, grinding his knuckles.

'You are helping,' said Lord Broghan, who stood beside his father. 'Your presence here is essential as we decide what to do.'

'And what *are* we going to do exactly? My uncle, Magister Kohl, lies dead while my brother fights for his life. By rights I should take an army and march on Vermire. That's where he's taken her, mark my words!'

Drew had heard enough about Vermire to know that he never wanted to visit it. A city port of murderers and pirates, it had enjoyed great business during Leopold's reign, the ships that sailed from the city stealing on the Lion's behalf. But if Vankaskan *had* taken Gretchen there then that was where Drew was heading.

'Let's not talk of armies, Mikkel,' barked Bergan. 'The last thing we want is war. Your brother lives; hold on to that thought. We're close to chasing the Lion and his cronies from Lyssia for good. So Vankaskan has been bold and played his hand – he's only one therian. The other four Wererats are holed up with Leopold, remember?'

Bergan pointed out of the window in the direction of Highcliff Keep while Broghan nodded gravely.

'We'll find them. There'll be nowhere to hide.'

'I pray so,' said Mikkel. 'Know this: the Rat's mine!'

'Send word to Stormdale,' suggested Bergan calmly, gesturing at Mikkel's chair with an open hand. 'Tell them this terrible business. But please – keep your army there for now. If you marched your soldiers across Westland there might be panic across the Seven Realms. No, stay here, keep your voice in the Wolf's Council. If you leave it weakens us.'

Mikkel sat down, weaving his fingers together and resting them beneath his chin. Drew felt enormous sympathy for him. Thus far he had remained silent

'My Lord Mikkel,' said Drew. Everyone turned to face him. 'You act with great dignity. A weaker man might let his anger beat him, which is what Vankaskan wants. I'm grateful you remain here by our side.'

'You speak wise words, Drew,' said Mikkel quietly, nodding his head in a brief but sincere bow.

'If I do, I have your brother to thank for teaching me them.'

Manfred's life hung in the balance; if he died what effect might that have on the furious Mikkel? There were too many unanswered questions about the Wererat and his plans, specifically where he was taking Gretchen and how many were in his company. There was, of course, another way to get answers, but it wouldn't have been approved by the Wolf's Council.

Drew wished there were more members of the council. Those therians who'd fought in the Battle of Highcliff had all taken their places in the court of Traitors' House. But two of the lesser Werelords who had fought on that day had returned to their homelands – Count Fripp, the Badger of Bray, and

Baron Mervin, the Wildcat of Robben. Their presence now might have given their fellows more comfort in numbers, but instead their spirits were fragile. Even the normally flamboyant Vega was in reserved mood. A showman, a pirate, a ladies' man, a cold-blooded killer: he and Manfred might have quarrelled, but ultimately the sea marshal respected the old Stag more than Manfred had ever known.

Bergan looked tired. The Bearlord was a leader of men, not a bureaucrat, and Drew could see that he felt under pressure. The abduction of Gretchen had resulted in mobs gathering outside Traitors' House, clamouring for news.

The atmosphere lifted slightly when a knock at the door heralded the arrival of Captain Harker, freshly returned from his tour of duty. The soldier bowed to the assembled Werelords before striding up to embrace Bergan.

'My lord,' he said.

Harker looked battle weary and grizzled, having grown a beard since Drew had last seen the soldier a month ago. A soiled bandage was looped round his head through his dark hair.

'Earl Mikkel,' said Harker. 'I've spoken with the Watch. You've my deepest sympathies at your loss, and I pray for Duke Manfred's swift recovery.'

The Staglord nodded gratefully to Harker. The captain spied Drew suddenly.

'Your Majesty,' he said, bowing low.

'Not yet,' said Bergan.

'You can still call me Drew, captain. Anything else makes me feel like a pretender.'

'Very well . . . Drew,' he said. 'Have you been injured?'

Drew checked himself, having forgotten about his wounds; he was wrapped in bandages of his own. The injuries were already healing, but the poultices and drugs that Hector had applied were a precaution against any diseases he might have picked up in the sewers. He wondered how the Boarlord was getting on with his secret task.

'Something like that,' answered Drew. 'You seem to have been in a scrape yourself!'

'This?' said Harker, tapping the bandage across his brow. 'Business in the Badlands. Trouble in Vermire has been quelled, but as my company returned down Grimm's Lane we ran into some of Muller's Skirmishers.'

Sheriff Muller, self proclaimed Lord of the Badlands, was not a therianthrope. He was a mortal man, an ex-member of Wergar's Wolfguard. When the Wolf's army was disbanded he had turned to banditry to make a living. Chased out of West-land, he had unified the various bands of brigands. Now this small army was getting bolder, striking the smaller, less well protected settlements on Westland's border.

Harker continued.

'We ended up chasing them, which delayed our return. Apologies, my lord.'

Bergan waved the apology away.

'Any man who catches Muller, dead or alive, gets one hundred gold crowns. They treat him like some kind of saviour. I remember him well: a tough soldier, but a loose blade, unpre-dictable. He'll be calling himself a king before long!'

'Might Vankaskan have asked Muller for help?' said Drew. The others looked at one another, not having considered this.

'It's possible,' muttered Broghan. 'The Badlands do neighbour Vermire.'

Bergan nodded.

'Don't get too comfortable, captain. Your company may be turning round rather quicker than expected, I'm afraid.'

'Command me, my lord, and I'm there,' said Harker, his jaw set and eyes keen.

'Most importantly,' said Bergan, patting Harker's shoulder. 'My daughter; has she returned?'

'She has, and she's well. We'd have been lost without her.'

'Really?' said Bergan with a mixture of surprise and pride.

'Our main scout, Cooper, stumbled on a nest of adders out of Vermire. Got bitten bad. He'll live, but we were without a scout. Lady Whitley stepped up; we'd never have hunted down Muller's Skirmishers if she hadn't been along. Led us straight to their camp, concealed as it was. As good as any scout I've worked with.'

Bergan growled in the direction of his son.

'I thought she wouldn't be in danger?'

'She's back safely, isn't she?' said Broghan. The young Werelord received a dark stare from the old Bear as Bergan turned back to Harker.

'Thank you for returning my daughter safely, captain.'

Drew walked up to Harker.

'When you're ready to head back out I'd be honoured if you'd let me travel with you.'

Before Harker could reply, the Lord of Brackenholme spoke up.

'That won't be happening.'

Drew turned to look at Bergan.

'Pardon? You're not in command of me, Duke Bergan.'

'As Lord Protector I'm charged with looking after the safety of the Seven Realms of Lyssia. This includes making sure the heir to the throne of Westland remains as far removed from danger as is possible. I can't let you go.'

'*Can't let me go?* You're not my father. If I choose to go I shall.'

'Then you'll find me blocking your path.'

'And me,' said Mikkel. 'You have lessons to complete.'

'*Lessons to complete?*' Drew could feel his own anger rising now. 'With respect, Mikkel, my teacher is currently under the watchful eyes of our magisters as he clings to life. He's hardly in any state to chase me with blunt steels.'

'Then I'll take the lessons myself,' bellowed Mikkel, no longer keeping his anger in check. 'You're just a boy! There's no way we'll let you risk the future of Lyssia on some foolish adventure.'

'This is not an adventure,' snarled Drew. 'It's a friend going after a friend. And I'm not a child any more. You can't hail me as the man who dethroned a tyrant in one breath and then swaddle me like a baby in the next!'

'Let us use our other resources to find Gretchen,' said Broghan. 'Surely you can see that it's folly for you to endanger yourself?'

Drew's blood was up. He'd been told what to do and where to go by the senior Werelords for a month now. He looked to Vega for support, who suddenly found the pommel of his cutlass very interesting.

'Have you nothing to say?' he asked the sea marshal. 'You've an opinion on most matters.'

The count looked up, his smile dazzling as ever.

'I actually agree with Drew,' he said, to everyone's surprise. 'Let him go and find her. He's been blessed by Sosha thus far, why should it stop now?'

Bergan clapped his hands sarcastically.

'Terrific. There's the voice of reason: dependable as ever, my dear count.'

Vega shrugged.

'I say what I see. Drew has come through everything that's happened to him thus far, from the Dyrewood, the serpent and my own regretted treachery. The lad can fall into a net of fish heads and come up smelling of Spyr Oil.'

Drew nodded his thanks.

'This isn't up for discussion,' said the Bear, thumping the tabletop with his fist and making them all jump. 'I made a promise to you and the people, Drew, that I shall keep you safe from harm. You stay and that's an end to it.'

Drew snatched his cloak up, fastening the clasp hastily round his throat.

'Where are you going?' asked Bergan, eyes narrow and suspicious.

'I desire the company of friends,' said Drew, pointedly. 'Don't worry yourself, Duke Bergan. I'm not planning on jumping the walls. There's a Boarlord and Lady of Brackenholme who might calm my spirits. I feel . . . on edge.'

He bowed to them.

'Drew,' said Bergan quietly. 'You must understand. I do this for everyone, not least your mother, Queen Amelie. She's only just found you again after all these years. Don't let her mourn you for a second time.'

Drew winced; he hadn't expected such arguments from Bergan. He turned and walked out of the chamber, slamming the door behind him.

He was halfway down the stairs when he found Whitley coming up the other way.

'Drew!' she cried, her face lighting up. His step quickened at the sight of her, and his dark mood instantly subsided. Arms open, he danced down the remaining step, embracing her.

'Oh, it's good to see you, Whitley,' he said, holding her at arm's length to appraise her. Was she taller since he'd last seen her a month ago? She looked grown up, wearing a studded leather jerkin and long knee-length boots. Bracers were laced over each forearm and she wore a huntsman's dagger on her hip. Her brown hair was tied back in a thick braid over her shoulders, out of the way of her face. She was filthy from weeks on the road, but her smile was as warm and bright as ever.

'And you, Drew. I was on my way to see my father – I believe Captain Harker came ahead of me. There seems a lot of activity at the gates with the Watch. What's going on? What have I missed?'

Drew looked back up the stairs the way he'd come, chewing his lip. Hector might have made some progress by now. Could he confide in Whitley? As guards walked past them up the stairs and staff came down the other way, Drew leaned in close to Whitley.

'Walk with me,' he whispered. 'There's something I'd like to discuss with you.'

5

Autopsy

Their booted feet splashed through puddles as they advanced down the corridor. The whole cell block had been abandoned since the Wolf's Council had taken control. Under Leopold it had teemed with prisoners. Three floors underground without a hint of natural light, the Pits, as they were known, had been emptied by Bergan immediately. Prisoners who had been jailed for over a decade had been brought to the surface, driven mad by their pitch-black confinement. The Wolf's Council had voted quickly to close and collapse this whole floor, reducing it to rubble to ensure it could never hold humans again, regardless of their crimes. Only the pressing matter of prising Leopold out of the keep had stopped them from getting on with the task.

Drew lifted his torch and looked back as they neared the corridor's end. Its fluttering flame illuminated the barred chambers as they passed. Recognizable shapes, draped in white sheets, lay on benches in the abandoned cells. The cold atmosphere kept the chambers refrigerated, reminding Drew of the butcher in Tuckborough who'd had a room where he kept his meats to stop them from spoiling. Mack Ferran would regularly sell animals to the man, and the cold room had always put Drew on edge.

Nobody had followed: the staff were quite relaxed within Traitors' House. The huge doors at the entrance to the old prison were well guarded, but once inside the tower it was relatively easy to move about freely. Since the Pits were currently being used as a makeshift mortuary by the military, there was very little need for people to head below. Unless, of course, they were transporting the dead.

'Is this it? No guard?' asked Whitley as they halted at the end of the corridor. Three stone steps led up to a squat wooden door. A faded sign was nailed to it, indicating it had once been a guardroom.

'What is there to guard?' said Drew.

Whitley shrugged and reached for the handle, but Drew moved quickly, snatching her hand and holding her back.

'What is it?'

'Beyond the door,' said Drew. 'What you might see. I don't want you to panic.'

'What will I see? It's just Hector meditating, no?'

'It's more . . . animated than that.'

'I don't understand,' said the girl, suddenly hesitant, pulling her hand away.

'I suppose you have to see for yourself.' He grabbed the

iron ring handle, turning it and pushing. The door creaked open and Drew entered, beckoning Whitley to follow. Her steps were small and wary.

Compared to the cells they'd passed, this room was more austere. Two torches spluttered on either side of the doorway, and Drew immediately holstered his into a spare bracket. A bunkbed stood against each of the three walls, and a writing desk with a rotten old ledger gathering dust and a mangy quill drooping from a dry inkpot were by the door. In the centre of the room was a heavy table, no doubt used by the guards in every aspect of their lives for eating, drinking and gambling. Drew was more concerned about what currently lay upon it.

A white sheet was draped over the corpse, stained brown in many places where blood had soaked through. Hector had his back to them, sitting cross-legged on the floor, but Drew could see the circle of yellow brimstone he'd carefully traced around the table. Communing with the dead was outlawed throughout Lyssia, although it was still practised in more remote societies. The Guild of Magisters, keepers of arcane knowledge, had banned it long ago. A handful of Dark Magisters, twisted and perverted by the power magick held over them, had killed in order to simply question and command a corpse. It couldn't be tolerated. But in this instance, as Hector had informed Drew, it seemed entirely necessary.

Hector was incanting, chanting the same words Drew had heard once before, one awful night in the Wyrmwood. While searching for the kidnapped Gretchen, Drew and Hector had encountered a tribe of Wyldermen, savages who worshipped the great Wereserpent Vala. The Wylderman Shaman had been slain, but their encounter didn't end there. Hector had raised the man from the dead, questioning the corpse to find where their friend had been taken. Drew felt goosebumps race across his flesh. In Hector's right hand Drew could see a long black candle, its flame shifting with their entrance, while his left palm held a pool of melted wax.

'What's he doing?' whispered Whitley, nervously. Drew felt her hand close round his, and he held hers tightly.

'Communing.'

'But that's a crime! Isn't it dangerous?'

Drew didn't want to tell her what he'd witnessed when Hector had raised the Wylderman Shaman.

'Don't worry, Whitley; he knows what he's doing.' He put a reassuring arm round her and positioned himself slightly ahead of her, just in case anything went awry like last time.

Hector's chanting stopped suddenly and he curled the wax-covered hand into a tight fist. The hot wax poured down his forearm, his sleeve falling back to the elbow. He brought his fist down once. Twice. Three times.

'Look!' gasped Whitley, her trembling finger pointing to the table.

The sheet shifted slightly, as if a breeze had fluttered by. Only Drew knew there were no breezes down in the Pits. This was a crypt, for all intents and purposes, as good as airtight.

Hector's voice was quiet and confident.

'Rise, creature, and answer to your master's bidding.'

Captain Brutus's corpse suddenly sat upright on the table, like a puppet on strings still covered by the shroud. Drew and Whitley instinctively stepped back, but Hector remained on the floor, legs folded and fist still planted firmly on the ground. He was showing tremendous restraint considering this was the corpse of the man who had slain his father. The cockiness that Hector had shown with the dead shaman had gone, replaced by a cautiousness that Drew welcomed.

'Where am I?' gurgled the corpse. The torchlight lit the sheet up, the body's silhouette visible through the material. Drew was grateful the sheet remained on the corpse for Whitley's sake. The rats had done a good job of stripping the captain's flesh and burrowing into the body's chest.

Although the torso remained relatively motionless, there was a rising panic in the corpse's voice as its head twitched this way and that as if scanning the room.

'The dark. They're in the dark,' it rasped. 'All around me. Claws and teeth.'

'They're gone now,' said Hector to the corpse of his father's killer. 'They're dead. The rats are all gone.'

'No, no, no,' whined the dead captain fearfully. 'They're all around me.'

'They're gone. They can't hurt you now. You're . . . dead.'

Drew felt Whitley's hand tighten about his, almost cracking his knuckles.

'Dead?' murmured the corpse, apparently only semi-aware of its fate. 'Then why do I feel their teeth and claws? Why can I hear them screaming?'

Hector looked over his shoulder at Drew with an expression that said *what do I tell it?* Drew shrugged, shaking his head.

'Ask about Gretchen and Vankaskan!'

Hector turned back and cleared his throat.

'Your master — where did he take our friend?'

The corpse of Brutus didn't answer, still glancing about frightened, the sheet rustling. Hector raised his voice.

'Lady Gretchen! Your master took her: what plans did he make?'

The dead captain snapped back to attention at his shout.

'The woman. We took her. Never told us plans. Never asked. Just obeyed.'

Hector shook his head, annoyance rising.

'Where was he heading?'

'South,' said the corpse. 'We were heading south.'

So south it was, thought Drew. What was south of High-cliff but the Longridings, land of the Horselords? Did the rat have allies there?

'Where, exactly?' asked Drew.

Hector took up the question. 'Why is the south so impor-tant to Vankaskan, your master?'

The corpse gurgled a low laugh, the ribcage in its open chest grating.

'Why do you laugh?' asked Hector. It ignored him, its shoulders now rocking as it began to lose control. 'Why do you laugh?' shouted the Boarlord.

'Vankaskan not my master,' spluttered the corpse. 'Prince Lucas my master.'

Hector turned to Drew, his expression a mixture of surprise and concern. Neither youth had even considered whether Lucas was behind the abduction — it appeared to be the hand-iwork of the Ratlord, even down to the sewers as a route of escape. Both Drew and Hector knew firsthand how unhinged the prince was. If he'd got his claws back into Gretchen who knew what his intentions were.

'If Lucas is with Vankaskan and has Gretchen . . .' began Drew.

'The south,' continued Hector, his head snapping back to Brutus's corpse. 'Where does he head to?'

'Bast,' hissed the dead body of the captain, its half-eaten tongue licking the once-white sheet. 'Bast.'

Hector, Drew and Whitley looked at one another. Bast: the jungle continent to the south of Lyssia. Leopold's homeland.

'We have to stop him,' said Drew. 'If he catches a ship south, we'll have lost them.'

'We must send word to the towns and ports along the Cold Coast,' said Whitley. 'Have them alerted to Lucas and Vankaskan, make sure they can't charter passage.'

'And Cape Gala?' asked Hector. 'We've had no word from Cape Gala since Leopold was dethroned. What if he *does* have allies there? What if Duke Lorimer is a friend to the Lion?'

Drew looked past Hector and back at the corpse on the table. Hector followed his gaze back to the animated soldier. Brutus's body seemed to be weaving where it sat, lurching one way and then the other as if evading a series of blows. Its wailing had begun once more.

'What's the matter with it?' asked Drew. Hector didn't answer; he was looking left and right around the body, as if anticipating whatever imaginary foes the dead man faced.

'They bite!' cried the corpse. 'Teeth so sharp!' Its hands came up beneath the sheet. Through the dim light Drew could see the silhouette of Brutus's mangled limbs, fingers and thumbs missing from each hand.

'Hector?' asked Drew. Again, the Boarlord didn't answer, his own head flicking about now, around the room, over his own shoulder, behind Drew. His face was pale and his eyes were wide and white.

'Drew . . .' said Whitley, her voice thick with terror.

'Hector!' shouted Drew. He'd seen the chaos of communing before. He had to end this before it went the same way. Drew leapt forward and dropped to his knees beside Hector, whose head flashed about, his mouth slack and gibbering. Brutus's corpse on the table was shaking now, battered from side to side by an invisible force. Drew could hear a ripping, shredding sound. The corpse was screaming now, dying all over again.

'Hector, make it stop!' he shouted, shaking him. 'We have what we need!' When Hector didn't respond, Drew slapped him hard across the face. The body was lifting into the air now, appearing to levitate, bouncing against the tabletop. Drew smacked Hector once more.

'*Hector!*'

The Boarlord suddenly snapped to, his eyes blinking back into focus.

'Yes,' he babbled. 'Make it stop. Make it stop.' He opened his left palm, black with the liquid wax that remained hot against his flesh. He held it up at Brutus's corpse as it thrashed about, tormented by its invisible attackers.

'Return from whence you came!' he shouted, and slammed his palm into the ground. Instantly the body stopped its demonic dance, collapsing in a heap of torn flesh and bone on to the table, the sheet slowly fluttering as it settled over it once again.

The room was quiet, but for Hector's low sobbing. Drew glanced up at Whitley, then turned and hugged his friend.

6

Under Cover of Darkness

The white stag danced in the breeze, its body rising and falling
as it raced across the grey field. The flag of Stormdale flew at
half mast above Buck House as the occupants within mourned
the loss of one of their lords, and prayed for the recovery of
another. The guards at the gatehouse were in a sombre mood
after the day's events. Some had been first on the scene along
with the Wolf and the Boarlord. Others had received news of
Magister Kohl's death later in the day when taking their posts.
Each of them grieved and each wanted to hunt the killers
down, unaware that within the mansion, that very hunt had
already begun.

Drew had kept his bedchamber window open so he could
make a swift exit – he didn't want to wake the house. The
bells of Brenn's temple chimed to mark midnight, an hour as
good as any to depart. His balcony provided a view of the

harbour and the whole of the Low Quarter, the grand houses of Highcliff's wealthiest hugging the cliffs all around. The waxing moon was pulling hard tonight – he could feel it in his bones, a dull ache that begged him to take on the beast. Manfred's lessons stood him in good stead at times like these. The Wolf wasn't conquered, but Drew felt in control as never before. The opportunity to run on all fours might arise beyond the walls.

Below, in the courtyard, Hector waited. The Boarlord was Drew's way out – he was more than aware that Bergan didn't want him to leave. But the two of them couldn't do this alone. Drew fastened his cloak about his shoulders, the dark woodland green of Brackenholme an ideal camouflage for the wilderness. Not ideal within Highcliff, but his quarry wasn't in the city. It was heading south and already had a head start. Picking up his backpack, he slung it over his shoulder before opening the chest at the foot of his bed. It was empty. It was gone.

'Looking for this?' whispered a voice. Drew jumped up, his eyes searching the shadows. It was Queen Amelie, dressed in a long grey nightrobe, and in her hands she held the Wolf-shead blade. Her faced was etched with worry, every line thrown into contrast by the moonlight.

'The sword of Mack Ferran, isn't it? A good sword wielded by a brave man in the defence of the realm. Wergar's sword, Moonbrand, disappeared when he died.'

Her voice was sad as she looked at the sword, thinking of happier times. Drew could think of nothing to say – he hadn't intended to be discovered making his escape. This threw his plans into chaos. It was probably only a matter of time before she called the guards. Amelie looked up suddenly as if sensing his tension.

'Was that your plan, then? To disappear?'

'I'm sorry. I was afraid you'd try to prevent my leaving.'

'Is that what troubles you?' asked Amelie, stepping closer. 'That I might raise the alarm?'

'Will you not?' asked Drew, his voice cracking with emotion.

She handed the sword across to him by the scabbard, the hilt within reaching distance.

'Take the blade, Drew. Find Gretchen. Stop this evil.'

He didn't take it, unsure whether she was testing him. Amelie's mood could change quickly. Fifteen years in mourning, being medicated by Leopold, had left her a fragile woman.

'But, Mother,' he whispered, the word still odd to his lips. 'What if the evil is being carried out by . . . your other son?'

He couldn't hide the truth: he and Lucas were brothers, sons of the same mother. Utterly different, but inextricably connected to the heart of Queen Amelie. If the two came to blows – and chasing after Gretchen might lead to that – that could lead to the death of one of them.

'Lucas was always troubled. A priest of Brenn warned us that his birth was surrounded by dark omens, and Leopold had the priest killed. Lucas was always kind to me, but others? I witnessed my son beating his tutors as a child, having servants flogged. There is too much of his father in him. I love him, Drew – nothing can change that. But I know he has done wicked things. If you can pull him back from the brink, then I beg you to try to do that, for my sake. But if his soul is so damaged, so irretrievable . . .'

She couldn't finish the sentence, the sword and scabbard beginning to shake in her grasp. Drew took the handle, taking the weight, and sword, from her hands. He stepped close and embraced her, allowing her to cry. He spoke quietly, his words chosen carefully.

'You have my word, Mother, that if need be I'll stop his torment.' He kissed her gently on the forehead.

'You know why I have to do this, don't you?' he went on. 'I can't trust someone else to fight my fight.'

She brushed her hand across his face.

'Oh, Drew. You're more like your father than you'll ever know. But his world was black and white, full of only friends or enemies. You see all the shades of grey.'

Drew looked to the balcony and back to the queen.

'I'm sorry to put you in the middle of this, Mother, but I must go. Time is against us.'

'One more thing, Drew,' she said, reaching into her robe, pulling a white metal signet ring from her pocket and handing it to him. 'It was my wedding gift to Wergar, and now it's my gift to you.'

The ring bore the image of an enraged wolf, teeth bared and ready for battle. Amelie smiled as Drew traced his finger-tip along the metal, lingering over the details.

'I had Duke Henrik of Icegarden set his greatest smiths to work on it, and they didn't let me down. It was blessed by the elders of Shadowhaven. Wergar never took it off.'

'It's incredible,' said Drew, slotting it on to the middle finger of his left hand. 'It fits perfectly.'

'The metal was enchanted deep within the Strakenberg, Henrik told me. It will change when you change, Drew, growing and shrinking as you shift.'

The queen was more animated than Drew had ever seen her before, speaking wistfully about the past.

'There are no greater metalsmiths in Lyssia than those you'll find beneath the Whitepeaks,' she continued. 'The Sturmish guard their secrets well. Henrik's father, Ragnor, charged into battle wearing an enchanted gauntlet, fashioned into a bear's paw. The White Fist of Icegarden they called him. There was a time when all the ancient Werelords carried Sturmish artefacts on to the battlefield. Take this ring, and keep it close.'

Drew regarded Wergar's ring before dropping to one knee, bowing his head before the queen. She stepped forward and pulled him to his feet, hugging him once.

'Go now, quickly.'

Drew ran to the balcony, took hold of the climbing vines and disappeared over the edge. Hector watched nervously, glancing toward the gatehouse. Drew dropped gracefully to the dusty ground.

'What kept you?'

'Goodbyes,' said Drew, pulling his friend toward the gates. As they neared, the captain of the guard came out to meet them.

'My lords,' he said. 'I have guards prepared to escort you to Traitors' House. They wait in the barracks – let me fetch them.'

This wasn't what they'd planned. Hector had told the gate guards that Drew was needed for an emergency meeting of the Wolf's Council. Any other reason for removing the heir to the throne in the dead of night would have met with disapproval. The guards were under strict instruction to keep an eye on Drew – Hector had even signed the orders. The two had hoped to depart alone. Guards would draw attention and, more importantly, they weren't heading to Traitors' House.

'That's not necessary,' said Hector. 'Lord Drew and I can make our way to Traitors' House alone.'

'May I speak freely?' asked the captain, anxiously. He was a heavy set man, with a mop of red hair tumbling over his brow. He looked like a seasoned campaigner, and a very capable warrior.

'Please do.'

'With respect, my lord, Duke Manfred left with the same destination earlier today and we know what happened to him. It would be remiss of me to let you leave without my men-at-arms.'

Hector prickled, struggling to reply to the captain's logical response. A lapse in duty had led to tragedy and the last thing the guards needed was more bloodshed. Drew decided to step in and pull rank.

'Captain Graves, isn't it?' Drew said. Graves nodded, clearly pleased that the future king remembered his name.

'Your offer is generous,' said Drew. 'But I can assure you that your men aren't needed. The people responsible for the attack earlier today have already fled. They're beyond the walls and every minute we're delayed they move further from our grasp. Thank you, captain, but keep your men here and guard Queen Amelie.'

Drew started to walk past, but Graves wasn't giving up. He lifted a hand before him, Drew's chest bumping into it.

'I'm sorry, my lord, but I cannot let you leave alone. By order of the Wolf's Council.'

Drew was impressed by the man. Ordinarily it would be good to know that Graves was a stickler for detail, especially with his mother in residence and Manfred recovering. But now the man's stubborn sense of duty was proving a huge hurdle. He hated himself for what came next, but they had to pass.

'The Wolf's Council serves *me*, captain,' he snapped. 'Stand aside.'

'Word from the Lord Protector himself,' said Graves, straightening his back. 'You're a flight risk, my lord. The Wolf's Council fears you'll attempt to depart Highcliff.' He looked past Drew, standing to attention like a good soldier.

Good old Bergan, thought Drew, as Hector reached inside his collar and pulled out a disc on a chain. The wolf medallion glinted in the moonlight. The soldier glanced at it.

'You recognize the amulet, captain?' Hector said coldly. 'Good. I *am* the Wolf's Council. Now stand aside and we'll see you upon our return.'

The guard didn't move immediately. His eyes kept settling upon the medallion. Gradually his nerve buckled and he stood to one side.

'Apologies, my lords,' he said, bowing his head. 'Guards: the gate!'

Drew glowered at Graves as he passed, although he wanted to commend him for standing up to them. With a man like Graves in charge of Buck House and the safety of his mother, Drew would rest easy. The gates swung open and the two Werelords paced on to the cobbles of Lofty Lane.

Once they were out of earshot, Drew spoke to Hector.

'When I'm gone, you make sure Graves isn't punished. Better still, award him a medal.'

The walk to the Tall Quarter took almost an hour. At every junction they inevitably met the City Watch. Werelords or not, the curfew stood, and on half a dozen occasions they found themselves facing guards with halberds lowered. Each time Hector stepped forward to answer their questions. As a member of the Wolf's Council he could move freely around the city. He also knew that Bergan's order to prevent Drew from leaving the city meant he'd be stopped if recognized. Drew travelled with his hood up and face obscured, looking like a regular soldier of Brackenholme.

The two therians took a wide berth around the army encampment, but couldn't miss Highcliff Keep as they passed. Ships had been anchored below at the foot of the cliffs, monitoring any movement, while in the city above the army had placed great braziers along the edge of the moat, letting the fires burn through the night. This kept the walls illuminated until morning, and any attempt to escape would be seen. Somewhere within the keep, Leopold and the remaining four members of the Rat King hid from them, plotting their revenge. Drew shivered at the thought.

Reaching Pious Road, a broad avenue that ran through the Tall Quarter, the two youths headed south-east, sticking to the shadows and trying to make up time. They should depart without further delay.

'Are we nearly there?' asked Drew as they passed the stone steps that led to Brenn's Temple. The old church stood like a looming sarcophagus, its tall doors open as was the tradition of Brenn's order: 'A haven to all, his door shall never close'. Drew hoped he'd never have to take him up on that offer.

'Almost,' huffed Hector. He was still out of shape, the weight he'd lost on their recent perilous adventure having reappeared. Highcliff life could make a man soft.

They rounded a corner and there it was: Hammergate. Drew's heart quickened. Hector still strode in front, drawing any attention that came their way. Two torches burned on either side of the gate, lighting Hammergate's arch. A guardroom was built into the wall to the right, but the duty guards were gathered in the street. The four of them looked their way as the youths turned the corner, readying their halberds.

'Who goes there?' asked a tall, lanky one, who had a swaggering stride as he stepped forward. The other guards followed him

'Lord Hector, Magister to the Wolf's Council,' replied Hector, striding confidently forward and showing them his medallion. He'd been through this routine before and found the deception got easier. 'You can stand down.'

The lanky fellow stepped further forward, his colleagues standing their ground behind.

'We have our orders, Lord Hector,' said the soldier, leaning on his halberd. He seemed pleased to be correcting a Werelord.

'Nobody's to leave or enter the city during the curfew. I'm afraid you'll have to wait until the morning.'

Drew clenched his fists beneath his cloak.

'On whose order?' asked Hector, already knowing the answer.

'The Lord Protector. Take it up with him would be my suggestion.'

Hector was about to challenge the impertinent guard when they were interrupted by a voice from behind.

'My lord!'

A figure in a hooded green cloak, the same cut as Drew's, appeared from within the stable block across the road. The staff slung across his back marked him a scout. Drew was grateful his own hood was up because his grin within was wide.

'Our horses are ready,' said the young scout, bowing. The guards showed no alarm.

'Your horses are going nowhere, lad,' said the guard, smiling. 'Not without the approval of Duke Bergan.'

'My apologies,' said the scout, reaching into his hip satchel. Tugging loose a scroll he handed it to the guard. 'Duke Bergan's seal.'

The lanky guard held the scroll to the fire, letting the flames reveal the red wax: the Tree of Brackenholme. There was no mistaking the Bearlord's personal seal. He grimaced.

'This is most unorthodox. We're under special instruction to stop anyone from leaving.'

'Well,' said Hector. 'As you can see our scouts are also under special instruction. They carry a message, direct from the Wolf's Council, which needs to reach Brackenholme as fast as possible. Stand down.' The guards behind the soldier began to relax. They weren't about to push the situation, not if Bergan was involved. The soldier begrudgingly handed the scroll back.

'Lad,' said Hector. 'Fetch your horses.'

Whitley smiled.

'Yes, my lord,' she said, and hurried into the stable block. It amused Drew no end that it wasn't just him who so readily mistook Whitley for a boy. He'd mistaken her as such when they'd first met in the Dyrewood, only discovering a month ago that he was in fact a she. With her hood up and head down, she looked like any other scout of the Woodland Watch, and who would question one that carried the seal of Brackenholme? She emerged from the stables a moment later leading two light horses by their reins. With delight Drew recognized Chancer, the faithful mount of Whitley's that had helped them so long ago.

'Good work,' whispered Drew to Whitley as he checked his gear on his horse. 'The scroll's a nice touch.' She leaned back into him as she straightened her saddle.

'A perk of Father being Lord Protector; it wasn't difficult to get to his writing desk. One never knows when an important looking document might be useful.'

'Why did we pick Hammergate?' Drew quietly asked.

'It's usually quiet. It was used by one of Leopold's deserters the other week. I wasn't expecting the guards to be so diligent, that one in particular, impertinent fellow.'

The guards moved the locking timber from its moorings, sliding it to one side. The tall stubborn soldier glowered, refusing to help. The three friends stepped through the gate, leading the horses out of the city. Whitley gave Hector her best manly handshake, trying not to attract further attention. Drew followed, squeezing Hector's black gloved hand tight.

'I'll miss you, Hector,' he whispered, his voice choked. 'Bergan's going to come down on you like a rockfall. Will you be all right?'

'I'll be fine,' he said quietly, his own words catching in his throat. 'What harm can I come to within these walls? It's you two who are facing the dark and dangerous road. Take care of each other. And find Gretchen. Bring her back safely, and bring yourselves back too while you're at it.'

Drew and Whitley climbed into their saddles, saluting Hector just once. Then they were riding, putting distance between themselves and Highcliff. Drew looked back at his friend as their horses picked up speed. He felt an ache in his heart at the thought of perhaps never seeing Hector again. A moment later the Boarlord was lost from sight, as the walls of the city disappeared into the night and Drew's attention was drawn to the open road ahead.

PART II

The Talstaff Road

I

Breaking the Boar

Hector stood on the tiled floor of the library, hands behind his back. He kept his gaze fixed on the ground, letting his eyes wander over the mosaic depicting the settling of Highcliff city. All manner of beasts could be spotted within the picture: wolves, bears, boars, stags. Lions were conspicuously absent. The art was a celebration of all that was great about Westland, commissioned by a long dead warden of Traitors' House. The old library now acted as a court, with Hector on trial.

'Well?' said Duke Bergan. He sat in the middle of a long bench on a raised dais in the room. Count Vega and Earl Mikkel sat on either side of him, with Lord Broghan beside the Werestag.

'Have you nothing to say?' added Mikkel. 'You've betrayed the trust of this council and put Drew's life at risk.'

'With respect, my lords, Drew can make decisions for himself. If he wants to go after Gretchen, we shouldn't stand in his way.'

'He is but a boy, as are you,' boomed Mikkel. The Staglord, famous for his temper, was behaving true to form.

'I wasn't considered a boy when you vouched for my inclusion on the Wolf's Council, my lord.'

'What a grand idea that's proved to be,' grumbled Mikkel.

Bergan stamped his foot. The council was silenced, turning to the Lord Protector. He looked hard at Hector from beneath his bushy eyebrows, his temper in check, unlike that of the Staglord.

'When you took the role of magister to the Wolf's Council, Hector, you became part of a select group of Werelords who were sworn to protect Drew and the future of Lyssia.'

Hector opened his mouth, but Bergan raised a hand to silence him.

'By helping Drew leave the city, in the manner you did – scheming and betraying your oath – you've jeopardized all that we work towards. Furthermore, you've let my only daughter join him on his mad quest. Do you know what they're up against if they catch up with the Rat? You worked for Vankaskan – you know what he's capable of! What might he do to Gretchen if Drew gets to him before we do?'

Hector knew Vankaskan all too well. A sadist who delighted in torturing others, he was a monster for sure, but he wasn't pulling the strings.

'Vankaskan won't harm Gretchen,' said Hector. 'I promise you.'

Mikkel began to object, but another raised hand from Bergan brought silence.

'What possible assurance can you give?'

'Because Prince Lucas still commands him. It's Lucas who's behind this abduction and it's Lucas who flees to Bast.'

Bergan's eyes widened as Mikkel leaned forward in his seat, spit flying from his mouth as he shouted. 'How in Brenn's name could you know that? What would you know about the whereabouts of Lucas? Vankaskan acts alone and heads to Vermire as I've said all along!'

'Whoever is behind this, east is the way they've gone, I guarantee it,' said Broghan. 'Father, let me take Harker and six of our best branches. The Great West Road – fast and straight, that's how he travels. I must go immediately if I'm to catch him.'

Bergan ignored the others, while Vega kept his own counsel, silently stroking his chin. The Bear and the Shark looked to one another. *Were they thinking the same thing?* wondered Hector. Finally Bergan spoke.

'How is it you can make such a statement, Hector? How can you know, beyond doubt, who is behind the kidnapping of Gretchen and where he intends to take her?'

Hector's gaze fell to the floor again, his cheeks hot, the telltale blush of shame creeping across his face.

'Answer him, lad,' said Mikkel.

Hector's stomach knotted. He'd known it would come to this all along. He glanced up to see Bergan staring at him. The Bearlord nodded. *He knows about the communing!* Hector cursed himself; they'd been in such a hurry to escape the scene of horror in the Pits that they hadn't tidied their mess up. He'd left the corpse, the markings from the ritual; only the Wolf's Council had access to that part of Traitors' House. He'd been caught red-handed. *Or is that black-handed?* he asked himself. Hector's mouth was dry, and he could feel nausea coming on in a great dark wave as he answered.

'Questions.'

'What?' asked Mikkel.

'Questions,' replied Hector, again.

Mikkel turned to the others, confusion racing across his face.

'Is he mocking us?'

'He doesn't mock us,' said the old Bearlord, dropping his head and shaking it sadly. 'He's answered us.'

'He's been asking questions,' added Vega, finally joining the debate. 'Haven't you Hector? And this isn't the first occasion is it?'

Mikkel looked no wiser.

'I don't follow,' said the Staglord gruffly, anger rising in his voice. 'What does he mean?'

The Bearlord looked up at Hector, his face full of thunder.

'It appears our magister has been communing.'

Broghan and Mikkel gasped in unison.

'That's outlawed!' cried Broghan.

'Witchcraft is what it is!' snapped Mikkel. 'Kohl practised magicks for sixty years, healing cantrips, blessings and such. I can't recall a single occasion when he tampered with the dark arts.'

'Hector, what were you thinking?' asked Broghan, trying

to catch his gaze, but instead the Boar kept his eyes on the ground, fighting back tears.

'Your father would be ashamed of you,' said Mikkel. 'As are we all.'

'I'm not ashamed of him,' said Vega, rising and stretching.

'Stay seated,' said Broghan to the sea marshal.

'I don't think I shall, young cub,' said Vega. 'My back aches from sitting on that bench and I can no longer feel my buttocks, the poor things.' He rubbed his rump, smacking life back into it.

'Remember where you are!' shouted Broghan.

'Oh please,' said Vega, exasperated. 'We sit in a musty library berating a boy whose only crime is helping a friend.'

Hector chanced a look up, while Vega took the focus away from him. Broghan was snarling, while Mikkel put a calming hand upon his shoulder. Only Bergan still stared at him, eyes twinkling, face in shadow. The Bearlord rose from the bench, all order gone. He slowly walked to Hector. The others fell silent behind him.

Hector dropped his head as Bergan approached, only for the the Bearlord to take his chin between thumb and forefinger and raise his face up. Bergan was a giant, literally a bear of a man. His huge red beard didn't hide his face; it made it bigger broad nose, ruddy skin, dark brown eyes and heavy brow. The hand that held Hector's jaw could probably fit easily round his head, and was just as likely to crush it in an instant.

'Hector,' he whispered. 'It was the corpse they brought out of the sewer, wasn't it? Brutus?'

Hector nodded.

'Is this the first time?'

He considered lying, but with the Bearlord staring at him with those big, fierce eyes he felt compelled to tell the truth. Hector shook his head sadly. Bergan continued.

'In times of old, the magisters who practised communing were executed, considered corrupt in mind and spirit. Burned, beheaded, stoned, drowned . . .'

Bergan leaned in close, whispering into Hector's ear.

'I heard of one magister, a Horselord I believe. They poured molten silver into his mouth. Can you imagine?'

Hector thought he might vomit. His head swam and his legs felt unsteady. Bergan took a firmer hold of his jaw.

'Steady, Hector. Don't be falling down now.'

'My Lord,' said Hector, his face streaked with tears. 'I've only ever communed to help our cause. When my friends are endangered I do what I can to help. I've never communed for selfish reasons, I swear!'

'I've always thought of you as family, Hector. Your father was like a brother, and I've watched you grow up from being a young Boar to a true Werelord. Until today I imagined Huth was proud of what you've become. But this? You've done something incredibly foolish.'

'You're too hard on him,' interrupted Vega. 'He communed. So what? It was with good intentions. If he hadn't we wouldn't know that Lucas was behind this fiasco and fleeing south to Bast as we speak. We should thank him!'

Bergan didn't turn to the captain of the *Maelstrom*, keeping his eyes on Hector instead.

'He has taken a great risk in doing this, Vega. Communing,

the dark arts of magick – they're like a drug, I'm told, addictive at that. No cause is reason enough to speak with the dead. A line has been crossed, and I fear it cannot be uncrossed.'

'You speak in riddles,' sighed Vega, striding down the dais to join Bergan. 'Let the boy be. He's learned his lesson.'

Bergan let go of Hector and stepped back.

'You've left us with no option. I say this with regret.'

Duke Bergan held his hand out.

'The amulet, Hector. Hand it over.'

Hector looked at Bergan, his eyes wide with astonishment. His gloved hand closed round the medallion that marked him as one of Drew's most trusted, a fellow of the Wolf's Council.

'Please,' he implored. 'Not that. I'm so sorry, but don't take the amulet. I can do better, you have my word!'

'We had your word before, lad,' said Mikkel, his eyes narrowed.

'I'll give it again,' said Hector. 'I can make this right!'

Bergan's face was hard, his decision made.

'Your word means little now, I'm afraid.' His open hand twitched, fingers beckoning. 'You can still have a role here, Hector. There's important work that needs doing for the Wolf's Council. But some of our business will be behind closed doors, and you won't be present, son.'

'Show us you can be trusted again and you can take your place once more,' added Mikkel.

'I promise you,' said Bergan, nodding in agreement. 'The amulet can be yours again. But you must prove your loyalty to us.'

Hector lifted the chain of office from round his neck. He

held it for the briefest moment, taking one last look at the medallion, before dropping it into Bergan's palm. Bergan turned and walked back up the steps to retake his seat. He looked down to Vega who still stood beside the shamed Boarlord on the mosaic.

'Are you rejoining us, Sea Marshal Vega?'

The count snatched up his cape and cutlass from where he'd draped them over a bookcase.

'I have more pressing business in the harbour. I believe there are two drunks arguing over the ownership of a broken lobster basket.' He didn't look back as he stormed out of the door. 'Good day, gentlemen.'

Mikkel glowered as Broghan pointed after the Wereshark.

'Vega's a liability,' said the young Bearlord. 'He shows a constant lack of respect for this council.'

'I thought he'd have tired of playing government by now,' said Mikkel. 'This must be the longest the Shark has stuck to anything in his life. I'm almost worried about him!'

Mikkel and Broghan laughed, unaware of Bergan's quiet mood. The Bearlord still stared at Hector, who looked back, a broken man. Hector didn't particularly care what Mikkel and Broghan thought of him. The Stag's temper often got him into trouble, while the young Bear was a good but naive man in Hector's eyes, desperate for his father's approval.

But Hector could remember childhood summers in the company of Bergan and Lady Rainier. He and his brother had grown up alongside Whitley, treated by Bergan as his own. He saw how disappointed the duke was, and it broke his heart.

'Have you noticed any . . . ill effects, since this communing, Hector?' asked Bergan.

'What do you mean?' asked Mikkel.

'I remember Baron Huth mentioning it years ago,' explained the Bearlord, watching Hector all the while. 'Once a magister taps through to the other side, he can leave himself open to . . . forces. Perhaps we've nipped this in the bud quickly enough, Hector. Nothing ails you, does it?'

Hector shook his head. He could have mentioned the darkness in the Pits, but figured he'd had enough trouble for one day.

'Nothing ails me, my lord,' lied Hector.

'You may leave then,' said Bergan warmly, though his smile looked hollow to Hector.

Bergan continued. 'Might I suggest you take the rest of the day for yourself? Fresh air will clear your head.'

Hector nodded and walked to the door. They didn't wait for him to leave, getting back to the business of Drew immediately.

'Father,' said Broghan. 'Let me take those six branches as I said. Harker can have them ready to ride within the hour. If we leave now we may catch them on the road south.'

'It's a fine idea,' agreed Mikkel. He coughed sharply and suddenly and the Boarlord glanced back at them. The Staglord was looking his way. *Did they think he was eavesdropping?*

'Tomorrow, Hector,' said Bergan. 'I'll see you then. Go now.'

Head bowed, the shamed Lord of Redmire left the room. He trudged down the staircase, each step jarring. As he passed guards he felt their eyes upon him, judging him. He heard them whispering, sensed them pointing. He'd never felt so miserable in his life. His dark mood seemed to radiate outwards, gloom descending everywhere he looked: shadows and darkness.

The darkness – if he'd mentioned that to Bergan they wouldn't have let him leave the room. They'd probably have him put under armed guard, for his own safety. Deep in the Pits, questioning the corpse of Captain Brutus, he'd seen them. Out of the darkness they had appeared, shadows taking on an apparently solid form, black gaseous shapes with teeth and talons. The dead soldier's spirit had drawn their attention, and they'd feasted on him, killing him again. To die once horrifically was unthinkable, but twice?

Some had ignored the corpse, lured to the power Hector channelled. They'd circled like a pack of dogs, searching for a weak point to attack. He'd felt blind terror, his heart seizing up, waiting for them to strike. Then Drew had slapped him, brought him round. He'd killed the ritual and the shadows had vanished.

Only now, even in daylight, by firelight, wherever there were shadows, he saw the beasts in the corner of his eye. He'd turn his head, but they'd be gone, tricks of the light. Just thinking about the shadows brought a pain behind his eyes, like knives to his mind. His left hand balled into a trembling fist as he fought fresh tears. *No*, he thought. *Don't let them see you cry.* He turned his fist over and slowly unfurled it.

The black mark had started small, insignificant at first, but it had irritated him. He'd thought it was just a burn initially, brought on from his communing in the Wyrmwood. The black wax had seared the flesh, but the wound hadn't healed. On board the *Maelstrom*, he'd communed again, that time with his father. The mark had grown – only slightly, but larger nonetheless. He'd tried not to rub it, but it was always there, an itch that needed scratching. Out of habit he would rub it with the thumb of his right hand, unaware he was doing it.

Since he'd communed with the corpse yesterday the mark was considerably bigger, roughly the size of a gold crown. The flesh around it looked sore from the wax, but the blackened skin was easier to examine now. It wasn't burned at all. He could see every detail of the skin's surface. And it didn't hurt. He thought it would feel hot and tender, but it felt cool to the touch. Cool and numb. He traced his thumb over it in a slow circle, following its edge around his palm.

'Don't let them get to you.'

Hector looked around, snapping his hand closed. Count Vega stepped out of a doorway that led on to the first floor. *Has he been waiting for me?*

'Come, I'll walk with you,' said the sea marshal.

'They haven't got to me,' sighed Hector as they descended. 'No more than they're entitled. It was stupid.'

'You were being a friend. You risked something for Drew and Gretchen,' said Vega. 'Surely that's worth something? To have power and not use it is criminal. You could have left things to fate, but you did something about it instead.'

'I've been an idiot.'

'No,' snapped Vega, grabbing him by the arm and turning him to face him. 'You've been brave.'

Hector tugged himself free and trudged down the remaining steps, arriving on the ground floor. Still the staff looked his way. His cheeks burned with embarrassment. He needed to get back to Bevan's Tower, his home in Highcliff; get away from the glares. The tower was the Lord of Redmire's residence when in the city, named after an early Boarlord.

'Hector,' said Vega as they walked through the double doors out of Traitors' House. 'I'd be proud to call you a friend, if I were Drew. He's hunting Lucas now, and that's thanks to you. Sleep easy tonight, little Boar.'

Vega patted his back before striding off down the road in the direction of the harbour. He bowed to a trio of young ladies who passed by, bringing a chorus of giggles and blushes.

'You need anything at all,' he shouted back, saluting as he went. 'Just call for me!' In a moment he was lost in the noisy crowd.

Hector was rubbing his palm once more. Suddenly aware, he shoved his hand into his pocket, as if the black mark were a physical manifestation of his shame. His spirits had picked up slightly after Vega's kind words. He wondered where Drew was now, how far behind Lucas he was. If anybody could save Gretchen it was Drew, and he had Whitley to help. Of course, the communing had been risky, but what option had Hector had? He'd done the right thing, and he'd do it again if he had to. His mind wandering, he stepped out into the street.

The carriage was almost upon him when the shriek of a passer-by alerted him to the danger. Hector stumbled as the carriage bore down, unable to get out of the way. The team of four horses pulling it reared up, hooves kicking as the driver hauled on the reins. The carriage bounced, its wheels bucking as it juddered to a halt. The clattering of hooves on cobbles sounded like swords hammering plate mail, the din deafening Hector as he staggered clear. Gradually the horses calmed, the driver breathing a sigh of relief as they settled. Hector looked back at them as they snorted and stamped, their skin coated in sweat.

Back on the paving, Hector looked at the carriage. Two men sat on the driver's bench, one short and one tall, each of them glowering at him. He recognized the carriage immediately. Its panelling was marked with faded red paint that was cracked along its length. The window pane in the door was shattered, a piece of cloth wadded into the splintered glass to keep the elements out. Redmire's carriage of state had seen better days. Hector recalled his father telling him how his mother had arrived at their wedding in it. He'd kept it for sentimental reasons, never using it again after his mother had passed away. To see it in Highcliff now, in this condition, sickened Hector. When the carriage door opened his stomach dropped further.

'My dear brother,' said Vincent, smiling as he emerged, with Baron Huth's golden chain of office standing proud on his chest. 'Fancy running into you like this!'

2

The Scent

The quiet was unnerving, the countryside still sleeping. The Talstaff Road was empty – not surprisingly considering the ungodly hour. Only the crazed or the desperate travelled before dawn, and these riders were far from mad. The two Greencloaks rode side by side, keeping the pace brisk as they tried to make up time on their quarry.

Drew and Whitley had been travelling through the rolling hills of Westland for a week now, with no sign of their enemy. There were few people on the road, bar the occasional trader's caravan or farmer heading to market. On each occasion the pair asked the strangers if they'd seen anyone on the road fitting the description of Lucas, Vankaskan or Gretchen, but none had. This raised the question of how the trio were travelling. Drew was sure that someone would have seen them or passed them. Had they been wrong to head south? Had Brutus's corpse been mistaken?

They stopped briefly at noon, simple trail rations of cured meat and flatbread staunching their hunger until the evening.

'I wonder how Hector is faring,' said Drew, washing down his food with a swig from his waterskin. He handed it to Whitley. Invariably, many of their conversations revolved around the Boarlord and what might have become of him.

'Hopefully fine,' said Whitley. 'My father's an understanding man. He'll realize that Hector's intentions were good.'

'You think so?' said Drew, staring back the way they had come. 'I have to say I'm worried. I've seen how your father deals with those who disagree with him. He shouted me down when I suggested going after Gretchen.'

'I'm sure he felt he was doing the right thing,' said Whitley, stoppering the waterskin.

'As did Hector, but that'll count for nought.' Drew squinted as his gaze drifted over the meadows, cloud shadows racing over the whispering grasses.

They made good time in the afternoon, the horses opening their stride and quickening the pace. To the east was the vast Dyrewood, stretching in every direction as far as the eye could see, flanking them on their journey south. To be so close to the great forest stirred all kinds of emotions in Drew. As wild and savage as that time had been, his life had been so much simpler: eat, sleep, survive. The Dyrewood was where his life as a Werewolf had really begun, after fleeing the farm on the Cold Coast. He shivered, thinking back to that dreadful night.

The trees grew in size as the woodland receded into the distance. Somewhere at the heart of the giant forest was Brackenholme, city of the Bearlord. Drew hoped he would see it again; it felt like a city he could one day call home.

They pushed the horses until the afternoon gave way to evening. Drew didn't want to waste any time, although he could feel tiredness setting in, taking hold. Still he stayed awake, focusing on the road ahead. Over the noise of the hooves he could hear his voice being called.

'Drew . . . . *Drew!*'

Snapping his head back he turned in the saddle. Whitley had pulled up and was frantically waving. He pulled hard on his reins, turning his horse and returning to the scout. As he approached, Whitley led Chancer off the road. Drew fell in line behind her. She had jumped out of her saddle and slowly advanced on foot, head lowered. The ground was uneven as the grassy bank rose.

'What is it?' he said, keeping his voice low.

'Two things,' she said, looking back. 'The horses are exhausted. It's dark now and if one should stumble and break a leg, we're ruined.'

'But we're losing time, stopping now. They're getting further away!'

'Keep pushing these horses and you'll kill them. They need rest. We need rest.'

Drew said nothing, but begrudgingly agreed with a cursory nod.

'What's the other thing?'

'Tracks,' she said. 'Someone's camped here.'

Drew looked up from where he sat in his saddle. The incline rose to a hilltop. He hadn't noticed it when he'd ridden by. He stayed silent, watching Whitley work. Soon they were at the top.

The hillock had indeed been used as a campsite. Shrubs and bushes crowned the crest of it, providing cover to anyone resting there while affording a view of the road. A fire-pit had been dug, and the grass worn thin over the area. Whitley handed her reins to Drew before investigating the campsite.

She crouched, putting her hand into the charred remains. She sniffed at the coals, crumbling them and rubbing them into her palms. Scrambling around the fire's edge she rooted through what lay around, including two charred sticks.

'They made a spit,' she said, waving one at Drew before tossing it. 'And there are stripped bones scattered about too, looks like wild boar.'

'They were here last night?'

'The opposite. They camped here today.'

'Today? So they're travelling by night?'

Whitley nodded, rising from her crouch and pacing a wider circle around the camp.

'It makes sense, if they're trying not to be seen.'

Drew chewed his thumb, watching Whitley as she prowled the deserted camp. He wasn't sure what she was looking for, but he had faith that she knew what she was doing. She bore little resemblance to the frightened youth he'd met in the Dyrewood. She now had the confidence and assurance of a seasoned scout. Her time with Captain Harker in the Badlands had allowed her to mature in many ways.

'I count twelve horses,' she said eventually after examining the edge of the site. 'As many bedrolls too.' She walked back and took Chancer's reins from him. Drew turned his horse and started out of the campsite.

'Where are you going?' asked Whitley.

'The Talstaff. If they've been here through the day and they're travelling at night then that means we're right behind them, surely? If we move now we can catch them!'

'Drew, are you not listening to me? The horses are exhausted, as are we. We've pushed them all day long.'

'But we're so close!'

'And we'll get closer, but this fire tells me they left this site hours ago, at dusk. They're long gone.'

Drew snarled with frustration.

'I could go on ahead. On foot. You could catch up when you've rested.'

'Drew, this is madness. Get out of your saddle. Eat. Sleep.'

'But . . .'

'No buts,' she said, her voice stern now. 'If you caught them up now what good would you be? You're exhausted; Lucas, Vankaskan and their men will be rested. It's suicide. Let's rest while we can. We can face them on our terms, when we can fight them at full strength.'

Reluctantly Drew stopped. Grabbing his saddle he swung off his horse, landing shakily. She wasn't wrong. He was tired. His legs throbbed and his back ached, and no doubt Whitley felt the same.

'How do you feel?' he asked.

'Why do you think I suggested we rest?' she smiled, taking

his reins and leading the horses to the edge of the camp. Drew unpacked his bedroll and rations.

'Cured meat again?' offered Drew, waving a stick of grey meat in her direction. Whitley grimaced, but took it, settling down beside him.

'I'd suggest foraging for rabbits, but that'd mean starting a fire.'

'Is that a problem? A fire would keep us warm.'

'It'd attract attention. Lucas got away with one in the day, but at night it'd bring trouble. There are plenty of brigands in the Kinmoors who might look for a camp to raid off the Talstaff Road.'

'I hadn't thought of that.'

'That's why you have me,' smiled Whitley, winking.

The day had been long, and hungry though they were, they had to ration their food. Whitley sat opposite Drew on her bedroll, licking the last taste of cured meat from her fingertips. She noticed him watching.

'Sorry,' she blushed. 'I know; it's no way for a lady to eat.'

'Duke Bergan would be mortified!' he exclaimed, and she began to giggle.

'I'll tell you what; while we're out here can we just concentrate on being a soldier and a scout? I've had a gutful of etiquette in Highcliff this past month!'

They laughed out loud together. It was a pleasant feeling.

'Look!' she gasped, pointing.

The Wolfshead blade was whipped from its sheath and its tip cut through the air in the direction she pointed.

'You can put that away,' she snorted, jumping to her feet and dashing to the bushes. Feeling foolish, Drew got to his feet and followed.

'What is it?'

'Black-hearts!'

When Drew caught up he found her rummaging through a bush, plucking dark blue berries from the foliage.

'Oh, you mean bilberries,' he said, grinning. She looked back at him, her mouth already brimming with the small, sweet fruit.

'No, I mean what I said; black-hearts. I don't know what you call them out on the Cold Coast but in the Dyrewood there's only one name for them. And I like to think if the Dyrewood is home to all trees that it's home to all bushes as well, so black-hearts it is!'

Drew chuckled, joining her as she stripped the bush of its ripened berries. They tasted delicious. They ate what they could, each filling a pouch with additional berries for the road tomorrow.

'This is the life, living off the wild,' sighed Whitley. Drew watched her as she feasted. She was so at ease, relaxed. So different from how she had been when they'd first met. She caught him looking.

'What?' she asked, smiling.

'Oh nothing,' he said, looking away, abashed at having been spotted. She gave him a dig in the ribs with her elbow.

'Come on, what?'

'You seem very . . . content,' he said, cocking his head as he appraised her. 'Do you remember when we first met? You seemed out of your depth; a million leagues away from being a scout, but look at you now!'

'Let's just say that meeting you was an epiphany, Drew,' she said, snatching up the remaining berries, depositing them into her pouch and drawing it shut by its string.

'A what?'

'A revelation,' she said. 'When we met I was still a child, one who had been pampered for too long. Yet you and I are close in age. You'd survived in the Dyrewood, alone, for months. That trip into the forest with Master Hogan was my first away from Brackenholme. When I got back it was like the blinkers had been removed; I could see at last, and knew what I wanted.'

'And what was that?' asked Drew, as they stepped out of the bushes. A chill breeze blew through the campsite. As warm as the summer days were, the nights were still cool. Whitley pulled her cloak about her shoulders.

'Freedom,' she said, simply.

Drew laughed, bitterly.

'What's so funny?' she said, punching him in the arm.

'We're both after the same thing but heading in different directions. You're a noblewoman and you want to live wild and free. That's how I started out, but I seem destined to wear a crown.'

She hesitantly put an arm round his shoulder.

'You'll get what you want, Drew, I'm sure of it.'

'Will you remain a scout?'

Whitley laughed.

'My mother and father humour me presently. He'll have

been furious that I joined you on this journey. He was angry enough that I was gone for so long with Captain Harker. No, he won't be pleased at all. Broghan's the important one. He's the heir to the throne who'll follow Father. Me? I'll be married off when the time's right. Father won't want me to come to any harm, not just because I'm his daughter, but also because of the stability of Brackenholme.'

'To be forced to marry just seems so wrong.'

Whitley watched him sit down and moved to the opposite side of the fire-pit.

'Well,' she said quietly. 'We don't always get what we want.'

They were quiet for a time, each lost in their own thoughts. Drew considered his future. Who would they want *him* to marry? Bergan had probably already got the wheels in motion, plotting some union that would benefit the whole of Lyssia. Gretchen had been betrothed to Lucas. Perhaps that was the intention of the Wolf's Council, to pair the two of them up in light of the Lion's demise. The thought of marriage to Gretchen caused his heart to quicken, and not in a pleasant way. He shivered at the thought, still unsure of how he felt about her, or she about him. She thrilled and terrified him. Infuriating and unpredictable though she was, he missed her company.

'I hope Hector's all right,' whispered Whitley.

'He will be. He's resourceful, and safe in Highcliff. No harm can come to him there, not with Lucas and Vankaskan fleeing. It's Gretchen I'm worried about.'

'You think a lot of the Werefox, don't you?'

'I've grown to,' he admitted. 'I couldn't stand her when we first met. That journey from Redmire was chaotic to say the least. We were at one another's throats most of the time, with poor Hector stuck in between.'

'That must have been fun for poor Hector,' smiled Whitley.

'Brenn bless him, he endured a lot. The poor chap had just lost his father and had the two of us bickering like children.'

Whitley considered her words carefully, keeping her eyes on the firepit.

'You know how she feels about you, don't you?'

'Pardon?'

'Gretchen,' said Whitley, kicking at the dead coals with her boot heel. 'She told me.' She looked up, staring straight at him.

'She did?' said Drew, suddenly unnerved. What had Gretchen told Whitley? Did he want to know?

'I'm sorry. I didn't mean to speak out of turn.'

'You didn't,' said Drew, waving her apology away with a hand.

There was an awkward silence, as Drew picked at the hem of his cloak and Whitley looked anywhere but at Drew. Whitley spoke first.

'The horses,' she said, raising a finger as if she'd just remembered. 'Better get them settled for the night. There's much to do!' She jumped up and hopped over to them.

'Yes,' said Drew, calling after her as she busied herself with a task that could have waited. He sat there in the dark, head swimming with thoughts of his friends. The road ahead, following the Fox's scent. The Boar left behind, back in the city. And the scout by his side, unearthing his feelings. Gretchen, Hector, Whitley; they all vied for his attention.

'Much to do indeed.'

3

The Lords of Redmire

Hector couldn't sleep. He might have been the only living soul in the room, but he wasn't alone. He could hear voices, whispering in the dark. The windows were open, faded curtains flapping in the breeze. The city was quiet, the curfew keeping the people off the street, and Hector felt he must be the only person awake in Highcliff. As the night had drawn in the voices had arrived, creeping out of the woodwork, whispering through the floorboards and hissing beneath the bed. Hector's nerves were in tatters, his mind desperately trying to convince him that he was imagining them, although a cold dread told him they were very real.

Intent upon ignoring them, he had busied himself with paperwork from Redmire, spreading the scrolls and ledgers across his bed. Not only had Vincent arrived unannounced, he'd also brought a chestful of bills that needed settling. Since

Redmire had been sacked by Captain Brutus during the last days of the Lion's regime, the town remained in disarray. The palisade was ruined, people were homeless, the old hall had burned to the ground – the home of the Boarlords was in dire need of assistance, and it was Hector's duty to make sure that happened. Still a friend of the Wolf's Council, he was better placed than anyone to ensure some emergency monies headed to his people.

Having left his treacherous twin behind when he and his friends had fled down the Redwine, Hector had assumed that Vincent would look after their people. But judging by the fact that his brother was now in Highcliff, intent upon frittering away what money Baron Huth had left, Hector could see the people of Redmire were being neglected. He'd pressed Vincent on who he'd left in charge, and he'd been very non-committal on the matter. As far as Hector could tell, Gerard, the captain of the house guard, had assumed some kind of ministerial role and was carrying out the lord's law in Redmire. Vincent had avoided leadership, instead merely ensuring that taxes were still collected from their people, regardless of their poverty. When this money was gone, he'd borrowed from Redmire's more affluent citizens. Since he'd turned up at Bevan's Tower with a crate-load of debt, it was clear to Hector that he'd exhausted their generosity. Now it was left to Hector to sort out the mess while Vincent seemed in no hurry to return to Redmire.

Hector had spent the last few days lying on his bed, writing more than eighty personal letters to creditors, his words gradually getting more scrawled and illegible as time had worn on.

Dark stains marked the quilt where he'd knocked the inkpot over from jumping when he'd heard noises in the night. Two candles flickered on tables on either side of the bed, almost melted down to their stubs. Hector found himself worrying that he was being too frivolous, burning two candles instead of one. He cursed his brother's greed, forcing Hector to be the sensible one, having to think of thrifty measures to save coin. This was no way for a Werelord to live.

'Hector . . .'

That was the clearest voice he'd heard all night. It came from near the door, either in the shadows around or beyond it. He withdrew his dagger. He'd been mocked for the purchase of the gaudy knife, but he was grateful he had it now. Holding the blade in his shaking hands gave him a touch of courage.

'Go away!' he cried quietly. 'Leave me alone!'

'Hector . . .'

Hector wiped tears from his cheek. Was he mad? Another shadow moved in the corner of the room. His thoughts rushed back to the corpse in the Pits and the swirling shadows that taunted him, threatened him. It was all well and good for him to commune with the dead when he was in control, choosing the terms, but what could he do when they chose to commune with him? He couldn't shut them out. You couldn't hide from the dead.

He could hear giggles now, beyond the door.

Perhaps if he confronted the shadows head on, he might be able to banish them. He gripped the dagger in his sweating palm. He knew the warding cantrips, he'd scoured the arcane books in search of something that might protect him from the spirits. He started to whisper the ancient words over and over as he clambered off the bed. With his free hand he picked up a candle stub, its flame barely alive upon its tin dish. His battle with the dead shaman had been a warning, alerting him to the dangers of communing. The encounter with Brutus in the Pits had been a reminder. Hector was grateful that Bergan had punished him, awakening him to the perilous path he was on. He was finished with communing, finished with the dead. The danger was too great.

The giggles continued, only his name occasionally breaking up the ethereal laughter.

Hector crept across the room, floorboards creaking beneath bare feet as he approached the door. He repeated the warding chant, trying to feel confident, protected. The words of magick had been written in a long-dead language, the dialect and pronunciation alien to all but magisters. The Dragonlords had been the first to harness magicks, and most of the knowledge had died with that extinct race. What scraps remained had been protected for centuries by the Magisterial Guild across Lyssia, closely guarded by only a few. Hector's eyes widened as he approached the door. He held the dagger pointing out from his belly in a white-knuckled grip. Placing the candle on the sideboard, he reached for the doorknob.

The giggling shifted to frantic whispering, quickening as his hand neared, as if in panicked discussion with another. The brass handle was cold to the touch. Hector's fingers closed round the metal ball. The mechanism clunked as the latch slowly lifted.

The voices stopped.

The corridor was empty, but for the long rug that covered the floor. Picking up the candle he stepped out, holding it before him. His hand trembled, causing the already flickering light to sputter almost out of existence. The short passage led from the lord's bedroom to a sweeping staircase that circled through Bevan's Tower, past the guest rooms below and down to the ground. He shuffled down the corridor, stumbling over the rug's furled edge and up to the banister. Leaning over the rail he peered down into the darkness. In the dim light he could make out the large hall at street level. He blinked, unsure whether he'd seen movement.

'Is anyone there?' he called, regretting it immediately. *You fool, Hector. If there's an intruder down there then they know you're coming now.* Cursing, he set off downstairs, no longer attempting to be quiet. He let his feet slap the marble steps, deliberately rapped the stone handrail with his dagger. When he got to the first floor he contemplated knocking on Vincent's door, but then thought better of it. The resentment Victor had always shown towards Hector seemed to have grown since their father's murder. If anything, Hector would have been more justified in resenting his brother, as it was Vincent's deceit that had brought about Baron Huth's death at the hands of the Lionguard. Hector wasn't about to provoke Vincent. Hector might have been older by a matter of minutes, but Vincent was the bigger brother, both physically and in personality.

Hector continued to the ground floor. As he approached the bottom he could discern noises coming from the back of the hall, giggling. The shadow creatures. Hector gripped his dagger in a nervous sweaty palm as he advanced.

He remembered the feasts his father used to throw in the hall of Bevan's Tower, where the great and not-so-good of Leopold's court would assemble and take advantage of his hospitality. Now the place felt like a tomb. Dust sheets covered many pieces of furniture, mirrors remained blanketed and cobwebs hung all around. Busy with Wolf's Council duties since arriving, Hector had been living, dining and sleeping solely in the lord's chambers, leaving the rest of the tower to continue gathering dust.

He walked through, glancing about, mumbling his protection cantrip with every step. A breeze gusted through, causing dust sheets to dance like a host of ghosts. Where was the wind coming from? He hadn't left any windows open. Hector walked towards a window that overlooked the garden, feeling the cool night air as he drew nearer. It was wide open. Another gust rushed in, racing over the candle and snuffing it out. Hector's heart froze as the darkness smothered him.

A giggle behind him.

Hector moved fast, spinning and dropping the candle. He held his left hand up, palm out. Show the devils the black mark, he thought. Show them who the magister is. Show them who's in command.

'*Return from whence you came!*' he screamed, his face white with fear and anger.

The room was quiet, for a moment. Slowly the giggling returned. As Hector's eyes adjusted to the dark, he saw two shadows moving, peeling away from the hall's blackest corners.

One was tall and rangy, its movement spindly like a twig man. The other was short and squat, lurching, giggling all the while. Hector wanted to run, but his legs failed him; he wanted to scream, but his voice had vanished. The taller shadow stretched its arms out as if it might embrace him, before bringing them together swiftly.

Clap. Clap. Clap.

A slow handclap, like the kind given to a poor jester; a tired applause tinged with malice. The shadow's fat companion continued to giggle, waddling closer, ahead of its partner. Hector hadn't expected a shadow to be able to clap.

The men materialized, shadows solidifying. The tall figure wore a leather coat that hung to his knees, tied round the middle by a chain-link weapon belt. His slitted eyes glinted at Hector from his pockmarked face as he continued his hand-clap. The squat fellow had a stagger to his step, his fat legs stumbling as he closed in. He wore a thick woollen vest covered in stains, his hairy arms bare from the shoulder down. His face was wide, blubbery lips fixed in an idiotic grin. His giggle wouldn't stay in, spilling out of his mouth at every opportunity. Hector thought he recognized the men, but couldn't place them. Either way, he felt in terrible danger.

Hector backed away, bumping into a sheet-covered table and sending some chairs balanced on it crashing to the ground. He shrieked, bringing his dagger up as the tall man advanced. The short man scuttled round the table, kicking the upturned chairs aside. They circled him, closing in.

'Get back!' Hector shouted. 'Brenn help me! Get back, or you'll feel my blade.'

'That's no blade, little pig,' said the tall man, reaching behind his back. When his hand re-emerged it held a long knife, one side razor sharp, the other serrated. The starlight that filtered through the window danced along its length. It looked lethal. Lethal and well-used.

'Ibal,' said the tall man. 'Show him yours.'

The fat man swiftly whipped out a sickle. The crescent blade flipped as he tossed it from one stumpy hand to the other, giggling continuously.

'Stop it!' gasped Hector, unable to hide his fear. 'Stop it, please!'

'Stop what?' said the tall man, looking about and shrugging. Hector stumbled over a fallen stool, wheeling backwards and crashing to the floor. The jewelled dagger was gone, skittering along the floor. Quick as a flash the fat man named Ibal was over him, his head twitching as he loomed above. The tall man appeared behind, staring down, twirling the knife.

'Leave him, lads,' came a familiar voice. 'That's one of your lords. Show some respect.' Both men stepped away as footsteps approached. From his position Hector was relieved to see Vincent appear over him. Hector raised his hand for assistance but the younger twin stepped past towards the window.

'It's as cold as a crypt down here,' he said, slamming it shut. 'Were you both born in a barn?'

Ibal giggled louder than ever while the tall man simply stood still, staring as Hector struggled to his feet. He noticed the tall man had his dagger, appraising its worth by the starlight.

'A barn would be a palace in comparison,' rasped the tall man.

Vincent took the dagger, inspecting it himself. He chuckled and handed it back to a grateful Hector.

'What woke you, brother?'

'I heard voices,' said Hector. 'Outside my room. What were you doing up there?' Hector stared at the tall man, finding courage now his brother was present.

'Don't know what you mean.'

'You were up there, you and him. Outside my room.'

The man shook his head and looked to Vincent.

'We did no such thing, my lord. Haven't strayed from the hall as you instructed.'

Vincent shrugged at Hector.

'There you have it. I don't know what you heard, Hector, but it wasn't these fellows. You must be hearing things, eh?'

'Who *are* these men?' said Hector in an urgent tone to his brother. He could feel a sickening sensation taking hold. It was bad enough that his brother was in league with these rogues. Worse still, that neither of them had been upstairs. Whatever he'd heard and seen in the darkness was connected with the communing. His world was unravelling, the lines between the living and the dead blurring.

'I thought I'd introduced them. My apologies, Hector.' He gestured towards the sinister duo. 'These are my personal guard, Ringlin and Ibal. They drove me here, remember? They're the first of a new Boarguard. They'll stay here with me while we sort out our business. It seems Father's soldiers didn't have the stomach for real work under me; they've near enough disbanded. Thank goodness we have Gerard back there running things. You know he wants to become Sheriff of Redmire? Sounds like revolution.'

'Sounds like someone cares about our people. Gerard's a good man, and if Redmire needs a Sheriff he has my blessing,' said Hector, following his brother towards the disused fire-place. Vincent collapsed into a sheet-covered chair, a cloud of dust erupting as he landed.

'I hope you're not suggesting I don't care about Redmire. The only reason I'm here is to resolve the business of ascension.'

'Ascension? I don't follow.'

'Why, the throne of Redmire, dear brother. Father, Brenn rest his soul, is gone. We need to ensure my ascent to the throne is approved quickly. I seek counsel with Bergan tomorrow. I shall have the whole affair tied up swiftly.'

Vincent looked very pleased with himself. Hector was aware of his henchmen moving behind him, drifting in and out of his field of vision. Cold sweat pooled on his neck and chest. His head pounded with worry and he was overwhelmed by nausea.

'I wasn't aware there was anything to tie up,' said Hector, nervously. He moved back to the fireplace so he could keep an eye on Ringlin and Ibal. 'Besides, don't forget that Redmire's throne is mine by rights, to give up should I wish to.'

Vincent smiled, nodding. He was suddenly animated.

'I know, I'm a bit previous aren't I? Of course, once you've renounced your claim, witnessed by Bergan or Mikkel, I can get on with arranging a coronation. Father had property in

Highcliff, did he not? It might be worth selling those estates and businesses off, ploughing that money back into Redmire upon my return.'

'That's important revenue our family depends upon. Selling it would bring a quick windfall, but leave us in a dire state long-term. I can't agree,' said Hector, catching his breath before continuing.

'Besides which, I haven't decided to abdicate.'

'You're a magister, Hector, happier in the company of your books, no? You'd struggle to run your own social life, let alone a court. I, on the other hand, have been groomed for this role. Who shadowed Father these last four years? And who vanished from the map, a skulking servant for that rat, Vankaskan? You're not cut out for ruling. Leave that to me.'

This was more than Hector could take.

'I shall not,' said Hector, indignantly. 'I won't let you ruin Redmire. If you continue as you are doing you'll destroy Father's hard work, as well as your reputation. I know right from wrong, and I know what's best for Redmire. For everyone's sake I think it best I keep an eye on things for the foreseeable future.'

Vincent's response didn't come immediately. He rose from his chair, pausing to brush the dust off his dressing gown. He smiled at Ringlin and Ibal. Hector glanced round to see their response. When he turned back Vincent's face was inches from his own.

'I'll make this easy for you,' said Vincent quietly. He put his hands on Hector's shoulders, the grip tightening. 'You'll renounce your claim to the throne.'

'And if I don't?'

Vincent squeezed hard, digging thumbs and fingers through the material of Hector's gown. The magister saw dark, russet hairs emerging from his brother's sleeves, spreading over his broad hands as he gripped. He bared his teeth, snorting, forcing his brother down. Hector felt his knees give, legs buckling as he dropped to the floor. Vincent held on, his brother kneeling in his shadow. Vincent's chest heaved now, his breath hot and laboured as his ribs cracked and shifted. Hector watched, horrified, listening to the bones of his brother's head popping and grating. Hector had never learned to control his therianthropy; the fact that Vincent had mastered it was news to him.

'I shall have the throne of Redmire, Hector,' said Vincent, the teeth of his lower jaw jutting from his mouth: the tusks of the Boar. 'There are two ways this can happen. You step down like a good boy, or I claim it as the only living heir.'

He released his grasp, sending Hector headlong into the fireplace. His brow hit the brickwork, his temple splitting instantly. He looked up as Vincent stepped over him to join his men. Hector no longer recognized him. This wasn't the boy he had grown up with, once a friend, always a brother. He wanted to cry, for his father, for Redmire, even for Vincent. Hector scrambled to his feet, head streaming with blood as he staggered from the hall. Grabbing the handles of the great doors he threw them open, nightclothes flapping, and slipped and stumbled into the gardens beyond.

'That's right,' called Vincent, the rattling laughter of Ringlin and Ibal chasing Hector out into the night. 'Run along, little lordling. You've lots to do! Busy work this abdication business!'

4

By Royal Command

Despite the gloom of the caravan's interior, the dark stain on the floorboard was still visible. Lucas's men had made no attempt to clean up the murder scene, leaving the blood there as a chilling reminder of what they were capable of. A bunkbed was the only comfort, every inch of space having once been packed with goods for market. These now lay in some ditch off the Talstaff Road, alongside the bodies of the merchant and his guards. It was sickening to imagine the boggy trench as the last resting place of those poor souls, whose only mistake was being in the wrong place at the wrong time. Stripped bare, the caravan was little more than a mobile jail cell, its prisoner the Fox of Hedgemoor.

Gretchen grimaced, looking away from the grisly stain and peering through the window grille in the rear door. She could see the road, the horizon bouncing as the caravan sped along.

It was growing lighter now, their journey through the night surely ending soon. She could hear the morning chorus over the sound of the horses and wheels, birds chirping as they announced their passing. Occasionally the groans of the injured soldier on top of the caravan could be heard, but they fell on deaf ears – his companions showed no sympathy. Gretchen was finding the whole grim experience disorientating. To be abducted and imprisoned was one thing, but sleeping in the day and travelling at night was a world away from what she was used to. She hadn't wasted today, though. Far from it; she'd been busy.

The nails on her hand were still cracked and broken, but the slashed fingertips were well on their way to healing. She thanked her therian powers of recuperation. In the past she'd have quit anything that caused her pain. In the last two months, though, she'd discovered a resolve she'd never realized she had. Drew had inspired this. She smiled, thinking of the young Werewolf. Where was he? Did he know she lived?

Vankaskan had procured the caravan earlier in the night, not long after setting off, when he came across a campsite the poor merchant had set up. He and his two men-at-arms had welcomed the Werelords' party, but regretted it immediately. The merchant's guards had tumbled to the floor with crossbow bolts skewering their bodies, while the Wererat had gone after the merchant as he'd scrambled into his caravan. The poor fellow had managed to fire a crossbow at one of the prince's men, injuring him gravely, but it hadn't prevented his slaughter at the hands of the Rat. The soldiers had stripped the wagon, dumping the bodies in the ditch and killing the campfire. By the time they'd departed any passers-by would have been unaware of the horrific events.

She felt inside the rim of her boot. Her sore fingers brushed against the head of the six-inch rusty spike. It had been jutting out of the wall, worked proud when the van was ransacked. The broad head with its sharp edges had been the point of purchase for Gretchen to seize it by. Once left alone she'd spent the night coaxing it free, working at it with tattered fingers. Finally the spike slid free into her bloody palm, a grim reward for her night's work. Only one question remained. Was she prepared to use it?

'Good morning, my angel!'

She spun about. Prince Lucas's head hung upside down from a hatch in the roof. He was smiling broadly, blond locks tumbling around his face. He manoeuvred round the opening, grabbing its edge and falling head first, graceful as an acrobat, into the caravan. He steadied himself upon landing.

Lucas sat down upon the bunk, patting the mattress, gesturing her to join him.

'If it's all right I'd rather stand.'

'Don't be silly,' laughed Lucas. His gaze hardened. 'Sit down, I insist.'

Reluctantly she joined him, smoothing her dress over her lap. She'd been using her red cloak as a blanket, but now she wrapped it about her body modestly. She was still wearing the low-cut white summer dress from Highcliff and she didn't want to encourage the young Lion. When all was said and done she was a girl in the company of killers. Although she wanted to keep Lucas at arm's length, her safety also depended upon him.

'Your mood seems pleasant.'

'Why shouldn't it be?' he said, placing an arm round her. She shivered at his touch as he continued.

'Reunited with my intended and heading towards freedom. Why shouldn't I be happy?'

'Does the fact that innocent men lie dead, at both your hand and command, not concern you?'

'I don't know about *innocent*! That fool Kohl worked for those pigs in Traitors' House, an apt name if ever there was one. I'll lose no sleep over his demise.'

'He was an old man!'

'He was an old traitor. He sided with the Wolf, that makes him an enemy to us all – to you, to me, to my father the king.'

'And the others?' she said, struggling to keep her composure. 'The merchant? Your Rat killed him and his men, Lucas.' She pointed at the floor. 'That's where he died. See how his blood still marks the wood?'

Lucas wouldn't look, instead taking her trembling hand in his.

'I wouldn't know about that. I didn't witness the poor fellow's death – I was keeping you company on the road if you remember? I can only imagine that the hapless chap did something foolish to provoke my loyal Lionguard. The last person one would want to enrage is my old friend Vankaskan, wouldn't you agree?'

Lucas didn't lie. He'd been on the horse beside her when the camp was attacked, while Vankaskan led the assault. But the notion that three men might make a stand against ten was preposterous. She thought better of telling him so, choosing silence instead. She had to pick her battles with the prince.

'You seem anxious, my love,' he said, stroking her hand. Her skin crawled, but she didn't pull away. Offending Lucas was not something she wanted to do.

'Don't worry, my sweet,' he went on. 'No harm shall come your way. You have to understand, these men would give their lives for you and me. They are loyal soldiers of the Lionguard, forever oath-bound to my father. Trust me. Once we're south we'll have nothing more to worry about.'

He kissed her cheek, his lips lingering for a moment too long. She felt his breath against her skin as he inhaled, taking in her scent. She shuddered, her body unable to suppress her fear.

'I see you need your rest, Gretchen,' he said. 'We'll stop soon, and then perhaps we can stretch our legs, away from the men. Wouldn't that be nice?'

She looked hard at him. He smiled at her earnestly. Lovingly. She couldn't quite fathom how damaged he was and could hold her tongue no longer.

'After all that's gone on, you continue this courtship as if it were the most normal thing in the world, surrounded by cut-throats! These "loyal king's men" you speak of – each one is a villain! And you trust them? You're as mad as they are!'

The back of his hand struck her across the cheek. She crumpled against the mattress, the blow taking her by surprise. She'd never been hit before. He stood, his balance assured as the caravan bounced, his hand curled into a fist.

She whipped out the spike of metal, raising it before her defensively.

'How *dare* you!' he roared, face red and eyes bulging. 'You dare question my sanity? I'm the only sane one in this world of cowards and turncoats! And what do you intend to do with that scrap of metal? I hope it's silver, for your sake!'

'There are other ways in which a Werelord can be harmed, Lucas!'

She snarled, baring her teeth as her face took on the aspects of the Fox. Her cheekbones hollowed as her features sharpened, her mouth, jaw and ears beginning to shift and stretch, the pain unbearable. Still she let the beast in, feeling strong now, energized.

Lucas staggered back as the Werefox transformed. This was new to him, something he hadn't expected from Gretchen. He looked shocked and shaken by her change. *Could she actually fight him, transformed?*

Lucas began to grow, his shoulders broadening and straining under his shirt. His head filled out, blond hair beginning to break through the skin of his jutting jaw. His breathing changed, sounding like there were suddenly too many teeth in his mouth, heavy and sharp, grating against one another.

The Werefox let out a sharp bark, a reminder to the Werelion that she had a bite of her own. He bellowed back, the air thick with spittle as he unleashed a mighty roar in her face. She cried out, her morale broken, fear hitting her like an avalanche as the Fox swiftly faded. She dropped the spike on the floor where it clattered at Lucas's feet.

'Silence!' he shouted. He pointed a clawed finger at her.

'Never question me again! I'll let that go just this once. Know your place, Gretchen; by my side.'

He shrank, and as quickly as the Lion had come it departed. He ran his now human hand through his hair as he calmed himself. Suddenly he was the precocious young prince again. He bent and picked up the spike.

A noise at the hatch made them both look up. A dark shape appeared, dropping in and crunching into the wall as the caravan bounced along. Vankaskan's wretched face appeared from within his cowled cloak.

'Apologies for the intrusion, but I heard screaming,' said the Ratlord. 'It would be most ignoble of me not to investigate. Is everything all right?'

Gretchen turned away. She found the man revolting. His greasy black hair hung in unwashed ringlets about his face, further emphasizing the white of his skull-like face. She especially disliked the way he always looked at her, as if she were a tasty piece of meat he might take a bite out of.

'It was nothing,' said Lucas, still glowering at Gretchen. He handed the spike to the Wererat. 'Gretchen chose some inappropriate words. All is well now,' he said, smiling as if they'd had a lovers' tiff.

'You know,' said the Wererat, making no attempt to quieten his voice. 'If the lady is unwell I have medicines I'd be happy to prescribe to make her more . . . comfortable.'

Gretchen turned quickly.

'Lay a hand on me and I'll tear out your throat with my bare hands!'

Vankaskan laughed, a sinister noise that ended in a coughing fit. His eyes bulged, as if her words were the funniest thing he'd ever heard.

'My dear lady, I'm nothing if not your humble servant. Please, accept my apology if my words offended you. Know I'm here, if you need me.'

Vankaskan patted Lucas on the shoulder.

'Your Highness,' he said. 'I'll head up top if you have everything in hand. If you'd like to join me, that would be splendid. I would talk with you.'

Lucas nodded as the Rat climbed back out of the hatch. Gretchen's heart thundered like a galloping horse, her throat sore from screaming.

'Let's stay civil for the remainder of our journey, my love,' Lucas said. 'Remain calm, or we'll end with worse than tears.' He stroked her face, brushing a tear away. 'Yes?'

She nodded, flinching at his touch. The prince hauled himself out of the caravan, leaving the Fox of Hedgemoor alone on her bunk.

Slamming the hatch, Lucas slid the spear through the handle, locking it shut. Staying low he clambered over the roof, past the injured soldier, Bussnell, towards the driver's seat. The soldier banged his bald head on the caravan, cursing through his bloodied throat. Lucas ignored him, rejoining his friends at the front.

Captain Colbard, a hulking northman with a colourful past, sat at the reins. A Badlands bandit in his youth, he'd taken the king's coin instead of a walk to the gallows, making a name for himself on the battlefield. When Vankaskan recruited

Lucas's personal guard, Colbard had been the first appointment. There was little the brute couldn't bring down with his axe. Since Captain Brutus was now dead, Colbard was his natural replacement. The northman glanced briefly at his prince before looking back to the road.

Vankaskan was seated beside the captain, moving up as Lucas joined him. The prince tossed the Wererat the rusty spike before collapsing into the seat. He rubbed the back of his hand where he'd struck Gretchen.

'She's got claws, that one,' said the Ratlord, playing with the piece of metal in his hand.

'That's exactly why she must be my bride,' muttered Lucas. 'I need a strong woman to raise my heirs, not some shrinking mouse. Spirit like hers is rare among Wereladies. She's perfect.'

'Perfect or not, be careful. Don't let your guard down with her.'

'She wouldn't dare disobey me. I am still the son of the king, and she has been raised to respect her betters.'

'I'm just saying,' said Vankaskan. 'I have my medical case.' He patted the black leather bag at his feet.

'Medical case?' laughed Lucas. 'It holds your tools, does it not? I thought the fat pigboy took your medicines?'

Vankaskan sneered, spitting into the wind in disgust. The phlegm spun back, spattering Colbard's shoulder. The captain didn't react.

'I'll enjoy gutting that wretch when the time comes,' Vankaskan snarled. 'No, it's a medical case. Any good surgeon needs drugs as well as tools. I've all kinds of medicines in this box of tricks.'

'Hopefully it won't come to that,' said Lucas, as the injured Bussnell moaned behind them. 'Isn't there anything you can give him?'

'That one's a clot,' said Vankaskan, clearly in earshot of the wounded soldier. 'I'm not wasting anything on him. He's more hindrance than help.'

Bussnell was one of the more hapless soldiers of Lucas's Lionguard, injuries frequently finding him. He had taken the merchant's crossbow bolt in the throat, and the group had endured his wails throughout the night as they travelled. He was in a bad way.

Lucas cast his eyes over the soldiers who galloped along on either side of the caravan.

'Is Sorin back? He's done well to catch us up.'

'That's what I wanted to discuss,' said Vankaskan. 'He waited for a few hours as ordered, and it appears I was correct. He counted two riders coming south, down the road. They wore the Greencloaks of Brackenholme; scouts without a doubt. They even found our campsite. I imagine a larger force follows behind.'

'Then it's fortuitous that we found this caravan. Gretchen was dragging her heels – if we'd continued letting her dictate our speed of travel they might have caught us by now. Good work, Vankaskan.'

The Ratlord smiled, staring down the Talstaff Road, deep in thought.

'Sorin must be ravenous if he rode all night to catch up. Give him extra rations when we stop to camp,' said Lucas.

'He's earned it,' said Vankaskan. 'Perhaps we should leave

something for the Bear's scouts to stumble across. A reminder of who they hunt.'

Lucas looked puzzled as Vankaskan climbed back on to the roof of the caravan. He heard Bussnell cry out for the Were-rat's help as the Lord of Vermire crawled over him. When Lucas spied Vankaskan raising the rusty spike over his head, he turned his eyes back to the road. The Prince of Westland concentrated on the clattering hooves of the horses, allowing them to drown out the cries of the dying man.

'I'm glad he likes me,' muttered Colbard, cracking the reins.

Lucas shivered, and nodded.

5

Shelter from the Storm

The storm pursued the two riders as they travelled along the Talstaff Road. A cloudburst had struck as they packed up camp that morning, prompting them to set off more quickly than they'd planned. They were moving while it was still dark, but Drew was relieved to be back on the road. Now, a few hours later, Whitley drew them off the road, having seen something that caused alarm. One crow taking flight from a ditch might have gone unnoticed, but when a dozen took to the air it caught the scout's attention.

The crows were feasting on three fresh corpses. One of them lay on his back, his face already stripped by the carrion birds. His companions lay face down in the stagnant water. The back of one had been pierced by crossbow bolts while the torso of the third was covered in savage cuts. He wore the clothes of a merchant, now daubed with mud and blood.

Further inspection of the camp revealed abandoned goods crates, while caravan wheels had rutted the earth leading back to the road, heading south. It took Drew little time to determine what had happened.

'This is Lucas and Vankaskan's doing.'

'How can you know that?' asked Whitley, gagging at the sight of the fresh corpses.

'No self-respecting bandits would leave behind the spoils of their attack like that. Whoever attacked these men wanted the wagon, by the look of things. And they didn't mind killing to get it.'

Whitley nodded in agreement, turning Chancer away from the bodies as Drew's horse followed.

'Let's keep moving,' she said, 'before these cursed rain clouds wash away all trace of their passing.'

The downpour was unrelenting, the weather keeping most travellers off the road. The horses picked up their pace, both riders pushing their mounts as they tried to close on their quarry. Lucas and Vankaskan might have a wagon, but nothing could compete with the speed of a light horse on the open road. They stopped briefly in the afternoon where the Talstaff Road was intersected by a flooded ford, the fresh water from the Kinmoors refreshing their thirsty mounts. Drew and Whitley crouched to fill their waterskins, the rain still hammering down on to the hoods of their green riding cloaks.

'It might have been easier to chase them by boat,' muttered Drew. 'I've never seen so much rain.'

'I'll try to get a fire going tonight,' said Whitley. 'See if we can dry our clothes off.'

'I wasn't complaining. I'll happily take all the rain, floods and bad weather Lyssia can throw at me if it means getting out of the city.'

Whitley stoppered her waterskin, watching him thoughtfully. She smiled grimly at him, her wet hair clinging to her brow.

'You're running away, aren't you?'

Drew shook his head, surprised at the comment.

'I'm running after Gretchen. That's a very different thing.'

'Oh, don't mistake me, I'm with you on this. We want to find our friend, bring her home safely. But there's more to it for you.'

Drew was honestly puzzled by Whitley's comments, and squinted at her through the rain.

'You're a different boy, out here. It's like a huge weight has been lifted from your shoulders. You're back in familiar territory.'

Drew shrugged, stoppering his own waterskin.

'I'm in my element. I know this world, the Cold Coast, the Kinmoors. You and I both know I don't belong in Highcliff.'

'But you do, Drew – you're the future king of Westland.'

'My friends come first, Whitley: you, Gretchen, Hector.'

'But Lyssia needs you too. The people need you.'

'You sound like your father now,' he grunted.

'Now you're just being mean,' she laughed. 'Don't misunderstand me; it's a noble cause, chasing after a friend like this. How could you stay in Highcliff when someone you love has been kidnapped?'

Drew wanted to say something about the word 'love', but he didn't get the chance.

The Bearlady continued. 'But when we do find her, if we rescue Gretchen, wherever that might be – what then? Will you return to Highcliff with us? Answer truthfully, Drew. This is me you're talking to.'

Her smile was there again, rivulets of rainwater racing over her lips. Drew shivered, thinking for a moment.

'I honestly don't know.'

She began to laugh as she straightened, and he raised a hand to draw back her attention.

'I'm not going to lie to you about how I feel, Whitley. I never asked for any of this.' He cast his hands about him.

'I'm still the boy from the Cold Coast. I've been forced to change awfully quickly lately, and my world's been turned on its head. Is it so strange that I don't want to be king? That I want to return to my roots?'

'But that's just it,' said Whitley. She prodded her forefinger into the damp cloth of his cloak, jabbing at his heart. 'Your roots are in here. You're a Wolf, Drew, and there's no escaping it, just as I am a Bear. That is our destiny. We're therians, Werelords, and we were born to rule.'

'You wouldn't understand,' he said, stepping towards his horse.

'Wait,' she said, grabbing him and pulling him back. She looked cross. 'I understand better than anyone, Drew. I've been running from something too – a life in court as Lady of Brackenholme. True, I wear the clothes of a scout of the Woodland Watch, but who am I really deceiving? When the day comes I'll be married off, a political arrangement between the houses of Werelords, whether I want to or not. That's *my* destiny. The only difference between us is that I've had more time to get used to the idea.'

She smiled sadly at Drew, and he nodded. He must have looked miserable, for she stepped forward and hugged him. He squeezed back. His breath felt strangely shallow, his heart suddenly beating hard within his chest. Could she feel it, hammering to burst free? Suddenly uncomfortable in their embrace, the two pulled apart, smiling awkwardly at one another.

'We'd best push on,' Whitley said, swinging up into Chancer's saddle effortlessly.

'Yes,' nodded Drew, struggling to find words. He clambered into his saddle and soon fell in behind her.

They travelled until nightfall in silence, lost in their own thoughts as the first stars blinked into life overhead. Eventually they pulled off the road, heading towards a small wooded area to the east of the Talstaff. With the tree canopy providing shelter from the rain, Whitley set about tethering the horses and hobbling them for the night.

'Would you like me to go and fetch some firewood?' Drew asked, immediately cursing himself for sounding like a child.

Whitley smiled over Chancer's saddle, nodding. 'If you can find any that's dry enough to burn. I think it's for the best, we're sodden. It might attract attention, but we'll catch our deaths if we sleep the night in soaking clothes.'

Drew set off immediately, happy to be alone, albeit briefly. His mind hadn't wandered too far from their earlier embrace. Whitley was his friend – the last thing he needed was to confuse his feelings for her. It was bad enough that he didn't know exactly where he stood with Gretchen, but for him to be unsure about his relationship with Bergan's daughter made his head and heart ache. He only hoped she hadn't noticed how awkward he felt.

He stumbled through the undergrowth, foraging for dry branches and tossing back those that were damp. Whitley was right, of course, about all of it. He was running. Dangerous though it was, he was delighted to be on the road, each day's pursuit of Gretchen drawing him further away from Highcliff and his responsibilities to the Wolf's Council. He was Drew Ferran, a farmer's son — what did he know about ruling a kingdom? The most he'd been called on to do was count his flock each night before turning in, and that suited him fine. He'd stop Lucas, and he'd rescue Gretchen, and then he'd be finished. Let Bergan rule Lyssia — he was already doing a fine job as Lord Protector. The more distance he put between himself and Highcliff, the easier it would be to simply fall from the map when the chance came.

A lightly rapped knock on the back door of the wagon caused Captain Colbard to stir where he sat. The soldier yawned, rising from the steps to stretch for a moment before turning and taking the key from his pocket. Sorin slept on the floor nearby, a tough-as-nails fighter and the closest thing Colbard had to a friend. The Lionguard had taken it in turn to watch over the Lady of Hedgemoor while they camped, remaining on watch for a couple of hours at a time. It wasn't the most difficult military duty any of them had attended to, babysitting a spoiled princess and taking her bucket from her when it needed emptying.

Prince Lucas's party had camped during daylight hours once more, away from the prying eyes of travellers. Rumours regarding the fate of one of their own, Bussnell, had passed between the soldiers. All agreed that Vankaskan had done the right thing in ending the hapless man's life, but the subsequent ritual the Ratlord had carried out on him had turned their stomachs. They'd left the corpse behind them, a surprise for the scouts of Brackenholme who followed. Colbard shivered; dark magistry was something the big northman would never grow accustomed to.

The girl knocked on the door again, a dainty, gentle rap. *Her latrine must be full.* He chuckled at the thought, thinking of the whip-tongued therian lady having to relieve herself in a bucket like a lowly peasant.

'Hold your horses, I'm coming,' he grumbled. He yawned again and turned the key in the lock.

The door was the first thing to hit him and set him stumbling from the wagon steps. Just as he was about to right himself he felt the hard, steel rim of the bucket connect with his jaw, sending him reeling back to land on top of the still sleeping Sorin. He barely caught sight of Gretchen speeding past as his companion cried out in agony. In a moment the whole camp was awake.

Whitley reached across both horses, taking their reins and looping them through one another. She chewed her lip, shaking her head and muttering to herself as she worked.

'How do you get yourself into these situations, Whitley?'

The sensations were wholly new to her, a queasiness rising in her stomach when she thought about Drew and their embrace. No good could come of those feelings. She crouched low, passing the reins through a rope, which she proceeded to tie round a fallen tree.

Life in Brackenholme Hall had never felt comfortable for Whitley. She'd never enjoyed the company of people, preferring the outdoors, wanting to be exploring the woods and fields, not holed up inside a stuffy palace. She had joined the Woodland Watch for that very reason, to get away from the politics of court life.

Gretchen was her friend, the one therian lady her age she had known. They didn't have much in common, as Gretchen was very much a lifelong princess while Whitley had always played the tomboy, but they felt like family. She owed it to the Fox to help her in any way she could. *That* was why she was on the road with Drew. *That* was the only reason she'd agreed to come with the Wolf.

'Keep telling yourself that, Whitley,' she muttered to herself, not believing it for one moment.

A twig snapping beneath a footfall made her rise suddenly. She turned round, surprised that Drew was back from his hunt for firewood so quickly.

Two pale blue eyes flashed in the darkness as dirty hands reached out to her, fingers grasping and teeth bared. She tried to jump back but not before a hand took hold of her cloak, clenching into a fist. The attacker pulled her close as Whitley struggled to unfasten the clasp round her throat. The blue-eyed man gurgled, opening his mouth to bite down on to her skull. The clasp opened just as the teeth closed, biting into a mouthful of hair. She screamed as she pulled herself clear, the hair tearing from her scalp.

She collapsed into the mud, looking up in time to see her assailant lurching quickly towards her. Whitley brought her legs round, sending him crashing into the mulch. She rolled over, trying to crawl away when she felt his hand snatch her ankle. She kicked back, struggling to loosen his grip, but he kept coming, drawing himself up her length, one filthy hand over another until he was on top of her.

The man was monstrous, blue flames dancing in his eyes, spitting her torn hair from his hungry mouth as he snapped at her. Black goo spilled from his jaws and Whitley turned her face to avoid it. His throat hung open, a flapping sheet of torn flesh, the stench of decay flooding over her. *Brenn help me, he's dead!* With horror her mind flew back to the risen corpse of Captain Brutus in Highcliff. She kept her arms locked, fending off the corpse, but her strength was failing.

Thoughts of Duke Bergan and Broghan raced through her head. She'd never learned to channel the Werebear, therianthropy being the domain of more aggressive Werelords, but she knew enough to call on it when in need. She couldn't change like her father and brother, but there were other ways the beast within could help. She felt her muscles growing, the Bear rushing to her aid and helping her hold the dead creature at bay. She growled, letting her attacker know it was in a fight.

The firewood clattered to the ground as Drew sprinted towards Whitley's scream. He tore through the undergrowth, hurdling fallen trees and ducking beneath branches as he closed on the campsite. As he ran he could feel the change taking him; canines growing, limbs transforming, stride lengthening as his human gait shifted into that of the Wolf. By the time he burst into the camp he was the beast born of tooth, claw and terror.

A large figure straddled Whitley on the forest floor, the girl struggling beneath its weight as the attacker wrestled with her, teeth snapping at her face. Incredibly, Whitley was holding her own, keeping the assailant from biting her. Drew didn't waste a moment, and with a mighty kick sent the figure clear of his friend. The brute staggered to its feet as Drew positioned himself between it and Whitley. He winced, his ankle aching where it had twisted with the impact. He pulled the Wolfshead blade free from its scabbard and focused on his enemy.

Big and bald, the attacker had been a northman once, but no longer. Its eyes burned with a pale blue fire that reminded Drew of Brutus; the risen dead. This corpse had been communed with.

It had clearly been a military man in life, its torso clad in a tabard and chain shirt that hung below its groin. Its neck flapped loose beneath the jaw, a great savage hole running from ear to ear across the throat, its chest soaked dark with a vast stain of blood. Drew squinted at the crest on the torn cloth, faint but visible – a rampant lion. What appeared to be the blunt end of a rusty metal spike protruded from its breast, buried deep in the corpse's heart. Drew pointed at the walking corpse.

'You work for Lucas?'

The bald cadaver worked its mouth, fat lips smacking, as if

unfamiliar with the notion of speech. Its teeth grated, bits of flesh catching between them as it ground its jaws, its voice gurgling.

'In life . . . and death. Serve Lion. Kill Wolf.'

The conversation was over as swiftly as it had begun, the dead soldier moving deceptively fast as it surged towards the Wolf. Drew wasn't as quick as he'd have liked, thanks to his ankle sprained from the kick. He lunged forward with his sword, running the dead man through the belly, the blade buried to the hilt. To Drew's horror the soldier didn't slow, instead backhanding Drew across the clearing. It may have been a corpse but it was as strong as an ox. The Werewolf crashed into a tree trunk and hit the ground with a crunch.

The dead soldier reached down to snatch at the transformed therian, the sword still lodged in its stomach, while the Wolf was still stunned from the impact with the tree. Before the corpse could bite into Drew's throat it felt the jarring rattle of Whitley's quarterstaff across the back of its head. The soldier's already torn throat ripped further as the head cracked to one side, sending the corpse careering away from her friend. Whitley stood over Drew as he gathered his senses, the dead creature letting out a gurgling cry as it came straight back at her. She jabbed the staff forward, crumpling the corpse's ruined face further, but it kept on coming, knocking the staff aside.

The ghoul snatched her up in its grasp, teeth gnashing at her as it struggled to bite her. If Whitley could get hold of the sword she might be able to stop it for good. She grabbed the handle of the Wolfshead blade and pulled, the monster's innards sliding out of the dark exit hole with the sword. Before she could raise it to strike, the corpse squeezed her hard with a bone crunching hug and the sword tumbled from her hand.

Drew leapt up from the floor, his senses fully returned, and not a moment too soon. The corpse had Whitley in its arms, a deadly embrace that was leading towards a hungry kiss at her throat. The Werewolf launched himself at the two of them, jarring his friend from the dead man's grip and sending them both in separate directions. He snatched up his sword from the ground as the soldier charged once more, showing no sign of slowing.

Drew brought the Wolfshead blade around, the steel flying towards the dead man's neck. The corpse brought its left arm up defensively, the longsword biting through flesh and bone as it broke the limb in two. Such a blow would have killed a living man, but the ghoul let the arm go, the parry having slowed the blade and allowed it to take hold of Drew with its remaining arm.

Drew felt the air escape his lungs as the dead Lionguard embraced him, the two of them crashing to the muddy floor, the big man on top of him. The Wolfshead blade was gone from his grasp, useless now, as Drew raised his claws round the dead man's shoulders, struggling to grab hold through the mud. The soldier's jaws snapped away, relentless, the good arm behind Drew pulling him in while the gory stump of its left arm battered at Drew's chest.

It took all Drew's dexterity to protect his fingers – the lost little finger from his fight with Vanmorten was a daily reminder of the dangers of battle. The teeth strained closer and the stench of death was overwhelming. Foul black drool spattered

Drew as he turned his face, avoiding the bite. Quickly, he worked his left arm forward, catching the beast under its jaw. He shoved the head up, the torn neck flapping open to reveal the man's severed windpipe. The head was barely hanging on, lolling on its shoulders. Bringing his right arm back, Drew launched a well-aimed punch.

The head landed ten feet away in a shower of dead leaves, the blue lights gone forever from the fallen soldier's eyes.

Drew dashed over to Whitley, his limbs and features already beginning to return to normal. She staggered to her feet, her face a mask of shock and exhilaration as they hugged one another.

'Did you see that?' she said, struggling to regain her breath after the battle. 'I managed to change! The Bear, it was there; it was with me, while we fought that monster!'

'I know, we made quite a team didn't we?' he grinned. 'Are you all right?'

'I'm fine,' gasped Whitley, wheezing. Her face was white, her body still coursing with adrenaline and the Bear. 'You're injured though, Drew.'

She pointed at his chest. Drew examined the blood on his leather breastplate, wiping it away, expecting to find the hole in the armour underneath. He hadn't felt the dead man's blow and didn't recall receiving a bite. The blood smeared away, revealing undamaged leather beneath. He felt across his chest and neck; no injuries. He looked up.

He could see the blood on Whitley now, rising from the collar of her jerkin. Her face was paler and he saw her eyes beginning to flutter. Drew hopped forward and caught her before she collapsed. As her head fell to one side it revealed a deep wound in her neck. She winced.

'I'm so sorry, I should have stayed with you,' Drew gasped as he inspected the bite. 'We need to get that seen to and quickly. It might go bad . . .'

Drew put a hand to her neck, trying to staunch the blood. He felt it pumping, pulsing between his fingers. Hopefully her therianthropic healing would set to work shortly. Drew cast his mind back to the rotten, disease-ridden mouth of the soldier.

'I know where we can go,' said Whitley as if reading his fears. 'I know who can help us.'

6

Hunting the Fox

'We're going in there?' asked Sorin, his voice catching in his throat.

The men stood looking at the line of dead trees that marked the perimeter of the Dyrewood. It snaked off in each direction as far as the eye could see. None of them wanted to be the first to enter the trees. Each of them had heard enough tales about the horrors and creatures that lurked within the Woodland Realm. The campsite was still visible behind them, abandoned for the time being. They could hear the whinnies and snorts of their horses, alarmed to have been left alone so close to the Dyrewood.

'The Haunted Forest; that's what they call it,' whispered another of the Lionguard.

'Haunted or not we're going in,' barked Colbard, nursing his jaw. 'She can't have got far. She's just a girl, remember; a stupid, spoiled one who knows nothing about life outside a throne room. We'll soon flush her out.'

The soldiers spread out, saying their prayers before disappearing into the dark, leafless domain of the Dyrewood.

From her hiding place Gretchen could hear their voices as they approached, calling to one another, big brave men afraid of the shadows that lurked within the ancient forest. *And so they should be*, she thought to herself. There were any number of dangers waiting to take their lives within the Dyrewood; poisonous plants, suffocating serpents, cannibal Wyldermen. All inhabited the wilds of the Woodland Realm, but none were the worst threat to the lives of the Lionguard at this moment. Gretchen gritted her teeth, determination set like stone. Today they faced the Werefox.

They were correct about one thing – she could only get so far into the forest. The first fifty feet or so around the Dyrewood's outer edge was marked by a barrier of tangled thorns and thickets, impassable by anyone but the most experienced woodsmen. Beyond the dead trees and razor sharp vines was the deep green sanctuary of the forest, but it might as well have been a hundred miles away from Gretchen. Her passage was halted by the vast nest of thorns, and she'd have to bypass the Lionguard before she could find another way in. She looked at her hands, blood dripping between her knuckles where they were clenched into fists. She tried not to think about the pain and instead focused on the approaching Lionguard.

The soldier was ten feet away, oblivious to her presence.

His eyes searched the black forest floor, as he cut away at the tangleweeds and risen roots with his shortsword, trying to hack his way through. Occasionally he jumped when he saw movement, only for a small animal to scurry away through the undergrowth. A nearby companion shouted something at him, and the soldier cursed him back with a frightened laugh. It was dark and gloomy and visibility was deteriorating as dusk set in.

His eyes fixed on the forest floor, the soldier never saw the thorny noose descend and loop round his throat. The barbed hooks caught him clean round the neck, and Gretchen allowed herself to swing down from the other side of the tree bough above, holding on to the vine. Thorns became embedded in her palms as her body weight lifted the man into the air. He kicked spasmodically, dropping his shortsword as his hands grasped at the thick woody coil. He couldn't make a sound, his death rattle silenced by the thorny noose. Gretchen winced, looking away, as the soldier kicked one last time before ceasing his struggle.

She released the vine and caught his body as it dropped to the forest floor. Her hands trembled as her body reacted. *You've just killed a man, Gretchen.* She tried to concentrate. These men were killers, and she would mourn the murderer when time allowed. Picking up his shortsword, she checked her bearings. Two of the Lionguard worked their way through the undergrowth to the north of her, while to the south she could see five of them. Who knew where the rest were? There were still too many of them, cutting off her search for a way into the Dyrewood. She crouched low and tried to remain calm, blood pooling in her palm as she clenched the sword hilt.

Not for the first time that day, her thoughts went to Drew. She'd seen him transform, watched how he'd used his powers to aid him in battle. Lucas had changed to bully and terrify her, but Drew's lycanthropy was a weapon as great as any, and his to command. She thought back to her dear dead father, Earl Gaston, remembering the lessons he'd taught her about 'the change'. All therianthropes had the ability to transform, but some, the stronger, more physical ones, had greater control than others. Gretchen had rarely allowed the Fox into her life, scared of what it was capable of, restricting herself to flashes of teeth to intimidate others. Now she needed to embrace her animal within.

Ever since her capture the Fox had been waiting patiently inside Gretchen for its moment to come forth. When she'd faced Lucas in the caravan, it had felt as if she'd opened her mind for the first time and lifted a latch. Now she let the cage door swing silently open, the beast advancing freely. Her skin burned and itched all over as she felt hairs beginning to break through the surface. She gritted her teeth, grating them as they broke free from her gums, and rose up, long and needle-sharp. She wanted to shout out, but held back her cry, all too aware that a scream would end her escape before it had truly begun. The blood ceased flowing from her palms as they toughened round the sword's grip, dark claws ripping free from her fingertips. The pain began to subside as her body settled. It wasn't a complete change like those she'd seen from the greatest Werelords, but it was a start. She felt strong, fit, faster than she'd ever been in her life. Buoyed by this new confidence she scanned the undergrowth for her enemies.

'Where's Mayhew?' asked one scruffy looking soldier, suddenly aware that his companion was missing.

'He was there a minute ago,' shouted Colbard, a little further away. 'Mayhew?'

The scruffy soldier didn't get the opportunity to call out again. The Werefox burst through the undergrowth at his feet, her shortsword catching him in the stomach before her paw snatched him round the mouth. She dragged him to the floor as he let out a muffled wail.

'McLeod?' This was Colbard again, but the soldier didn't reply. He was already dead. The big captain turned his axe in his hands nervously.

'Come on lads, she's just a girl! She can't harm you!'

The old campaigner was ready for her when she came at him, raising his axe up to her as she leapt through the briars at him. The partly transformed Werefox turned in the air, bringing her shortsword down to deflect the weight of the axe blow, but it still sent her tumbling through the thorns. The captain might have killed her if she'd been any other foe, but he was under strict orders. She was to remain unharmed, even if she did somehow manage to maim or kill his men.

He hacked furiously at the tangle of dead ivy and thorny vines, ripping at them to try to get near to her, but she was moving again, away from the Lionguard.

'Move your backsides you lazy lot! She's getting away!'

Gretchen could see her opportunity now. Only one more soldier remained ahead of her and then she'd have them all at her back. Even if she continued running along the outer edge of the forest, she could still lose them. There was no way they could keep up with her now that she'd taken on the Fox. The soldier ahead could see her coming and raised his sword warily, trying to block her path as she tore through the undergrowth. She threw the shortsword at him, which he parried easily, but the distraction allowed her to hit him with an uppercut. Her fist connected squarely with his jaw, sending him tumbling into the bushes.

She dived beyond him and the way ahead was clear.

Gretchen could hear a noise in the undergrowth ahead, something larger than the animals that had caused the soldiers alarm earlier. She changed the angle of her path to avoid it, keen to avoid any other encounters that might allow her kidnappers to recapture her. Her heart quickened, so close to freedom.

In the excitement of this first ever change and her battle against the Lionguard, Gretchen realized she had forgotten one important factor. Of course, the guards weren't going to harm her. She was the prisoner of Lucas. She'd forgotten all about the Lion Prince.

At that moment the Werelion exploded from the black forest beside her, roaring as he came. The thicket was shredded as he ran, his brute strength breaking its thorny hold on him. She stumbled, primal fear coming to the fore in the face of a greater, more ferocious killer. He snapped his massive jaws at her as he neared, his body closer to that of a lion than a man now. His paw caught at her, tearing down her side and causing her to bark with pain. She immediately went into a tumble, getting caught up in the brambles and hitting the forest floor.

'Why do you run, my love?' bellowed Lucas, a malicious smile splitting his face. He actually seemed to enjoy the hunt. Gretchen struggled to free herself from the ivy that held her fast as the Werelion bore down on her.

'I didn't think she had it in her,' rasped Vankaskan from the shadows, drawing Gretchen's attention briefly. His large black shape had emerged through the trees, greasy black pelt glistening with oil as his red eyes blinked, emotionless. A weight on her torso brought her attention back to Lucas. His huge paw pinned her across the chest.

With her last ounce of strength she brought her right paw up to strike him. She'd tried to strike Drew once, when she'd first met him and the boy from the Cold Coast had infuriated her. But he'd been too quick for her. He'd caught her hand in his own grip and held her fast. Lucas was no Drew.

The clawed hand flew straight and true, tearing three long bloody strips across the left-hand side of his face. The transformed prince let out a terrible scream of agony as he brought both his paws up to his head, staggering back. She scrambled backwards, struggling to free herself from the vines, helpless before the Lion. He glared down at her, his eyes wide with rage. She no longer recognized the blond-haired prince, and it was clear he no longer recognized her. He was about to lunge at her neck when the Wererat darted in swiftly to pull the young Werelion back.

'Let go of me, Rat!' he bellowed. 'I'll kill her! Dirty little dog!'

His jaws gnashed with bloodlust, his mind fractured. Gretchen lay still, petrified. For once, she was grateful that Vankaskan was there to keep the prince at bay. Her body reverted to its human state as the Ratlord stood between the two of them, the remaining soldiers of the Lionguard beginning to gather round. Vankaskan opened his palms in a show of peace, stepping over to the prince. The Wererat whispered to him as the Lion swayed violently from side to side, trying to see past the Rat to Gretchen.

Gradually the prince calmed, staggering away as the Ratlord remained guarding the girl. As Lucas stumbled back towards the camp, his anger subsiding thanks to the Wererat's words, Vankaskan snatched Colbard's cloak, tearing it off the northman's shoulders. The Ratlord threw it down to the shivering Gretchen.

'Put that on, girl. You have placed yourself on the wrong side of your fiancé. If you want to live I suggest you do exactly as you're told from now on. Understand?'

Gretchen nodded, eyes frantic, fully aware of how close she'd just come to death. Colbard reached down and snatched her by the wrist as his men watched, cursing the Fox of Hedgemoor and dragging her back to the wagon.

PART III

Of Blood, Flesh and Bone

I

The Lord of Thieves

Duke Bergan stood with his hands behind his back, barrel chest puffed out as he stared at Highcliff Keep. He kept his chin raised, eyes peering up at the ramparts from beneath bushy red brows. An arrow bounced off the ground ten feet away, ricocheting into the air. More than two dozen additional arrows lay about or stood embedded in the earth around him.

'Lord Protector,' said a soldier, his voice strained with concern. 'Might it not be an idea to retreat and join us behind the barricade?'

The man's name was Reuben Fry, an archer from Sturmland who'd once been a member of the Lionguard. When Leopold had been overthrown he'd been among the first to take the new oath to the re-established Wolfguard. Not only was he their best shot, but he also had the keenest eyesight. Rumour had it that he was descended from the Hawklords, but Fry wouldn't comment on the matter. He peered out from behind a palisade wall they'd constructed close to the gorge that circled the castle.

'Nonsense,' said Bergan, taking a lungful of air. 'I'm not going to let Leopold's lackeys interfere with my daily constitutionals. Besides, let them fire. It's their ammunition they're wasting and I see no silver arrowheads.'

'He's got some good archers in there, my lord. It's only a matter of time before one of them finds their target. They might not kill you but they could put you out of action.' The man was clearly concerned for Bergan's safety. The Bearlord unhurriedly returned to the barricade.

'Very well,' he said gruffly. 'How many arrows have they lost? I counted around thirty.'

'Closer to forty, my lord,' said another man, smiling. Four other soldiers stood behind the barricade, which was studded with arrows on the side facing the keep.

'Excellent,' said Bergan, slapping the man's back. 'Keep up the splendid work, lads. If one of those archers so much as spits over those battlements I want to know.'

The soldiers saluted as Fry escorted Bergan away. Within moments the two of them were walking through the High Square. Since the siege had begun, the square had been transformed into a temporary military base, tents used for armouries, dining, billeting and healing filling every quarter. It was a fully functioning army camp.

'Any sign of him this morning?' asked Bergan, nodding to the soldiers who stopped and saluted as they passed.

'Yes, my lord,' said Fry, quickening his stride to keep pace. 'Saw him myself at daybreak. He's there every sunrise lately in addition to each sunset. He's worse at night, raging along the battlements. His men leave the ramparts so he can run riot. If you're in his way, you're going over the wall. He's different at dawn, though.'

'Different? This is Leopold, remember? The man's fury knows no bounds.'

'He stands calmly with the sun at his back, staring out to the horizon of the White Sea.'

'Out to sea, you say?'

'Yes, as if looking for something. Maybe he's expecting a ship to sail into the harbour and spirit him away. He's been seen there every morning for the last five days.'

'The only ship that'll spirit him away is death's raft to the underworld! You say he's calm in the mornings?'

'Yes, my lord. Calmest I've ever seen, and I served him for a number of years.'

The duke stroked his beard, twisting the red locks.

'Keep your eye on him, Fry. Could just be me getting twitchy, but I'd rather be cautious than reckless.'

'He'll do nothing without my seeing it, my lord,' said the Sturmlander, bowing. Six Greencloaks stood nearby, waiting for their liege. Bergan clapped his hand round Fry's, shaking it vigorously.

'Good man,' he said, turning to depart. 'And Fry, have you no captain working the archers?'

'Not strictly speaking, my lord. I'm overseeing them presently, as Captain Harker has gone chasing after Lord Drew.

They're responding well, but we could do with a senior officer. They'll only put up with me barking orders for so long!'

The archer smiled at the duke. Bergan wagged a finger as he departed, calling over his shoulder as he went.

'Well volunteered, man! It's Captain Fry from now on; deal with them as you will!'

Bergan disappeared into the crowd, Greencloaks flanking him, leaving a perplexed yet proud Reuben Fry, Captain of the Wolfguard, behind.

The duke's head buzzed as he walked to the Crow's Nest. Count Vega had nicknamed the wooden tower on account of its height and position in the city. The lofty scaffold was the command post in High Square, directing the allied armies' movements. Bergan's thoughts revolved around the Werelion and what his next move might be. Leopold was boxed in, going nowhere. Why hadn't he surrendered? He should have done so by now, surely? It was nearly six weeks since the siege began – what was the Lion waiting for?

Bergan left his Greencloaks and pounded up the steps of the Crow's Nest. Six flights up brought him to a covered platform that allowed views of the whole city, especially the keep. He was pleased to see Mikkel and Vega present, in addition to Hector. The young Boarlord had been working hard to prove himself, seemingly recovered from a recent illness. Bergan knew the lad wanted to right his wrongs, the shame clearly visible on his washed-out face. A part of the Bearlord regretted punishing Hector so harshly, seeing how much weight the youth had lost, but this was pushed aside by his greater feelings of relief. Relief that they'd stopped Hector before it was too late.

Magistery was an ancient art and the responsibility that went with it immense. A great deal of a magister's work involved knowledge and healing. It was typical that Hector should have wandered off the lawful path to investigate necromancy. The late Baron Huth had schooled Hector in healing, but the old magicks of Vankaskan had played their part in his education too. True, the communing had provided the answers they needed to rescue Gretchen. But at what cost to Hector? Time would tell.

'It's good you're all here,' said Bergan, shaking hands with each of them. He gripped Hector's leather gloved hand, giving it a hearty squeeze. 'I'm especially pleased to see you here, son. How are you feeling?'

'I'm fine thank you, my lord. It's good to be up and about once more.'

It had been a peculiar time for all the Werelords since the disappearance of Whitley and Drew. Bergan had decided that silence was the best policy regarding the missing pair. Knowledge of their leaving was carefully guarded – if the people of Westland discovered that Drew was missing before he'd even been crowned there'd be uproar. Instead, the Werelords let the people believe Drew was still in residence at Buck House under heavy guard. After the attack on Manfred and Kohl it was hardly surprising that he wouldn't be appearing in public.

After Hector had been removed, the Wolf's Council had sent Broghan after Drew and Whitley. He was a good leader and it was his sister who'd gone missing, so Bergan couldn't imagine anyone better to be charged with the task of bringing her safely home. He took six of Brackenholme's best branches, with Captain Harker as second in command. As one Werelord left another arrived – Vincent of Redmire, Hector's twin, had moved into Bevan's Tower, alongside Hector. But soon after his appearance Hector had been found wandering the streets, fevered. Mikkel had Hector moved to Buck House where his staff could nurse him alongside the recuperating Duke Manfred.

Bergan wasn't sure it was coincidence, Hector falling ill as his brother arrived. The arrogant Vincent had big plans for Redmire, informing the Wolf's Council of his intentions straight away. He wanted his father's title and throne. One could understand his reasoning. Hector was a magister, not a leader of men. He lacked the charisma of a ruler, making an unlikely baron in Bergan's eyes. But Bergan struggled to imagine Vincent taking power. There was something about him that raised the Bearlord's hackles.

'It's good to see him, isn't it?' said Mikkel to the council, patting Hector's back. 'Maybe I can have my house back soon, eh?' He gave the magister a playful dig, but Hector merely smiled wanly.

'Leave the boy alone, Mikkel,' sighed Vega. 'The last thing he needs is your gurning face knocking him sick again.'

'How's your brother?' Bergan asked Hector, cutting to the chase.

'I haven't seen him,' said the Boarlord. He was still pale and looked sickly. 'Not since my . . . incident. He hasn't been to see me, if that's what you mean.'

'I was just wondering if you'd been back to Bevan's Tower yet. He'll be making that place his home if you're not careful!'

Bergan only half joked; Vincent had informed the higher social echelons of Highcliff that he'd be in the city for a while. But Bergan wasn't about to let Hector know about Vincent's visit to the Wolf's Council; it might tip him back over the edge. Vincent would no doubt have been making himself very comfortable in the tower.

'Has he been to see you?' asked Hector, his voice shaky. Duke Bergan shrugged.

'Only to congratulate everyone on the defeat of the Lion. He speaks on behalf of Redmire, Hector.'

'Were you aware of this?' added Mikkel. Hector shook his head, rubbing his gloved hands together as if fighting the chill. The young magister had taken to wearing black, as if in mourning, with only his brown woollen cloak of Redmire breaking the effect. It perplexed Bergan. It was the tail end of summer, yet Hector was dressed for winter. Perhaps the fever still gripped him.

'I wasn't,' he muttered. 'He wants Redmire for himself. I know I'm a magister; that is my calling. But by rights the throne is mine to give away, is it not?' The others nodded. 'So I think . . . it might be best if I keep hold of it for a while longer. Let things settle. For everyone's sake . . .'

Hector trailed off. The news must have irked him, reasoned Bergan. He'd have been furious if he were in Hector's boots but then, Hector was no Bear.

'Good idea,' said the Bearlord. 'It's the wisest thing to do. Your father would approve.'

Two soldiers of the Wolfguard appeared at the top of the staircase, one young and one old. They looked splendid, grey game pelts lining the edges of their black cloaks, the silver Wolfshead roaring on their black tabards. Bergan had been pleased to see many soldiers of the old Lionguard taking the oath. There had been many who'd asked to switch allegiance from the armies of Stormdale and Brackenholme, men who had once served under Wergar but had left when he was slain. This was their chance to return to the black and serve his son. The soldier who spoke was one such man, the white-haired Crombie.

'Lord Protector, we have the prisoner you requested below.' Crombie was the chief jailer at Traitors' House, overseeing the release of prisoners. He also ensured that those who belonged there were cared for humanely.

'Bring him up.'

Crombie called his men and chains rattled as the prisoner was led up. Mikkel was glowering already, so Bergan gave him a nudge.

'I can't help it,' grumbled the Staglord. 'Of all the rogues we released from Traitors' House, this is one villain we rightly kept in.'

'Regardless, let's keep this civil. We may need his help more than once before we're done.' He turned to Vega. 'You're sure he can help?'

'There's no harm in talking with him, is there?'

The prisoner's head emerged first, flanked by the Wolfguard. He was bald, the right side of his face heavily decorated with the tattoo of a sea serpent that coiled around his brow and cheekbone, its jaws opening round his mouth so its teeth closed round his. He smiled as he approached with small steady steps. Without the tattoo he might not have looked threatening, although the manacles round his throat, ankles and wrists told a different story. The guards were taking no risks; Bo Carver, Lord of the Thieves Guild, still had many friends in Highcliff.

'Vega,' he smiled. The guards let go, leaving him to stand alone as they stepped back.

'How are you, Bo?' said the sea marshal, breaking with etiquette and striding forward to grasp him by the hand. Carver laughed as Vega shook his wrist, the manacles jangling furiously. Mikkel looked outraged by the Wereshark's behaviour, although Bergan was getting used to it.

'You know Carver?' spluttered Mikkel.

'Indeed,' laughed Vega. 'This scoundrel and I used to sail together on the *Harbinger*, my father's schooner. Only it turned out young Bo couldn't cut it – jumped ship in Highcliff and made this place his home. Isn't that right?'

'I saw an opportunity, Vega. Like any good pirate would, I took it.'

'Yes,' said Bergan, cutting in at last. 'As I recall you killed that old thief Gwillem in the docks. He was the boss of the Highcliff thieves, wasn't he?'

'You make it sound dirty. It was a fair fight, instigated by him I might add. With no leader for my brethren I stepped into the role, backed by a couple of influential supporters.'

'I heard he died with a knife in his back,' said Bergan.

'Knife fights can end that way,' replied Carver.

'I've never known a man more deadly with a dagger,' said Vega. 'Are you still dangerous with a longknife?'

'You still dangerous with that smart mouth?' asked Carver.

'And this murder made you the top thief in Highcliff?' asked Mikkel, still clearly disgusted by Vega's friendship with the rogue.

'Lord of the Thieves Guild, if you please.'

'You make it sound like a lawful organization! And you're no lord for that matter!'

'One doesn't need animal blood coursing through his veins to be a lord, sir,' said Carver, smiling slyly.

Bergan placed a hand on the furious Mikkel's shaking shoulder.

'Enough,' he barked. 'This bickering gets us nowhere.'

'I quite agree,' replied Carver, smiling at Mikkel as the Staglord stepped down. Vega backed away now to stand with his therian brothers.

'Do you know of any way into or out of Highcliff Keep?'

The Werelords turned to Hector, surprised that the direct question had come from the young Boarlord. Hector's cheeks were crimson and he looked like he was about to apologize. It was no longer his place to ask questions. Bergan spoke quickly.

'You heard the Lord of Redmire, Carver,' he said, deflecting attention from Hector. Bergan pointed at the castle. 'The keep – are there hidden exits?'

'You brought me all this way to ask me that?' he said, his voice slightly incredulous.

'Answer the question. No games.'

'What's it worth?'

'You're in no position to barter,' scoffed Bergan.

'I'd say I am, actually,' said Carver. 'My life in Traitors' House could certainly be more comfortable. Am I really likely to escape? Is there a need for these chains?'

'You killed a guard two years ago.'

'Ah,' qualified the prisoner, raising his manacled hands to waggle a finger. 'I killed a *Lionguard*, a real bully too. They don't count.'

Bergan caught sight of Vega smiling as he strode up to the thief. The top of Carver's head reached just below Bergan's beard and his chest was as wide as the thief's shoulders. Carver found himself eclipsed by shadow; his confidence wavered.

'Answer my question and I'll consider moving you to more comfortable quarters.'

Carver peered round Bergan to look at his old friend Vega.

'Is that the best offer I'm getting?'

The captain of the *Maelstrom* nodded, his face now serious. Carver pulled back.

'It's a deal,' he said, holding a chained open palm up. Bergan placed his huge hand round the thief's, sealing the deal.

'The Cold Coast wasn't always cold,' said Carver. 'From Highcliff up to Vermire and beyond, this land was forged by volcanoes thousands of years ago. The Fiery Coast it should have been named, so the men of the Whitepeaks say.'

'You're very learned for a thief,' sniffed Mikkel.

'You're very ignorant for a lord.'

Bergan growled to quiet the pair. Carver continued.

'Let's just say I've always been interested in what's under our feet; what lies beneath Highcliff. As Lord of the Thieves Guild

I needed to know how to get in and out of places. Why else would you have brought me here today? The smiths of the Strakenberg, the mountain Icegarden sits upon, would tell you this far better than I. There are tunnels the whole length of the Cold Coast, formed from the lava flows that became Westland. There's a world below you'll never see – unless you look for it.'

'So these tunnels,' said Bergan. 'They're under Highcliff?'

Carver nodded, animated now, talking about something that clearly excited him. Bergan was impressed. As thugs went Carver was very intelligent. This also made him dangerous.

'Indeed. You'll know about the sewers, mostly man-made, but some of their creators made use of the natural fissures in the rock. I used to have a map that showed every tunnel and cave system that the thieves ever charted.'

'There's one that leads into the castle?' asked Mikkel, animosity replaced by curiosity.

'Not that we ever found. There may well be a hidden path, but where, I couldn't say.'

Bergan stared at the man, assessing him.

'He's telling the truth,' said the Bearlord.

'Thank you,' laughed Carver. 'There may be a tunnel, but the Lion doesn't know about it. If he did, he'd be gone by now, wouldn't he?'

'Depends on whether he wants to surrender Highcliff. He fought hard for that crown and won't give it up lightly.'

Hector stepped forward. He'd been taking notes on what was discussed. He raised his quill tentatively.

'Sorry to interrupt, my lords. But if he *does* know of a way out of the castle – which he might not – then isn't it possible that he's sent for help?'

'It's possible,' said Bergan. 'But what allies does he have? Who can he turn to? It'd take a large bag of gold to persuade anyone to fight for him. He has no gold or friends any more.'

'Still,' said Vega hesitantly. 'Perhaps I should send some patrols out into the White Sea.'

'He watches the sea every morning,' said Bergan.

'Then I'll send the fastest vessels we have. It's scouting, that's all. If Leopold has friends lurking out there in the ocean, I'll be sure to find them.' Vega clapped his hand into Carver's. 'Thanks for this, Bo. I'll see about getting some wine and . . . *treats* delivered to you.'

'A pardon wouldn't go amiss,' said Carver as the guards led him away.

'One thing at a time, Carver,' said Bergan. 'The Wolf's Council thanks you for your assistance.'

'Of course it does,' he called back, as he disappeared down the steps.

'Where does this leave us?' asked Bergan.

'Still in the harbour,' said Vega.

'Meaning?'

'While the game's afoot, whatever it is, we're moored up going nowhere. My sailors see dark omens everywhere, warning them that war comes. Something's happening, and soon. We need to stay on our mettle.'

'It's good to hear you enthuse, Vega,' said Bergan.

'It's good to have something to do,' said the Pirate Prince. 'Sitting in port for two months can bore a man to death.' The Wereshark made his way to the stairs, thinking aloud. 'Once the scout ships are gone, I'll mobilize my fleet, if you can call it that. You might want to raise some taxes if you want a proper presence in the ocean. I could have rallied an armada from the Cluster Isles to put the navy here to shame, if Leopold hadn't put that fat Kraken Ghul on my throne. Ramshackle is too kind a description for what currently sails in the name of Westland.'

With that last comment the sea marshal disappeared, heels clicking rapidly down the wooden steps as he hurried to the *Maelstrom*.

'He's like a different man,' grunted Mikkel. 'I have to say I prefer this version.'

'He's has a strategy. Vega's many things, but most of all he's a man of action.' Bergan turned to Hector, his quill still scribbling on parchment. Mikkel nodded to Bergan, prompting him.

'Do you need help moving your personal effects back to Bevan's Tower, Hector?'

Hector's quill nib nearly splintered. He was on edge, and Bergan didn't like it. He knew brothers could fight, but was worried that this bad blood between the Boars ran deeper.

'I can do it myself,' said Hector, steeling himself. 'I shouldn't put this off any longer.' He turned to Mikkel. 'My lord, I'll send a runner to fetch my belongings from Buck House. Thank you for the hospitality you've shown me while I convalesced. I shan't forget your kindness.'

Mikkel started to shake Hector's hand and then embraced the young Boar. Bergan smiled. Mikkel could be an obstinate fool but deep down he was a warm-hearted fellow.

'Brothers can fight, I know,' Mikkel comforted Hector. 'I've lost track of the number of times Manfred and I have locked antlers. I love my brother with all my heart, and knowing how gravely wounded he was . . . well, I'd give anything to take his place now. Once you've spoken with Vincent you'll forget what you ever crossed words over.'

Hector's smile was strained.

'I'm sure you're right, my lord. If you'll excuse me?'

Bergan could tell Hector's voice lacked conviction. He alone accompanied the Boarlord to the staircase. He spoke to the young man in quiet tones.

'If you need anything, don't hesitate to ask. Anything at all.' He jabbed Hector's shoulder with a finger.

'I shall my lord,' said the Magister. He rubbed his gloved hands together once more before trudging down the stairs of the Crow's Nest.

'What is it?' said Mikkel.

'I worry about what awaits him.'

'Family affairs, Bergan,' said the Staglord, leaning on the wooden balcony and staring out over the city. 'Not our place to meddle – it's for the brothers to sort out. Blood's thicker than water and all that.'

'It's the blood I'm afraid of,' said Bergan.

2

Sibling Rivalry

Hector stood outside Bevan's Tower, the brass key to the great door in his trembling grasp. He looked back through the gardens to the gate in the wall, which he'd deliberately left open. If he had a change of heart he could make a dash to the street. The gardens were badly overgrown after years of neglect, weeds choking the rosebushes, strangling the life out of them. Hector stroked his throat tentatively. People milled past in the street beyond the gate, oblivious to the Boarlord's anxieties.

He unlocked the door.

The main hall had seen a great deal of recent activity. The dust sheets were gone, and the hall was transformed into a room for feasting once again, although it appeared that a debauched affair had already taken place. The remains of a banquet covered the great table and the floor was littered with half-eaten food, broken crockery and smashed glasses. A small stray dog lay beneath the table, gnawing on a discarded bone. Hector clapped his hands to shoo it away, but it growled, guarding its prize. Hector ignored it; he'd pick his moment for that little fight.

It horrified Hector that Vincent could treat their home in such a manner. He glanced into the kitchen to find, once more, a room in disarray. Plates cluttered every surface and the door into the herb garden was wide open and swinging in the mid-morning breeze. That explained where their four-legged guest had come from.

Hector cautiously went upstairs. When he got to the first floor, which Vincent had taken for himself, he took a moment to catch his breath before knocking at his twin's door.

'Vincent?' he said, his voice cracking with nerves. The last time they'd spoken he'd scrambled away with a bloody brow and a deathly fever. His head had mended but the fever still had its claws in him. He called once more and, when no reply came, turned the handle, swinging the door open and stepping into the room.

The chambers looked like a paupers' wash house, clothes heaped and draped across the floor and furniture. Once again the leftovers from various meals littered the room, leaving few areas where one could see the floor.

'Vincent!' Hector called, peering into the bathroom. A riot appeared to have taken place. The smell from the privy was awful. He backed out of the chambers.

The second flight of stairs up to his own chambers took twice as long to climb as Hector pondered what awaited him.

Sweat rolled down his face and he whipped the glove off his left hand to wipe it out of his eyes. He glanced at the black mark on his palm, shivering, before tugging his glove on again. He crept down the short corridor to the door, taking the handle and swinging it open.

The party had visited every corner of Bevan's Tower. Hector's quilt had been kicked from the bed, the sheets beneath were soiled. His writing desk had been rifled through, paperwork and letters were torn and heaped about. Hector cursed; all his good work had been undone. Every corner had been desecrated, nothing was untouched.

The locked drawers on the desk had been cracked open and the coins Hector kept in the bureau were gone. Vincent had thieved the money, leaving Hector penniless. His head suddenly snapped to attention.

Hector dashed over to the wardrobe that dominated the inside wall of the room. Opening the door he felt around the base. His fingers found purchase round the loose board. Prising it up he moved it to one side. The brass box was still there. He felt his heart rate quicken. It was unspectacular looking, a foot long, with handles on either end. He glanced nervously over his shoulder, as if he were a villain carrying out some terrible deed. *Perhaps I am*, thought Hector.

Twisting the latch gently he flipped open the lid. He sighed when he saw that the contents were still there. He traced his hands over the documents, his fingers lingering over the black candles. Hector patted the pouch of brimstone. He'd made a promise to Bergan and the Wolf's Council, one he intended to keep, but he wasn't ready to let go of the box just yet.

Hector snapped the lid shut, replacing it in the base of the cupboard. He patted the board back into place, backing away and closing the door again.

It was going to be a busy day.

By late afternoon both the hall and kitchen were clean, emptied of the detritus that Vincent's entertaining had left behind. Hector lit a bonfire in the courtyard, burning the rubbish as he went. The dog had put up more of a fight than he'd expected, eventually being chased off by the irate Boarlord with a broom. He'd soon returned, his insolence broken, and now followed the Lord of Redmire around like a faithful retainer.

The hall restored to its former beauty, Hector's next task had been to clean out his own rooms. The soiled bedsheets had ended up on the bonfire with the rest of the refuse, as he'd systematically worked through his bed chamber and bathroom, removing all signs of Vincent and his cronies.

Left to his own devices, Hector reflected upon the last week. The small dog proved to be a very capable listener as he busied himself with chores.

'I know Vincent will make a move for the title, but will he really hurt me if he doesn't get his way? We rarely see eye to eye, but I can't imagine him physically harming me.'

Hector rubbed his head where he'd split it on the fireplace. The little dog cocked its head.

'Perhaps this was *my* mistake. I've always been clumsy. Maybe I misunderstood Vincent that night,' reasoned Hector.

'Of course Vincent wants the throne, but he'll only push

things so far. This has been a foolish mistake on both our parts. There's nothing the sons of Baron Huth can't resolve when we put our heads together.'

He was grateful that Mikkel had taken him in. The last thing he remembered that night was fleeing from Bevan Tower, fever raging and head spinning. The next thing he recalled was waking up in Buck House. He was later told that he'd been found wandering the streets by the City Watch. Hector had never blacked out before, and the episode caused him great alarm.

The dog followed Hector as he finished sweeping the door-step of Bevan's Tower, dispersing the dust clouds into the garden. The hound stayed clear, remembering its previous encounter with the broom.

'Brenn only knows why Vincent's taken those rogues Ringlin and Ibal into service. If I can just get Vincent alone for a moment I'm sure I can set things straight. He may not agree, but he'll always listen. This day's work has really blown the cobwebs away. I'm beginning to feel like my old self again!'

A passing cloud caused gloom to descend over the garden. Hector watched as the shade lifted again, the sun's rays returning. He shivered as sharp shadows appeared. Hector returned indoors, the dog following.

His week in Buck House hadn't been spent entirely in bed. Hector had been able to browse through the library of the late Magister Kohl. Hector reached his left hand out to the dog. It sniffed at his gloved hand, staying away. Keeping it there Hector tugged the right glove off with his teeth, holding the bare hand out alongside the other. The dog moved to it straight away, licking his palm. Hector smiled, ruffling its fur. He slowly stopped stroking the dog as his thoughts returned to the shadows.

'Viles. That's what the phantoms are known as, so the books of Magister Kohl say. They're spirits of wicked men who refused to move on, trapped between worlds, latching on to sources of magick among the living. Necromancers are, understandably, an attractive host for a vile to haunt, being as close to the dead as a soul could be. A practitioner of the dark arts, a competent one, might never encounter a vile. I, however, am not competent . . .'

Hector could trace his predicament back to his encounter with the dead shaman – the minute he'd messed up the ritual he'd left himself open to attack. He was a marked man to the dead. The dog let out a low growl, as if mention of viles struck a chord.

'Knowing what the entities are removes some of the fear. I'm looking for them now, trying to decipher who the spirits were in life. They still chatter and giggle in the dark, but their torment isn't as great as it was. Having a name for them's half the battle: knowledge is power, and I'm determined to learn more.'

The little mongrel growled, baring its teeth nervously. Hector's hand wavered over its head.

'Steady, mutt. You've nothing to fear.'

'Hasn't he?'

Hector looked back to the front doors where Vincent stood, flanked by his lackeys. He was silhouetted by the daylight behind, all three faces shrouded in darkness. Hector struggled to his feet. The little dog kept its belly low, hiding behind him. Hector was determined this conversation would go better than their last.

'It's so good to see you, Vincent. I didn't hear you come in. How long have you been there?'

Vincent unfastened his cape, tossing it over the banister at the bottom of the staircase. It tumbled untidily to the floor.

'Long enough to hear your confession to that cur.'

Vincent's voice was disapproving. Hector strode up, arms open. He couldn't have heard him, surely?

'Confession? I don't follow, brother.'

Vincent backed away as Hector tried to embrace him, leaving the magister grasping at air. His stomach lurched as he watched Vincent manoeuvre past him. Red wine stains marked his jerkin, red eyes telling their tale of his excesses.

'Enitities? Spirits? Monsters in shadows?' Vincent said, his voice laced with horror. 'Dear Brenn, Hector; what have you become?'

'I . . . but . . .' Hector stammered, unable to explain quickly enough. 'It's not what you think.'

'What on earth would Bergan say if he knew you practised the dark arts?' his brother scoffed. Ibal grinned manically while Ringlin sneered.

Hector shifted nervously, disappointed at how swiftly the exchange had deteriorated. He eyed the henchmen warily, the small dog trembling against his boots. He had to keep Bergan out of this, the Bearlord's complicity was serious business. Hector felt the traitorous colour rise in his cheeks, telling Vincent all he needed to know.

'He already *knows*, doesn't he?' exclaimed his brother. 'And yet still keeps you close? How embarrassing for this Wolf's Council!' He turned to his companions for support. 'Surely the people wouldn't want a necromancer working in their own government?'

'I'd be horrified at the prospect, sire,' said Ringlin quietly, never taking his narrow eyes off Hector. His fat friend giggled in agreement.

'Please, Vincent,' said Hector, following his twin into the hall. 'Nobody else need know of my mistakes.'

'Ah, but Hector, these things have a habit of getting out! Father would be so disappointed in you; sullying the good name of Redmire.'

'Show mercy,' implored Hector. 'I've been unwell, and whatever mistakes I've made were made with the best intentions. Thanks to my communing we know where Gretchen is. That's where Drew is, right now – on her trail, trying to rescue her from Lucas and Vankaskan.'

Vincent staggered into the table as if struck by a heavy blow.

'What news!' he gasped dramatically, his face a show of distress. 'Our future king? Beyond the walls of the city? Missing?'

Hector felt nauseous. He'd said too much; he knew it as soon as the words left his mouth. But how else could he secure his brother's compliance other than by telling him the truth? Judging by Vincent's histrionics, his compliance didn't seem likely.

'Necromancy used by the council? The Lion and the Rat behind the abduction? Deception about the whereabouts of the Wolf? The people need to know! What a shambles! Oh, this is too much!'

'Some restraint, Vincent, I beg of you!'

'You beg of *me*?' shouted the younger twin, advancing quickly on his brother. His little performance of concerned citizen was gone in an instant. He was back on form; hard, focused, self-centred. Hot spittle hit Hector's face.

'You're a disgrace! A spineless mess and a sorry excuse for a Werelord. Drew, Gretchen, Lucas, the actions of the Wolf's Council – this stuff is *incendiary*, Hector. Can you imagine what chaos this information would cause in Highcliff, throughout Westland? There'd be rebellion! The people wouldn't stand for that old fool Bergan running things under the pretence of the Wolf. Lord Protector! The old Bear can't even protect that shepherd friend of yours who plays at being regal!'

'Please,' sobbed Hector. 'You have to realize what we battle against. The Lions are behind this business, all of it. You know what monsters they are – they ordered our father's death! Bergan can hardly be charged with failure when Drew shows such determination to go after Gretchen. She's like a sister to us. Can you not see that?'

Vincent took hold of Hector, pinning him against the wall as he spoke quietly.

'I can forgive all of this, Hector.' He smiled, his face suddenly that of a loving brother. Tears rolled down Hector's face as he nodded eagerly.

'Renounce your claim,' said Vincent.

Hector's mouth fell open, his eyes wide.

'But . . .'

'No buts. Renounce your claim, and this information won't leave the room.'

Hector looked past his brother to the two rogues.

'What about those two?'

'They are members of the Boarguard,' said Vincent, straightening his brother's clothes and patting him. 'Honest and loyal, the pair of them; I vouch for their silence.'

Hector doubted it, but he was in no position to argue. He cursed himself for having told Vincent the business of the Wolf's Council.

'Give me some time to step down without losing face, Vincent.'

'I don't have time, and neither do you. Count yourself lucky I don't go to a street corner and announce all this news to the people right now! No, time is not a friend to either of us. I expect you to stand down immediately, and with that you buy my silence.'

'But I'll willingly step down, Vincent. Please, just give me a month to sort out my affairs.'

'I'll give you a week. After that I start talking. Let the people decide whether you and your friends are fit to govern. Seven days and seven nights, Hector. After that? No more sleeps . . .'

Vincent's smile was cruel and self-satisfied. Hector dared not breathe, waiting for his brother to move. But he just stood there, blocking any means of escape.

A sudden knocking at the front door caused them all to turn.

'Hector, I would talk with you about bad omens – sailors are such a superstitious bunch!'

'Come in!' shouted Hector. Vincent sneered as the door opened. It was Count Vega.

'A few sage words from a magister would put them . . .' The sea marshal's voice trailed off as he entered the room. He looked quickly between the four men, recognizing the threat. Instinctively his sword arm shrugged his cape clear of his weapon. Vincent immediately took a step back. Vega settled his gaze on Ringlin.

'Everything all right, Hector?'

'Ringlin. Ibal. Come – let's drink, dine and make merry,' said Vincent, swaggering off towards the kitchens. 'Let's toast my health, the future Baron of Redmire!'

The men followed Vincent, the fat one clapping his stumpy hands as he went, the tall one glaring at Vega as he strode by. Hector slid down the wall to the floor, the small dog jumping into his lap, their miserable friendship sealed.

'What in sweet Sosha's name was all that about?' asked Vega, crouching down beside the young magister.

'Brenn help me, Vega,' Hector whispered. 'What have I done?'

3

The Wound That Would Not Heal

'That's Haggard, then?' asked Drew, looking across the Longridings towards the distant walled city. The sun hung low in the west as it slowly descended from the heavens. Whitley was squinting and struggling to see the city. Drew took for granted his own heightened senses, as well as the training he'd received at the hands of Mack Ferran. His role as a shepherd had often depended upon seeing: the land, the animals, the horizon.

'You see it?' she said.

Drew nodded slowly.

'City of the Ram?' he replied.

'You were paying attention after all.'

Drew looked back the way they'd come, half expecting to see Duke Bergan charging into view at any moment. He was amazed they'd got this far without the Wolf's Council tracking them down. It was only a matter of time before the council caught them; Hector had never intended to keep their route secret.

He looked at Whitley with concern. She slumped in Chancer's saddle, somewhere between the waking world and the dead. Her skin had a sickly pallor, red rings circling her bloodshot eyes as she struggled to keep them open. Her therian healing had meant the difference between life and death for the young scout, the wound at her neck having become infected all too swiftly. If she'd been human, she would have been dead by now.

The attack by the dead Lionguard felt more like a year ago to Drew as opposed to a few days. The burden of protecting his sick friend while staying on Gretchen's trail weighed heavy on his shoulders. Whitley's injury showed no sign of recovery, and the bite festered. All Drew could do was keep it clean; a cure was beyond him.

'Drew,' said Whitley, drinking heavily from her waterskin as she slouched on Chancer behind him. 'We shouldn't be going there. We need to go south. Cape Gala's where they've headed with Gretchen.'

'You won't make it to Cape Gala. That wound needs looking at by someone who knows what they're doing. You said so yourself; Baron Ewan will help.'

The two of them had stopped in Cheaptown a few nights earlier. They'd quickly discovered that Lucas's party had been through a couple of days previously. Ten or so men, they'd numbered, or so Drew and Whitley were told. Cheaptown's healer had tended Whitley's injury, but he lacked the medicines to cure her. He agreed with Whitley's suggestion – Ewan of Haggard would help. An old magister, there was little the Ramlord didn't know about medicine. Werelords and humans alike had heard tell of his skilled magistcry.

'We don't have time,' insisted Whitley, wavering in her saddle. Drew steadied her. 'Just leave me here, someone will find me and take me to Haggard, I'm sure.'

'Don't argue, Whitley. We go to Haggard, City of the Ram.'

Drew dug his heels into his horse's flanks and set off once again, leading Chancer along behind.

It took the remainder of the day to reach Haggard, along a road winding through the rugged foothills. Drew took comfort in knowing that the Lord of Haggard was an old friend of Whitley's father. It seemed that Bergan's paw had a long and influential reach. The swifter Ewan could tend to his friend the better – every moment they delayed made Drew fear that Gretchen would be gone across the sea, shipped off to Bast like some spoil of war.

He would have his moment with Lucas. There would be a reckoning. Drew had considered what he might do whenever he encountered his half-brother again. He'd made an awful promise to their mother. Prince Lucas was unwell, and there was no cure for his sickness. Well, perhaps one, mused Drew grimly. If the moment came, he wasn't sure he could carry through with the deed. He wanted to give the Lion a chance to redeem himself, but feared it was too late.

Haggard was a rough, windswept city, perched along the

cliffs that staggered into the sea. It was much smaller than Highcliff, covering the same kind of area as Tuckborough, with stocky walls surrounding it. Drew's father had dealt with men from Haggard in Tuckborough. He'd heard they were honest, straight-talking folk, typical of those who inhabited the Cold Coast and the Longridings. As they were well known for their hospitality, Drew wasn't surprised when a welcoming party awaited the duo as they approached the gates.

'Well met,' called Drew, hailing them as they neared.

Drew counted six soldiers on the road, spears carried loose in hand. He was surprised to see that they didn't wear a uniform, unlike those he'd encountered in other cities. These men seemed rougher, more casual than one might expect from a City Watch. The hairs on Drew's neck began to prickle. Something wasn't right. Only one bore any insignia, and that was illegible, its paint scratched away on his battered breast-plate. Even in the half light of dusk he recognized these men as mercenaries. Two manoeuvred past him towards Chancer, who let out a nervous whinny. Drew twisted, looking back as one reached up to grab Whitley by the thigh, giving her a hard jostle.

'Please don't,' said Drew. 'She's unwell and needs the help of Baron Ewan.'

'Does she now?' said one guard, taking hold of Chancer's reins. He was short and stocky, the only one who looked like a local. His short blond beard was stained red. *Wine*, thought Drew. *What kind of guard drinks while on watch?*

Drew tried to remain calm, but felt his irritation level rise.

The last thing he wanted was to cause a scene at the gates, especially as the Ramlord was a friend of Bergan's.

'Sir,' he continued politely. 'My lady is gravely ill – I'm told the baron can help her.'

'You scouts from Brackenholme, then?' asked one man, a tall, dark-skinned fellow who carried a shortsword on one hip and a coiled whip on the other. A southerner, from overseas; the last kind of soldier one expected to see in a quiet Lyssian city like Haggard.

Drew smiled nervously, raising a hand to his cloak.

'You recognize the Green of the Woodland Realm, sir?'

'That's a yes then?' replied the blond-bearded man behind who now tugged at Chancer's reins. Whitley slumped to one side, almost falling from her saddle. 'Whoah! Now then, girlie!' he laughed, slapping Whitley on the thigh with a fat hand.

'Don't touch her,' shouted Drew. The southerner reached for the reins of Drew's horse, causing Drew to tug them away from his grasp. His horse took a step back in response, hooves clattering the cobbled road. Drew caught sight of Whitley sliding from her saddle into the arms of the bearded man as his friends jeered.

Drew reached for his sword. One of the soldiers saw this, levelling his spear at Drew.

'Unhand her!' roared Drew, unable to contain himself a moment longer. His anger had got the better of him and he could feel the Wolf rising. Before he could give in to his lycanthropy the world turned. The horizon tilted dramatically as his horse reared and he began to tumble backwards, falling from the saddle. His body sped down, head first, towards the hard road. He might have cushioned himself from the fall if he'd been able to free himself from his saddle, but his feet remained fixed in the stirrups. The last thing he saw was the soldier's spear, buried deep in the neck of his screaming mount, as the ground rushed up to meet him in a blinding, deafening crash.

A bucket of icy water in the face brought Drew's rude awakening. Immediately he was scrambling backwards on the floor, temporarily blinded, as his bare back hit a cold stone wall.

'Wake up, boy,' barked a gravelly voice. Drew blinked, shaking the water from his face as he squinted around the chamber.

The tall, dark-skinned guard from the gate stood immediately above him, the empty bucket swinging in one hand, a torch brand in the other. Drew spotted the pommel of his own longsword, the Wolfshead bouncing against the soldier's hip. It wasn't the guard's voice he had heard, though; that belonged to someone else. Behind the soldier Drew could see a railed partition, metal bars running from the jagged ceiling to the rough stone floor to provide one long communal prison cell. The whole chamber was some kind of natural cave, possibly situated directly beneath Haggard itself. A single barred door, now open, was the only exit. The only other light in the prison came from the torches that spluttered along the curving wall beyond, disappearing up a winding staircase. The huddled shapes of a great many other prisoners lined the back wall of the cavern. They all kept a respectful distance from Drew and his captor.

A short, broad-shouldered man crouched beside Drew, a bloody cloth in his hand. Drew knitted his brow, gasping as he felt torn skin pulling away from his skull. The man with the cloth shook his head from side to side, willing Drew not to struggle. He had bushy grey hair and a short beard, worn in the style of the men of the region. Below the man's jaw Drew could make out a metal ring circling his throat. The guard threw the bucket to the floor with a clatter and stepped away to reveal another man standing in the darkened doorway.

'The girl upstairs,' said the man in the shadows, his voice rough as sandpaper. 'Who is she and what ails her?'

Drew suddenly raised a hand to his constricted throat. His fingers brushed the cold metal ring there, lingering over the bolt that sealed it shut. *No shape-shifting for me then*, he realized. *Unless I'm in a hurry to meet Brenn.*

The man in the shadows nodded to the guard. The kick caught Drew square across the jaw, his head bouncing off the floor and his mouth filling with blood. The grey bearded man beside him reached forward with his bloody cloth to mop Drew's face.

'Leave him,' barked the man at the door. 'He has a tongue in his head. He'd better use it quickly before Djogo here cuts it out.' The dark-skinned soldier grinned, patting the Wolfs-head blade on his hip. Drew struggled to his knees.

'I shall only speak with Baron Ewan,' he spluttered. 'Call off your dog and take me to him.'

'You'll only speak in the presence of the Ramlord, eh?' said the gravel-voiced man. 'Interesting.'

The speaker grunted, his face lost in shadow. He shook his

head from one side to the other, the white hair on his head catching the torchlight. He snarled, teeth gnashing as his chest pumped and strained. His back arched, and his shoulders bulged within his robes. The stocky man who crouched beside Drew looked away. Only Drew and the brutal guard kept their eyes on the transformation. When the change was complete the Werelord's head had slumped against his chest. Slowly he raised it. The silhouette of the horns was unmistakable as he took a cloven-hoofed step into the cell.

In his years of tending sheep Drew had faced down rams before and had never found them frightening, with or without their enormous horns. But Baron Ewan was more than a man, more than a ram. He was a Werelord, and a monstrous one at that. The cloven foot that stepped into the chamber was connected to a muscular grey leg that disappeared into his open red robes, dark shaggy wool hanging around his exposed midriff. His chest heaved with the effort of the change as he bent low to enter the cell, manoeuvring his horns through the doorway. One of the thick horns clanged against the metal bars, ringing dully like a mournful bell. His face was suddenly illuminated by the guard's torch; long and grey, with a mop of wiry white hair that tumbled over his sloping brow. His teeth were yellowed and cracked, grating against one another as he turned his lips, preparing to speak. Most frightful of all were the eyes; globs of dirty gold bulging from the sides of his face, pupils splitting the eyes like rectangles of jet.

'Speak!' spat the Werelord as he towered over Drew. The young Werewolf could hardly breathe. Leopold, Vanmorten,

Vala – all the monsters he'd faced had been terrifying. But the Ram looked like a demon. Drew struggled to find words.

'Whitley,' he said quickly. 'She's Whitley, Lady of Brackenholme. Duke Bergan's daughter. She said you were a friend of the Bearlord.' His words were out before he'd considered them, such was his desire not to anger the Ramlord further. He only just managed to stay his tongue and keep his own identity secret. The bearded man by Drew's side looked up at mention of Whitley and Bergan, glancing wide-eyed from Drew to the monster.

'A Werelady; here, in Haggard?' growled the beast. 'And a valuable one at that! Good fortune just falls into my lap, does it not, dear Ewan?' The Werelord reached down and patted the crouching old man on his head. Drew looked at him, struggling to comprehend.

'Leave the boy, Ewan,' added the towering Werelord, leaving the cell. 'He's worth nothing to me. The girl on the other hand . . .'

Drew's head was spinning. If the short, grey-haired man who'd cleaned his wound was Ewan . . . then who was this monster, commanding the Lord of Haggard? The horned therianthrope stood outside the cell and stroked the long white hair that curled down from the end of his chin.

'Lady Whitley,' he chortled, his laugh rattling like a bag of stones. 'I witnessed her birth before Bergan chased me out of Brackenholme. I really should become reacquainted with her.' He looked back at the crouching Ewan. 'Come along, Sheep: this scout is insignificant! I've an investment that requires your attention upstairs.'

Ewan struggled to his feet and followed the Werelord out of the chamber. Last to leave the room was the guard, who bent low to offer a word of warning to Drew before leaving.

'I'm watching you, boy,' he said. 'No silly ideas, or it'll be more than your tongue I cut off, right?'

The guard closed the door, rattling the heavy key in the lock as the Werelord and his companions made for the stairs. Drew scrambled up, finding courage as the entourage departed.

'If that's Baron Ewan,' called Drew, pointing at the short, bearded man. 'Then who the devil are you?'

The Werelord stopped. He turned to look at Drew with those demonic eyes, leaning against the bars to let his long curled horns scrape along their length. The sound was like knives against slate.

'I'm Count Kesslar, boy,' he replied. 'Goatlord of Haggard, dealer in blood, flesh and bone and rightful Lord of all the Longridings.' He smiled, revealing his broken yellow teeth as Drew felt the fear wash over him once more. A foul golden eye winked at him.

'But devil will do just fine.'

4

The Goats and the Rams

There were few places as miserable as the cavern below Haggard. Many centuries ago the caves had been used by the Ramlords to store their ill-gotten gains. The Werelords of Haggard hadn't always been peaceful, taking to the seas in more violent times to raid their neighbours and seafarers. That was the way in the Old Age, Werelord battling Werelord. With the dawning of the New Age a more enlightened approach was embraced by Lyssia's therianthropes, with only a few still clinging to the older, savage ways. The caverns of Haggard had been transformed into grain stores. The prison bars were a recent modification added by the castle's current custodian.

Kesslar was a confident beast. He hadn't bothered to post guards in the jail, instead leaving the captives to their own devices. The locked door was immovable, so the only way out would be with the key. Of the hundred prisoners, seventy or so were locals – fishermen, farmers and tradesmen – the fittest men and women of Haggard. The remaining thirty were what remained of Haggard's regular army. In among these survivors sat three therian nobles. News of Drew's true identity had been very well received.

Lord Dorn sat staring quietly at Drew and Baron Ewan as they spoke in whispers. Dorn was the son of Duke Brand, the Bull of Calico, and he was every bit the giant his father had been. Broad-shouldered with the build of a grown man, it was hard to believe he was the same age as Drew. The young Bull had been sent to study under Ewan. In return, Ewan's son, Eben, lodged with Brand as his ward. The relationship was beneficial to both noble houses, each Werelord treating the other's son as their own.

'It's a blessing Eben isn't here to witness this,' Ewan said, looking up at the ceiling. 'I should have buried this cursed room years ago. I'm sorry you paid a visit to my spoiled city, Drew. You'd probably be in Cape Gala by now if you hadn't have made this excursion.'

'I'd have been dragging Whitley's corpse behind me if I had. We came here so you could heal her. Certainly, we've run into some other . . . difficulties, but my friend will live, my lord, thanks to you.'

Ewan waved Drew's praises away.

'It's what I do.'

'So, you're a magister?' asked Drew. 'My friend Hector, Baron Huth's son – he's one, and a talented healer.'

'I'm a magister of sorts, although I lost my way a long time ago. I was never one for sitting in a stuffy library behind a mountain of books. I wanted to see the world. I quit my studies and adventured – the only thing that stayed with me was herb lore. I joined up with your father on many campaigns, travelling alongside him all over Lyssia. I got my sword wet, but for the most part my journey was one of peace. I gathered healing practices wherever I went, cataloguing them. By the time I returned to Haggard, I'd a reputation as a great healer. Can't shake it off, no matter how many folks I poison!'

Drew liked the Ramlord a lot. It hadn't taken him long to reveal his identity to Ewan; Drew was a fine judge of character and the Ram didn't disappoint him. He was relieved to hear that Whitley had responded well to Ewan's medicines. She was on the mend and would be walking again within the day.

'Again, I offer you my profound thanks for healing Whitley,' said Drew earnestly.

'I can only partly accept your thanks, Drew. It seems the union of my drugs and her therian healing has accelerated her recovery at a rate faster than I'd have expected. How did you say she came by the injury?'

'I didn't,' said Drew, shivering at the memory. Ewan leaned in, expecting to hear more.

Drew continued.

'We were attacked off the Talstaff Road by a man. Only, and this will sound crazy, I know . . . he was dead.'

Ewan didn't look at all surprised, instead nodding sagely and stroking his beard.

'I'd recognize necromancy anywhere. There was an evil to that wound, something unnatural and wicked. I hope there are no lasting after-effects from her carrying such a foul bite for so long. She's clear of it now, but one has to be very careful when dealing with dark magicks.'

Drew nodded, but remained silent. He wanted to say something about Hector, but thought better of it. His friend had suffered so much through the ritual of communing and speaking with the dead, and although Ewan seemed to know about the dark magicks, it didn't seem right to discuss Hector's personal business with the Ramlord. He returned the subject to Whitley.

'And she's responding well to conversation?' Drew asked.

'Responding? She won't stop asking questions. No, there's nothing wrong with her that a bit of sleep won't cure now. I've told her what's happened to you, and she knows all about Kesslar. She needs to rest now – there's really nothing she can do. Kesslar will be questioning her in the morning.'

Drew prayed that the Goatlord would treat her with respect but feared the worst.

'What's he going to do with us?' asked Drew wearily.

'Kesslar's ship, the *Banshee*, was due in last night.' Ewan pointed towards a tunnel beyond the bars. 'He'll march you to the harbour and then take you with him to Brenn-knows-where. He's taking me as his personal physician. I'm spared the hold, I'm told. You'll be thrown in with the others – he may have special plans for Dorn . . .'

The young Bull looked on, his large brown eyes emotionless.

'What special plans?' asked Drew.

'Kesslar's a slave trader, Drew. He picks up people from

across Lyssia, transporting them overseas. Nobody knows who he trades with – some say it's the Catlords of Bast. But he's spoken of an arena called the Furnace on more than one occasion, gloating about what a spectacle Dorn will provide for his friends.'

'Arena?'

'He wants me to fight,' said Dorn quietly. Drew was surprised by his soft, honey-toned voice. 'I'll give him a show all right. The minute they take this collar off I'll gore him a new hole.'

Drew had no trouble believing this – even in human form the Bull-lord was the image of the perfect athlete; tall, muscular and deadly.

'Of course,' said Dorn. 'If he knew what *you* were, he'd probably ship you off in your own boat, guarded by twenty of his best. Your value to a skin-trader would be immeasurable. Keep silent on that score, Drew.'

If Kesslar was in the habit of making a spectacle out of a Werelord, then Dorn was right. *Imagine the fee he could demand for the last of the Wolves – the rightful king of Westland.*

'If Kesslar's such a despicable man – why did you let him into the city?'

'Haggard's a peaceful place these days,' said Ewan. 'It's more a town than the once splendid city it used to be. My guards stand on the gates counting the grain wagons that roll in and out. We have nothing worth thieving here. Little did I realize that my people were the very thing he intended to steal.'

Ewan's head fell to his chest and Dorn continued the story for him.

'Haggard used to be a shared seat of governance, Drew. The Goats and Rams worked together as one – after all, theirs is a kindred heritage. Kesslar's older than Baron Ewan by twenty or so years – by the time Ewan took his title he was the junior partner in Haggard. The city was Kesslar's.'

'Haggard was never enough for the Goat, though. His aspirations took him further afield: Highcliff, Brackenholme, even Icegarden in the frozen north. And in every city he visited, he left betrayal in his wake.'

Ewan, having regained his composure, picked up the tale again.

'Wealth is everything to Kesslar. With wealth comes power and swords. He corrupted and conned Werelords across Lyssia and fled before he answered for his crimes. Haggard is just a port of call. He's stripped it of all its worth and now he'll move on.'

'But how did he get into the city? You must have had some clue he was coming?'

'He knew about this cavern, and the way to it from Haggard's Bay below.'

'They came in the night,' said Dorn. 'Slipped through the tunnels and up into the castle. The garrison didn't know what hit them, and how could they?' The Bull craned his head towards Ewan, catching the old Ram's eye. 'You shouldn't blame yourself, uncle.'

Drew looked around the chamber. Those prisoners who were still awake regarded the Werelords with sad and weary eyes. They were broken men, their pride and lives taken when the Goat had stormed their home.

'None of you should feel any shame!' he said, loud enough that anyone who was awake might hear his voice, but not so loud to alert the guards upstairs. 'These cowards who've taken your city – if they'd faced the men of Haggard head-on I don't doubt for a second you'd have given them a fight they'd remember until the end of their days, if they survived it.'

He noticed the men rising where they sat, raising their heads, patting one another's backs. Wives rubbed their husband's shoulders, squeezing them with love and reassurance. The people of Haggard embraced. Drew's blood was up, thinking about these poor unfortunates, buried beneath their city, destined to be shipped a world away. He stood tall making sure he caught the eyes of his fellow prisoners, nodding to anyone who looked back, letting them know they had his respect.

'He could do that, too,' whispered Ewan.

'Who?'

'Wergar. He could inspire men. You're a good man, Drew. I wish we'd met in happier times.'

'I'm nothing like Wergar,' said Drew, suddenly reminded of who he really was. It was all well and good speaking to these prisoners and giving them back some dignity, but who was he at the end of the day? He was still just a farmer's boy from the Cold Coast. His bluster and bravado ebbed away.

'You obviously never met him, that much is clear,' smiled Ewan. 'Sure, he was a bigger man, and he had a voice like rough gravel, but he could move men with his words. You have that gift too.'

'I have a curse, my lord, that's all it is to me. I never asked to be born the son of Wergar.'

'Well who in Lyssia *does* get to choose who their parents are?' laughed Ewan. 'You are what you are, Drew. You can't run from it. You should be proud of your heritage, young man.'

Oh, if you only knew what I think of my heritage, Baron Ewan, thought Drew, settling once more on the cold floor. He wanted to run from that heritage. He wanted to run and never look back.

5

The Key

Haggard Castle once had a splendid throne room, home to the great and good of the Longridings. Merchants and nobles wined and dined there, keen to earn favour and fortune. The port of Haggard's Bay provided a harbour for ships from every edge of Lyssia. It was relatively recently that the Horselord city of Cape Gala had replaced Haggard as the capital of the Longridings, and many still considered Haggard the beating heart of the grasslands, carved out of the rock it grew upon. But times had changed.

Now, Count Kesslar's 'court' slept where they fell, littering the floor of the throne room. Bodies slumped around the chamber's marble pillars. Spent ale casks lay about, the soldiers having done their best to empty the castle's cellars. A figure slept upon the throne beneath a fur blanket, an ancient grey mastiff dozing at his feet, its dirty muzzle resting on its paws.

Whitley crept silently towards the throne's stone dais, stepping gingerly between the slumbering guards. She counted twenty, each fearsome looking and armed to the teeth. She'd seen men like these before, rolling through Brackenholme, hitting taverns and causing chaos before they picked up jobs on departing caravans.

Kesslar's men had underestimated Whitley. Lying in bed, convalescing after Baron Ewan had treated her injury, she was the last person any of them expected to be creeping around the castle in the middle of the night. She'd appeared close to death upon arrival, only attracting the attention of Kesslar once he discovered she had value. The daughter of Duke Bergan was clearly worth a great deal to the Goatlord.

Kindly old Ewan had been the first person she laid eyes upon when she regained consciousness. He'd quickly informed her of the predicament she was in, where Drew was imprisoned and who held the key that kept him locked away. It was all immaterial, Ewan had said – she was too ill to get out of bed, let alone plan a daring escape for her friend. She needed a full night's sleep, and then they'd face what the new day brought when her energy had returned.

That wasn't good enough for Whitley.

The Goatlord's men had made merry until the early hours, drinking and carousing. When the noise subsided, Whitley waited for a further hour before creeping from her bed wearing nothing but the nightdress she'd been given. The guard who had been posted outside her door had departed long ago to join his brothers in their cups. After all, how much guarding did a sickly young girl require?

A sweeping staircase led down directly into the throne room, where Kesslar's small army of hired swords lay sleeping off their festivities. This was their last night in Haggard, according to Ewan, the Goatlord intending to set sail with his prisoners the following day. Whitley spied the stairwell that led down to the cavern beneath the castle, but that wasn't where she was heading. Drew would have to wait. She had to pay someone else a visit first.

Whitley was far from recovered, her body still weak as it fought the diseased wound from the dead soldier. The last week had been surreal as she'd slipped in and out of consciousness, battling the bite. Whatever medicines Baron Ewan had used had clearly done the trick, bringing her back from the brink and allowing her Brenn-given Bearlord healing to take effect. She felt a coldness inside, her mind's eye still recalling the feel of the corpse's teeth at her neck. She stepped gingerly, channelling Master Hogan's lessons on stealth and stalking as she paced silently across the throne room.

She was fifteen feet from the dais when she noticed the mastiff stirring. It let out a low growl as it chased something through its dreams. A nearby soldier shifted at the noise, rolling over where he lay. Whitley's eyes were wide with fear. One of the men directly beside her rolled her way, causing the girl to hop forward, her bare feet landing with a quiet slap on the flags. The dog growled again. A dark-skinned hand fell out from under the blanket, waving down sleepily and swatting the dog's muzzle, instantly silencing it. Whitley caught sight of the keyring on the captain's hip, the prize she sought. As the hand moved back Whitley breathed a sigh of relief.

Djogo, Baron Ewan had called him. He was from a remote island in the southern seas, so hot that a man's blood could boil, the Ramlord said. Kesslar's rogues had arrived two months ago. Apparently, Djogo's first act had been to beat Baron Ewan's head butler to within an inch of his life for simply questioning Kesslar's commands. That had captured the castle staff's attention. He was fiercely cruel and the captain of the mercenaries. While Kesslar slept in the lord's chambers, Djogo slept with his men. He was one of them: a killer.

Confident that Djogo and the mastiff slept, Whitley prepared to take another step. A wave of dizziness washed over her, skin slick with cold, clammy sweat. The nightdress clung to her, restricting movement, causing her anxiety to rise. The fever still had a grip on her. She let her mind focus on the task at hand; Djogo and the keyring. What would Drew do? How would *he* get the key? Her friend acted on impulse, on instinct. He channelled the Wolf.

Whitley closed her eyes, surrounded by the sleeping soldiers, and once more invited the Bear to join her. Her senses began to heighten, her hearing and vision becoming swiftly acute. Unused to shifting, she stopped short of attempting any further transformation; she needed to remain in control, preserve her energy.

As she stepped closer to the dais, the old mastiff opened its eyes suddenly. It was no longer the human scent the hound picked up; instead, it sensed the presence of the Werebear. She froze five feet away as it stared at her. *Was it going to bark?* She narrowed her eyes, unblinking, and bared her teeth, staring the mastiff down. Its confidence broken in the face of a more powerful beast, the dog lowered its jaws to its paws with only the slightest whimper. It remained on its belly, fearful, as the intruder approached its master and reached for the keys.

Drew looked up suddenly as he noticed a shadow fluttering down the spiral staircase. The other prisoners also saw it, their fearful eyes watching on. Maybe it was Djogo, returned to inflict more misery on Drew. *Let him come*, he thought. *I don't need claws to give that monster a fight*. He crouched low.

A slim figure emerged from the stairwell and dashed to the bars, feeling along until its hands closed round the door hinges. Drew heard keys jingle as the stranger fumbled with a ring of them, trying one after another. A key went in, the stranger struggling with the mechanism before trying another. This happened repeatedly. Drew noticed that the figure was bare-foot, faint torchlight from the stairs catching the pale skin as the girl desperately searched for the right key.

'Whitley?'

The figure looked up. Drew could now clearly see the outline of the young Werelady in the dark, clad in a pale white nightdress.

'Drew!' gasped Whitley, joy ringing in her voice. 'Give me a moment . . .'

Inspired, Whitley continued trying keys as Drew rushed up. Those prisoners who had been sleeping began to stir as the excited murmuring of their friends woke them.

'Where did you get the keys from?' asked Drew, looking towards the staircase and praying that nobody appeared. She was taking a monumental risk.

'Djogo.'

'Djogo?' said Ewan. 'How in Brenn's name did you get them off him, my lady?'

'I had some help,' she whispered as a key turned noisily in the lock. Before Drew could press her, Whitley had opened the door and rushed to embrace the young Werewolf. She shivered in his arms, her body still raw as it fought the fever.

'Thank Brenn you're safe, Whitley,' said Drew, hugging her close.

Drew ran his fingers round the collar he wore, feeling for the point where the circle of iron was joined.

'I don't suppose we can get these off?'

'There are smiths in the city, but now isn't the ideal time to call upon them,' smiled Ewan grimly.

Dorn rose, towering over Drew and holding out a hand.

'Drew of the Dyrewood,' he said. 'You would do me an honour in allowing me to fight by your side.'

'It's you who honours me, Dorn,' said Drew, his blood racing as adrenaline flowed.

'What do you intend to do?' asked the Bull as they stepped out of the cell.

'We can rule out shape-shifting,' he said. 'That's unless you were planning on losing your heads.'

'Fight,' muttered Ewan, the idea a distant memory. 'It's been so long.'

'The Goat has butchered Haggard,' said Drew, reminding Ewan of what he'd lost. 'Your subjects are beyond that staircase.' He looked to everyone in the room, addressing them all. 'Each of you has family up there; loved ones, children, parents. You had lives. You had a city. They can be yours again.'

The men and women stirred now. They were beginning to believe. Not all of them would come. Some were injured, others were terrified, and rightly so. He counted around forty who were prepared to fight.

'Let's take back our city,' said Ewan. 'Take back Haggard.'

The people assembled behind Ewan. They bowed, whispering his name and seeking Brenn's blessing.

'What's the plan?' he asked Drew.

The young Werewolf took Whitley by the hand.

'Stay close to me, Whitley,' he said before turning to the others. 'Tell me everything you can about the castle, quickly. This'll be dangerous, but we can hurt the Goatlord. It's our turn to have surprise on our side.'

Ewan and Dorn nodded enthusiastically as the small but determined crowd gathered outside the jail cell, plotting their attack.

6

The Battle of Haggard

They came like the White Sea breaking against the Cold Coast, flooding the throne room in a swift unstoppable wave. There were no battle roars, no warnings. They moved with a single and deadly purpose. The soldier who lay nearest the stairs was pounced on, hands strangling the life from him. His sword and knife were taken and they were on to the next one. It wasn't until the fifth soldier managed to cry out that the alarm was finally raised. By then eight of the Haggard men had blades in their hands. Kesslar's army had been savagely awakened.

Djogo stood on the dais, awake quickly and off the throne. The old mastiff lifted its head, barking out a late warning. Djogo furiously kicked the hound, sending it stumbling down the steps, as he watched his men retreating through the room, chased from the chamber by the farmers and fishermen of

Haggard. When he saw that his keyring was gone he strode down the steps, cursing, whipping his newly acquired sword from its scabbard. It would be good to try the blade out – he'd been waiting for an excuse to bloody it.

A man of Haggard was pounding a splintered chair over a soldier's back. The guard crumpled beneath the blows, his assailant realizing that the fight was his. He never saw the battle through to its end though – a sword emerged from his stomach, driven through from behind. He was dead before he slid from the steel.

'On your toes, Purney!' snarled Djogo at the man, looking over the combatants. There weren't as many of the prisoners as he'd first thought. His men were armed and armoured against a handful of half-starved yokels; why were the idiots cowering? *They should be stacking heads on the throne.*

He caught sight of five of the prisoners disappearing up the broad stairs at the far end of the hall, the flight that led up to his master's bedchambers. One of the men was Ewan and he had the scout from Brackenholme with him, plus a girl in a white nightdress. The Bearlord's daughter? Djogo grinned, grabbing Purney by the neck, pulling him close.

'Spread word. They're a handful of wretches, that's all. You're not fighting an army; you're fighting some rats from the cellar. Kill them all.' He released his grip on the soldier as Purney puffed out his chest with newfound confidence. 'I've got some mutton needs mincing.'

Drew and Whitley were ahead of Baron Ewan and his men as they arrived on the first floor. Drew knew exactly where he was heading, the old Ram having told him where the Goat would be sleeping. He had to move fast – the clamour below would disturb Kesslar soon enough. Drew dashed up to two heavy double doors, snatching at the handles and flinging them open.

His hopes of taking the Goatlord by surprise had come to nothing. Open doors on to the balcony allowed the first light of day into the room, heavy drapes flapping in the cold morning wind. There was no sign of Kesslar in the bedchamber and the room was deserted. Whitley staggered past Drew, collapsing against the bedframe to catch her breath. Still recovering, the exertion of channelling the Bear and freeing Drew had exhausted her.

'He must be down there, with his men,' said Drew, cursing his luck.

'Perhaps he's made a run for it,' said Whitley, lurching towards the balcony.

'Wait!' shouted Drew, but it was too late.

Emerging from the billowing drapes, Kesslar darted into the bedchamber, snatching Whitley by the throat. He retreated quickly to the balcony. Drew made to follow and the Goatlord squeezed Whitley's neck, warning the young man to back off. Kesslar looked over the low stone wall as the battle of Haggard spilled on to the courtyard. Dawn's early light illuminated the Goat's craggy face as he chortled. He didn't appear to be concerned by the turn of events – he actually seemed to be enjoying it.

'Let her go,' said Drew, as calmly as possible.

The Goatlord's hunched shoulders gave him an exaggerated

and ungainly stoop. His white hair was slicked back against his head, curling round his neck. A pointed white beard in a similar style to Ewan's made his drawn face look even longer, with sagging bags hanging below his heavy lidded eyes. The eyes had a wild look to them, a pronounced squint causing them to look outwards in slightly different directions.

'You're behind this, are you, boy? Very inventive.'

Kesslar straightened his right arm, shaking Whitley by the throat like a ragdoll. Her eyes were wide, looking desperately in Drew's direction. She still looked terribly ill, her face pale and scared.

'I'm sorry, am I not following the script?' said the Goatlord, sweeping his free hand out over the courtyard dramatically. 'I can't lie in bed while your cohorts run roughshod over my city. I'm prone to improvising, you see? Like this!'

He dragged Whitley towards the balcony's edge.

'No!' shouted Drew as Ewan and his men arrived at his side.

'Ah, Ewan! Found a backbone at last have you?'

'Let her go!' yelled the Ramlord.

'You dare command me? Take a look below, cousin. Your army of peasants is running out of steam. And bodies for that matter!'

Ewan walked warily forward towards the balcony, watching Kesslar all the while. Drew shifted over to see for himself, peering over the Ramlord's shoulder. Kesslar didn't lie.

The sky in the east was mottled red as daylight began to creep over Haggard. Drew counted a handful of dead prisoners in the courtyard and Kesslar's soldiers were now armed and shielded. A dozen or so prisoners clung together, defending one another with their stolen weapons. They looked up desperately, spying Ewan on the balcony, as more soldiers of the Goat appeared, their net closing.

'Are you just going to stand and watch them get butchered, Ewan?' asked Kesslar. 'You can put an end to this now. I'd rather not see all my stock put to the sword, but if I need to teach you a lesson . . .'

'Don't!' said Ewan. 'Please.'

Kesslar's grin revealed those cracked yellow teeth. The fighting below had ceased momentarily as all looked up to the balcony. Surrender was moments away. Drew placed his hand on the Baron's shoulder giving him an understanding squeeze.

'It was a good fight, wasn't it?' said Ewan, before turning to Kesslar. Drew looked out over the city again, and beyond the walls.

'Kesslar,' began the Baron. 'You have my . . .'

'Wait!' said Drew, gripping Ewan hard. 'Look!'

Ewan followed Drew's gaze over the rooftops. Over thirty men on horseback were riding towards the city up the steep cobbled road, unmistakably Greencloaks; the best six branches of Brackenholme's army. At their head rode Lord Broghan, with Captain Harker at his side.

Kesslar eyes bulged with surprise, and he wasn't the only one surprised.

'Broghan!' screamed Whitley.

The Greencloaks charged. Kesslar dragged Whitley into an embrace, holding her before him. The gate captain shouted a warning to the soldiers in the courtyard, but they were struck by indecision, unsure whether to attack. The thunder of hooves echoed through the streets, as the Goatlord's men began to panic.

'How quickly the tide turns, Kesslar,' said Drew. 'Let her go.'

'Kill them!' yelled Kesslar to those below.

Broghan's Greencloaks emerged at the top of the court-yard, the riders quickly surveying the battleground. The bodies of butchered civilians lay in the dirt, while the armed mercenaries of the Goatlord stood over them, swords and spears still dark with blood. Broghan caught sight of his sister in the arms of Count Kesslar. Before the Bearlord could issue a command a dozen arrows rained down on his company from the walls. The captain at the gate hadn't sat idle, having spread word to his archers. The Woodland Watch split formation, riding for cover as arrows flew. Haggard was beginning to look crowded as combatants from three sides waged battle.

'Kesslar,' repeated Drew. 'Let her go.'

'Who are *you* to command a Werelord?' roared the Goat, his face distorting as horns broke free from his brow. Whitley squirmed as Kesslar's chest pushed into her back, his lungs bursting as he changed. She could hear his ribs breaking apart and reforming, flesh tearing and hooves hammering as the Weregoat emerged.

Before Drew could answer there were screams from the door. The men who had escorted Ewan upstairs fell. One savage blow had taken them both out, the Wolfshead blade scything through the back of one before becoming embedded in the other. Djogo ripped the sword free as the body tumbled.

Kesslar stamped his hooves excitedly, his horns now completely grown as he stood to his full height.

'Oh, splendid, Djogo! Splendid!'

The men fighting in the courtyard could see Kesslar now and were both horrified and in awe of the sight. Kesslar's soldiers made a rush for Haggard Castle, disappearing indoors. The Woodland Watch rushed after them, the heavy doors slamming shut as they were barred from within. As the men of Brackenholme and Haggard tried to enter the castle below, the deadly game played out above.

Kesslar gestured to Drew, his gravelly voice thick with hatred.

'Kill him! And then that fat lamb Ewan!'

'My pleasure,' said Djogo, spinning the Wolfshead blade as he closed on Drew.

Drew backed away as Djogo tried to close his escape routes. Ewan stumbled clear as the southerner strode past, staying out of reach. Djogo managed a smile for the Ram.

'Your turn will come, old man.'

Four of Kesslar's men appeared in the doorway, fresh from the fight.

'Men of the Dyrewood, sire,' shouted one of them, panting for breath. It was Purney, Djogo's man from the throne room.

'I'm not blind!' yelled Kesslar.

'The doors are barricaded, master, but for how long, who can say? There's thirty of 'em, as well as the locals. They might be a match for us. Maybe we need to make tracks?'

'Hold your tongue, Purney. I'll decide when we're leaving. And as long as I have this pretty thing,' he said, sniffing at Whitley's hair, 'we have something to bargain with.'

The mercenaries began to advance, closing on Drew.

'Back!' shouted Kesslar. 'Watch as your captain shows you how to gut one of these men of the Dyrewood.'

Drew had nowhere left to run. At his back was an ornate fireplace, the coals from the night's fire still glowing. In front of him was the brutal looking Djogo, whip curled on his hip, shifting Drew's sword in his grip as he neared. *If he sticks me with it,* thought Drew, *it won't be the first time. It hurt but it didn't kill me.* It was small comfort – Djogo looked like a seasoned killer and probably rarely missed.

The slaver smiled at his friends, who cheered him on. Drew must have looked harmless. Wrong. Taking the initiative, Drew leapt. His fist cracked Djogo's jaw, sending him spinning back a few steps. Drew pounced on to his back, tugging the man's whip from his hip. He threw it about his throat and pulled tight. Instantly Djogo staggered backwards towards the fireplace. Drew yanked at the leather with all his might, but the southerner's neck muscles bulged like hardened teak.

Drew felt the hard edge of the mantlepiece strike his shoulders as Djogo launched him into it, driving him back against the stonework. His grip on the whip went slack as air escaped his lungs. As if the impact wasn't enough, he felt the back of Djogo's head crash into his face. Blood erupted instantly as his nose shattered and he went limp against the southerner's shoulders. Djogo stepped forward casually as Drew collapsed with a crunch.

Drew could hear the men's laughs as Djogo paced around him. His vision was blurred as he looked up, his face inches from the dying fire. To the side he could see a dejected Ewan and a stamping Kesslar, Whitley limp in his grasp. He could feel the Wolf straining to break out. If he unleashed it he'd be dead in seconds, strangled by the iron collar round his neck, saving Djogo the grisly job.

'Finish the child off and get on with this old fool,' Kesslar rasped, kicking a scared looking Ewan to his knees.

'As you wish,' snarled Djogo, turning to Drew as he reached towards the fire. He raised the sword as Drew stumbled to his feet, punching Djogo in the face with what strength remained. He clutched a fistful of sharp hot coals in his hand, leaving them behind in Djogo's face. The big man screamed in agony, striking Drew and sending the young man back to his knees. Many of the coals fell away, but a number found the flesh and remained, smouldering, embedded in his face. One wicked shard protruded from Djogo's left eye, blood hissing against the white hot rock.

Drew's hand was peppered with hot studs of coal also, but he didn't care. He threw the villain his most brazen smile, his face bloody from his broken nose. Djogo lost whatever self control he still had, but by now Drew had resigned himself to the end. The irony of being killed by that sword wasn't lost on him. He closed his eyes, waiting for the blow.

Half-blind, Djogo poured his fury into the swing. It was brutal and unorthodox, but either way it was aimed where it needed to go. He'd beheaded many men over the years –

deserters in his old lord's army, rivals in the gladiatorial arena, enemies on the battlefield. He might have baulked at the task of slaying a youth, but not this one. If ever anyone needed his head removing it was this Dyrewood scum. The sword descended on the boy's neck, swift as lightning.

Sparks flew.

7

Unleashed

The reaction to the blow was mixed. Baron Ewan looked away, while Whitley, choking, closed her eyes in horror. Kesslar let loose a bellowing bray, his soldiers cheering. Djogo staggered back, almost dropping the sword as he lifted a hand to his ruined eye. The boy's body lay in a heap on the floor in front of the fire.

Djogo grabbed the coal in his eye socket, giving it a sharp tug. It made a popping sound as it tore free, his hand swiftly staunching the blood flow. His men stepped up to congratulate him, aware that their commander was gravely injured, but Djogo ignored them and turned to the body.

'What's the matter?' wheezed Kesslar, kicking Ewan forward. 'You've another one to do here, remember.'

'A moment,' said the killer. 'I need to check something.'

Something wasn't right. The sword had hit the youth in

the neck. He'd felt the sword bite home and the body crumple. But the head hadn't come free. And where had those sparks come from? He kicked the body over, expecting to see the mess his gruesome handiwork had created painting the flags. Instead he saw the boy intact, and two broken pieces of pig iron on the floor.

The sparks. The collar. Shattered.

Djogo's four companions gathered round the corpse. The Goatlord stared, but not at the boy or collar. He was looking at the sword in Djogo's grasp.

'His head ain't come off!' said Purney.

'The collar . . .' began Djogo, ignoring his men as they kicked the body.

'Forget the collar,' snapped Kesslar, loosening his grip on Whitley as he took a lurching step forward. 'Where did you get that?'

Djogo looked at the sword in his hand.

'The sword?'

'Am I speaking another language? Yes, the sword! It's a Wolfshead blade! As carried by Wergar's closest guard. Where did you get it?'

'From the boy,' said Djogo.

'What boy?'

'This boy,' said Djogo. The four soldiers began to slowly back away.

'Boss . . .' began Purney. At that moment a grey clawed hand shot up from the floor, catching the man in the neck. In a split second Purney was catapulted into the air, his head crashing into the ceiling before his body hit the floor. The other three scrambled away, stumbling into one another. The first was grabbed by the ankle, the monster spinning him across the floor into the fireplace. The guard screeched as he rolled in the hot coals, skin smoking. The remaining two flanked Djogo.

Drew rose, still mid-change, the Wolf's arrival bringing a second burst of energy. He felt alive, for the first time in ages. His lips peeled back as drool dripped from between ever-sharpening teeth. His torso rippled, dark hair shooting from the greying skin, as the claws of his bare feet scraped along the slate flags. Yellow eyes blinked balefully.

'It can't be!' bleated the transformed Kesslar, still squeezing Whitley, his shield against the monster.

'Oh, but it can,' smiled Ewan.

Djogo grabbed his men, shoving them forward.

'Come on, lads. He's a boy under all that fur. Let's have him!'

The men rushed the Wolf, their weapons raised and slashing. Drew took a blow to the shoulder as he dropped to one knee, using his crouch as a springboard to propel himself into one of them. The Wolf carried the man through the air as they landed with a splintering crash on to a table, the wood showering down around them. Drew snatched up the fallen man's shortsword, hurling it back across the room like a throwing knife. It hit the remaining guard in the leg, sending him toppling to the ground in agony. That left just him and Djogo.

'Now,' growled Drew through his bared teeth. 'Back to you. And me.'

Djogo looked at the Werewolf and then back to his defeated

soldiers. He grabbed the handle of the shortsword that protruded from his guard's thigh, tugging it out. Kesslar had begun to work his way round the edge of the room towards the doorway.

'You go nowhere, Kesslar,' Drew snarled. 'Not finished with you.'

Regardless of his size and monstrous presence, the Goat seemed in awe of the Wolf. Whether the sight of him had reminded the count of an encounter with Wergar years ago, Drew would never know, but faced with a transformed lycanthrope Kesslar panicked. Baron Ewan moved to cut the Goat off, blocking his route out of the room. Kesslar returned to the balcony, peering worriedly over the edge, Whitley still held tight in his grasp. The young woman from Brackenholme was limp now, the Goatlord forgetting his strength as he held her about the throat.

Djogo took this moment to lunge at Drew, aiming for his guts. Drew turned into the thrust, but not quickly enough. The Wolfshead blade tore a thin strip through his hip, separating muscle. As the man passed, Drew lost his footing for a moment as the pain hit him. The southerner's shortsword flashed past too, tearing another wound along Drew's torso. The half-blind warrior whirled, weaving and hacking with the swords, as Drew found himself retreating. The man was deadly with weapons, more competent than anyone he'd faced before. His missing eye was helping to even things up, though.

Djogo and the Werewolf circled one another. The great door of Haggard Castle rattled as Lord Broghan's men hammered at it, using everything to break it down.

'They'll be in soon,' snarled Drew. 'Give it up. Drop your weapons. Release Whitley!'

Kesslar looked at Djogo. He nodded before lifting Whitley over his head by her long brown hair and hips. Throttled by Kesslar until she'd lost consciousness, she dangled in his grasp, arms and legs loose, as he tottered on the balcony. Drew advanced towards him, the Wolf disappearing. His jaws began to retract, the teeth shortening, his build beginning to revert to that of a human.

'Stop there!' warned Kesslar, staggering over the low parapet.

'Please!' begged Drew, but he could see Kesslar was beyond reason, gripped by a furious anger. His hooves slipped, Whitley's body lurched. If he took another step, both would be over the edge.

Ewan acted fast, jumping up from where he crouched on the ground he snatched at Kesslar's ankles. His hands gripped the Goatlord's boots, stopping him in his tracks, but his body lurched forward. The Goat wailed, releasing Whitley. As her body was propelled forward Drew leapt. The stone courtyard was thirty feet below them, a fatal fall for anyone, including an unconscious therianthrope.

Time slowed as he passed the Goatlord, braying furiously at the old Ramlord. Whitley's body floated through the air over the balcony. Throwing an arm out, Drew followed Whitley through the air. His right hand caught her ankle, but his body kept moving. The stone banister hit Drew's stomach, briefly halting his momentum, before he tipped over the edge after her.

Drew's plummet was halted suddenly and violently. He felt his left arm might tear from its socket as Ewan's strong hands closed round his ankle. The jerking stop almost made him release Whitley from his grasp, and Drew screamed as he strained to keep hold. She dangled upside down for what seemed like an eternity. Drew could feel his bloody hand losing its grip on her boot. The men of Haggard and the soldiers from Brackenholme who surged against the great door looked up, Broghan moving through them to stand below.

'Let her go, Drew,' he cried, his men gathering round him, dropping their weapons. 'We've got her!'

With a gasp Drew relinquished his grip, watching as she fell through the air. The men caught her, safely handing her into the arms of her brother. Ewan hauled Drew back over the edge of the balcony, the youth crumpling to the floor, exhausted.

'You all right, lad?' he said, holding Drew's face in his leathery hands. Drew nodded, glancing past the Werelord's shoulder.

'Where's Kesslar?' The two of them looked towards the open doorway.

'Can't let him get away,' grunted Drew, struggling to his feet.

'Damn them!' screamed the Goatlord, striking out indiscriminately at his men as he rushed down the sweeping staircase, Djogo close behind.

'We need to leave this dungheap now,' said Djogo, the only

soldier immune to the count's fury. As Kesslar's long-time second in command, he was used to the Goat's wrath. 'They haven't all escaped. At least fifty were recaptured – they've already been sent to the *Banshee*. We should leave with what we have.'

Kesslar ground his teeth with irritation as he glared around the hall. Eight of the prisoners who'd survived the fight stood beside the throne, recaptured. Armed soldiers surrounded them, spears and swords readied. The castle's great door shook with the impact of the Woodland Watch's makeshift battering rams.

'Kesslar,' repeated Djogo. 'We need to leave. Now.'

Kesslar stepped towards the eight men. He recognized one of them, the big brute from Calico, Lord Dorn.

'Ah, Brand's boy,' said Kesslar. The young man was tall but, changed into the Goat, Kesslar dwarfed him. The other prisoners cowered, backing into the soldiers' weapons, as the Goatlord menaced them. Dorn's body was criss-crossed with open wounds from where he'd battled Kesslar's small army. How many had the young Bull taken down? The impertinent oaf stood his ground, staring back with calm eyes. Quick as a flash the Ram butted him, sending the young Werelord staggering into his companions. The Bull looked up, stepping forward defiantly again.

'You don't deserve the Arena,' spat Kesslar at the Bull-lord. 'Djogo; the Wolfshead blade.'

Reluctantly the southerner handed his new weapon over to the count. Kesslar's soldiers advanced, some raising their weapons, others drawing them back. The prisoners recoiled.

The Weregoat weighed the blade for a moment, before turning back to Lord Dorn.

'I need you to pass a message on to Baron Ewan and the Wolf.'

Drew and Baron Ewan stumbled downstairs, just as Broghan's men finally splintered the great door of the castle. Greencloaks and the surviving members of Haggard's militia rushed into the hall, swords up and bows drawn. Captain Harker dashed up to Drew, clapping him on the back.

'It's good to see you, Drew! Looks like you're neck deep in trouble again.'

'Trouble doesn't come close, Harker. Your timing's impeccable. A moment later and I dread to think what would've happened. How did you know we'd be here? We're some way off the road to Cape Gala.'

'We stopped in Cheaptown a couple of days back,' said the captain, walking with him as Ewan strode ahead into the throne room to survey the carnage. 'You made an impression; they said you were heading this way.'

'How is Whitley?' asked Drew.

'She's all right. Broghan is with her outside.'

'Where's Kesslar?'

'Your guess is as good as mine. I was hoping you could tell us . . .'

'There are tunnels,' said Drew, gesturing to the back of the throne room. 'They lead down to Haggard's Bay. We should pursue them before they escape.'

Their conversation was disrupted by a sudden cry. A crowd

of men was gathering round the marble throne. As Drew and Harker approached some turned, shaking their heads sadly, weeping and retching. They parted to reveal a sight that made Drew's blood run cold. The butchered bodies of a handful of prisoners lay strewn over the throne and dais, their blood pooling over the steps. Ewan crouched before the seat, shoulders hunched, rocking to and fro.

Drew wanted to put his hand on the baron's shoulder, whisper words of comfort and sympathy, but he could find no words. He looked at the pile of bodies, feeling bile rise as he recognized the corpse of Lord Dorn. He lay slumped on the top of the heap, face down, a sword sticking out of his back like a flag on top of a conquered mountain.

Drew looked up at the sword, eyes streaming as hot tears burned his face. The Wolfshead roared back at him.

8

No More Sleeps

Count Vega leaned back perilously in his chair, wondering if anyone would notice if he fell off it. He looked out of the window beside him. Highcliff was swallowed by the night, the darkness broken only by lights twinkling in windows like diamonds on a black sheet. He was enduring the arguing of the Lords of Brackenholme and Stormdale, spit flying and fingers jabbing, wondering how he managed to get himself into these situations. *There's a reason I shouldn't meddle in the affairs of landlubbers.* Vega had been told from a young age that 'dirtwalkers', as his mother referred to them, were complicated. Stick to the seas, boy, she would say; that was a Sharklord's home. Not cooped up in a stone tower watching a Bear and a Stag go at one another. *And these two are friends!*

'Stand down, Bergan!' shouted Mikkel. 'I'll put you on your rump if you don't show some respect!'

'You're acting like a child,' roared the Bearlord. 'This is *not* what your brother would want!'

'You think I don't know my own brother?' Mikkel turned to Vega for support. 'Do you hear him, cousin?'

Vega raised his gloved hands in a show of non-participation.

'I'm "cousin" all of a sudden, now? Count me out, children.' The wooden chair legs struck the stone floor hard. Bergan and Mikkel looked at him expectantly.

'But Vega,' said Bergan. 'As part of the Wolf's Council . . .'

'Oh spare us the talk of the Wolf's Council,' interrupted the Earl of Highwater. 'Drew is gone, Brenn knows where, and there's no sign of him returning. All the while we sit here doing nothing when we should be mobilizing our armies.'

'Don't you see, Mikkel, how much we need strength in numbers here? Our combined forces can hold the city presently, defend the walls against invasion if need be. If you uproot your men to return to the Barebones you'd leave us short-handed here. We don't have the manpower to defend Highcliff alone.'

'I need to make sure my people are safe.'

'Then send another messenger, but don't leave on the off-chance that there's a threat. Leopold can rage to his heart's content in the keep – he's going nowhere. And nobody has come to his aid.'

'Nobody's come to his aid . . . *yet*,' corrected Mikkel.

Bergan threw his hands in the air.

'I give up! Go to Stormdale then, ready your army against an imagined foe. Leave us in a weakened state. But let your brother stay here. Don't drag him across Lyssia in such a fragile state.'

Mikkel sneered. Vega watched him, waiting for him to say something else provocative. He wasn't fond of Mikkel, but he respected him. However, it was clear Mikkel wasn't thinking rationally. If the captain of the *Maelstrom* was ever going to get involved, now was the time.

'I've a few words to say on this matter, and then you'll see my cape disappear out of the door.'

The Werelords turned, eager to hear what he had to say.

'Exciting, isn't it, all this?' he smiled. Bergan glowered. Vega continued.

'I've taken my fleet out to sea. We've seen nothing alarming. However, sailors are superstitious. They've been telling me of the dark omens they're seeing: gulls flying low, blood red skies in the east, dead fish in the nets; I'm not so ignorant as to ignore them. A lifetime at sea teaches a man – and a therian – to respect the old ways. Something's coming.

'I don't know whether leaving is wise; couldn't say. But I agree with Bergan: dragging a sick Manfred to the Barebones is sheer folly. Leave him in the care of his healers here Mikkel, and as soon as he's fit enough to travel he can decide for himself what he wants to do.'

Bergan and Mikkel stared at one another. Bergan held his hand out, waiting for Mikkel to take it. They joined palms, shaking their agreement.

'As soon as he's fit to travel?'

'As soon as,' nodded Bergan. 'I really can't persuade you to stay? Must you leave in the middle of the night?'

Mikkel nodded, immovable in his will.

'I've let the grass grow beneath my hooves for too long. War is coming. I can smell it on the wind.'

'Then Brenn be with you, brother,' said Bergan, hugging Mikkel.

'And with you.'

Vega rolled his eyes. *What a bunch of tender-hearts!*

'Sorry to spoil your moment, children, but I've someone to find. I haven't seen Hector for days. I don't know about you but I'm concerned.'

'The boy still isn't right,' said Mikkel, picking up his grey cloak. 'He's not been the same since his tomfoolery in the Pits.'

'He needs company,' said Bergan. 'Hiding away in Bevan Tower like that. I'm not sure Vincent's the right fellow to be looking after him, either.'

You don't know the half of it, thought Vega.

'My feelings exactly. So if you'll excuse me,' said Vega, bowing in his typically flamboyant manner, 'I must away.'

Vega didn't wait for further goodbyes. He bounded down the steps of Traitors' House, three at a time. He *was* concerned about the young Boarlord. Hector had been in pieces the previous week when he'd last seen him, and Vega had no trouble recognizing a bully when he saw one. Vincent was menacing his twin, pushing the young magister until he got what he wanted: the throne of Redmire. Hector was losing his mind, fearing what his brother might do next. There was something distinctly wicked about Vincent, and Vega wasn't sure how low he'd stoop in order to get what he wanted.

★

Hector blinked, trying to see through the mist as the dark water slapped around his waist. He was naked, cold and didn't know where he was. He could feel the mud sucking and shifting beneath his feet as he tried to stay upright, like sands shifting in a tide although the pool's surface was still. He could see no bank, no matter in which direction he looked. All he could see was the black water and the dirty yellow mist. The air had a familiar, pungent smell to it. Sulphur. He ran his hands through the water, feeling a resistance like oil. He struggled to keep his rising panic down.

He didn't know this place, and it scared the life out of him. *How did I get here? Why am I here?* He took a step forward and felt something move under his foot. Something *beneath* the sand. Next he felt something brush his ankle, beneath the black water. Something sharp scratched at his skin, like a trailing claw or tooth. He spun, splashing.

'Where am I?' he screamed, looking up as the sulphurous mist thickened. He wiped his eyes with his left hand as he tried to keep his balance with his right. The yellow cloud was choking him, causing him to splutter and wheeze. There were more motions beneath the surface, something moving between his legs, jostling him. His eyes were hot, stinging. As his vision cleared he looked at the palm of his hand. The black spot that marked the centre of his palm was growing rapidly, spreading, spilling over his skin like ink tipped from a pot. In seconds his fingers were black and the darkness was spreading up his arm.

'No!' he yelled, plunging his arm into the water as if removing it from sight might make the darkness go away. But the moment it disappeared below the surface he felt a cold, dead hand grasp it. Hard. He tugged back, trying to release himself.

'Let go!' he cried, but there was no release. He felt something scurrying up his bare back; a long, shadowy hand, snaking out of the black water. Viles! The hand grabbed his shoulder and pulled him slowly down towards the water. He tried to pound it off with his right hand, but couldn't make it release its grip. The hand below the surface continued to drag him down, his chin getting closer to the black liquid.

'Please!' he begged, as more hands appeared around him, taking hold where they could. His throat, his jaw, his chest; the fingers gripped all over, digging in as they dragged him down, down, into the black water. He opened his mouth for one final cry, but never made it, the black water rushing over his scream and racing down his throat, as cold as death itself.

Hector rose, crying out, gasping for air and reaching for the ceiling. His hair clung to his face, dripping with sweat. The bedsheets were soaking, stuck to his warm, damp skin. It took him a moment to realize that, firstly (and most importantly), he was still alive and, secondly, he was in his bedroom in Bevan's Tower. His throat was dry and sore. He must have been screaming while he slept, his nightmare intruding on the real world. His eyes searched his darkened room, looking for viles. They were everywhere, always watching, waiting to torment him. Then he saw the shape sitting on the bed. A large, dark shape.

'Get away, demon!'

'Is that any way to speak to your brother?'

Hector's eyes adjusted to the gloom. It was indeed Vincent, legs crossed neatly and arms folded on his lap. There was no sign of Mutt, the faithful little dog Hector had befriended. The stray had taken to sleeping on the foot of the bed, but had clearly been scared off by Hector's twin brother.

'What time is it?' asked Hector.

'Late,' replied his brother, rising. His movements were slow, purposeful. 'More nightmares?'

Hector didn't reply. His brother had returned each night since his ultimatum, though Hector hid away to avoid contact with him. He'd kept the room locked, but a glance past Vincent revealed an open doorway and a broken lock. He'd forced his way in. Tonight of all nights.

'I couldn't help but hear from downstairs. Awful racket. I was worried for your safety. And sanity.'

Hector looked at his sheets. The bed was soaking, his skin freezing. The fever still wouldn't relinquish its grip. He couldn't find his pillow. He looked back to Vincent suddenly.

Vincent held the pillow above him. For the last week, each night he'd tormented Hector, reminding him of how embarrassing he was to their household, their father's memory and the people of Redmire. Each night he'd reminded him that his time was running out. The words of his ultimatum still haunted Hector's thoughts:

'*No more sleeps.*'

Vincent squeezed the pillow. He plumped it, punching it with his balled fist, smiling at Hector. Hector's body trembled, his shivers revealing just how scared he was. Suddenly, Vincent was over him, the pillow inches from Hector's face.

'Whatever's the matter, Hector? You look so . . . nervous!'

Hector's wide eyes stared at the pillow. Vincent craned closer, the pillow descending.

'Do you want your pillow?'

Hector wanted to cry out but was paralysed with fear. Vincent had told him he'd have Redmire one way or the other. Nothing would stand in his way.

'Please, Vincent. I beg you, don't!'

'Don't what?' hissed Vincent

'The pillow. Please don't!'

Vincent sat upright suddenly.

'This?' he said, pointing to the sodden bundle of feathers and cotton. 'You thought I meant to suffocate you?'

Vincent laughed, flinging the pillow on to the bed. Hector didn't join in, still fearful for his life. Vincent clapped his hands, shaking his head and wiping away tears.

'Oh that's a good one, Hector. That *is* amusing!'

Vincent stopped laughing. He moved fast, hands open, then closing swiftly round his brother's throat. Hector's eyes bulged as he felt the grip tighten.

'If I were to kill you, brother, I wouldn't use some filthy pillow. I'd want to be sure. I'd want to see your face. I'd do it with these . . .' A squeeze. 'Two . . .' Another squeeze. 'Hands!'

Hector's legs kicked into action, his knees connecting with Vincent's elbows and dislodging his grip. Hector rolled off the bed in his drenched nightshirt, landing on his discarded clothes. He fumbled among them, gasping for breath. Vincent laughed.

'Come come, brother, I was just playing a game. Let me help you get up.'

Vincent reached to grab at Hector who was scrambling through his belongings. The magister spun round, holding a blade up defensively in his trembling hands. Vincent took a step back, warily, before bursting into another chorus of laughter.

'That? What are you going to do? Tickle me with it?'

Hector held his gaudy jewelled dagger up, handle close to his chest, the blade pointing outwards. It was decorative; there was nothing practical about it. The jewels would bite into the holder's grip if one used it in earnest. It would probably do the wielder more damage than an intended target. Hector started to circle round his brother, making for the door. He saw a small shape on the floor, the outline unmistakably that of Mutt. The little stray could have been sleeping, but Hector knew better: the dog was dead.

'Please, Vincent,' he mumbled, mucus and tears mingling over his trembling lips. 'I'll go first thing in the morning. I'll tell Bergan, I'll tell them all. Everything's yours. I want none of it. But please, no more.'

Vincent's face contorted as he followed Hector, the magister stumbling as he backed into the corridor. The torches from the hall below illuminated the stairwell, throwing light up to the top floor of Bevan's Tower.

'I've given you so many chances and you've refused them, like the stubborn fat little pig you are. I've waited long enough, Hector. I'll take the throne tonight.'

'Tomorrow,' begged Hector. He shuffled back down the corridor, following the old tattered rug towards the landing and staircase. 'Don't do this, Vincent. On my life I promise, it's all yours. First thing in the morning, I'll do it.'

'You've said this before and you've lied each time . . .'

'I've been so sick, Vincent. So very ill. Tomorrow, I'll do it, I promise.'

Vincent advanced slowly, shaking his head as he followed him down the corridor. Hector could hardly see him. Vincent was a teary blur as he shivered and stumbled, nearing the balcony that overlooked the entrance hall two floors below.

How he wished his friend was here now. How he longed to see Drew again, the one fellow who felt like a true brother to Hector. He cried aloud as he thought of him, wailed as he realized he'd never see his friend again. He prayed to Brenn that Drew was safe, that he would find Gretchen. He felt his back bump into the stone banister as he came to the end of the old rug. He glanced down.

The figures of Ringlin and Ibal looked up from below, waiting expectantly. Through his tears, Hector saw the tall one wave, as a friend might to a passing acquaintance in the street. Hector turned back to Vincent.

'Drop your toy dagger, brother. It won't help you now. I wonder what they'll say? Everyone knows you've been poorly, sick in the head. Goodness, what else would explain your interfering with the dead? Nobody would blame you if you ended it all. Nobody would even miss you.'

'That's not true! I have friends!'

'The members of your precious Wolf's Council?'

'Not them,' whispered Hector, swaying against the banister. He lowered the dagger to his side, resigned to his fate.

'Who then, the Wolf? Where is he now? Chasing across

Lyssia after one of his *real* friends. No, Hector, you have nobody. You're nobody. You won't be missed.'

Vincent strode forward, his arms up, palms open, prepared for the final shove.

'No more sleeps.'

Vincent was a couple of steps from Hector when his leading foot caught the curled up edge of the long, frayed rug that ran down the corridor. It propelled Vincent into a stumble, arms flailing as he lurched forward. Instinctively, Hector brought his hands up to catch his brother, forgetting the other's wicked intentions for a split second. In that moment they were just two siblings again, one falling while the other tried to catch him.

The two collided on the banister in an embrace, Vincent's arms round Hector.

The doors of Bevan's Tower swung open suddenly as Count Vega ran in unannounced. Ringlin and Ibal turned to him quickly at the foot of the staircase, hands moving to their weapons. Vega's cutlass flew gracefully from its scabbard, but the Sharklord followed the gaze of the two rogues back to the drama high above.

Vincent and Hector looked into one another's eyes, their faces almost touching. There were mirrored, twin expressions of surprise and horror. They slowly pulled themselves apart, Vincent wheezing and snorting, spit dribbling from his mouth as he looked down. Hector mouthed the word 'no' repeatedly, but nothing came out. They both stared down.

Hector's fist was flush with Vincent's left breast, the hilt of his gaudy dagger flat against his brother's chest. The knife wasn't silver but the injury was massive; a sword didn't have to be silver to slay a Werelord. No therianthropic healing could reattach a severed head, and little could be done for this wound. The blade was buried deep within Vincent's heart, having found a clean and uninterrupted route between the Boarlord's ribs. Their eyes met once more, tears welling as brother looked upon brother. Hector's hopes for forgiveness were dashed as Vincent's face contorted into an expression of rage and hate. He tried to speak, mouthing obscenities and curses, but he too was dumbstruck.

Vincent's hands clawed Hector's face, tusks jutting from his jaws as dark brown hairs struggled to emerge from his face. He squealed and grunted, scraping at Hector's crying eyes with darkening fingers. The onlookers below watched as Vincent leaned further back over the balcony. Hector could hold him no longer, and released his grip.

'I'm sorry,' he whispered. 'Please forgive me, brother . . .'

As Vincent toppled over the banister, Hector could see his mouth contorting as he found his voice in the final moment.

'Never.'

Hector leaned over to watch his twin's descent, as Vega, Ringling and Ibal all stepped back. Vincent landed head first on the mosaic tiled floor below with a sickening crunch. Vega staggered forward, disbelieving as he stared at the grisly sight of the dead Boarlord. He looked up and saw Hector, leaning against the banister, dangerously close to following his brother over the edge. From the corner of his eye he caught sight of Vincent's two henchmen disappearing out of the door, fleeing from the scene of their master's death. Vega ran up the staircase towards his young friend, hoping to get to him before he did something foolish.

Hector stared at Vincent's broken body, limbs twisted into impossible positions, a dark pool spreading round him where he'd hit the ground. The tall stairwell seemed to be rotating, spinning, as his head thundered. He could feel he was slipping towards unconsciousness. A fall, yes. That would do it. They'd understand. Before the darkness came he saw the viles creeping out of the shadows below, long black claws pawing at Vincent's corpse.

No more sleeps.

Then darkness.

PART IV

The Storm from the South

I

An Open Heart

The men of Brackenholme lay round their campfires, settling down for the night while a handful remained on watch. Two of the Greencloaks had been killed in the battle of Haggard, and the rangers had delayed their departure from the City of the Ram to bury their fallen. Each man shared the grief, as the bond between the men of the Woodland Watch was like that of brothers. The mood was sombre and reflective, with talk brief and to the point. But by the fire at the centre of the camp, one group were deep in conversation, their mood anything but subdued.

'You should have *waited*,' said Lord Broghan, pointing an accusing finger across the fire towards Drew. The young Wolf shook his head.

'I can see we're never going to agree on this, Broghan, so I suggest we cease talking about it.'

'You acted recklessly, Drew, without the permission of the Wolf's Council.'

'I don't *need* the permission of anyone! If I want to rescue my friend, I shall, and nobody can stop me. I'll do what I like, thank you very much, Broghan.' He pointed north. 'Highcliff doesn't command me. Nobody does. I'm a free man.'

'A free man?' laughed Broghan. 'Drew, wake up! You're the most important and potentially powerful Werelord in Lyssia!'

'Brother, keep your voice down,' said Whitley from where she sat beside him. 'The men are trying to sleep.' Behind her, wrapped up in his bedroll, Baron Ewan slept, his snores punctuating their discussion.

'Stay out of this, sister,' snapped the young Bearlord. 'Do you not know right from wrong? You're as irresponsible as Drew, assisting him on this foolish errand. I'm sure I don't need to tell you how disappointed Father is in you.'

At this, Whitley rose to her feet. Captain Harker, who had remained silent throughout the heated discussion, stood respectfully as the Werelady rose.

'I'm sure our father is very proud of *you*, Broghan,' she shot back. 'Loud, argumentative, opinionated; you sound more and more like him each day.'

With that, she stormed away from the campfire. Broghan sat there, his face turning purple. Harker sat down again, keeping his eyes fixed on the fire so as not to further enrage his liege lord. Drew simply stared at the Bearlord.

'Nothing is ever black and white, Broghan,' said Drew, standing and stretching with a sigh. 'You need to start seeing all the shades of grey.'

With that he walked after Whitley, leaving the Lord of Brackenholme to glower into the flames.

He found her perched on a low outcrop of rock to the east of the encampment, overlooking the vast Longridings ahead of them. Small fires twinkled in the grasslands, as other travellers settled down for the night. To the north they could just make out the dark expanse of the Dyrewood as far as the eye could see. Somewhere to the south lay Cape Gala, the city of the Horselords. They'd be there tomorrow. Drew still hoped they'd find Gretchen there, but was all too aware that their chances were slim.

'Mind if I join you?'

Whitley smiled, pulling her knees up to her chest and folding her arms over them.

'You grew tired of the conversation with my brother, too?'

Drew sat beside her, his legs hanging over the rock ledge.

'He's unrelenting when he gets a thought in his head. He just won't let it go, will he?' said Drew.

He pointed towards the fires in the dark.

'Horselords?'

'I doubt it. The Horselords tend to live in the cities and towns of the Longridings now. There was a time when they lived in the fields with their people, but that was long ago. It's more likely they're peasant camps. Possibly even Romari.'

'Romari?'

'Oh, you'd like the Romari, Drew. They're always on the move. Like you,' she added, digging him in the ribs.

He smiled.

'On the move?'

'They're a travelling people, an ancient culture. They passed through Brackenholme occasionally, trading their goods, never staying long. That's not the half of it, though.' She leaned in close to whisper conspiratorially.

'*They worship the Wolf!*'

Drew was taken aback.

'There's a whole society of people out there who worship me?'

Whitley laughed.

'Don't get ahead of yourself, farm boy. The Wolf is a holy symbol to them; they hold the beast in high regard. It's a leap to believe that they'd treat you like some kind of living god!'

'Just as well,' sighed Drew comically. 'I've enough on my plate without worrying about being worshipped.'

The two were silent as they watched the night sky, the moon slipping in and out of the clouds above them.

'He's right though, isn't he?' said Whitley suddenly.

'Who's right?'

'Broghan. What we did was thoughtless.'

'You really think so?'

She nodded.

'It was foolish to run after Gretchen the way we did. We were ill prepared for what lay ahead. Horses, trail rations and riding cloaks; that's all we took with us. That and a noble cause.'

'So a noble cause is a bad thing, all of a sudden?'

'Not a bad thing, but a folly if it gets us killed, Drew, and it nearly did. The encounter with that Lionguard corpse, the bad business in Haggard; if the dice had landed any other way we might both be dead. We're lucky to be here, both of us.'

'I believe we make our own luck, Whitley. I knew it was going to be dangerous, and I warned you about that. You didn't need to accompany me all this way. You could have turned back any time you liked.'

'You'd have got lost.'

'I'd have stayed on the Talstaff Road. I'd have been fine.'

Whitley looked annoyed.

'So you're saying I should have stayed in Highcliff? That I've been a hindrance?'

'Brenn, no!' gasped Drew, uncomfortable with the conversation's change of direction. 'I didn't mean that at all. If you hadn't freed me from that jail beneath Haggard I'd be on Kesslar's slave ship by now.'

Whitley sighed long and hard, lowering her chin on to her knees.

'Yes, but if I hadn't been injured in the first place, we wouldn't have ended up in Haggard at all.'

Drew put an arm round her.

'But we were able to free all those poor people. Look at the good we did in Haggard – don't you think it was worth it?'

'But it further delayed our pursuit of Gretchen and her kidnappers.'

Drew shook his head and gave a bitter laugh.

'We could sit here all night, contemplating the "what ifs" and " maybes". No good crying over spilled milk; that's what my ma used to say. We have to deal with each new day as we find it, Whitley, and not worry about the last.'

She leaned in to him, letting her head fall against his chest. Drew didn't move, keeping his arm round her shoulder.

'You're a good friend, Drew. I'm going to miss you.'

'Miss me?'

'You're not coming back, are you?'

Drew was shocked into silence, thinking about how he could reply. He floundered for an answer.

'I knew it,' she whispered. 'You're a lousy liar, Drew of the Dyrewood.'

'I honestly don't know what I'm going to do. All I'm concentrating on is Gretchen and getting her back from Lucas and his men. Beyond that, if we succeed, who knows? But Highcliff – they don't really need me, Whitley. Your father would be better as king. Even Broghan, for that matter.'

'By right the throne of Westland is yours. You should take the crown.'

'It would never sit easy on this farm boy's head. Please, Whitley; tell Broghan nothing of my intentions.'

'You can't keep running, Drew,' she said. 'You can't escape what you are. No matter how far you run, your destiny will catch up with you.'

The two fell silent. *Perhaps Whitley is right*, thought Drew. *Perhaps this is our last night together.* They'd be in Cape Gala tomorrow. One way or another, the chase was over for them. It was clear that Broghan intended to escort Drew back to Highcliff once their business in the city of the Horselords was concluded. Drew didn't intend to give him the opportunity, and Whitley knew that. The only decision Drew had to make was whether he'd be jumping on a ship and sailing to Bast to rescue Gretchen, if indeed that was where Lucas had taken her, or disappear once again into the wilds of Lyssia.

As if sensing what he was thinking, Whitley stirred against his chest, sitting upright. He looked into her eyes. He'd first met her in the Dyrewood months ago, mistaking her for a boy as she'd scouted for a monster with her master, Hogan. Drew had been the monster. They'd come a long way since then, as a whole world of friends and enemies, Werelords and royal conspiracies had opened up for Drew. Whitley had been there at the beginning of his new life. Now he might be leaving her, forever. *Is this the last I'll see of her?*

'Be careful, Drew, whichever path you choose.'

Drew's stomach knotted. He couldn't be sure whether it was a trick of the light, the night casting shadows over her face, but her eyes had never looked deeper, darker. *How did I ever mistake her for a boy?*

Whitley leaned in suddenly, about to rise, but Drew misread the movement. He dipped his head, heart racing, and kissed her on the lips. She pulled back immediately, eyes wider than ever, shock writ large across her face.

'I'm sorry . . .' he spluttered, suddenly aware of his blunder. His cheeks shot crimson instantly, and he felt a sickness rise like a tidal wave. *Fool!*

Whitley backed away, tugging her cloak round her as she struggled to her feet, legs unsteady. Her face was pale, her eyes looking anywhere but at Drew. He began to get up, but she raised a hand to halt him.

'No, please. Please. Stay there. It's best . . .' she said. She seemed to consider saying something else before changing her mind, drawing her hood about her face and turning quickly to head back to camp. Drew sat there watching her go, feeling his friendship with Lady Whitley crumbling to ashes around him. *She was just getting up, not wanting to steal a kiss! What have you done?*

He looked up at the moon, almost full, overhead. He felt a growl in the pit of his chest, a reminder of what simmered beneath the surface. He glanced over his shoulder at his departing friend. He wanted to call out but only a whisper escaped.

'Goodbye.'

2

Cape Gala

Drew stared down the Talstaff Road, the ancient lane winding through the Longridings to Cape Gala ahead. The scale of the merchant city took his breath away. Piers and wharves thrust into the sea, homes, towers and warehouses occupying them. Some stretched hundreds of yards into the shimmering water, with smaller walkways and jetties running off them. The city appeared built upon stilts thanks to traders and sea captains who jostled for the best positions along the waterfront, pushing it further into the Lyssian Straits. At the city's centre, beyond its looping palisade wall, Drew could see a gaggle of taller buildings, including High Stable, the citadel which he'd been informed was the seat of power for the Longridings.

Although the road ahead appeared empty, the same could not be said of the road behind. Drew looked back towards his travelling companions. A line of Greencloaks trailed, accompanied by a handful of soldiers from Haggard. Baron Ewan rode alongside Lord Broghan, deep in conversation, while Whitley rode directly behind them on Chancer, her eyes fixed on the horse's mane.

Not a word had passed between the two friends since their encounter the previous evening. Any hope Drew held that they might be able to act as if nothing had happened soon vanished, as Whitley did her best to avoid him while the party breakfasted. Since they'd been on the road she'd ensured that she travelled behind her brother, putting as much distance between herself and Drew as possible. She looked up suddenly, catching sight of him. Drew looked back to the road, too embarrassed to hold the girl's gaze.

The Longridings were quiet. Cape Gala, though splendid at first glance, looked sombre to Drew, as if storm clouds rolled in from the sea. The seasons were turning, summer giving way to autumn already, the tall grasses now yellow and dry. Was it really autumn again? Had it been a year since he'd fled the Ferran farmstead? He felt the stubble on his jaw. He was a boy no more.

A rider trotted up alongside him. It was his old friend Captain Harker, commander of the Woodland Watch and Duke Bergan's most trusted soldier.

'He's worried,' said the soldier as he pulled alongside Drew.

'Broghan? So would I be, turning up unannounced with a small army.'

'We're hardly an army. We're rangers first and foremost, guardians of the forest and the road.'

'Well armed and expertly trained fighters, though.'

Harker looked surprised.

'Not shy about speaking your mind any more, are you Drew? I remember the wild lad we encountered on the Dymling Road not so many moons ago.'

Harker was one of the first people Drew had met, along with Whitley and Hogan, after living wild in the Dyrewood. There was a connection between them that went beyond their social standing.

'As you say, that was a long time ago, and I'm only stating the facts. You turn up in Cape Gala with a small force like this and you'll put noses out of joint, as I understand the Longridings haven't said one way or the other whether they approve of Leopold being deposed, or a Wolf taking the throne. We could be walking into trouble.'

'Chances are Lucas has already fled to Bast, taking Lady Gretchen with him. I know you've come all this way to rescue her, but sometimes the best intentions count for nought. The most I hope for is that the Horselords can tell us when they left and which port in Bast they sailed to.'

'You really think they've gone?'

The captain shrugged, sympathetically.

'They must be a week ahead of you with all your diversions and distractions.'

'Still, I've a bad feeling in my bones. Why haven't they sent anyone out to escort us? That's what they *do*, isn't it?'

'Don't worry, Drew. Broghan knows what he's doing. I'd follow him into the heart of Omir; he's not daft.'

'I never said he was daft. Overconfident though, that's another thing. This feels like walking into a trap.'

'You worry too much,' said Harker, patting Drew's shoulder. 'Try to relax. The Horselords are a welcoming bunch. I promise.'

Drew hunkered down in his saddle, his nerves on edge. By the time he'd caught sight of the first ramshackle huts that surrounded the city, it was too late to turn back; the Horselords knew they were coming.

The citadel of High Stable was the tallest building in Cape Gala. Most of the city's buildings were of wooden construction, whereas this stocky tower was built on firmer footing – stone transported from the Barebones centuries ago. Its colour alone made it stand out from all the rest, cold and grey against the weatherworn timber surrounding it. Merchants' towers crowded round it, brazen in their show of wealth. Gold and bronze, the colours and currency of the Longridings, were on show for all to see, a world away from the makeshift homes that huddled outside the city walls.

Drew had counted hundreds of huts beyond the palisade, where the homeless of the Longridings had set up house. The gate guards had demanded they wait while an escort from High Stable rode them in. By the time the escort arrived the Greencloaks had been surrounded by a mob of hungry peasants. Drew had given the remains of his provisions to the crowd and was instantly scolded by the guards for almost inciting a riot.

It was late afternoon when they dismounted in the gravelled courtyard that circled the citadel, their mounts led away by the Horselords' staff. If a horse required care, Cape Gala was the place to be. The party handed over their arms, each man passing his bow, sword and dagger to bronze-armoured soldiers. Drew was the last to hand over his Wolfshead blade, taking a moment to wrap the pommel in rags before relinquishing it. Four guards transported the weapons in chests to an exterior building, where they would be kept until leaving High Stable.

Satisfied their rides and weapons were in safe hands, Broghan nodded to a handful of them: Ewan, Drew, Whitley, Harker and a couple of Greencloaks. The seven continued on, unarmed, into the citadel, while the rest gathered outside. Drew kept his left hand, which bore Wergar's ring, hidden within his cloak. He remained at the rear, head bowed and hood half-raised. Whitley did likewise, the two of them remaining anonymous like regular scouts of the Woodland Watch. She wore her hair tied up and braided, just as she had when the two had first met in the Dyrewood. The group strode up a sweeping set of stone steps towards an open portcullis. Tall white wooden doors stood open on either side, guards standing to attention between them. Drew couldn't shake the feeling that something was amiss. He watched the bronze-plated guards as they walked by, full helms obscuring most of their faces, although their eyes watched the visitors intently. Drew recognized the look: fear.

A series of staircases carried them up four or five floors of the grey tower to the court itself. Staff stopped to stare, similar looks of concern gracing their faces as the party entered the most sacred chamber of the Horselords.

The courtroom was a sprawling affair, a mixture of rising

and sinking steps on many levels interspersed with cold columns of rock. Twenty nobles stood or sat around the circular hall, the chamber built for debate, no point more prominent than another. All were supposedly equal in the court of High Stable.

'Welcome to our court,' boomed a rumbling voice, 'Broghan, son of Bergan and Ewan, son of Edwin.'

A tall, long-faced man stepped forward, other nobles joining him at his side. His thick grey hair tumbled down his back in tightly bound golden hoops. The others wore theirs in a similar fashion although none wore as many trinkets as the speaker. In their long, cream robes, they reminded Drew of priests. Broghan bowed, dropping to his knee, while Ewan tilted his head respectfully. The nod that passed between the Ram and the speaker told Drew they were acquainted.

'Duke Lorimer,' said Broghan, rising. 'I bring greetings from my father in the north.'

'From Brackenholme?' asked Lorimer, arching an eyebrow as he teased an answer from the Bearlord.

'Not directly. He currently resides in Highcliff, Your Grace.'

'Ah,' said Lorimer, clicking his fingers. 'That's right. I'd heard of this; something about your father seizing Westland?'

Drew felt the hairs on his neck stand on end. He didn't like the sound of this, and judging by the awkward look on Broghan's face, neither did the young Bearlord.

'That's not the case, Your Grace. My father's taken the role of Lord Protector, providing counsel to the young Wolf before he takes the throne. He speaks on behalf of his fellow Werelords, I assure you, and makes no move for Westland. His heart lies forever in Brackenholme, but he cannot ignore the plight of his neighbours.'

'As I understood, it was hardly neighbourly kindness that took him to Highcliff,' countered Lorimer as his companions nodded. 'News travels fast, Bearlord. Let us not confuse the situation; it sounds like a clear case of the Bear seizing power from the Lion.'

'With respect,' said Broghan, through gritted teeth. 'The Wolf's Council act as guardians of the northern realms in the Wolf's name.'

The Lord of the Longridings laughed haughtily. One of his companions stepped forward, stooped with long thinning hair.

'Pick your words carefully, cub,' said the old Horselord. 'The Wolves are gone. Whoever you've pushed on to the throne, he's certainly no Wolf. Just a puppet to dance to your tune.'

Broghan's face coloured with anger. He turned to Drew, about to point him out.

Drew's eyes widened. *No, Broghan, say nothing!* Ewan stepped in before the Bearlord could speak.

'Viscount Colt,' said the Ramlord, raising his palms outwards towards the old Horselord in a sign of peace. 'You misunderstand what my friend tells you. Whatever news you've heard, I assure you it's incorrect. Dukes Bergan and Manfred work alongside the only surviving son of Wergar. A grey Wolf still lives. Of that there's no doubt, and he is an ally to all honourable and loyal men of Lyssia.'

Drew was relieved to see that Ewan appreciated the need

to keep his identity secret, at least until they knew where they stood. Lorimer lifted his hand, signalling his intention to speak.

'How is it you've allied yourself with this . . . this would-be Wolf, Ewan?'

'He's a friend of Haggard. My cousin, Kesslar, made an enemy of him after the Wolf protected my people against him, at great risk to his life. We all know what kind of beast Kesslar is. This Wolf – Drew is his name – stood up to him. He faced the Goatlord, as man and beast. He's the Wolf returned.'

'I don't trust this talk,' muttered Viscount Colt, turning to Lorimer. 'And you'd do well to steer clear of this business, nephew. You knew Wergar, but he's gone. And you've known Leopold all these years, too, through feast and famine.'

'Aye,' called another Horselord, a blond-maned youth, barely older than Drew. 'We've been held down long enough, first by the Wolf and now by the Lion. If they fight in the north, let them fight I say. This is our chance to break free of their reign.'

Drew's eyes flitted around the room as the crowd cheered. Colt pointed at the young Horselord who'd just spoken, nodding with approval.

'Lord Conrad speaks with wisdom beyond his years. We have an opportunity. Let us follow the example of Duke Henrik in Sturmland; cut away from the Union. We should ride out alone, lose our greedy neighbours. What's left of our crops? The Lion has taken everything from the Longridings. If we're to recover then we must do so alone. Now is the time for the Kingdom of the Longridings!'

There was an enormous cheer, as the Horselords snorted and stamped their boots in approval. The noise was deafening as their feet clattered the stone floor. It sounded like a cavalry charge, as if the Werestallions' hooves were hammering across a battlefield.

'The Longridings!' they cheered.

'King Lorimer!' they roared.

Drew wasn't scared – the atmosphere felt volatile, but not dangerous – but he was worried by the separatist talk; the Horselords seemed to think that Duke Henrik, the White Bear of the North, had already split from the Union of Realms. As his gaze swept the chamber, Drew spied bronze-armoured guards moving round the courtroom's edges. One man, certainly not a guard, was dressed less formally in a battered brown jerkin with a longsword at his hip. His nose was badly broken, and he seemed to watch with great interest from the back of the chamber. *Why is he armed when we aren't?* Drew couldn't decide if he recognized the fellow.

'But the Lion's dethroned now!' shouted Ewan. 'Don't you see? The Lion stripped your land bare, but Drew is different. He understands the people!'

'If he's truly a Wolf,' said Lorimer, the crowd quietening instantly. 'That makes him Wergar's cub. You and I knew Wergar, old friend. We fought alongside him. You remember what he was capable of. Are you honestly trying to tell me this boy could be different?

'You'll be my friend until I ride over the last meadow, Ewan, but don't challenge me on this. I do this for the Longridings. You've seen the shanty towns. It's time to reclaim our land and look after our own. I'd suggest you do the same in Haggard, cousin.'

'So that's it?' asked Ewan. 'The Longridings is an independent realm now? How long will you survive alone, Lorimer? Who will you trade with?'

Colt put a bony knuckled hand on his nephew's shoulder. 'Anything is better than servitude to a fat king in Westland.'

Broghan shook his head wearily, curling his fists with frustration. He glanced at his disguised sister and Drew before looking back to Lorimer.

'Leopold's son,' said the Bearlord, struggling to hold back his anger. 'What of him?'

'I don't follow,' said Lorimer.

'We aren't here to beg you to remain in the Union. We're hunting Prince Lucas and his cohorts. They came to Cape Gala.'

'Is that so?'

'It is so,' snipped Broghan angrily. Ewan turned to him, throwing a cautionary glare.

Keep it in check, Broghan, thought Drew. *Don't do anything foolish*.

Broghan continued, controlling his breathing.

'Lady Gretchen of Hedgemoor, daughter of the late Earl Gaston, was abducted by Lucas and Vankaskan, the Wererat. We've been charged with tracking them down and retrieving Lady Gretchen. We believe they're heading to Bast. Please tell me they haven't set sail yet?'

Broghan spoke earnestly. His single-mindedness in his mission was unshakable. Drew found himself watching the young blond Horselord while the others stared at Duke Lorimer. The blond therian looked to the ground, anger on his face as Lorimer spoke.

Odd, thought Drew.

'I'm afraid if Prince Lucas has been through Cape Gala, then he's done so unnoticed. We're a vast city, Lord Broghan, with many ways in and out. The shanty town covers every entrance, keeping my guards occupied day and night, making access on the road relatively easy. Especially if one flashes the bronze.'

'So you're saying he's been and gone?'

'What I'm saying, young Bear, is that I wouldn't know. Thousands pass through this city every week. Three people could easily move quickly through Cape Gala, from foot to boat.'

Drew looked for the broken-nosed man but couldn't see him. *Why do I know that face?*

'Then this was a wasted expedition,' snapped Broghan.

'Not entirely wasted,' Viscount Colt chimed. 'When you return to Westland you can pass on our secession from the Union to your father.'

Ewan put a hand on Broghan's forearm. The young Were lord seemed to shimmer where he stood, threatening to channel the Bear at any moment. The Horselords recoiled, the guards beginning to step forward. Even Harker and Drew moved to put their hands on the therian, trying to calm him. He knocked their hands clear, taking one heavy step towards the elderly viscount. Colt looked scared, as the sound of swords being drawn from their sheaths hissed around the hall. Spittle foamed at Broghan's lips as his teeth sharpened.

The gentle hand of Whitley on his wrist froze him where he stood.

'No, brother,' she whispered. 'Don't.'

That was all it took. The Bear retreated, the beast back in its cage as Broghan staggered back, exhausted with unspent anger. Ewan checked he was all right before turning back to the Horselords. Swords returned to their scabbards as the tension subsided.

'Apologies on behalf of our northern friend,' said Ewan. 'It has been a taxing time on the road as he has chased these villains down. Alas, it appears to have been to no avail. May the men of Brackenholme and Haggard lodge with you this evening?'

'I insist you stay in High Stable, Lord Broghan,' said Lorimer. 'You are our guests so long as you are here.'

'There are barracks for the Greencloaks,' rasped Colt quickly.

You want to keep us where you can see us, thought Drew. He looked once more for the familiar broken-nosed man but to no avail.

'I shouldn't imagine you'll want to be staying too long,' said Colt. 'The road north is long and I'm sure your Lord Protector is keen to hear the news of our separation.'

Others joined Colt as he chuckled, keeping it low after Broghan's outburst. Drew noticed that Lorimer and the blond Horselord, Conrad, didn't laugh.

Drew followed Broghan, Whitley and Harker out of the

chamber, the two Greencloaks supporting the exhausted Bear-lord. Broghan looked shattered, the act of keeping his therian side in check having exhausted him twice as much as a full transformation. Drew glanced back, noticing the Horselords dispersing. Conrad had joined Lorimer, who was already deep in conversation with Ewan about the events in Haggard. If there was any way he might influence Lorimer, now was the time. The younger Horselord stared back, watching him leave. Before Drew turned he spied Colt at the back of the chamber, talking to a figure behind a pillar. The man in the brown jerkin had reappeared; why did he hide?

The doors closed as the six northerners gathered under the watchful eye of the bronze-plated Horseguard. Harker whispered under his breath, taking Broghan's weight from his men.

'As far as they know you are just a scout, Drew. Keep it that way. Stay with the men until we can get word out of here. Whitley?'

'I'll stay as well,' she said to Harker, aware they were being observed. 'Keep an eye on my brother, captain. We'll see what we can find out on the street regarding Gretchen and Lucas. We just need to lose our escort first. Someone's bound to have heard something.'

Harker nodded.

'Drew, you're in charge of my men now, at least until I send word in the morning.'

Drew was astonished. He was used to working alone, or at the most with a couple of friends. But thirty-odd men under his command?

'I can't. I'm not cut out for this!'

Harker leaned in, smiling at the bronze-armoured guards as he spoke through clenched teeth.

'Drew, you are the future king of Westland. Tell these men what to do. They'll follow.'

With that Harker set off with the Horseguard, supporting the weary Broghan across their shoulders as he hobbled along. Drew, Whitley and the two rangers from Brackenholme watched them depart. Slowly they made their way down the grand staircases before leaving the citadel through the open portcullis, joining their fellow Greencloaks in the gathering dusk.

3

The Bows of Saddlers Row

Drew felt all eyes on him as he strode down High Stable's steps. He nodded to the assembled rangers of Brackenholme. The Greencloaks looked calm, awaiting orders, as a Horseguard rode up on a white steed. Five more guards waited at the gate.

'This way, gentlemen,' he said. 'We'll escort you to your lodging. You're down Saddlers Row, near the docks.' He turned his horse, about to make off.

'A moment,' said Drew, quickly checking his companions' weapon belts. 'We were told we'd get our weapons back when we left High Stable.'

'My captain had them sent on to your barracks, along with your horses. You'll find them waiting there for you.'

Drew looked to Godric, one of Harker's more senior men. The old ranger tipped his head and shrugged.

'Can't say I'm happy about going anywhere without my sword and bow, sir, but if that's what they've done . . .'

Whitley looked displeased. Clearly the idea of going anywhere without Chancer was unpalatable for her. Drew rubbed his chin, fighting the urge to run indoors and fetch Harker. He'd know what to do. He turned back to the Horseguard.

'Lead on,' said Drew, shaking his head. He saw little point in arguing. What was done was done; the weapons and horses had been sent ahead. *But if anything's gone missing they'll see my anger all right.*

The Horseguard joined his companions at the gate. The Greencloaks stared at Drew, waiting for the word.

'You heard the man,' Drew said awkwardly, clapping his hands. 'Saddlers Row. Near the docks.' As one the six branches of the Woodland Watch turned, following the riders across the courtyard. Before long they were marching down a lane that skirted the waterfront, traders on one side of the road and the harbour on the other. The procession cut quite a dash, a string of brilliant green capes and cloaks fluttering in the evening breeze. Locals stopped what they were doing to watch the rangers stride past. Drew felt great pride as he made his way up the line.

He wondered where Gretchen might be. Had Lucas gone straight to Bast? The prince was so angry – Drew had witnessed it first hand – and his stomach lurched at the notion of him laying a finger on Gretchen. And Vankaskan – was he still whispering words of poison into the young Lion's ear?

Two of the Horseguard rode at the front of the group while

four fell back to the rear, keeping the rangers moving along. Drew noticed that the streets were growing quiet, as the hour was late. They saw fewer locals as they walked away from the trading and residential streets and into a warehouse district. He noticed a wooden post swinging from a street corner; Saddlers Row. The barracks had to be close by.

Drew looked at Whitley who was walking between him and Godric. She kept her head bowed, looking down at the cobbles. Was she aware he was trying to catch her eye? He wanted to speak to her about the other night, wanted to say something, anything, by way of explanation for his actions. It had been a terrible mistake, that's all – a misunderstanding.

'You tired?'

Whitley nodded wearily. The tension between them was palpable. It had been a very long day.

'We'll be there shortly.' He looked at the grizzled ranger. 'What say we give our friend first choice of bed, Godric?'

'Drew, you don't have to . . .' said Whitley.

'Let's not argue about this,' he began, before Godric expertly interrupted.

'Sounds like an excellent idea, sir,' smiled the ranger, tapping the tip of his green hood with a scarred hand. 'I'm ready for a bunk myself. Weeks on the road aren't good for old bones.'

Drew noticed there were very few lights along this stretch of Saddlers Row. There was no sign of life and certainly no evidence of the barracks yet. One of the rangers stumbled in the twilight, a raised cobble tripping him. Drew was about to call to the riders up front when he noticed they'd pulled some distance away. He looked over the heads of his men towards the rear, searching for the four riders who'd followed. There was no sign of them.

'This isn't right,' muttered Drew. Godric quickly picked up on Drew's feeling of unease. The two lead riders suddenly galloped, hooves clattering as they disappeared down the road.

Sensing an ambush, Godric was about to alert his men, but the words never left his lips. The first volley of arrows had already filled the air, one of them finding a home in the old ranger's throat. He was dead before he hit the cobbles at Drew's feet.

'Take cover!' screamed Drew as he snatched Whitley by the wrist. The unarmed Greencloaks were already running to find shelter, but the road was wide and the ground treacherous in the dark. They ran for the nearest buildings and alleys, unaware that they were running directly towards their ambushers. More arrows flew, too many finding their targets.

Drew and a branch of rangers dashed towards the waterfront, sprinting blindly, weaving as they ran. One of the men spun, an arrow appearing with a wet snap through his breastplate, its feathers flush to his back. Drew kept Whitley close, pushing her before him and putting himself in the way of the arrows as they neared the wooden jetties. Another man tumbled, an arrow splintering through his leg. Drew ran on as he heard the man scream. He could see the launches and piers now that criss-crossed their way along the docks, reaching out into the harbour. A fine mist had rolled over Saddlers Row. Cursing, Drew skidded to a halt, passing Whitley to a Greencloak.

'Run quickly, find a boat! Keep Whitley safe!'

'Drew, no!' cried the Lady of Brackenholme as the man struggled with her towards the jetties.

'I'll find you,' he yelled before running back.

He'd run twenty yards through the fog when he saw the wounded ranger, trying to drag himself towards the water-front. Drew caught sight of armed men through the mist, walking through the dead and dying Greencloaks. Of the Horseguard he saw no sign. These men looked like brigands, acting with ruthless precision. They carried melee weapons – swords, knives, axes and cudgels. Their deadly tools came down, silencing the cries of those men of the Woodland Watch who had survived the ambush. One by one the injured were dispatched.

Drew crouched low, dragging the stricken man towards the sea front. The ranger let out a cry as the arrowhead through his calf caught on the ground. Three of the killers looked up at the sound, one of them pointing Drew and the man out through the mist. They closed on them fast.

Drew kept moving, pulling the wounded ranger back. At the last moment he yanked him clear and stepped forward, chest heaving as he faced the three men. He measured up his opposition.

On his left was a short fat one; out of shape. He was a hired heavy judging by the cudgel in his stubby hands, hardly a weapon of choice for a trained fighter. The other two, however, demanded Drew's attention. The one in the middle was a hulking northman, the kind you avoided eye contact with. His grey beard was shorn close to his face, his bald head shining with sweat. He had a crescent moon axe in his hands, dark with the blood of Brackenholme. To his right was the mystery man from High Stable. *Where do I know you from?* Drew gritted his teeth with frustration and fear. The broken-nosed man held a longsword in his hands, its tip suddenly rising to point at Drew.

'It's you!' he rasped, and in an instant Drew remembered. He was back in the sewers beneath Highcliff, fighting two villains in the dark. This was the fellow who'd survived and escaped.

'Sorin, he called you,' said Drew. He could make out the Greencloak still crawling, edging closer to the water's edge. They were maybe ten feet from the first wooden pier. 'Your friend, remember? He's dead now, in case it interests you.'

Drew could feel the Wolf's blood coursing through his body, filling him with a furious fire. He allowed it to build, keeping the transformation back until the last moment so it would be sudden and explosive. Already hairs sprouted over his body, muscles expanding, teeth sharpening, but in the half-light of mist and dusk it was impossible for his enemies to see this.

'Who is he?' asked the big northman, squinting through the gloom at Drew.

'He's the one I told you about, Colbard!' said Sorin. 'Killed Brutus in Highcliff.'

'Afraid not,' said Drew, backing away and following his crawling comrade. 'Brutus was done in by the rats. But then, you'd know all about vermin. How is Vankaskan?'

'What would *you* know about the old Rat?' grunted Colbard.

Drew glanced down again. The ranger was almost to the edge of the dock. *A little further, just keep them occupied.*

'I know you and Vankaskan work for Lucas and I know he has Lady Gretchen. Where is she? And what kind of hold does Lucas have over the Horselords that they let his dogs run riot through their streets?'

Colbard spat on the ground.

'Hardly in a position to ask questions, are you boy?' He shifted the axe in his hands, spinning the big blade as blood flicked from the steel. A leather loop on the end of the haft kept the weapon attached to his wrist. 'I get smart-mouthed when I have a weapon at hand. I know you aint got no weapons on you. You sick in the head or something?'

The big man laughed and his companions joined him. Drew could see their shadowy companions dispatching the other rangers. Hopefully more had escaped. He brought his attention back to the trio.

'Duke Bergan and the Werelords shan't stand for this. You and your masters should have fled when you had the chance.'

'Fled?' snorted Sorin 'He thinks we're fleeing! Quite the opposite, lad. We're the welcoming committee.'

Drew didn't understand what the rogue meant. *Welcoming committee?*

'Who are you greeting?'

'Oh, they'll be here any day now. You won't believe what's in store for the Bear and his friends. What a shame you're not going to live long enough to find out!'

'Answer my questions and you walk away with your lives,' snarled Drew, his voice deepening now.

'Was he this confident in the sewer?' asked Colbard, genuinely astonished. 'He's got some guts, I'll give him that!' The three stepped forward, weapons poised.

'Does it matter?' said Sorin. 'He's an unarmed halfwit. He'll be just another dead ranger in a moment.' The broken-nosed killer brought his longsword back.

'Who said I was unarmed?' growled Drew, letting the Wolf rip free.

It was the fastest change he'd ever undertaken, and it felt fluid and focused. The three men paused, caught by surprise. A moment was all Drew needed. The Wolf hit the trio like a tidal wave.

He went for Colbard's axe first, grasping the blade with dark clawed hands and twirling it in the man's grip like a spinning top. The big man watched in horror as the axe – and the loop round his wrist – spun repeatedly in his sweaty palm, his wrist locking with the momentum of the blade. The axe continued to spin, through and beyond the physical limit of his joints. First the wrist snapped and the elbow swiftly followed as the torque of the huge weapon threatened to rip his arm out of its socket. Colbard staggered to the ground, screaming like a stuck pig, the bones of his arm in pieces.

The fat man lunged clumsily with the cudgel, taking a wild swing at Drew's head that might have proved fatal if he'd been human. As a therianthrope he allowed the wooden club to bounce off his head, jarring him only slightly as he brought his changed face round to growl furiously at the man. The Werewolf's unmistakable roar rose up from Saddlers Row and raced to every corner of Cape Gala. In that moment, the Horselords knew that the Wolf was in their city. The fat man stumbled away in terror, wisely deciding that this fight wasn't for him. That left Sorin facing Drew.

'I'm not scared of you,' blustered Sorin, although his trembling voice said otherwise. He held his longsword up, striking a defensive pose in case the Werewolf lunged. Drew looked beyond the broken-nosed rogue and saw the shadowy shapes of Sorin's companions beginning to draw in, lifting their bows. He had to make the most of this chance.

He turned on his heel and snatched up the injured ranger, aware that Sorin was on the back foot, unprepared to strike.

'Stop him!' screamed Lucas's man.

Cradling the wounded man in his arms, the Wolf dug his claws into the earth and sprinted towards the first wooden pier, his feet pounding the planks along its length. No sooner had he set off than he heard the flight of arrows through the air. The missiles rained down upon him, but he didn't look back. He felt three arrows hit him hard and deep in the back. Fatal strikes to a human, but to a lycanthrope merely painful wounds. Drew had endured worse before now.

There was no sign of any other Greencloaks. He prayed that at least some had got away.

'Hold on,' Drew growled to the injured man, hoping to get them away from the chasing pack. There were boats he could jump on to, try to hide in, but both were bleeding – heavily – and they'd be sure to leave a trail. Behind he could hear the Lion's men, shouting to one another as they covered all escape routes.

Drew found himself at the end of the pier with nowhere left to run.

'You strong enough to swim?' he said to the man in his arms, his features reverting back to human. He couldn't keep the change up for long, the beast devouring his energy voraciously. He looked down at the Greencloak.

The man's eyes were open and glassy as he peeled away from Drew's chest. Two of the arrows that had struck the Werewolf had punched their way clean through his torso, finding their mark in the hapless ranger. One had made a clean hit to his heart. The only comfort Drew took was that it had probably been a swift death. He crouched over the pier's edge, lowering him into the tide, and watched his body sink into the dark waters.

He looked back down the pier, golden eyes burning. His superior night vision allowed him to clearly make out the approaching men. There were ten, arrows nocked, with possibly more behind. Sorin was in the middle somewhere. They couldn't see him though, crouched on the jetty, shrouded in the sea mist.

Drew winced as he felt the arrows in his back and chest grate against ribs and organs. He could stay and fight, take more injuries and hopefully defeat them. But it wasn't a sure thing; he thought of Dorn and how he'd seen first hand how a relentless attack with unsilvered weapons could slay a Werelord.

Or he could run and recover to fight another day. These were lackeys after all. The true villains were inside High Stable, seducing the Horselords. If Lucas and Vankaskan were there, then perhaps Gretchen was too.

Drew scanned the harbour one last time. *Dear Brenn, please look out for Whitley.* He thought about Sorin's words — the 'welcoming committee'. *Who was coming to Cape Gala?* As if in answer there was a rumble of thunder and a flash of lightning out to sea, over the Lyssian Bay. With a final glance back at the advancing soldiers Drew slipped off the pier and disappeared silently into cold, dark water. He was a lone Wolf once more, and it was time to take the fight to the real enemy.

4

Beyond the Gates

Trying to enter Cape Gala was a formidable task. A man of money could easily secure passage, a flash of bronze would turn the head of most guards. A man-at-arms could sway them too, a sword for hire was always welcome in the city of merchants. But a man with nothing would be barred entry, the shanty town his only welcome port. Trying to enter was difficult if you were a nobody, but leaving was a different matter.

Whitley bided her time, watching the guards patiently as they prepared to open up the gates. She'd been hiding across the street for half an hour, waiting for the next caravan to leave or enter the city. The rainclouds ensured her task was miserable as well as dangerous. She knew it was late, but she also knew the gate was in constant use. The shouts of the homeless floated over the palisade, reminding those within that all was not well across the Longridings. Those lucky enough to have rooves over their heads did their best to ignore the cries, turning a deaf ear to their brothers' misfortune.

The grinding of hinges heralded the gate's opening, four guards stepping up with their polearms lowered, keeping the mob at bay. A big wagon waited to enter, its own guards surrounding it as the horses stamped their hooves impatiently. With the gates fully open and the guards holding back the crowd, the horses advanced, pulling the wagon in.

Whitley dashed forward, feet flying through puddles, a shadow flitting past the wagon, past its guard and straight past the City Watch. One of the soldiers saw the girl, as her head bumped the side of his halberd before she was swallowed by the crowd. The guards retreated, their faces set and grim. The gate slammed shut.

Whitley was running now. She didn't know where to, only that she needed to get away from Cape Gala and the villains who'd killed her friends. She and the three Greencloaks who had left Drew had taken a rowing boat. Quist, a tall graceful woman from the easternmost edge of the Dyrewood, had assumed command, structuring a plan of action as she rowed. They would take the water out of the city, get beyond the walls and make camp. One of them would go on up the River Steppen before striking out on foot back north. The other two would wait beyond the walls of Cape Gala for any sign of fellow survivors, guarding Whitley in turns. Get out, regroup; that was the Woodland Watch's way when things went wrong.

They hadn't consulted Whitley, though. She had been

dragged on to the boat against her will. Drew was on the shore somewhere, facing awful odds and possible death. Their friendship had been built on looking out for one another, and she wasn't about to leave him behind, regardless of Drew's blundering advance the previous evening. At the first opportunity she'd jumped off the boat and swum back to shore, the cries of the rangers disappearing behind her.

She'd returned to Saddlers Row, creeping through the mists that clung to the harbourfront. By the time she'd arrived back at the scene of the ambush, there was no sign of battle, no sign of her fallen comrades or Drew. The enemy had disappeared and the street was quiet. The only clue was a couple of street cleaners brushing the road and splashing buckets of water over the cobbles. She'd shivered, panicked and soaking, more scared than ever, wary of every movement in the shadows as she'd made for the gates out of the city.

The only notion she now had was to hide. Get to a place where she wouldn't be noticed, couldn't be found – she refused to be used as bait again. She'd seen the shanty town earlier. As Whitley ran in her still-damp clothes she glanced back to check if she was being followed, putting distance between herself and the gate. She was deep into the shanty town now. Fires burned between huts and tents as people gathered under tarpaulins to shelter from the rain.

With her eyes glancing behind her and not ahead, it came as little surprise to Whitley when she ran headlong into a man. What *did* surprise her was the force with which the man took hold of her wrists. Whitley struggled, trying to pull free, looking up at the fellow who blocked her path. He was tall, well beyond six feet, with weatherbeaten skin and long black hair. His grip was like iron while his face remained impassive. Whitley kicked at the man, who responded by suspending the girl at arm's length. Swiftly he spun the scout, tucking her under his arm as one might carry a rolled rug, his other hand clamped over her mouth. Then he was off, through the camp, the young Werelady firmly held: his prisoner.

The man carried Whitley for a couple of minutes, immune to her struggles, kicks and muffled shouts. The people they passed paid them little attention. When they did look up some of them nodded to the tall man, showing no surprise at the fact he was striding around with a girl under his arm. They obviously knew him, but Whitley couldn't work out whether they respected or feared him.

Eventually they arrived at the shanty town's outskirts, where the marshes of the River Steppen met the settlement. The air was thick with mosquitoes, big ones compared to the tiddlers back in Brackenholme. The man strode silently up to an animal-hide tent that perched near the swamp's edge, tugging back the door flap, crouching and entering. Once inside he placed Whitley on the ground and moved back to the tent entrance, leaving the girl standing alone, fearful.

The tent had a musty smell, as if the skins it was made from hadn't been cured properly. Incense burned, perhaps to mask the odour of decay, but it was fighting a losing battle. Thick sheepskins were piled on the opposite side of the tent, a bed for the inhabitant, and a small fire burned within a circle of stones in the centre, a copper cooking pot suspended over it by a spit. The liquid inside bubbled and steamed, as the withered hand of the tent's owner stirred the contents with a wooden spoon. The old woman sat cross-legged on the skins.

'Sit down, girl,' said the woman in a dry, husky voice. She patted the floor beside her. Whitley had never seen so old a person in her life. She was short and squat, her back terribly hunched and malformed as if she'd spent her life stooping. She worked a hand against her throat, hidden among a bundle of colourful scarves. Her thin grey hair – what was left of it – was scraped back from the top of her head and hung scraggy round her shoulders. Liver marks speckled the leathery skin of her face and hands and her toothless gums banged into one another, her tongue running their length as she sniffed at the stew.

Whitley looked over her shoulder. The tall man remained.

'Don't worry about Rolff. He doesn't bite. Apologies if he seemed rude. My dear friend is mute, you see?' She tapped her throat with a bony finger. 'Can't speak a word, poor chap.'

The tall man, Rolff, nodded sombrely to Whitley, as if by way of an apology. Her heart was racing. She still wasn't at ease.

'Please sit. I insist.'

Reluctantly Whitley sat, but not beside the woman. She settled down on the opposite side of the pot to her, her eyes wide as she watched her every move. The scout was already looking for escape routes.

'That was a brief stay in Cape Gala, young one. Were the Horselords not to your liking?'

Whitley felt her stomach flip. How did she know their movements?

'I have friends everywhere, child,' she said, as if reading

Whitley's thoughts. 'The people of the shanty town look after one another. There are few who enter or leave through those gates who aren't noticed. Especially when they travel with such a large, armed group. Tell me, where are your companions?'

Whitley didn't answer. The old crone stopped stirring briefly to put her hands together, as if in prayer. 'I don't want to alarm you, child. Difficult as it might be for you to believe, you have nothing to fear from us. We are not your enemies. And we are not blind to the comings and goings of the Werelords.'

'You know about the Werelords who came?' asked Whitley, suddenly emboldened to ask questions of her own.

'Have a drink girl.'

The woman's beady eyes twinkled as she picked up two tin cups and sloshed the stew into both, handing one to Whitley. The old woman slurped her own cup of broth encouragingly. Whitley took a sniff and a sip. It was a meat and potato stew and she was starving. She wiped her mouth against her still damp sleeve.

'You'll be catching your death in those wet clothes. Rolff, pull a cloak from the trunk.' The tall man walked away from the tent flap to a chest and Whitley glanced at the doorway, torn between her meal and freedom. Again, it was as if the old woman read her mind.

'Finish your broth, child, before you consider making good your escape,' she chuckled.

Whitley continued eating the first hot food she'd had since breakfast. She wondered what time it was. It had to be the early hours of the morning. What had become of Drew? How could they have parted with so much unsaid? She prayed he yet lived. What of her brother, Broghan? And why was the old woman so interested in her and her friends?

'Who are you?' asked Whitley, before tucking into the broth once more.

'I'm known by many names,' said the crooked lady. She scratched at her throat again, clearing her voice with a dry cough. 'But you may call me Baba Korga.'

Whitley had heard of Babas before – wise women from Romari communities across the north. Her childhood nurse-maid had been Romari, trusted utterly by her parents. Rosa had been a proud lady who had instilled in Whitley respect for her elders. Rosa's lessons had stayed with her, and she looked at the old woman with fresh eyes.

'How do you know so much about me and my friends, Baba Korga?'

'Very fortunate is the young girl who can call the future king a friend, is she not?' said Baba Korga. Whitley shivered; she'd as good as named Drew. 'The people of this settlement are my eyes and ears. When you soldiers from Brackenholme arrived it caused quite a stir. Baron Ewan is a familiar face throughout the Longridings, and word spreads fast across the grasslands. Did not the young Wolf free Haggard from the tyranny of Count Kesslar?'

Whitley nodded, confirming the rumours.

'You see, child. There's no faster messenger than word of mouth. A pebble can cause a ripple that spans an ocean. The Wolf is here at last, and the people await him.'

It was beginning to make perfect sense to Whitley. She'd

teased Drew about the notion of the Romari worshipping the Wolf, but he hadn't been far wrong.

'You know he's a good person, don't you?' said Whitley, keen to show her loyalty to her friend.

'Of course we do,' said the woman, waving her bony hand dismissively. 'He's the one Werelord who can unite the continent again. The Seven Realms lie broken with the Lion defeated; only a strong king can mend them.'

'That's Drew! Don't get me wrong, he can be stubborn when the mood takes him. But he is so big-hearted, so loyal to his friends.' She found herself blushing as she described him, thinking back to their first encounter in the Dyrewood. 'He's like a hero from the old storybooks.'

Baba Korga nodded, her toothless smile creasing her wrinkled face further.

'Well, my girl. It seems he's had a profound effect on you. You understand, then, why it is of the utmost importance that we help your friend escape that city, yes? Many lives depend upon him. Where is he now?'

Whitley dropped her head. The last time she'd seen Drew, he'd been dashing into battle against insurmountable odds. She prayed he was still alive.

'I don't know. He was fighting the scoundrels who attacked us. There were so many of them. I'm worried he might not . . .'

She couldn't finish the sentence, the words catching in her throat. She suddenly comprehended how much the boy from the Cold Coast meant to her. The Baba reached across the fire, her fragile hand resting on Whitley's shoulder comfortingly.

'All is not lost, child. The Werelords have their powers and the magisters have their tricks, but there are older magicks in this world. People visit me when they need to know things. I provide answers, I divine the truths from the lies. Your friend Drew still lives. He's within that city.'

She pointed a bony finger into the dark. Whitley's face instantly brightened.

'You can help me find him?'

'We can,' nodded Baba Korga. 'We have friends who can get you back into the city and Rolff here will protect you. But we need *you* to go and find Drew and bring him to me. He'll listen to you. Even if Rolff could speak I can't imagine Drew trusting a complete stranger. What is your name, child?'

'Whitley,' said the Lady of Brackenholme, holding her cup out for another helping of the hot broth. The crone spooned another portion into the tin beaker.

'Go into Cape Gala, Whitley. Bring your friend to us, to safety. We Romari have always honoured the Wolf. He is a brother to our kind. Bring him so we may aid him as he saves this world.'

Whitley nodded, relieved to be under the protection of the Baba and her people.

'How do we get in?'

'Drink up, Whitley, and I'll tell you.'

5

The Broken Heart Tavern

A curfew may have hung over Highcliff, but the hardened reveller could always find a watering hole, if he knew where to look. With the bells of Brenn's temple marking midnight, a lone figure crept through the Low Quarter. Clad in a long black cloak, hood up, he flitted between shadows as he slipped through the night. The City Watch were absent from the docks, their attention focused on the wealthier quarters. If they'd stopped the man in black, they'd have been surprised; the last person one might expect to find wandering the docks at this ungodly hour was a Lord of Redmire. Even more alarming was the conversation he was having with himself.

Beneath the cloak Hector's hands curled round the jewel encrusted handle of his gaudy dagger, the white knuckled grip of his bare right hand clasped over the black-gloved left. Stepping into a darkened doorway he waited a moment to see if anyone followed him.

What's the matter brother? whispered Vincent. *Are you afraid you've been rumbled? Is the game up?*

'No,' said Hector, his voice trembling. 'I fear there might be footpads nearby, keen to see the inside of my wallet.'

Don't they know the Lord of Redmire is penniless?

'Your doing. Not mine.'

They'll be in for a nasty surprise if they dare threaten the great Hector, Wereboar of the Dalelands, won't they? How does that blade feel in your piggy hands, brother? Heavy?

Hector shifted the dagger from right hand to left, wiping his sweating palm on his breeches. As always, Vincent knew just what to say.

'Don't worry about me, brother. I can take care of myself.'

Took care of me, didn't you? the voice hissed.

Hector glanced up the cobbled street, towards the Tall Quarter; nobody was there. It appeared even thieves were honouring the curfew tonight. He set off again, turning down an unlit alleyway. The uneven floor of the passage was slick with fish guts, but it cut through to where he wanted to be: Brandy Lane. A little way down he caught sight of his destination, the Broken Heart Tavern.

Are you sure you want to do this? It's not too late for you to scurry home. These aren't children you've come to play with, brother.

Indeed they weren't. Hector knew who was in the tavern, suspected they were capable of terrible things, but he couldn't leave them free to talk. They were loose ends and consequently needed tying up. He'd waited until late in the evening so they'd be in their cups when he entered, the booze hopefully slowing their reactions. Hopefully.

They're killers, hissed his brother, the dark voice licking his ear like a cold blade. Hector flinched, raising a hand to brush his ear nervously, as if chasing away cobwebs.

When his brother had been stabbed and fallen to his death in Bevan Tower, Hector had imagined he'd finally be rid of him. It had been a terrible mistake, an accident, but it had happened nonetheless. He should be gone now, ending the torment for the young magister. How could he have been more wrong? With cruel irony the viles that had gathered round Vincent's corpse and had worried his spirit loose, claiming it as one of their own. That very night Vincent had visited Hector while his mortal body was carried away to be disposed of by Count Vega. Only this Vincent had a new body, born of hate and night and death.

Vincent's vile followed Hector's every twilight step, waiting for the sun to slip away before jumping upon him. It clung like a parasite, a cloak far darker than the black hooded cape Hector wore this night. With dawn the vile would dissipate, retreating to the shadows once more to leave Hector alone. But the relief was only fleeting. Hector could not hide from the night. Darkness would always find him.

'Killers or not, I need to parlay with them.'

The voice giggled in his ear.

Listen to yourself – 'parlay' – how ridiculous you sound! This is not some game for noblemen you enter into, Hector. These men are ruthless. Why do you think I hired them?

'You hired them because you were a fool, Vincent, and it's my job to tidy up your mess.'

The spirit hissed as Hector dashed across the street. He'd lost most of the puppy fat that had dogged him throughout his adolescence, but he was still out of shape. Having eaten little recently, Hector looked ill. His face was pale and his cheekbones sunken. His eyes were red-rimmed through lack of sleep as a result of his brother's nightly visitations. He knew he'd neglected to look after himself, but he'd be able to set that right. All he needed was to find a way to banish this vile.

He stopped outside the tavern's side door.

Turn back, came the whisper, a note of concern creeping into the vile's voice. Hector ignored it, raising his right hand to rap sharply on the frame. A wooden slat suddenly flew back, revealing a pair of squinting eyes. They looked him up and down, regarding him suspiciously.

'Help you?'

Hector didn't speak. He raised his right hand to reveal the signet ring Vincent had taken from their dead father. His twin had been wearing the ring around town, using it to gain entrance into all manner of places. Hector was under the impression that the ring carried some weight at the Broken Heart Tavern. If it didn't this would be a very short escapade. Thankfully for Hector the ring registered with the doorman, who slid the hatch back and unlocked the door, allowing the magister entrance.

Very clever, Hector.

Hector ignored the voice, passing the brute of a doorman who re-locked the door and gestured to a staircase that disappeared below ground. Hector nodded and stepped downstairs, his heart thundering like a Sturmish smith's hammer. The doorman watched the visitor descend.

The flight of stairs ended in a cellar. Barrels flanked him, the smells of stale beer and damp were overwhelming. A trail of tobacco smoke hung at head height, rolling out of an open door ahead.

'You came here to relax?' he muttered.

I came here to win money. They're all idiots down here who want to lose their coins.

'This was where you lost our money.'

Stop moaning, you little girl. Always whinging, crying like a baby . . .

'Shut up!' shouted Hector, just as a man appeared at the doorway, surprised at the magister's outburst. Hector smiled awkwardly as he stood to one side. The man shuffled past, giving him a wide berth.

'Shut . . . up . . .' whispered Hector, as he stepped through the doorway.

The room beyond was thick with smoke, with snugs and nooks on each wall that should have held barrels. With the curfew still in effect the barrels had been removed, freeing the cellar up as a gambling den. Each compartment now housed seats and small tables where men gathered to play various games: dice, mumbly-peg, deadly six, bones. A large lady sidled past with a tray of drinks on one arm. There were maybe twenty men in the room, some just here to get drunk while their friends cursed or cheered at their luck. Hector squinted through the foul smoke.

'Are you sure they'll be here?'

They're always here. They know no better. Money, Hector; gold drives a man.

'There they are!'

Four men sat at a round table as the steady *thunk-thunk-thunk* of a short-handled knife hit the wooden tabletop. Hector recognized the fat one straight away – Ibal. The giggler had his hand on the table, pudgy fingers splayed, stabbing the blade into the wood between each digit. Two of his companions threw insults as they tried to put him off, a pile of coppers wagered in the table centre. To his credit Ibal smiled and ignored them, concentrating on the task at hand. Beside him sat Ringlin, reclining against the bench they shared while puffing on a thin reed pipe. None of them had noticed Hector.

What will you do now, Hector? Kill these two – and then what? There must be two dozen men down here. You'd never get out of here alive.

Hector looked over his shoulder at the vile, an ethereal shadow hanging from his back. His throat was dry, his lips cracked and parched. His hand trembled under the cloak as it clutched the gaudy dagger.

What are you waiting for? Go on, coward. See how you fare against these two. If you think every murder will be as easy as mine you're in for an awfully big surprise, brother.

Hector tried to push Vincent from his mind as he stepped to the edge of the table. His knee caught the tabletop, knocking it. The knife came down and nicked Ibal's thumb with a wet *snick!*

'What the . . .' began Ringlin, going silent when he saw who stood over them. Ibal stuck his thumb in his mouth, sucking at the wound. He stopped when he saw Hector.

A white-haired man opposite reached out, grabbing the

coppers, dragging them across the table to empty into his lap. Ringlin never took his eyes off Hector as he spoke.

'Leave those coins, Poom. That game is void. You and Ibal may play again once we've attended to . . . *business.*'

'That was a fair win,' said the one called Poom.

'You can leave the coins or you can get a better look at the knife,' said Ringlin, still staring at Hector. 'Your call, old man.'

Begrudgingly Poom pushed the coins back into the table's centre, squeezing out and making for the bar. His companion followed him, mocking him all the way. Ringlin cast his hand to the now vacated seats.

'Please sit,' he said casually, but his eyes told a different story. They were narrow, trying to read Hector. Ibal was much the same, watching Hector with a mixture of fear and loathing.

They're wary of you? Unbelievable! Murdering me has made you fearsome, brother.

'Hardly,' said Hector.

'What's that?' asked Ringlin.

'Nothing,' said Hector awkwardly, sitting down on the bench opposite. His cheeks were flushed with colour as he realized they'd seen him talking to nobody.

'I can't say we were expecting to see you again, Lord Hector,' said Ringlin, his hands falling under the table. 'A little out of your depth, aren't you?'

That'll be him reaching for his long knife. You know the one — serrated edge, good for gutting pigs with. And Ibal has his sickle, remember?

'I know,' said Hector.

'You know?' said Ringlin. 'Then why come? Our business is closed since your brother . . . died. You remember that, don't you? We do.'

Ibal nodded, finding his voice with a gurgling giggle.

'I remember all too clearly,' said Hector. 'It was a terrible accident.'

He tried to block out the shrill laughter of the vile in his ear as Ringlin spoke.

'Count yourself lucky we never went to the authorities with what we saw. Would make for an interesting chat with the old Bear, wouldn't it?'

'He wouldn't believe you.'

'Mud sticks. Your reputation is already in pieces. A rumour could destroy you, let alone something that truly happened, Piggy!'

Hector's mind clouded quickly, ears thrumming as a headache struck out of nowhere. Everything in the room shifted and faded as his thoughts focused on Ringlin. He couldn't hear what Ringlin said, but he could make out his expressions well enough; smug smiles and sneering taunts. Hector found his left hand rising from beneath his cloak with a will of its own, black-gloved fingers reaching across the table. Immediately he felt the vile disengage, leaping across the table at his command and slithering round Ringlin's throat like a black noose. Instantly the rogue's eyes widened and his mouth stopped flapping, his hands shooting to his neck.

'Don't call me that.'

Hector heard his voice as if a stranger had said the words.

It was deep, alien, but it had come from his mouth. As he realized something awful was happening his ears popped, the sound in the room returning instantly. The vile was suddenly back on his shoulder, its grip on Ringlin released. The man fell forward, spluttering as he tried to gather his composure. Hector shook his head, trying to straighten his senses, hurriedly bringing his gloved hand back below the table. Ibal watched the two of them with wide eyes, his giggling silenced for once.

What was that? screeched Vincent in Hector's ear.

'I don't know,' mumbled Hector, shaking his head.

Ringlin rubbed his throat, staring at Hector with newfound fear.

'What do you want from us? We'll say nothing, you have our word. We owe your brother nothing.'

Dogs! spat the vile. *You owe me everything! You were penniless thugs when I met you. You're not shy of coin now! Kill them, Hector. Kill them now!*

Hector ignored his dead brother. He cleared his throat, still reeling from the darkness that had assailed him.

'You entered into a contract with the House of Redmire. My brother may be dead, but he paid you well to serve the Boars.'

'He paid us coppers,' sneered Ringlin.

'Then stay with me and see gold,' said Hector, his voice serious as he stared from one man to another. The two put their heads together, Ibal whispering something into Ringlin's ear. The tall man nodded before turning back to Hector.

'What's to stop us from just walking away?'

'Honour and consequence,' said Hector. 'The honour of service to Redmire.'

'And what consequences if we don't accept?'

'Do I need to answer that?'

For the first time in his life Hector allowed menace to creep into his voice. It would have been out of character but for the performance with the gloved hand. He placed it on the table now, flexing the black leather-clad fingers into a fist.

Clever, Hector. Fear is the only language they understand.

'Gold, you say?'

'Eventually, in good time. In the meantime I'll see you're paid whatever Vincent gave you. You shan't go without.'

Hector rose, sliding the gaudy dagger back into its sheath and straightening his cloak.

'Gather your winnings. I'll wait for you upstairs.' With that Hector made his way back to street level.

I don't understand. Why would you want those turncoats working for you? They'll betray you the first chance they get.

'I shall treat them differently. Boundaries, Vincent; you made none and they took advantage of that. I won't make the same mistake.'

No, you'll make all new ones, sneered the vile. *And I'll be there to laugh when you do.*

'Interesting what happened in there, Vincent. The command . . .'

The vile fell silent for a moment.

My kind have never known of such a thing. What necromancy was that?

'I don't know, but I'll find out.'

Hector arrived upstairs, waiting for the men to join him. The doorman watched him with suspicion, but Hector was past worrying about what others thought about him this night.

But why Ringlin and Ibal? With all they know?

'Precisely because of that. I'll keep my friends close, but my enemies closer. You said yourself they're dangerous. I may have use for such fellows in the weeks and months ahead. I fear Lyssia is on the brink of something terrible.'

The two rogues arrived at the top of the stairs, grabbing their cloaks from pegs on the wall.

'Where to, boss?' said Ringlin, straightening the long knives in his weapon belt. Ibal patted the bag of coins at his hip, allowing himself a brief triumphant giggle.

'Bevan's Tower,' said Hector. 'And it's not boss. It's Baron Hector, Lord of Redmire.'

6

Power Play

Lord Broghan awoke suddenly as a fist hit his stomach. He winced as the hessian bag was whipped off his head and sunlight streamed into the courtroom of High Stable. A single manacle was fastened round his left wrist, keeping him chained to the wall. He struggled to rise. His arm was dislocated, his enemies having left him hanging from the wall since his capture. He struggled to focus his eyes, disoriented as blurred silhouettes passed before him.

'What is the meaning of this?' he shouted, raising his free hand to his eyes as he yanked on the chain. A huge bald north-man stood in front of him, his own right arm in a sling, his other fist still curled from the punch. The man wore a golden breast-plate that marked him instantly as one of King Leopold's men. His grin was framed by a dirty grey beard. He threw another punch, striking Broghan's stomach with a meaty thwack.

'Enough!' came a voice from behind the northman. The brute stood to one side, allowing his master to step forward. Broghan recognized the voice immediately: Prince Lucas, the Lion of Highcliff. The left-hand side of his face bore a trio of scars, a new addition since he'd last seen the boy.

'Still getting others to fight your battles, Lucas?'

The young Lion moved fast, snarling as he struck Broghan across the face with his fist. The Bearlord spat a glob of blood on to the floor, narrowly missing the Lion's boot.

'Kitten's got claws after all then . . .'

Broghan's eyes took in the chamber. He was standing on a platform at one of the higher points of the huge circular room. The wall he was chained to was beside a broad balcony that overlooked the city beyond. Gathered in the chamber below were the various Werelords of the region, all watching as the Lionlord strutted across the platform. Viscount Colt stood at the shoulder of Duke Lorimer, their brother Horselords standing around them. By the looks on their faces, there was little approval for Lucas's antics. Lord Conrad, the young blond noble, stood apart from the others, his own eyes trained on another captive in the room. Lady Gretchen stood on the opposite side of the chamber from Broghan on another raised platform, staring at him fearfully, a pair of red-cloaked Lionguards keeping watch over her. The Wererat Vankaskan stood beside her, grinning wickedly. There was no sign of Harker. And where was Drew? Where was Whitley?

Broghan's mind was addled. He recalled confronting Duke Lorimer upon his arrival and seeking the support of the

Horselords, but after that his recollections blurred. He'd struggled to keep the Bear at bay, passing out with exhaustion. Harker had taken him to a guest chamber and that was all he remembered. He'd woken up to a nightmare.

'Where is the Wolf?' roared Lucas.

'I don't know.'

'Don't lie to me, Bear! My men encountered him in the city. He caused a good deal of distress, especially to poor Colbard here.'

Lucas gestured to the big northman who rubbed his injured arm as if to stress the point.

Broghan laughed. *Well done, Drew.*

'Silence!' Lucas backhanded the Bearlord across the face.

'Prince Lucas,' cried out Lorimer below. 'Please be gentle with Lord Broghan. Remember, he is a brother Werelord, Your Highness.'

'Don't call him that!' shouted Broghan. 'There's nothing royal about this brat. He's a puppet, to his father and the rats. Have you taken leave of your senses, Lorimer, siding with these villains?'

Lucas moved to strike Broghan once again, but two of the Horseguard on the platform moved to stand in his way. The prince relented, but his look of hatred didn't change. He stepped back, joining the bald northman who had meted out the punches.

'I take no pleasure in hosting *any* of you in Cape Gala,' said Lorimer, his voice breaking.

'Hosting?' Broghan laughed incredulously, rattling the chain.

'You have to understand, Lord Broghan. My fellow Horselords and I have granted Prince Lucas shelter in return for his father's blessing. Independence is what we seek, not bloodshed.'

'Yet you side with a deposed king and his insane son? This is madness! You should be speaking with my father and the Staglords, working towards a better future for all.'

'A free Longridings *is* a better future, certainly for all in Cape Gala,' cried the elderly Viscount Colt, stepping out from behind the shadow of Lorimer. 'Westland gives us nothing.'

'You're wrong, Colt! Leopold has given you nothing – things can be different with the Wolf on the throne!'

'Enough,' said Lucas. 'The time for debate has passed, Bear. I've given our host my word that I shall spare your life as long as he is Lord of the Longridings. Contrary to what you may think, I'm a man of my word.'

'You're a child and a fool. You should have fled when you had the chance. My father and his allies won't stand for this. Lyssia shall not stand for this. You've missed your boat to Bast, cat!'

Lucas's laugh echoed round the chamber, building into a roar. The Horselords shivered below, the mortal men of the Lionguard and Horseguard flinching. Birds that roosted on the balcony took flight.

'You think we're *fleeing*?' He clapped his thigh, slapping the big northman on the shoulder as he wiped away tears of laughter. 'Look out over the harbour once again, Bear.'

Broghan let his gaze wander over the port. He hadn't noticed previously, but there they were. Six huge ships were anchored in the bay, a flotilla of smaller vessels pulling away from them as soldiers disembarked on to Lyssian soil. Prince Lucas clapped his hands together with delight.

'Fleeing? Ha! I'm here to greet family!'

Broghan gulped, looking frantically back across the room towards Gretchen. She stared back in horror.

'The Catlords come.'

There was no herald to mark the arrival of the Bastian soldiers. Fully thirty boats moored in the harbour and lightly armoured foreigners flooded on to the streets. The City Watch stood to one side, the men passing unopposed. The arrival of hundreds of golden-skinned warriors from Bast was beyond their knowledge and experience. Instinct told them to challenge the force, but doubt ensured that they watched them march by to High Stable, impotent and ineffective.

The storm clouds had long departed. Bright sunlight blazed down upon the warriors as they marched up to the citadel, watched by the populace. The men wore light mail shirts or breastplates and carried spears, swords and shields. Light sandals were laced on their feet while bracers protected their forearms. They looked deadly.

The Horseguard of High Stable were made of sterner stuff than the Watch. Refusing to let them enter, the Horseguard barred the doors to the foreign soldiers, who stood ready to force their way in if the order came. But there was no need, for Lucas's Lionguard moved quickly to see them opened. The protestations of the Horseguard ceased once the Bastians began to march into the courtyard. They stood by silently as the invaders entered High Stable.

★

The doors to the courtroom of the Horselords slammed open as fifty warriors entered the ancient chamber, fanning out and ringing the round room in moments. The Horselords looked furious. The last thing they had expected was armed soldiers entering their most sacred chamber.

'This is an outrage!' snorted Lorimer, his cry of disgust joined by other Horselords. They stamped their feet angrily, throwing their heads and gnashing their teeth. Facets of the Horses showed on their forms and faces – manes filling, nostrils flaring, shoulders broadening. Broghan watched, recognizing their performance for what it was – a gesture too late in the day. He caught sight of one of the Horselords who wasn't joining in the chorus. The young one, Conrad, just stood by, looking saddened.

Lucas danced down the steps with the eagerness of a child keen to impress his father. Six golden skinned men in fine battledress entered the room, full helmets covering their faces. Black horsehair plumed over the tops of the helms, trailing down their backs. The Lords of the Longridings shivered with revulsion. Between the six men strode a woman.

She prowled into the room, graceful and sleek, deadlier than the men who surrounded her. She wore little – a thin black dress that allowed the light through its material and revealed more than was decent in a Lyssian court. Horselords gasped at her attire as she slunk her way to the room's centre. Her black skin was so dark as to be almost purple, the sun's morning rays shining off the surface, her shaved head swaying as she stalked the room. Green eyes flashed as she cast her glare over all. She was the most fascinating woman Broghan had ever seen.

Lucas dropped to one knee as she approached. She lowered her hand and he took it. Broghan expected the prince to kiss it, but instead he rubbed it against either side of his face, marking his throat with her scent. Broghan shivered, finding the greeting perverse compared to the Lyssian tradition.

'Lady Opal,' said Lucas, his head bowed. 'Welcome to my kingdom.'

'Off the floor, Lucas,' she said wearily. 'It doesn't suit a Catlord to be on his belly, especially one who claims to own a kingdom.'

'But this *is* my kingdom, Lady Opal. Well, that is, my father's kingdom.'

'Of course it is,' she said drily, staring at the assembled Werelords. She briefly cast her eyes over Broghan. 'And don't call me Lady – Opal is the name I was blessed with, and that will suffice. I have no need for the ridiculous titles these Lyssians like to bandy about.'

Lucas nodded, embarrassed.

'Tell me,' she called out. 'Who's in charge here?'

Duke Lorimer stepped forward from where he stood with Baron Ewan, keeping his chin up as he approached the woman. *Good on you*, thought Broghan. *Let her know this is your courtroom. She should be bowing to you. That's the one thing you've done right so far, Horselord.* She looked him up and down, arching an eyebrow when she saw he refused to bow.

'I am Duke Lorimer, Lord of the Longridings,' he said stiffly. 'Welcome to Cape Gala.'

She nodded, gesturing with her hand that he should continue. He looked surprised, expecting her to introduce herself more formally. Opal wasn't forthcoming. Her six bodyguards in the horsehair helms stood to attention behind her like statues.

'I must say it's unorthodox to arrive in Cape Gala unannounced, and furthermore to enter High Stable with armed men. My people frown on such actions and it's a slight against our realm.'

'Slight or not, I see no reason to *announce* my arrival. You need to catch up, Horse. Times are changing. You'll answer to me now.'

'With respect, my lady, I answer to nobody. My only agreement is with King Leopold, and my allegiance lies with him until the Longridings takes its independence from the Seven Realms. This has been agreed in principle with Prince Lucas, in return for our favour to him. Soon, the Horselords shall answer to no one.'

'Whatever agreement you believe you have with the prince and his father, you may now disregard. You and the other Werelords of Lyssia have committed treason against our brother Cat by forcing him off his throne.'

Lorimer looked astonished.

'We Horselords did no such thing. We've remained neutral throughout the troubles in Westland, and remain so now.'

'Neutral is not loyal, Horselord,' she sneered, strolling round him as she stared down any who dared look at her. She yawned, revealing dazzling white teeth with slightly enlarged canines.

'We are a peaceful people, my lady. Ask Prince Lucas – he will vouch for our kindness.'

'I think I'm suitably informed,' she said, taking a silver shortsword from the scabbard of one of her bodyguards. She spun and lunged, dropping to her knee as she thrust, the sword disappearing up to the hilt in the duke's stomach. She twisted it once to the right, before dancing back in a single fluid movement. The sword whipped free, followed by a torrent of blood. Lorimer had hit the floor before the assembled Horselords could gasp.

The Werelords screamed, chaos breaking out in an instant as they rushed towards their dead liege. Opal's bodyguards stepped forward over the body, their weapons drawn, as their companions all readied their arms as well. The Horseguard were helpless, disarmed in a moment by Lucas's Lionguard. Broghan watched the chaos unfold, powerless.

'I might suggest,' shouted Opal, 'your immediate silence lest you suffer the same fate as this proud fool. You need to know our ... *displeasure* with your actions in helping the Wolf take the throne. Consequently, I expect you to learn from the lesson of your duke.' She nudged his body with her foot, which brought a fresh wave of gasps. She glowered and they were silent again.

'I expect your unwavering obedience henceforth. Nothing is too good for my men. Treat them like your fathers while they watch over this city in my absence. Prove your loyalty and you shall be rewarded.'

She walked up the steps towards the Wererat and Gretchen, Lucas at her shoulder.

'Gretchen, I presume?' she said to the Fox. The red-haired girl nodded, her face pale from the sight of the murder she'd just witnessed. 'You'll wait here in the custody of Vankaskan until we return from business in the north.' She turned to the Ratlord, 'I trust you can take care of matters in our absence?'

The Wererat nodded humbly.

'No task is too great, Your Highness.' He nodded towards the body of the slain Horselord. 'Lorimer. I have . . . *use* for his body. May I?'

Opal looked at Vankaskan quizzically for a moment, considering his strange request before shrugging and coldly nodding.

'He's hardly much use to his people any more. He's all yours. Who is that?' she asked, pointing across the chamber where Broghan stood chained to the wall.

'The Bearlord, Broghan,' sneered Lucas. 'Bergan's offspring, the traitor from Brackenholme who dethroned my father.'

'Interesting,' she said, handing him the silver shortsword. 'Kill him.'

Lucas looked shocked.

'You heard me, child,' said Opal, staring at Gretchen as tears welled in her eyes. She shook her head from side to side, sobbing openly, straining against her chains towards the distant Bearlord. 'This is where you start to scrape back some honour for Bast, Lucas. A slight against one Catlord is a slight against us all.'

She held the blade out again.

'Kill him.'

Broghan watched from where he stood, his heart shuddering as Lucas took the blade. The boy prince looked up across the round chamber, a flight of steps leading down to the pit at the bottom and then back up to the platform opposite. The Lion looked fearful; Broghan could see that from where he stood. All eyes were on the prince.

He began to stumble around the top of the circular chamber, following the curving wall, passing pillar and post slowly. It was maybe fifty feet in all. As he drew closer to Broghan the Bearlord could see the Lion's face changing slowly, from a look of dread to one of decisiveness. His choice made, he began to pick up speed. His golden mane emerged as he jogged, his teeth and jaws jutting and his body changing. The run became a lope, the sword raised high. By the time Lucas had covered the distance he was almost bounding, the Werelion leaping through the air with a roar. Broghan closed his eyes at the last moment, as the shortsword flew to his heart. Gretchen's scream was the final sound to hit his ears as the world fell silent and dark.

7

Blood and Rain

The storm from the south had taken hold of Highcliff and was refusing to relinquish its grip. The streets were slick with rivers of rainwater, racing down to the Low Quarter where they found the White Sea. The ships that were anchored clashed into one another, battling against the elements. The navy was at sea, leaving the harbour strangely quiet. As lightning flashed over the city, the lone figure of King Leopold could be seen, running along the battlements of Highcliff Keep, roaring angrily into the storm clouds. He was half-transformed, letting the rage take him as he celebrated the beast within. From the High Square, Duke Bergan watched.

The Raging Lion; that's how they used to describe him in battle, Bergan recalled. Back when he and Wergar faced him as younger men, Leopold had always been a sight to behold. He embraced the monster on the battlefield, discarding caution and giving in to pure aggression. He was a force of nature. Bergan only wished that force was spent now. There was something different about the old Lion's antics this night.

'Don't you feel it, Bergan?' roared Leopold, waving his clawed arms out before him, wheeling in the rain. 'Change is coming!'

'Change is here, right now, Leopold!' he bellowed up to the Lion. 'We are the change.' He cast his hand behind him at the assembled soldiers of Westland. They were diminished now, with the departure of Earl Mikkel's men, but they were still to be reckoned with.

'You had your chance,' yelled the king. Bergan glanced at the men who sheltered from the rain and enemy arrows behind him. Some blocked their ears when the Lion roared, terrified by the cry. Hector watched from a position nearby, his hood up and soaking wet. The young magister watched Bergan, nodding his support.

'It's over, Leopold! Stop prolonging the inevitable! How sick with starvation and disease are your men? Save their lives by surrendering your own!'

'Don't you smell it on the wind? In the rain, Bergan? You had your chance! I'm taking my city back! Your Wolf's Council is breaking around you, and you don't even know it! Run, Bear! *Run!*'

The Werelion laughed, smashing whatever he could find on the ramparts; crates, ladders, barrels. He lifted the splintered wood, tossing it wildly over the walls.

'Highcliff will be mine again!' he roared.

A voice called to Bergan from the barricades. It was Reuben Fry, the Bearlord's best archer and captain.

'I have him, my lord. I can take him.'

Fry had his longbow drawn back to its fullest length, the wood straining as the rain spattered the Sturmlander in the face. His fingers trembled as he held his aim, the arrow ready for flight. The silver head shone in the moonlight.

'Do it,' whispered Hector. 'If you have the shot, take him out!'

'No,' said Bergan, raising a hand to halt the attack. 'We won't stoop to the level of our enemies.'

'But we can end this now!' gasped Hector.

'No, Hector,' snapped the Bearlord. 'That isn't our way. Silver is outlawed. Lower your bow, Captain Fry. We'll find another way.'

The Sturmlander reluctantly lowered his bow, taking the rare arrow and placing it back into the mahogany box at his feet. Hector picked up the case and locked it shut, stowing it under his arm while he glowered at the duke through the drizzle.

'Brenn show us the way to defeat him,' whispered Bergan as the Lion continued to rage.

While other ships struggled against the storm and sea, one was in its element. The waves crashed against the fleet, battering it mercilessly as rain lashed down from the dark heavens. Almost beaten by the conditions, each vessel only just managed to remain in formation behind the lead ship, the graceful *Maelstrom* racing ahead as they struggled to keep pace. Count Vega stood on the deck, feet locked in position on the pitching ship as it scythed through the sea. His men ran about, preparing their ship for battle. The sea marshal kept his gaze fixed ahead, intermittently catching sight of their quarry.

The short, wiry figure of Figgis, his helmsman, manned the wheel. Small as the old man was he handled the great wheel with practised ease, holding it firm where lesser men might have been thrown from the deck. There was nothing Vega wouldn't trust his chief mate with, the elderly pirate having served alongside his father on the *Harbinger*. Indeed, Figgis had seen to the disposal of Vincent, the Boarlord, spiriting the body away from Bevan Tower in the dead of night. Vega didn't ask what had become of the corpse; he didn't need to. He had every confidence in Figgis that the corrupt Werelord's final resting place would never be uncovered.

Vega allowed his thoughts to drift briefly to Hector. He worried about him. The Baron of Redmire had already endured a terrible ordeal, witnessing his father's murder and being partly responsible for his own brother's death. The communing controversy hadn't gone away, a dark cloud over his reputation. Vega had watched him transform from a chubby, cheery young fellow into a shadow of his former self. The sooner he was reunited with Drew the better; separation from his best friend had been tough, and Vega imagined that with the Wolf back they'd see the old Hector again. In the meantime the Shark had taken it upon himself to keep an eye out for the young Boar.

The sea before them raged, mighty waves crashing over the bow, the horizon constantly dipping and shifting. Vega could no longer see the ship they pursued. He looked up the rigging of the main mast. The crouched figure in the crow's nest could be seen beyond the taut, straining sails, the icy rain whipping by like flying daggers. The boy was flinging his arms frantically, trying to catch their attention over the storm's roar.

'Figgis,' shouted Vega, pointing to the mast. 'The deck's yours.'

Figgis glanced up, nodding sharply as he returned his attention to the wheel.

The *Maelstrom* pitched hard to starboard, a mighty wave threatening to send her off course, but she wouldn't be denied. Vega ran, sure-footed and swift, leaping off a rail and grabbing the rigging, waves rushing by beneath him. In moments he was racing up the ropes towards the crow's nest. He could see the closest following ship of Westland's fleet was a tenth of a league behind. His fleet numbered thirty three ships, a mixture of galleons and converted merchant vessels called into service. Of those, ten were working warships, manned by experienced naval men.

The lone ship they chased had been spied off the south-eastern coasts of the Cluster Isles. There had been no mistaking it as a fighting vessel, equipped with light catapults and archers' decks. It carried a single black flag, marking it as a pirate ship, but something jarred for Vega. Its design and build told him it was foreign and a long way from home. And the black flag wasn't traditionally used by the pirates of the White Sea – he would know as Pirate Prince of the Cluster Isles. In the light of the omens his men had witnessed, it had been only right to approach the strange vessel, and when it raced off – hardly the action of an innocent party – the fleet had given chase. Vega had never lost a pursuit, and no storm from Brenn or Sosha was going to stop him today. The black flag must be close now. He would have his ship.

Vega scrambled to the top of the mast, where the cabin boy Casper held on for dear life. The *Maelstrom* was rocking now, the momentum with which the crow's nest swayed threatening to throw the cabin boy from his seat. Still the boy held on as instructed, one hand twined round the support rope within the barrel. Vega grinned, admiring his courage. The smile of the captain was all Casper needed to inspire confidence.

'What is it, son?' shouted Vega, clinging on as they pitched one way then the other in the rolling sea. The boy pointed ahead, over the crashing waves. The count followed his finger, spying the ship. It had turned hard to port, arcing away along a new line. Vega shouted over the screaming wind.

'She's trying to run, lad, but she won't make it! We'll have her, and there'll be no more talk of omens!'

The boy tugged at Vega before he could descend, pulling him closer to yell in his ear. There was a reason Vega had sent Casper to the crow's nest. The boy had the best eyesight on the *Maelstrom*.

'Not the black flag, captain,' he shouted. 'The others!'

Vega strained to look through the storm at the horizon. It was hard to tell their actual number, but as they loomed into view he figured there were more than a hundred ships. These weren't converted merchant vessels or requisitioned ships. These were galleons and men-o'-war. Vega could see the bare black flag flying from each ship in the mightiest armada he'd ever seen. That was when the copper dropped.

'The black flag,' he whispered, his voice carried away on the screaming wind. 'Onyx.'

The campfires belched dark smoke into the night sky, struggling to remain lit in the rain. Only the hardiest soldiers of Stormdale braved the conditions, maintaining the fires while their companions sheltered in their tents. Earl Mikkel stood by his tent door, grimacing. He allowed the flap to swing shut, stepping back into his command tent where his captain waited for him.

'Any word back from the scouts yet?'

'None yet, my lord,' replied the stocky Captain Harriman.

Mikkel was disappointed not to have heard back from his outriders yet. His small army of two hundred had camped north of the Great West Road, on the edge of bandit country. A smaller troop of soldiers might have been concerned about Sherriff Muller and his skirmishers, but a group this size had nothing to fear. Mikkel had sent half a dozen riders to alert various towns throughout the Dalelands of the developments in Westland and the stalemate with Leopold. Specifically he'd sent two on to the Barebones, one rider heading for his own town of Highwater while the other would continue on to the family stronghold of Stormdale.

'Odd,' grumbled the Staglord. 'I'd have expected to have had riders back from at least Hedgemoor and Redmire by now.'

'Perhaps the poor weather has kept them off the road?'

'Very amusing, Harriman,' smiled Mikkel. The men of the Barebones were as hardy as any in Lyssia. A bit of rain wouldn't keep them from their task.

A low rumble rolled over the camp, audible over the constant drumming of the rain on the tent roof.

'You hear that, my lord? This storm gets worse. Thank Brenn we brought the tents or we might have drowned.'

Mikkel nodded, looking down at the map that they'd laid out on a travel chest. He wondered where Drew might be, and if he'd managed to rescue Gretchen. It irked the Staglord that he'd been unable to exact justice upon Vankaskan. He only hoped, if the opportunity arose, that Drew could avenge Kohl's death and the maiming of Manfred.

The earl studied the map. Five days travel from Highwater, then he'd be back in his dear Shona's arms. He smiled. He'd missed his family and the mountain air. The rumbling continued, louder now, causing the pebbles that held the map down to dance and rattle along its surface. He placed a hand over a stone, feeling the tremors ride up through the chest below. Mikkel looked up at Harriman.

'That's not thunder,' he shouted, snatching his greatsword from its scabbard.

The Staglord yanked back the door just in time to see the first horseman riding through the camp, launching a spear from his hand. Twenty feet away the spear found its target in one of Mikkel's men, catapulting him into the wall of his tent. Enraged, the earl strode into the rain, embracing the Stag with each step. His ribcage groaned as his chest ballooned, muscles rising over his shoulders and neck as he snorted with fury. His face grew long, skin darkening as antlers ripped free from his head. A wicked arrangement of deadly spikes emerged, glistening with blood from his torn brow. In his hands he swung his greatsword, the now diminutive figure of Captain Harriman by his side.

Hooves thundered as hundreds of horseman galloped through the camp. Spears, arrows and blazing torches flew as the unprepared men of Stormdale staggered from their flaming tents into a hail of deadly missiles. Mikkel lashed out as one of the riders passed too close, the sword almost cutting the man in two. Another horseman followed, catching a chestful of the Staglord's antlers. Mikkel hoisted the man from his saddle, flinging him through the air as he collided with another rider.

'For Stormdale!' he bellowed, rushing into the melee as his men found their courage at last. Harriman ran beside him, his longsword slashing and parrying blows. The riders drew scimitars, the curved blades whistling through the rain as they hacked at the Staglord's men. The earl's soldiers were now greatly outnumbered, being whittled down by the over-whelming force.

Mikkel found himself surrounded by the riders, quickly separated from his men. No sooner did he bring down a rider than another replaced his fallen comrade. Each time he gored a horseman or battered one with his greatsword, he felt a rain of blows from behind. Scimitars hacked through the broad, bare flesh of his back, each one more painful than the last as the therianthrope struggled to keep his feet.

The Staglord caught sight of Harriman's body in the mud nearby, his eyes glazed over as the horsemen continued their murderous spree. His own vision blurred as he felt the scimi-tars striking him. The greatsword was heavy now, the unrelenting assault taking its toll.

A voice shouted in a language Mikkel didn't understand. Immediately the riders ceased their attack, drawing back, leaving Mikkel to drop to his knees in a bloodied puddle. He snorted, struggling to catch his breath, head slumped against his chest. *Thank Brenn*, thought the Staglord. *Mercy*.

'Parlay,' cried Mikkel, raising his heavy head as a single rider rode forward. His antlers made his head loll back and the Werelord release his grip on his greatsword and lifted shattered hands to his face. He tried to wipe the blood and rain from his eyes to better see the smiling rider on horseback.

'It can't be,' mouthed the Stag silently, instantly recognizing the horseman's origin. Mikkel's jaw went slack with horror at the precise moment the scimitar flew down, scything cleanly through the Staglord's neck.

PART V

Biting Back

I

The Uninvited Guest

Cape Gala was changed. Where previously the streets had been a centre for trade and commerce, they stood empty. The storm had passed, but a menacing cloud hung over the city. This was nowhere more obvious than at the citadel. Gone were the elegant corridors, open windows and cool breezes blowing freely through the courtroom of High Stable. In their place hung dark drapes blotting out the sun, the floor littered with waste and the Horseguard replaced by warriors from Bast. The Rat was now in residence.

With Vankaskan on the throne, the city bore more resemblance to the hideous Vermire far in the north, home to the Rat King. His position might only be temporary until the Catlords returned from Westland, but he would enjoy himself while it lasted. Vankaskan was all for indulgence, gorging himself on every whim and fancy that caught his eye. Colbard,

Sorin and the others had remained while Prince Lucas sailed north. They respected and feared the Wererat in equal parts, and as such were his trusted lieutenants while he governed the city. The soldiers from Bast were remarkably loyal, doing whatever the Rat demanded of them. Left to his own devices, he was free to pursue his passion: experimenting in dark magistery. In short, Vankaskan was very content.

The Rat hadn't strayed from the courtroom since Opal had left, making the place his own. His request for the body of Duke Lorimer had been met with widespread disgust by the entire court, but none dared question the Rat. They'd seen what fate awaited those who stood against the Lion's allies. Lorimer's wasn't the only corpse the Rat had seized. None sought audience with the Wererat, but all the Lords of the Longridings were forced to visit and swear fealty to him, an abhorrent act that Vankaskan delighted in. Nothing prepared them for the blasphemy they encountered within the once great courtroom of High Stable.

With all eyes on High Stable that evening, nobody noticed the shadow that danced along the rooftops of the towers and townhouses nearest the citadel walls. Crouching and hugging the slates, the figure crawled, jumped and skipped ever closer, searching for the ideal launch. He halted above an attic window, three storeys above street level. The roof leaned precariously out, overhanging the building below — the ramparts of High Stable almost thirty feet away and six feet lower.

Drew held his breath, controlling his heart rate. He heard

occasional screams escaping the stone tower. *What madness is going on in there?* He prayed they hadn't captured Whitley. His friends – Broghan, Harker, possibly Gretchen – were all in the citadel. He'd witnessed Lucas riding out of High Stable to the harbour, accompanied by frightful looking soldiers. With the Lion gone that left the Rat in command, and Drew was all too aware what Vankaskan was capable of.

Drew spied no guards on the wall. He wore little – torn leggings and a tattered cloak, everything else having been lost in the chaos that followed their ambush. It was time to let the beast come. He could feel his limbs elongating, toes and fingers growing, claws emerging as he clung to the tiles. Within moments he was part changed, his build dramatically altered into that of a wolfman. He took a couple of steps back, his lupine feet finding a better grip. He crouched, bouncing on his knees as he readied for his leap. With two quick bounds he was off the roof, his powerful legs launching him into the air and the street beyond. Broken tiles scattered behind him as the Werewolf flew through the sky, arms reaching forward as he covered the distance in one graceful animal bound.

Drew landed on all fours, claws digging into the stone walkway, his momentum almost carrying him over the wall and into the courtyard. Below he could see numerous people, all too busy to lift their gaze. If anyone had glanced up they'd have caught sight of a ferocious looking Werewolf trying not to fall into their midst. Drew retreated from the edge, staying low. He glanced along the wall, grateful for the dark of night and lack of guards patrolling. He let the beast recede, steadying his breathing to human levels and allowing his physique to return to normal. Drew studied High Stable with fresh eyes, the Wolf caged for the time being.

A loud wail echoed from the citadel. *What in Brenn's name is that?* Drew dashed along the wall, past an open stairwell where he heard voices approaching. *That'll be the guards, then.* High Stable's outer walls were circular, running around the central citadel tower in a great ring. There were the main gates at the front in the western section, plus two smaller gates to the north and south-east. He'd observed the citadel frequently since he'd set his mind on freeing his friends. Looking down from above, the eastern side of the great tower was the quietest area, a stableblock running along its length. Drew scampered round, finding a point where he could drop on to the stable's thatched roof. From here he could jump down to the courtyard. A convenient stack of hay had been piled in the corner at one end, allowing him a soft landing.

Emerging from the haystack Drew stayed in the shadows, surveying High Stable from the rear. He'd paid it little attention when he'd first arrived in the city, more focused on its occupants than the structure itself. Now he had to find a way in and avoid the guards for as long as possible. The citadel was maybe six or seven storeys tall. The large regal balcony of the courtroom was visible five floors up, black curtains flapping into the night. While the grand staircase rose up to the white wooden doors at High Stable's entrance, the back door was a more modest affair. A dozen guards were posted at the front to meet guests and remove weapons, whereas just one guard stood to the rear, chatting idly to the occasional house staff as they came in and out of the tower. *I guess that's my way in*, Drew figured.

Drew could see the guarded storeroom where his sword had been taken. Now wasn't the time to search for the Wolfshead blade. He was here to rescue his friends, and if that meant he had to do it with tooth and claw as opposed to his father's cold steel then so be it. He allowed himself a small prayer to Brenn, that the old sword would find its way into the hands of a noble and worthy owner, and said his silent goodbyes.

The opening of the main gates drew attention towards the front of the citadel, with even the rear guard wandering around the tower to observe what was going on. Drew could see a trio of caravans entering the courtyard, their colourful wagons marking them as entertainers. Sword-swallowers, fire eaters, snake charmers, musicians – the guards' torches illuminated the crude paintings along the wagons' sides. Soldiers escorted the caravan in with a ripple of excitement at the prospect of entertainment for the troops. It afforded Drew the perfect opportunity to dash across the courtyard and through the back door unchallenged.

A servants' corridor ran through the building, with doors on either wall. To his right he found an empty guardroom, a couple of bunks and little else. A rich brown cloak of the Horseguard hung from the wall on a peg. Drew snatched it up, tearing off his own tattered cloak and shoving it under a bunk. He opened the chest, finding a full bronze helm looking back at him. Pulling the cloak round himself he checked its length, happy to see that it covered most of his body. He put the helmet on, snapping it into place. At a glance he looked like a Horseguard. A more observant viewer might notice the bare feet, but Drew was grateful for the dark. He stepped back out of the guardroom.

A staircase rose up to the left of the back door, following the curvature of the citadel walls. Quickly he was up it, taking two or three steps in a bound, his bare feet slapping against granite. His chest was tight with anticipation. The last person he wanted to bump into was a servant or some other innocent. He wanted to find his friends and get out as painlessly as possible. Passing two landings, he figured he was close to the fourth floor and the Horselords' chamber. The staircase ended abruptly, leading into a sweeping circular corridor that Drew figured ran around the courtroom. He risked a glance, catching sight of the occasional noble and soldiers in the gallery before ducking back into the stairwell.

I can't stay here. Someone's bound to use the staircase at any moment.

Taking a deep breath he stepped into the wide curving corridor and set off round its edge, staying close to the outer wall and its tall windows. The corridor was gloomy, very few torches lit in the walls. The cold that struck up from the floor took Drew by surprise – there was something unnatural about the chill.

A cry from within the courtroom echoed around the gallery, causing the Horselords present to kiss their knuckles in prayer. Even the soldiers he passed looked shaken, Horseguard and golden-skinned southerners alike. They kept apart, passing one another and saying nothing. *What are these warriors doing in Cape Gala?* Drew's head thundered. Everything stank of disorder and chaos. *Where have they come from?*

Drew had almost completed a circuit of the gallery when he spied Baron Ewan. The Ramlord stood in a window alcove, talking to the young Horselord Drew had seen when they'd first entered High Stable. *Is it Conrad? If I can catch Ewan's eye I might stand a chance. He'll help. He'll know where Gretchen is.*

Drew edged nearer, keeping enough distance not to arouse suspicion but coming close enough to hear what they discussed. The Wolf's heightened hearing could aid him here. He stood against a wall to attention, as he'd seen other soldiers doing, praying his bare feet were hidden beneath his cloak's shadow.

'I can't stand by and watch this horror,' whispered the blond Horselord. 'He's making a mockery of High Stable. It is perverse and goes against Brenn's will. Someone should stop him.'

'And who would that be, Conrad?' asked the Ramlord. 'Are you going to stop him? Then what? You'd never get out of here alive.'

'Better to make a stand and die than live through this ghastly circus!'

'And if you fail, what then? You know it doesn't end with death. It'll be you he plays with next, and it'll be your hands and teeth that he sets upon your loved ones.'

'Vankaskan needs to be stopped, by whatever means necessary.'

'You should have left; nothing but death awaits man and therian in Cape Gala.'

'You're still here,' said the Horselord quietly. 'I'd have

thought you'd have returned to Haggard by now. Will you not fight them?'

'I've no fight left in me. The Catlords are our new masters, and we've nobody left to aid us. Your brethren diminish by the day, Conrad. Who will you turn to for help?'

Drew jumped as he heard Conrad snort. The Horselord's leg lifted, wanting to stamp with anger, and it took all his willpower to stop it. Drew was relieved. The last thing Conrad needed was to draw the attention of the foreign warriors. Ewan gripped his forearm to calm him.

'Your uncle's body's in there, Conrad. And there'll be more until Opal returns and puts an end to the Rat's madness. Who knows when that will be? Will there be any Horselords left by then?'

'Then we make a stand!'

'The time for the Longridings to make a stand has been and gone, young one,' sighed Ewan sadly. 'The enemy is within your home, feasting from your table and treating you as his servant. This is what we're left with – serving a new master. All we can do is look after our own. Return home, Conrad; go to your people, protect and defend them.'

'What will you do?' the Horselord asked, fixing his gaze on the Ramlord.

'Return to Haggard and take care of my wife and people. The Longridings is a broken realm now; Brenn knows what will happen to the rest of Lyssia. All we can do is look after our own. If that means servitude, then so be it.'

'Servitude? You surrender to these Bastians without putting up a fight?'

Ewan shook his head.

'The horse has bolted, if you'll pardon the expression. It's all about survival now.'

Conrad turned, bottling up his anger and strode away. He marched past Drew, disappearing down the darkened corridor. *I like him*, thought Drew as the Horselord vanished. Ewan stood alone by the tall window, looking down upon Cape Gala. Another scream, louder than any of the others, rattled through the corridor. The Ramlord clutched his chest, as if the shriek pierced his heart. Drew stepped closer, keeping his back to the wall.

'My lord,' he said.

'What is it, man?' muttered the Lord of Haggard. Drew checked that nobody was passing and the corridor was quiet. It was late and the night threw a dark blanket over High Stable. He lifted the helmet, turning back to his friend. Instantly Ewan grabbed Drew, pulling him into the alcove, banging into and almost toppling over a tall brass candlestick. He steadied the metal post with a trembling hand.

'Drew! What are you doing here? You should have stayed away!'

'Leave my friends? Impossible. I'd die for those people. Where are they?'

'Oh, Drew, it isn't as simple as that,' he sighed, his face etched with sadness and heartache. 'Everything's changed. The Horselords have been broken.'

'I heard that nobleman – Conrad? He spoke sense, Ewan. Band together; make a stand. It's the only way, my friend. Trust your fellow Werelords against this new threat.'

'Did you not hear? It's too *late* to make a stand.'

'It's never too late, Ewan. What evil is Vankaskan doing in there?'

'I fear that risen monster who bit Whitley was just the beginning.' The Ramlord clasped a hand on Drew's shoulder, squeezing tightly, a tear rolling down his face. 'Oh, Drew, you should never have returned to this ill-fated city.'

'I never went away. Now come, show me where he's keeping my friends.' He patted the Ram on the back and turned about, adjusting the helm on his head once more.

'The Wolf is the last thing the Rat will be expecting.'

Unfortunately for Drew, this was the last thing he said. A ferocious blow to the back of his head made blinding white lights flash in front of his eyes, his helmet ringing like a struck steel drum as he collapsed to the floor in an unconscious heap.

Baron Ewan stood over Drew's body, his ragged breath caught in his throat. He looked at the brass candlestick in his hands, dropping it with horror as he realized the full implications of what he'd done. It clattered to the ground, chiming like a struck bell. He lifted a shaky hand in the direction of the boy on the floor, wanting to touch him, wanting to check he wasn't dead.

Guards began to gather, as one of the warriors from Bast crouched, whipping the helmet from the head of the prone barefoot guard. Drew's dark hair tumbled loose, thick with blood from his head wound. His eyes were closed – the young therian was in a deathly slumber.

'Who is he?' asked the golden-skinned Bastian warrior, looking up at Ewan with cold, emotionless eyes.

'He's the Wolf,' whispered Ewan, his voice breaking as his heart screamed *traitor*. 'Tell Lord Vankaskan I've captured the Wolf for him.'

2

The Vagabond Players

Whitley peeked through the cloth wall of the wagon, watching the crowd of soldiers. A great many looked out of place compared to their companions. They were dressed in light armour, with small swords, spears and round buckler shields at their hips, and they outnumbered the Lionguard by four to one. Their skin was tanned the colour of the sun, almost shimmering with a golden sheen. Whitley figured they were from some faraway place. So what were they doing in Cape Gala?

They were gathered round the Romari performers known as the Vagabond Players, enjoying a rare evening's entertainment. Travelling the length and breadth of the Longridings, their usual audience was townsfolk and villagers, not military men. Currently a wiry old fellow was swallowing a sword, the steel disappearing inch by inch into his throat and torso. The soldiers held their breath as the sword descended, waiting for the basketwork hilt to hit his teeth before they let loose a gasp of appreciation. The old man took hold of the blade between bony fingers before slowly withdrawing it hand over hand, unsheathing it from his throat. As the blade emerged he bent double to bow, stabbing the earth at his feet with the rapier. The soldiers cheered and hollered as a trio of scantily clad girls joined the sword-swallower and began to dance.

Whitley let the cloth fall back into place as the dancing girls continued to entertain the soldiers. They were in a cramped chamber towards the front of the wagon, a fake wall allowing them to stow away. Similar smuggling compartments ensured that others were hidden within the other two caravans. The guards on the gate into Cape Gala had paid little attention, happy to see their bronze and wave them through, even taking a few coppers for their trouble. Whitley was relieved that Baba Korga had enough coins to make it appear the caravans had money. Once in, the matter of getting into the citadel's courtyard was easy. Parking outside a tavern near the barracks had ensured that the travelling players were brought to the Watch's attention. Once they offered a free performance the rest was easy – the guards couldn't get them through the gates quickly enough.

Whitley looked at her three companions in the carriage. The mute Rolff sat on the floor, legs folded, while the two Greencloaks crouched in front of him. Quist, the most senior surviving ranger, was pointing at the crude map she'd scratched into the floorboards with her dagger, indicating where they should try to enter the citadel. Her companion, Tristam, shook his head, jabbing towards the guards outside. He drew a thumb across his throat.

'We won't get past that crowd,' he whispered. 'They'll see us coming before we move. Too many of 'em.'

Whitley had reached Quist and Tristam via Baba Korga and her people. They'd sent a scout across the camp and into the marshes where the ranger had said Whitley would find them. Sure enough the two Greencloaks were waiting, the third woodlander, Machin, having continued north up the Steppen to send word back to Duke Bergan. Whitley had apologized to Quist for jumping from the boat, but the woman bore her no ill will. She was simply glad Whitley was alive, and delighted to hear she'd made contact with the Romari. Now they could put a plan into action and see about rescuing their friends.

'We can't just stay in these wagons,' hissed Quist as the old sword-swallower, Stirga, provided a musical accompaniment for the dancers on his lute. 'We need to move. We need to get in there and find them!'

Rolff clicked his fingers suddenly, causing the other three to look at him. Their attention captured, he reached behind, rummaging under the driver's seat at his back. He pulled out a leather bag which had a thick cork stopper at its neck. He handed it to Tristam. The ranger pulled the cork free and sniffed. Liquid sloshed inside.

'Odourless. Is it water?' Rolff shook his head. Whitley's eyes narrowed as she looked at Quist. The senior ranger was ahead of Whitley as she asked the question of the tall mute.

'Lunewine?'

The Romari nodded slowly.

'What's lunewine?' asked Tristam.

'It's a sleeping draught,' answered Whitley, thinking back to her herblore lessons with Master Hogan. 'You can distill it from the nightskull, a white flower that only blooms under a full moon. They grow deep within the Dyrewood, and there aren't many who know where to find them. How did you come by it?'

'He can't answer you,' whispered Quist. 'We should be happy we have it, regardless of how our silent friend here came by it. It's powerful stuff; poisonous in a large dose, but an effective sedative when diluted.'

'So we drug them? That can be done?' asked Whitley.

The Greencloaks and Rolff looked at one another, shrugging, nodding and eventually agreeing.

'I guess so,' said Quist. 'But getting it into their drinks is the difficult bit.'

Whitley reached across and took the leather bag from Quist, popping the stopper back into place.

'For you, perhaps.'

Tristam looked surprised, impressed by the scout's nerve. But the idea of sending the Lady of Brackenholme straight into the fray didn't please Quist.

'I can't let you go. Your father would have my head if he knew I was placing you in danger!'

'I'll be fine. I'm fast, I'm agile and I've always been stealthy – Master Hogan would never have taken me on otherwise. All three of you stand out in a crowd; you won't get ten yards without being spotted by the Lionguard. I, however . . .'

Whitley tied her hair back and tucked it into the neck of her dirty brown shirt picked up from Baba Korga, her boyish looks making her appear like any other urchin from the city's streets. Quist nodded slowly as Whitley hooked the pouch on to her belt. Rolff lifted the false boards out of the floor of the wagon. The scout stepped over either side of the hole, smiled at the three and then dropped out of sight.

She landed in the dirt below the caravan. The hoardings that rested round the wheels gave her cover as she shuffled towards the rear. Slipping between the performers' crates and provisions that had been unloaded, she was soon mingling with the Romari at the back of the wagons. Whitley wandered past the fire-eater as he oiled himself. The big man winked at her, and even though she was in a grave situation, Whitley couldn't resist grinning back. The lives of her friends depended upon her. For the first time since her terrible bite, Whitley felt alive. Whitley felt like a hero.

Taking a loaf of cherrybread from where it sat untouched, she slowly strolled away from the caravans and into the court- yard proper. The odd guard and servant walked past, completely ignoring her. She looked like any serving boy, the most unremarkable soul in High Stable. From within the tower she could hear cries and moaning, noises that made her skin crawl. She was transported instantly back to the dead soldier who had attacked her. She felt sick suddenly, nauseous beyond words.

Wanting to be away from the wails, she wandered back round the yard, drawing closer to the cheering soldiers. The men of the Lionguard were especially noisy, roaring at the three dancing women, while the southern warriors showed more composure. She saw the soldiers refilling their tankards from a couple of large barrels to the rear of the crowd. Whitley waited for her moment. *Not long now.*

The dancers withdrew suddenly as the music stopped. A flash of blinding fire erupted in front of the caravans as the fire-eater appeared from nowhere, belching a fireball into the night above the soldiers' heads. They hollered, crowding closer to the big, oily Romari as he guzzled a fresh mouthful of spirits. Whitley moved fast.

The lids of the barrels were off, a metal ladle hanging nearby to decant the wine. Whitley ripped the stopper off the pouch and emptied half the contents into one barrel, before finishing the job in the next. Shoving the empty skin back into her belt she stepped away, bumping instantly into a thin looking soldier in a dirty red cloak. His nose was badly broken, and Whitley gulped hard trying not to look alarmed.

'What are you doing, boy?'

The man grabbed Whitley by the ear, twisting it sharply. Whitley was on her toes, fearing her earlobe might tear off.

'Well? Speak!'

Whitley pulled the loaf of cherrybread out from behind her back.

'From the kitchens, sir. Cook told me to send it out to the captain.'

The man took the bread, glancing towards a huge man with his arm in a sling who watched the fire-eater. He sniffed the loaf, his broken nose twitching. He nodded, releasing Whitley's ear.

'Good lad. On your way.'

The soldier returned to the group, snatching up a bottle

from the floor and biting into the bread. Whitley's heart raced. She was all too aware of the peril she was in. She stumbled away from the crowd, the night lit up by occasional explosions of flames. There was nothing enjoyable about this. She no longer felt like a hero. The wailing in the tower, the memories of her attack, the vicious soldier and her narrow escape, Whitley had never known fear like this.

She followed the same route back to the caravans, looping out and away from the guards and skirting the tall flight of steps that led into the granite tower. As she staggered through the courtyard a young man in cream robes descended the staircase, aiming to intercept her. He was tall and wore a smart beard, his long blond hair tied in gold hoops down his back. She recognized him instantly from the encounter in High Stable.

'Young man,' he said, his voice low and hand raised as he tried to catch Whitley's attention. Whitley walked on, pretending not to hear; she was so close to the caravans.

'You there, stand still,' said the man, jumping down the last few steps and standing in front of the disguised girl. Whitley kept her eyes on the ground, cursing her ill luck. The man crouched quickly so that his face was level with Whitley's.

'Well if you won't look up I'd best get down to your level, eh?'

Whitley briefly looked at him. He might have a beard covering his square jaw, but he was young, not much older than Drew, handsome with blue twinkling eyes. Whitley felt tremendously wary, her heart beating frantically. He squinted at her. *Did he recognize her?* He smiled and winked.

'I'll tell you a secret,' said the man. He leaned in to whisper. '*I saw what you did.*'

Whitley's stomach lurched; he had to be bluffing. The man prodded the wineskin in Whitley's belt.

'I saw what you did with this . . . *Greencloak.*'

Whitley gulped, her throat suddenly very dry.

'Please, sir . . .' began Whitley, but the man silenced her swiftly.

'Shh. Don't worry. You're not in any trouble. What was in the wineskin?'

'Lunewine,' whispered Whitley.

The man nodded, scratching his beard while he watched the boozing soldiers. He looked towards the other side of the courtyard where a group of Horseguards had gathered.

'Where are your friends? You can't be doing this alone.'

Whitley chewed her lip. She was going to get them into so much trouble.

'Listen, son. You've nothing to fear from me. We share the same enemy and no doubt want the same thing. Somehow you've managed to get into High Stable, which is an achievement in itself. Let me help you get a little further.'

3

The Tightening Noose

The remaining members of the Wolf's Council stood on the viewing platform known as the Crow's Nest, looking out over a city in panic. From his position high above the Tall Quarter in the wooden tower, Duke Bergan could inspect the sea to the west, the countryside to the east, the Redwine to the south and Highcliff Keep to the north. All four points of the compass were a vision of chaos.

The remains of Westland's navy limped into the harbour, only its smallest and fastest ships returning. Of the warships that had set sail to banish ill omens, the *Maelstrom* alone remained. Bergan was yet to discover who had defeated them. The countryside in the east was alive with activity, as farmers and villagers from the surrounding hamlets tried to enter the great walled city. Behind, drawing ever nearer, an enormous dust cloud blotted out the horizon as an enemy of great might approached.

To the south the Redwine opened into the sea, the river teeming with small craft as they passed one another across the mouth. Some had packed up their belongings and made straight for Rushton across the water. Others came in the opposite direction, hearing that the countryside was no longer safe.

And directly north of the Crow's Nest stood the Keep. For weeks the walls had sat silent bar the Raging Lion. Now they bristled with life as Leopold's surviving soldiers prepared for one last battle. *Who was coming to aid them? What army approached by land? And what navy had devastated Vega's fleet?* Leopold could be seen racing along the ramparts, rallying his troops, the occasional sighting of a Wererat sending shivers down the spines of the Bearlord's men. The king might be feared, but the Rats were beasts of nightmare. And through all of this, the rain still fell.

Duke Manfred stood by Bergan's side, one of his remaining men securing his armour, Baron Hector looking on. The Lord of Stormdale's wounds were not fully gone. Hector had done what he could to aid the healers from Buck House, lending them his own knowledge of medicine, but the duke wouldn't remain in his bed. Highcliff needed defending and he wouldn't let an injury stop him.

'Go easy on the buckles,' said Hector as the soldier pulled them tight. The armour of the Werelords was commonly forged in Sturmland, bound by straps of unusual leather that allowed movement and stretch. If a therianthrope changed while armoured, the suit would move with the transformation, accommodating a shifted Werelord. The armour could be broken free via a series of hidden buckles, the location of which known only by the wearer.

'I'm fine, Hector,' wheezed Manfred, lying badly. His face was pale as he tried to smile. 'Any sign of Vega?'

'The *Maelstrom* has just moored up,' said Bergan. He turned back to the dustcloud in the east. 'I expect we'll see him presently and he can tell us what happened at sea.'

'Who is it?' whispered Hector, staring beyond the wall towards the approaching force.

Bergan glanced at the young Boarlord. He'd changed a lot in the last few weeks. Since taking on his father's title of Baron less than a week ago, he'd shown more drive and purpose, making himself available to the Wolf's Council as well as cleaning up the many messes Vincent had created for Redmire. He'd been so busy that Bergan hadn't had time to quiz him about the whereabouts of his brother. Perhaps becoming this new, mature Hector was his way of earning the trust of his fellow Werelords again.

'I've no idea who it is,' replied Bergan. 'But they're no friends of the Wolf.' He looked over his shoulder to Captain Fry who awaited orders.

'Captain, I'm handing the Crow's Nest to you. Respond to Leopold's volleys with arrows of your own by all means. Don't be cowed; give it back to him and then some. We still don't know how this is going to play out. Duke Manfred, Baron Hector and I are going to the walls. If Count Vega arrives let him know where we are. Let's see who dares scare the good folk of Westland out of their homes and villages.'

*

Hector followed Bergan and Manfred up the stairs of Kingsgate, the main gate into Highcliff. Soldiers ran past them, armour clanging as they gave the Werelords a wide berth. Bergan almost filled the stairwell. Wearing his full armour he was even more imposing than usual. Hector moved a hand over his own armour, a modest leather breastplate that featured an inlaid boar's head, its enormous tusks curving around his chest.

Oh, don't worry brother. You look every inch the warrior.

He ignored the vile, shaking it off as he stepped on to the ramparts above the gatehouse. It was dusk and there was a spark in the air, as if the storm might unleash lightning at any moment. The last stragglers from the outlying farmlands were making their way through the gates. On the horizon he could make out masses of figures approaching at speed.

'Horsemen,' said Manfred. 'From the Longridings? We never heard back from Lorimer, did we?'

'It may well be the Horselords,' agreed Bergan. 'But I'd be surprised; Lorimer, after all, is an old friend. Would he really weigh in on the side of Leopold? What allies does Leopold have in Lyssia, but the Rats of Vermire!'

Neither Hector nor Manfred had an answer to that.

You don't want to be here, Piggy. Death rides into Highcliff on steed and wave!

'Might they be allies?' asked Hector, trying to silence the voice at his shoulder.

'Unlikely,' said the Staglord. 'Word has it they've laid waste to a number of farmsteads on their way here. And look at the timing – they've arrived just as the fleet is wiped out. No, this stinks of betrayal to me.'

Bergan tugged at his beard, fingers twining between thick red whiskers.

'You know, if they've followed the Great West Road then there's a chance Mikkel spotted them. With luck he's got word to Brackenholme, the Barebones and the Dalelands. All is not lost.'

Hector nodded hopefully. The massed army drew closer. Soldiers shifted past to catch a better view, blocking his line of sight. He could hear the men gasping as the dust cloud cleared, revealing the enemy in all their glory. Hector shoved a soldier aside, something the Boarlord of old would never have dreamed of doing. The man turned angrily before seeing who it was, nodding by way of an apology. Hector stepped to the edge of the wall and looked to the east. His heart skipped a beat.

The approaching army was thousands strong, outnumbering the force that guarded Highcliff. With three hundred from Brackenholme and five hundred of the fledgling Wolfguard; there weren't even a thousand protecting the city, although they had the walls on their side. The soldiers looked nervous. Hector watched as they prayed to Brenn, kissing holy symbols that hung round their necks.

See how they make promises to Brenn now, at the end? My brothers and I shall feast this night for all the good their false words do them! This battlefield will be a banquet for my kin!

'Shut up!' grunted Hector, catching the ear of Manfred.

'They can't help it, Hector. If a man can't pray to Brenn on the eve of battle, when can he?'

Hector smiled politely and looked back over the wall. There were over a thousand soldiers advancing across the fields, horsemen following behind. To the rear of the cavalry he could see great wheeled catapults being pulled by teams of horses. Hector looked down the walls of Highcliff to the intermittent towers, relieved to see they were manned with siege engines of their own, loaded and ready to send boulders back to the enemy.

A roaring from the keep drew the attention of those on the walls. Leopold stood on the battlements of the ancient castle, straddling the crenellations, transforming monstrously for all the Wolf's allies to see. Arrows flew up from Fry's best archers, some hitting the target but doing little damage. His roar grew, deafening, shaking the spirit of everyone in Highcliff.

'I told you we should have used the silver arrow,' snapped Hector, cursing their missed opportunity. Bergan looked to him, his face stern.

'It's not our way, Hector. Don't speak of the matter again.'

Hector bowed apologetically, but he didn't mean it. They'd lost their chance, and all on account of Bergan's outdated moral code. It wasn't Brenn's way that forbade using silver. It was the Werelords' way. But why allow your enemy to make use of the deadly metal and not use it to arm yourself?

He's scared of change, Hector. It's too late, though. Tell the old fool his time's up. He should take that arrow and plunge it into his own breast, end it quickly. Better still, you could do it! You're getting good at it now, aren't you?

'Never!' said Hector angrily, getting an alarmed look from Bergan. He turned back to the advancing army. A lone rider broke from the ranks as they heard a commotion in the stairwell.

'Out of my way!' shouted Vega as he arrived on the tower

battlements. He was dishevelled, his usually smart clothes torn and stained. His cape clung to his skin, soaking wet from the rain and sea. Vega strode straight up to his fellow Werelords, embracing them quickly. Hector was surprised by this rare show of emotion from him; Vega was ordinarily so aloof, such a peacock. Lastly the Pirate Prince hugged Hector, squeezing his shoulders as he looked deep into his eyes. The look that passed between them spoke volumes.

'Are you all right, Hector?'

The Boarlord nodded. This was the first he'd seen of the captain of the *Maelstrom* since the Shark and his shipmate had carted Vincent's body away. Hector felt a shiver race down his spine, causing him to shudder involuntarily.

What are you quaking for? It's my grave he's walking over!

'So what happened?' asked Bergan of the agitated sea marshal. Hector could see the Wereshark's teeth were still sharp, as if he'd been part changed without returning fully to human form. Vega ran a hand through his wet hair, brushing the curling locks from his face.

'An armada, bigger than any I've ever seen before. It sailed north up the Cold Coast, sending scouting vessels on ahead. We gave chase and before we knew it were engaged with them. The fleet didn't stand a chance.'

He shook his head, struggling to hide his anger. The rider from the advancing horde was closer now, one sole emissary being sent to the gates of Highcliff.

'Can you send word to the Cluster Isles?' asked Manfred. 'They're your people, surely they'd help?'

'There isn't the time to ready a fleet, even if they listened to me. You forget that the Cluster Isles are still under the jurisdiction of Leopold. The Kraken sits on my throne there.'

'Where's this armada from?' asked Hector.

That's right brother. Cut to the chase. This is where it gets interesting.

Vega's face paled, defeat replaced by fear.

'Bast.'

Bergan and Manfred looked at one another, their faces mirroring Vega's.

'The Catlords?' gasped Hector.

Look at how scared they are now!

Hector had read about Bast. It was where Leopold came from, a jungle continent across the Lyssian Straits. All manner of Werelords ruled the tropical forests and mountains of Bast, but none were more feared or fabled than the Catlords. Leopold was the one that Lyssia knew, but his cousins numbered many. If *they* were sailing to his aid then it was grave news for the whole of the Seven Realms.

'It was the black flag of Onyx, Bergan.'

'Who's Onyx?' Hector wanted to know, but was struggling to be heard.

Manfred spoke over him to Vega.

'Surely the Panther hasn't come himself? He wouldn't leave Bast, would he?'

'We've turned on one of his kin. What do you . . .'

Vega trailed off, looking past Manfred, Bergan and Hector as the horseman rode closer.

'What's he doing?'

The Werelords stood together on the gatehouse as the rider

headed to the northernmost edge of the wall, staying at the limit of bowshot. He turned and galloped along the wall's length, passing Mucklegate, heading towards Kingsgate. A chorus of gasps and cries rose from the wall, building like a wave as he rode by.

'He's dragging something,' said Hector pointing.

The rider had a rope attached to the rear of his saddle, trailing behind his horse. The other end was attached to what looked like a root ball from a felled tree, the roots spinning and bouncing on the hard ground as the warhorse thundered by.

'More Bastians?' asked Vega as the horseman neared, the cries from the walls louder now.

Oh, no, whispered the vile in Hector's ear. He could feel its ghostly hands stroking his throat, tickling his jaw, running claws over his lips. *You're going to* love *this . . .*

'What does he drag behind his mount?' growled Bergan, his voice angry and fearful.

As the horseman finally became clear to the four Werelords, Bergan instantly threw a hand out to steady Manfred. The rider was unmistakable; eight feet tall and clad in animal hide armour. A wolfskin cloak billowed behind him as he clutched the reins with one hand, his other holding a huge wickedly curved scimitar high over his canine head. A Doglord of Omir.

The cries of the defenders were all around them now as they realized what the Omiri Werelord pulled along behind his warhorse. It wasn't a root ball or anything else from a tree. They weren't branches that spun, catching the ground and churning up puddles as the horse charged by. They were antlers.

The rope was attached to the severed head of Earl Mikkel, Lord of Highwater.

Manfred changed instantly, as did Bergan who struggled to hold the Stag back. Vega added his might to the Bearlord's, taking the distraught duke's other arm as he threatened to fling himself from the parapet. The Werestag's scream drowned the cries on the wall as the Doglord brought his scimitar down, slashing the rope and leaving the head to tumble to a halt as he turned his horse and returned to his troops.

Hector watched, dumbstruck and numb, as the voice rasped in his ear.

Who said Cats and Dogs couldn't play together?

4

Breakout

The doors slammed shut, silencing the moans from within the courtroom of High Stable. The Wolf captured. Who would have believed it? And betrayed by the treacherous old Ram too. His step brisk, Sorin set off downstairs. He cringed as he glanced back, the two Lionguards who were posted at the door looked sickly and troubled. *Better them than me*, he figured. *Last place I want to be is under Vankaskan's feet when he's got new toys to play with*. People were always so hasty in regarding the Ratlord as insane. He was far from mad. Vankaskan was driven, totally dedicated to the craft of magistry, and in particular the dark arts. He was now free to indulge his passion, and he was enjoying himself.

Sorin tugged the clasp of his dirty cloak round his throat, straightening his uniform as he exited the citadel. The soiled garment had seen better days, and Sorin found it an embarrassment that a sergeant of the Lionguard was forced to wear such a tarnished Redcloak. First thing in the morning he was going to get an order out to the nearest outfitter, have some new uniforms prepared for his men. Vankaskan had allowed Captain Colbard to recruit since they'd arrived, and they'd picked up a good number of ex-mercenaries who were more than willing to take the king's crown. They had thirty men at their disposal in the citadel now, with twenty more marshalling the City Watch on the gates into the Cape Gala. Added to these were the hundred Bastian warriors who'd put the fear of Brenn into the Longridings. High Stable was beginning to feel like a foothold for the Wolf's enemies. Sorin laughed to himself. *The Wolf. How brief was the mongrel's reign after such a promising fanfare?*

Stepping out of the tower he noticed that the Romari caravans were still present. Odd – they should have been turfed out by now, the temple having chimed two ages ago. His men were still gathered across the courtyard so he made his way over. There was no sign of the Romari and as he approached the soldiers he noticed that many of them were sleeping, slumped against one another. Some were woozily crawling, inebriated.

'What's going on here?' he yelled, causing some to stir. He dashed behind the caravans; nobody there, not even the dancing girls. A single slain Redcloak lay in the gravel, the deadly hole from a rapier thrust visible in the centre of his chest. Sorin ran back, his eyes widening with panic.

'Get up, the lot of you!' he screamed, kicking out indiscriminately as he made his way through them to the slumbering figure of Colbard, the broken-armed northman. He slapped the big captain and the grizzled warrior struggled to open his eyes. Inside the citadel they could now hear the clanging of steel.

'We're under attack!'

The fight had begun on the ground floor. A Redcloak who'd been to the privy had opened the door to the sight of a hulking Romari cutting the throat of his fellow watchman at the tower's back door. The Romari was fast, shooting the dagger from his wrist down the corridor where it landed squarely in the Redcloak's stomach. But not before he'd screamed.

Whitley slipped round Rolff as the mute giant dropped the dead Redcloak to the ground. She felt a hand at her shoulder propel her forward as Quist moved through the door behind her, ushering her on. Whitley held a dagger in her hand, not her choice of weapon. The scouts of the Woodland Watch were trained with bows and quarterstaffs for combat, but neither was appropriate for such confined spaces.

'The stairs, Whitley,' said the woman. 'The third floor; that's where the Horselord said the cells were.'

'That's where they're keeping them,' nodded Whitley, falling behind the ranger as she set off up the staircase that followed the wall of the citadel. Behind her came Rolff, then two Romari men and Stirga, the old sword-swallower, his rapier stained red from their encounter with the guard behind the caravans. The remainder of their party, led by Tristam and the fire-eater, Yuzhnik, advanced down the ground-floor corridor, hoping to secure the entrances and exits from the granite tower. Four of Lord Conrad's Horseguard would meet Tristam at the front steps. Whitley prayed that they kept their end of the bargain.

To her right Whitley caught sight of a landing on the first floor. One of the tanned foreign warriors saw them from down the corridor, already running their way having heard the scream downstairs. Behind him came two Redcloaks, swords drawn. Quist stepped off the stairs, pushing Whitley onwards with Rolff.

'Go with the Romari! Find them!'

With that Quist was gone. Whitley scrambled to keep up with Rolff, her heart beating nineteen to the dozen. The man behind kept a hand on her back, supporting her as she climbed.

Ahead on the second floor Whitley saw Rolff dip into the corridor that branched off, leaping with another knife raised. His belt was lined with them, three still tucked into the leather. By the time Whitley reached the landing she saw Rolff rising from the floor, the body of a dead Bastian at his feet. The big Romari was leading the way again, pushing on as they approached the third floor.

They emerged on to the third floor into the midst of a battle. There were maybe thirty well-armed Bastian warriors, carrying round buckler shields, short spears and swords. Five Redcloaks fought alongside them as they surrounded a dozen of High Stable's remaining Horseguard at the far side of the large guardroom. These Longridings men were struggling to stand their ground at the head of the main staircase. Swords and spears clashed as they were pushed back. This central floor was clearly the military heart of the citadel, with bunks lining the walls, anterooms for captains and even a door grille into a cell block. Two Redcloaks guarded the iron door, ready to join the fray if needed. One shouted an alarm as Whitley and her companions appeared from the servants' stairwell.

Rolff had a knife in each hand as eight Bastians pulled away from the main group, rushing the invaders. The Romari kicked a large table into them, causing them to break over and round it, losing their shape. He darted to the left of it, slashing and jabbing at the two who came round the side, as the Romari men and Stirga came forward in front of Whitley, daggers and rapier flashing. One of the warriors who dared to climb over the table got the sword-swallower's blade clean through the neck. Whitley stood still, not quite knowing what to do.

A Romari went down with a Bastian on top, his sword coming down in savage motions. His brother dived into him, bowling him off his feet as the Bastians waded in. Stirga leapt to their aid and suddenly Whitley was alone.

A gut feeling told her to move, and not a moment too soon, as a Bastian sword cut through the air where her head had been seconds before. She raised her blade as her attacker followed up the blow with another slash, knocking the dagger from her grasp and sending it flying. Whitley skidded round the table, ducking behind chairs as the warrior advanced, cutting her off from the rest of her party. The chainshirted fighter was shepherding her towards the Redcloaks at the door. They watched, waiting for the Bastian to make the kill.

Whitley's eyes searched for a weapon. A couple of swords hung from brackets just out of reach. She staggered into a stack of shields that tumbled around her, the warrior kicking them aside. Whitley scrambled back, knocking over stools and chairs, but the net was closing. She backed towards the corner of the room where spears and javelins stood stacked. The Bastian stepped on to a chair, propelling himself into the air and raising his sword high as he leapt down to deliver the killing blow. It was at this precise moment that the scout's back collided with the wall of spears, sending them clattering forward from their rack.

The warrior's sword never reached its intended mark, as an array of spears pierced the man through numerous points of his body as he landed on the projecting points, pinning Whitley beneath him. Beyond Whitley saw the guards from the iron doorway advancing, their companions all engaged with the Romari and Horseguard.

'Rolff!' she screamed, but her cry fell on deaf ears. The big Romari had his own problems, swamped and surrounded by the mob. The Redcloaks were wary now, having seen the Bastian butchered by a clutch of spears. Whitley struggled, unable to manoeuvre out from beneath the dead warrior.

'Please!' she cried, her voice rising in pitch. Her fingers scrambled for the Bastian's weapon on the floor. It was a short thrusting sword with a steel cup covering the hilt, perfect for close combat. She found the handle, pulling it along the flags, closing her fingers round the hilt.

The first Redcloak was about to pull the dead warrior to one side, ready to stab down. Whitley was ahead of him, though. The minute she felt the Lionguard tug the corpse, Whitley swung her arm out from below, ripping the shortsword through the air at his leg. She heard a wet *ssssnikt* sound as the blade tore through his hamstring, sending him toppling in agony.

The second soldier was less foolish, kicking the dead Bastian aside and drawing his sword back to strike. Instinct took over for Whitley, the Bear within leaping to her defence. She brought her legs back to kick out at the body of the speared soldier. With unnatural strength she launched her feet into the corpse's midriff, roaring as she kicked, sending the body and spears flying back over the Redcloak. By the time the soldier had struggled to his feet he was facing an armed Whitley, a spear in her hands, the head broken from the shaft.

The Redcloak grinned, fancying his odds; his sword against an urchin with a broken spear. It didn't occur to him for a moment that he was facing a trained scout of the Woodland Watch. Whitley grimaced back, turning the makeshift staff in her hands. The man raised his sword and brought it down fast. If he was expecting her to swing her weapon defensively to meet his blow, he was mistaken. Instead Whitley jumped at him, lightning fast, jabbing the staff forward with all her weight. The man took the brunt of the blow to his head, the splintered wood shattering his features. As he dropped his sword and brought his hands up to his broken face Whitley expertly swung the staff round her head, bringing the pole arcing round to strike him across the temple with a skull splitting crack. He went down instantly.

Before she could regain her breath, Stirga was at her side, the old Romari rifling through the guard's pockets searching for keys, but he found none. He held his hand out to Whitley.

'Haste, now! We must free your friends!'

The battle raged on the far side of the chamber. Nobody had noticed Whitley and Stirga, the intense combat providing enough distraction for them to carry out their task. Two Romari men lay on the floor, the contest having proved deadly for them. Whitley noticed Rolff rising from the floor at the back of the room from a pile of bodies. His gore-slicked chest and arms were scored by a dozen sword wounds but he was still standing. He stalked grimly over to them.

Whitley rattled the grilled door to the cell block.

'Locked. Don't suppose you can rip it from its brackets, Rolff?'

Rolff looked and sneered. Both door and frame were solid iron: no mortal could tear it loose.

'Here, let me,' said Stirga, pushing between them to inspect the mechanism. His hands went to a pouch at his hip, pulling out a couple of thin wire tools and blades. He slid them into the lock and started working at them. Whitley watched, impressed.

Rolff tapped Whitley on the shoulder, gesturing towards the fight on the landing. The Horseguard had been whittled away, with only four left standing, each of them badly bloodied. Around twenty of the Bastians remained, half of them closing in on the Horseguard while the others turned their attention to Whitley and the two Romari. Rolff stepped forward to buy them time.

Before he could join battle there was a thunderous noise on the main staircase, a clattering, banging crescendo of noise that grew and grew. The Horseguard surged forward, weapons rising as they faced their enemy with fresh confidence. Now the Bastians pulled back as they saw what raced up the staircase towards them.

Four Werestallions vaulted the remaining steps, fully transformed in all their glory. They were led by a blond-maned Horselord, snorting with fury and frothing at the mouth. He swung a greatsword in one hand, taking two of the Bastians' heads off their shoulders. He kicked out, his huge hoofed foot shattering the ribcage of another warrior who stood too close. Letting loose a war-cry he crashed into the Bastians, his stallion brothers joining him.

'That should buy you time, Stirga,' whispered Whitley.

The old Romari completed the lockpicking, and the grilled door swung open. A corridor that housed ten cells was beyond, each one locked by a steel bar across its wooden door. Hurriedly the three of them went down the passage, drawing back the bars and swinging doors wide. In each they found enemies of Vankaskan. Beaten Horselords and their wives and children shared cells with the Horseguards who'd survived the Ratlord's wrath.

Rolff pushed past Stirga as he made his way to the last cell in the corridor, snatching at the bar and yanking it back with a clang. He kicked the door open and stepped inside, Whitley right behind the mute giant. Her eyes lit up when she saw Gretchen, dashing across the room to where the red-haired young woman hung chained to the wall.

'Oh, Gretchen, you poor thing!' She looked up at Rolff and Stirga. 'Get these chains off her, please!'

Stirga moved quickly, setting to work on the manacles with his lockpick. Another figure, that of a man, hung from the wall opposite. Whitley hugged Gretchen as she tumbled into her arms. Rolff strode up to the male prisoner as Lord Conrad appeared in the doorway, now part changed and more human in appearance, although his face was still equine. He bowed towards Whitley, dropping his head low.

Whitley saw Rolff grab the other prisoner by his hair, lifting his head up warily, his dagger in his other hand.

It wasn't the Wolf. It was Captain Harker, Drew's friend. The man spluttered, squinting through puffed and blackened eyes. Rolff turned round as if looking for an explanation.

'If you're looking for the Wolf, he isn't here,' snorted Conrad. 'Vankaskan has him imprisoned in the courtroom. Others too. Brenn knows if we've time to save any of them! The evil, my lady; you cannot imagine!'

Whitley held Gretchen close as Stirga immediately set to work freeing Harker from his bonds.

'Try me,' gasped Whitley, squeezing Gretchen tight as the other slowly opened her eyes. 'Take us to Drew.'

5

City on Fire

'Incoming!'

The soldiers on the wall dived for cover at the Bearlord's warning cry, two members of the City Watch struggling to hide behind a raised stone parapet. Their choice of shelter was unfortunate. The boulder from the Omiri catapult hit the ramparts, shattering the defences and sending rock and crushed soldiers tumbling into the Tall Quarter. The walkway was reduced to rubble, other soldiers struggling to maintain their balance as the ancient wall crumbled beneath their feet. One unfortunate fellow tumbled over the outer side, landing amidst a crowd of wild Omiri, their scimitars slashing down in rapid succession.

Duke Bergan ran along the wall, roaring as he went, swinging his battle axe over the ramparts and sending the eastern warriors skittering with each blow. More frequently now the

Doglord's men were finding footholds along the wall, their catapults hitting their targets with increasing success. Bergan scanned the wall, dismayed to see fighting breaking out where the Omiri had scaled it. With ladders and grappling hooks flying up everywhere, it felt like they were putting out a forest fire with one leaking bucket.

And the Tall Quarter was literally aflame, civilians trying to put out the fires in the streets. For once Bergan was grateful for the rain, the only thing helping them on this terrible night. He looked towards the keep. Captain Fry had been ill-prepared for the ferocity with which the Lionguard had attacked: bolts, arrows, balls of flaming pitch were being launched into their midst. This was the Lion's last throw of the dice, and he gambled everything.

'Manfred! Stay where you are!'

He could see that the Staglord was separated from his personal guard, four soldiers in shining steel bearing the raised pattern of a pair of antlers on their breastplates, the last men of the Barebones in Highcliff. A well placed boulder had removed the wall between them and their liege. A troop of lightly armoured Omiri had clambered up the rubble, positioning themselves between the Staglord and his protectors. The four knights waded in, swords smashing down and crushing the enemy, limbs splintering with each swing, but they couldn't get to Manfred.

Manfred faced off four warriors on the ramparts of what remained of Kingsgate. Below, allied soldiers struggled to hold back the wave of Omiri that was funnelling through the broken gates. Bergan realized there was no getting through the melee on the wall and instead jumped into the Tall Quarter. Three soldiers of Brackenholme followed him, not an official bodyguard like Manfred's, but men who'd lay down their lives in the defence of Bergan nonetheless.

The Werebear ran towards the rear of his men as they were forced back, the enemy wedging itself in the shattered Kingsgate like a barbed thorn, immovable. Bergan's eyes fell on a two-wheeled hay wagon that had been pushed off the road. He threw his axe to one of his men, the poor fellow almost tumbling over with its weight. The Bearlord grabbed the cart, lifting it on to his chest, heaving it once more until it was above his head. He roared before throwing the wagon into the enemy ranks.

They toppled like skittles, knocked over, crushed, slaughtered by the splintering cart. Bergan snatched his axe back and with one bound leapt over his men, landing on the broken timber of the hay wagon. Axe, claws and teeth flew, shredding the Omiri about him into a red mist. His men surged forward, making up lost ground and using the shattered cart as a makeshift barricade. Other defences were brought forward; the broken gates, barrels, crates, even doors from houses.

'To me!' he roared as his soldiers found new hope. The morale of the attackers had wavered and the men of Highcliff pushed their advantage, causing the enemy to fall over one another. Bergan looked past the battle on the ground now, making for the crumbling gatehouse. He saw antlers tear into one of the warriors as Manfred fought above. The man's body was flung like a ragdoll, but another took his place.

Bergan leapt over the barricade and trampled the Omiri

underfoot as he ran to the gatehouse doorway. He ignored the scimitars and arrows, intent upon getting to his injured friend. The stairwell was a squeeze as the Werebear muscled his way up, his battleaxe drawing sparks as it bounced against brick-work. He emerged on the roof to find Manfred almost overwhelmed.

His armour lay in pieces, scimitar blows having hacked the straps to ribbons. His body was covered in wounds, both fresh and old. An antler was badly broken, lying severed on the floor, and his left arm hung limp at his side. The weapons weren't silver, but they were plentiful. The Omiri stopped their onslaught to regard the Bear, as the Stag wobbled unsteadily.

Bergan jumped forward, dragging his brother Werelord back, facing the attackers in his place. He held the enormous axe by its long carved handle, levelling the double-headed blade at the assembled Omiri. As one they backed off, refusing to engage.

'Fight me!'

The men looked over the edge of the wall, making room on the top of the gatehouse. Something approached. Something big. Bergan shifted the axe in his hands, readying himself for the forthcoming fight. A huge shape emerged over the side of the broken ramparts. In one giant, tanned hand he held a heavy scimitar. On his other arm he carried a sheet of metal, five feet high and hammered into the shape of a crude shield. The lowest edge looked razor sharp, and was stained red. The snarling Dog's head bore a mouthful of hellish teeth, canines bared as the beast prepared for battle.

'Bergan of Brackenholme,' the Doglord snarled. 'Fat old bear, you should have stayed in your treehouse.'

'Who are you?' said Bergan, ignoring the taunt. The two circled one another, weapons raised.

'I should gift you my name at the end? Before I kill you?'

'Stop being dramatic, Dog! Speak or shut up and fight!' This came from Manfred, crouched wheezing against the rubble of the stairwell. The Dog glared at Manfred before bringing his hateful gaze back on to Bergan.

'I am Canis, son of Canan, Prince of Omir.'

'Never heard of him,' said Bergan, turning to Manfred. 'You?'

Manfred shook his head.

'My father is the rightful King of Omir, you greenlander scum!'

'Oh, there are lots of rightful kings floating around lately, Canis. Try to keep up!'

'Quiet, Bear! I'll make your tree my first port of call once this battle is over. See how your people like Omiri steel!'

That was enough for Bergan. The Werehound's words had hardly left his lips when Bergan flung his axe forward, letting its head tear into the Doglord's massive torso. Canis collapsed as Bergan moved in, a claw tearing the Dog from his chest to his jaw. The Omiri Werelord staggered back, bringing his shield up to block any following blow. Bergan held back to see what damage he'd done, suspecting he'd opened the beast's belly. The full moon shone down as a smiling Dog's head emerged from behind his metal shield, jaw in tatters where the Bear had connected. Bergan smacked his lips, huffing anxiously, and prepared himself for the onslaught.

Bergan was one of the most powerful Werelords to grace

a Lyssian battlefield, but he was old. Canis was fast, his scimitar flying out once, twice, three times, slicing at last across Bergan's breast. The Bearlord stumbled back, almost colliding with Manfred, before hitting the Doglord in the jaw with the flat of his axe. The Bear opened his jaws and clasped them round the Dog's throat, biting deep and feeling the blood burst free. Canis dropped his scimitar and fought back, raking his hands into the Bearlord's face, pressing his claws into his eyes. Bergan clamped them shut, screaming as he let go, momentarily blinded by the Werehound's attack.

The Werebear staggered around the battlements, blinded, the Omiri slashing at him as he whirled past them. Canis picked up his scimitar, loudly barking for all to see and hear. There was a lull in the battle below as the combatants drew back to see the final blow. Bergan cursed; blinded at the last, not even seeing the deathblow come. Canis raised the scimitar overhead.

'For you, Father! For Canan and the glory of Omir!'

Suddenly Canis was choking for air, a pain in his chest as he struggled to breathe. Blood bubbled at his lips. Four sharp, black blades protruded from his torso, the broken antler driven deeply into his back. Duke Manfred stood at his shoulder as lightning flashed overhead and thunder instantly followed.

'You talk too much,' said the Lord of Stormdale, as he propelled his body forward off the battlements.

Bergan's eyesight was clearing and the surrounding Omiri's initiative was lost. He roared, jumping forward to where he thought they were. The men toppled off the wall, tumbling into the air rather than face the Werebear.

Bergan squinted at the injured Manfred.

'Thank you, old friend.'

'Thank me later,' wheezed the Stag, clearly in pain. He picked up his sword. 'Come, we must defend the walls. We *cannot* let these monsters through.'

The two Werelords stepped up to the crumbling edge of the wall, readying their weapons as a fresh wave of Omiri advanced.

Count Vega pushed his way through the soldiers, his companions on his heels. Just ahead he could see Kingsgate, where the fiercest fighting took place. The gatehouse had been bombarded by the Omiri catapults, the southern tower was a pile of rubble, while the north still stood. He caught sight of the Bear and the Stag on the roof, surrounded by savage warriors armed with spears and scimitars. He grabbed the nearest officer, the soldier blanching when he saw the partially transformed face of the Sharklord, dead black eyes and razor-sharp teeth inches from his face.

'What on Sosha's ocean are those two doing up there?'

'Holding the wall, sire!'

'Look around you, man, the wall is *broken*! The battle is *lost*! Why has nobody informed them?'

'I have, repeatedly!' yelled the soldier. 'My lord, I must return to the line, I'm sorry!' And with that the officer rejoined his men as they struggled against the onslaught.

'Stubborn Bear,' grumbled Vega, turning to the men who followed. 'Come on!'

Vega ran forward, his cutlass flashing and finding a target

with each flash. His cape was gone, lost in the battle, and his white shirt was torn to the waist. Reaching the stairwell beyond the barricade he took four steps at a time, swiftly arriving on the battle-ravaged wall.

There stood Bergan and Manfred, weapons swinging wildly, tearing at the Omiri with tooth, claw and blade. They were swamped. Vega skewered two warriors with one thrust, flinging them from his blade like dead bugs. His mouth bit down, taking an arm and a leg off another warrior before flinging the fresh corpse into its companions. The balance of the fight shifted dramatically.

Within moments the tower was clear of Omiri, the two older members of the Wolf's Council struggling to catch their breath. Bergan managed a nod of thanks to Vega, his face red with gore.

'Are you here to fight by our side?'

'No, I'm here to drag you away!'

'Never!' bellowed Manfred, staggering as an arrow hit home in his back alongside five others.

Vega put a hand on Manfred's shoulder, looking him in the eyes while the battle raged around and below them.

'Manfred, it's over. Brothers, can you not see? The city is fallen.'

The Stag and Bear blinked, looking around. The walls were overrun along their length, pockets of fighting now spilling into the city proper. The fires raged out of control at their backs, as the forces of Omir surged through the broken gates. They were overwhelmed.

'But, Mikkel . . .' began the Staglord, cut short by the Shark.

'Can be avenged another day. Come, we must move.'

Bergan noticed the three men at the head of the stairwell. Two were members of the Wolfguard, but the third was a prisoner, hands and throat bound by manacles and chains. His bald head bore the recognizable pattern of a sea serpent, filling the right side of his face.

'Carver,' said Bergan.

'I had to bring him. He can get the people out of here.' The Sharklord pointed out to the bay. 'The fleet draws close, they'll be here within the hour.'

Bergan stepped up to the Lord of the Thieves Guild who lifted his jaw defiantly.

'I have your word you'll serve us and the people of High-cliff?'

'You have my word I'll serve you until we emerge from the other side of those tunnels, Lord Protector. After that it's every man for himself.' He held his manacles up, tugging the chains taut.

'I don't have the keys,' said Vega suddenly, realizing his mistake. Before anyone could respond the chains were shattered, tiny pieces of twisted metal scattering along the tower top as Bergan's axe bit into the stone roof.

'You're pardoned, Carver. Don't make me regret this.'

Carver grinned, snatching up a fallen Omiri scimitar.

'Come, we have to move fast. There are three entrances to the catacombs: beneath Brenn's Temple in the Tall Quarter, the old fishmarket in the Low Quarter and the Garden of the Dead at the bottom of Lofty Lane.'

'The cemetery?' asked Manfred. Carver nodded, leading

them back down the stairwell, scimitar raised warily before him.

'I need to get the word out, don't know how many of my people have remained in the city, but if we're quick we can coordinate an evacuation. My lord, I may need to steal some of your men.'

'They can't be spared,' said Bergan. 'Haven't you noticed they're busy?'

Carver smiled as they arrived at the base of the guardhouse, entering the melee once more. The Omiri withdrew at the sight of changed therians, but only briefly; Vega could see over their heads that there were thousands, their injured replaced by fresh warriors. He looked at the soldiers of High-cliff, a battered army of the walking wounded. Where were their reinforcements?

As the Wolf's Council retreated Vega caught sight of a carriage hurtling up the street towards them. It was an ancient carriage of state, its faded red timber having seen better days. Two men sat on the driver's bench, one short, one tall, crack-ing the whip as they urged the horses onwards. Vega stood back as the carriage bumped to a halt and Hector, Baron of Redmire, opened a door.

'Get in! Hurry, my lords,' said the magister. 'Leopold lowers the drawbridge. I fear he and the Lionguard mean to join the battle.'

'I'll be waiting for him if he does,' snarled Bergan, his body returning to human proportions as he clambered in. Manfred directed his attending knights back to Buck House.

'See to Queen Amelie, have her prepare to leave at once!'

'Are you getting in?' asked Hector. Vega shook his head.

'No, I think Carver needs assistance, thanks all the same.'

Hector nodded and disappeared into the carriage, banging the roof to signal the drivers to ride on. Vega and the thief lord stood back as the carriage turned in the road, the battle of Kingsgate still raging at their backs. The Sharklord was astonished to recognize the two men who drove the carriage as the henchmen of Vincent, Ringlin and Ibal.

'What's the matter?' asked Carver.

'I'm surprised to see the company a Werelord is keeping.'

'You're one to talk. Come, we have business to attend to and quickly.'

Vega watched as the vehicle raced back towards the Crow's Nest, its drivers staring back as they passed. The tall one saluted the captain of the *Maelstrom* as the fat one giggled and the carriage was gone.

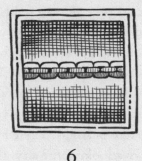

6

The Ratlord's Brood

The familiar smell of burning Spyr Oil woke Drew from his unnatural slumber. His face was slick with blood; his own. He raised a hand to his mouth, feeling for a wound but finding nothing. His fingers traced round his jaw, ear and beyond, finally discovering the matted lump of hair at the back of his head. The skin beneath had already healed, but the headache remained. The last thing he remembered was speaking with Baron Ewan and then . . . nothing. He winced as he rose from where he lay.

Another scent, hidden behind the Spyr Oil's aroma, was the sweet smell of decay. He felt the cool touch of steel against his left hand, a manacle keeping him chained to the wall. The linked length was forgiving, having allowed him to lie on the floor, but he was a prisoner nonetheless. He clenched his chained fist, Wergar's ring straining against the knuckles.

Drew's eyes and ears slowly adjusted to his surroundings. He was in the courtroom of High Stable.

He could hear the sounds of battle, the ringing of steel and rattle of swords echoing all around. The wall he stood against was at the top of a flight of curving steps that ran round the chamber, smoke and darkness obscuring the far side. He tried to get his bearings. There had been a balcony in the courtroom, overlooking the city. He looked behind, finding a wall of heavy blood-spattered drapes, alive with flies and their twitching grubs. The blood gathered on the floor, spreading out over the granite steps all around. *How many had died here?*

The moaning suddenly caught his attention. It was a low murmur, slowly becoming more insistent.

'Who's there?' said Drew, trying to see down the steps in the darkness. More moaning, responding in a chorus. *More than one?*

'Who is it?' He yanked at the chain, testing its strength. There were only two ways he'd be free of the manacle; with a key or by leaving his hand behind.

'You're awake.'

Drew recognized the rasping voice immediately, his mind racing back to a journey through the Dyrewood in the Ratlord's torture wagon.

'Vankaskan. Lucas let you off your leash?'

The Wererat didn't answer, setting Drew's nerves further on edge. He tugged at the chain again.

'If you were going to kill me you could have done it while I slept!'

'That would have been no fun. I'd be denying Wergar's offspring the death he deserves . . .'

'You're keeping me alive for a reason. You've been commanded to by Lucas, haven't you?'

Drew's voice lacked conviction. A fresh wave of moans rose in the dark. He could see dark shapes now, moving through the Spyr smoke below. He coughed and spluttered, the foul smells overpowering.

'You put too much faith in your importance, boy. As for me following commands, I've never responded well to orders. You should know you're mine, Wolf. Mine to do with as I like.'

Drew heard the grin in Vankaskan's voice.

'Show yourself then!' barked Drew, trying to remain in control. If the Wolf appeared he'd lose his manacled hand, something that didn't bear thinking about.

'All in good time. How's Hector?'

'Safe, far away from you and your vile teachings, that's for sure.'

'The seed is planted, Wolf. You cannot halt nature.'

Drew's feet slipped on the bloody floor. The chain jangled as he tried to stay upright. Again he saw the silhouettes below. *Were they coming closer?*

'Who's down there with you?'

'Down here? Oh, some of your friends, Drew. Would you like to see them?'

Drew heaved, the smell of death growing heavier. A fat bluebottle landed on his lip, threatening to disappear into his mouth. He spluttered and flicked it away. Below, in the dark, he heard the Rat whispering something; rapid, arcane words of magick.

'What's going on?' said Drew, yanking nervously at the chain again. Outside he could hear the shouts and screams of battle; what he'd give to have the Wolfshead blade in his hand. His attention suddenly focused through the smoke ahead.

A figure was crawling up the steps towards him, one stair at a time. It was heading straight for Drew through the darkness. Two dimly glowing blue eyes were fixed on him as it approached. Drew prayed it *wasn't* someone he knew. Whitley's injury at the hands of the risen Lionguard loomed large in his mind, the smell of the dead all too familiar. He'd known all along that the cursed soul was Vankaskan's handiwork. *He's done it in High Stable now?*

'Call it back, Vankaskan!'

He could hear the Wererat chuckling now.

'Go on, child. Go see your friend. Embrace him . . .'

The figure was eight feet away when Drew recognized it. *Had it only been a few days since he'd last seen him?* The skin was yellowed and pale, its jaw dark with a foul black liquid that pooled in its throat. It still had the frame of the Werelord, but it was now a mockery of the man it had been in life, a puppet for the Rat to play with; an abomination.

The body of Broghan raised a hand, straining to get to Drew. As it loomed closer, drawing itself upright, Drew could see the open wound in its chest.

'Oh, Brenn,' sobbed Drew, backing up to the wall. The dead Bearlord was a couple of paces from him now. Drew kicked the grasping hands away.

'Please, Broghan, don't!'

'You'll have to speak up,' laughed Vankaskan. 'His hearing's not what it used to be!'

The risen Bearlord opened its jaws, its pale blue eyes widening as its teeth clacked together expectantly – hungry. Drew brought his foot back.

'Forgive me, Broghan,' he whispered and struck out. The dead Bearlord's head snapped back and the body tumbled down the steps, crunching all the way down. Drew cried, shoulders shaking as the full extent of his predicament dawned on him. All the while Vankaskan laughed, breaking down into prolonged wheezes.

'You're insane!' shouted Drew. 'This is madness!'

'This is progress!' yelled the necromancer. 'Death shall no longer be the end. The dead shall walk the earth, *that's* what the prophecy says. And we all have a part to play. Me, commanding; and you, Werewolf, joining them. Can you imagine it? An army of the dead, with risen Werelords leading them into battle?'

'It's blasphemy!'

Drew saw a shape run up the steps, shaking off its robes, drawing the beast forth. By the time he landed at the top of the steps Vankaskan was fully changed, his clawed hand flying out and taking Drew round the throat. The Wererat was monstrous, long pink tail whipping about as he screeched into Drew's face. Drew felt stinking hot saliva spatter his face. He wanted to look away but the monster held his face inches from his slavering jaws.

'And I thought the dead smelled bad!' managed Drew. The Rat tightened his grip, instantly cutting off Drew's air supply.

'Always so smart with the mouth. Your father was the same, Wolf. What good did it do him?'

The courtroom door opened suddenly, light spilling into the great chamber as two figures rushed in. The beast slackened his grip, turning quickly to see what the commotion was. Great whirls of Spyr smoke disappeared through the open door in a gust, the drapes on the balcony suddenly flapping in the breeze revealing the night sky beyond. Full moon. Drew looked away, struggling to regain his breath.

'What is it?' screamed Vankaskan, furious at the interruption. Drew recognized Sorin and the big northman whose arm he'd broken. They both had their weapons drawn and looked around the dark courtroom for their master.

'We're under attack, my lord!' yelled the bearded northman, an axe in his good hand.

'Where are you, Vankaskan?' shouted Sorin. He took a step forward and pulled back immediately, a hand lunging at him from the gloom.

'Be careful,' spat the Wererat, his voice panicked. 'My children! They're down there!'

Drew moved fast, the distraction all he needed. He whipped the chain over the huge head of Vankaskan, as if he was lassoing a bullock on the farm. Then he threw himself past the beast, seeing the chain tighten with his body weight like a slipknot round the Rat's throat. Instantly Vankaskan was scrambling, huge arms reaching for his throat and trying to grip the links, but the thick oily pelt of his therian form prevented him from reaching the chain. Instead he tore at the fur, blood and flesh coming away in strips.

Sorin and Colbard had seen them now. They moved fast, skirting the walking dead and running up the stairs. The Rat's legs kicked and scrabbled against the bloody floor, his tail lashing out as the Lionguard arrived. Sorin saw the tail at the last minute, dodging clear, but Colbard wasn't so lucky, as the captain's legs were taken from under him in a sweeping slash. He toppled into the chamber, head first, landing on the second set of steps down. There was a crunch and a scream as he rolled over in agony, his other arm now broken at the elbow.

Drew saw the sword in Sorin's hand. *The Wolfshead blade!* Sorin kept his distance, resisting rushing in after seeing the fate that had befallen his friend. Below, Drew noticed some of the corpses moving through the open doorway. The bucking of the Wererat focused his attention. Unable to reach Drew, the Rat began to revert to human form, the only chance he had to reach the chain. By then it was too late.

Vankaskan's throat was ragged from his own claws, the bib of blood spreading down his gnarled, wizened torso and pooling in his groin. Drew jumped off the top step out into the chamber, feeling the chain go taut, the manacle jarring at the wrist. He heard something bounce down the steps as the headless body of Vankaskan toppled over.

The drapes were flapping now, the wind blowing through the courtroom. A couple of the dead had already disappeared into the galleried corridor, greeted by screams. But the others advanced up the steps towards the combatants.

Sorin moved fast, not giving Drew a chance to catch his breath. Sorin lashed out with the sword, forcing Drew off the top step and down one. The links went taut again. Drew strained out of reach of the swordsman, trying to draw him to his level. He glanced down, catching sight of the approaching monsters, blue flames flickering in their eyes. Duke Lorimer was nearest, the dead Horselord's blank expression ghostly in the gloom. Behind it he caught sight of other dead Werelords in their stained cream robes as they scrambled closer. There were a dozen of them. And there was poor Broghan's corpse in their midst, its neck broken at an impossible angle.

The Wolfshead blade. If Drew could disarm Sorin and get the blade, he might be able to shatter the chains. Draw him in close, feign weakness. Another leap and he'd be past the man's reach and on top of him. Hang back, draw him in, jump him.

Drew felt something he hadn't felt in a long time; hope.

He watched Sorin advance. And then stop. The wily rogue looked at Drew as if reading his thoughts and then stared at the mob of advancing dead. Colbard was scrambling to his knees, bouncing off his broken arms as he tried to avoid the hungry corpses. The dead closed round the northman, biting and clawing at him, pulling him down as they tore into him. Colbard's high-pitched scream echoed round the courtroom before ceasing suddenly. Sorin grimaced at the demise of his friend.

He began to back away. Drew could see his chance evaporating before his eyes. He *needed* the sword! He leapt, dashing up to the top step on the straining chain and lashing out at the man, but he was too late. Sorin was out of range.

'The sword, Sorin! For Brenn's sake! Throw me the sword!'

Sorin looked at the Wolfshead blade for a moment, then the dead. He looked at Drew. He slid the sword back into its sheath.

'Say hello to your father from me,' he shouted, running from the chamber. The dead watched him go and then turned back to Drew. And advanced.

Drew yanked on the chain futilely, his mind racing with blind panic. Some of the monsters had already started feasting on their dead master, tearing Vankaskan's body to pieces below him. That was Drew's fate. He was going to die like the Rat, devoured by the dead. He shook the chain again, cursing the manacle. He hadn't travelled across Lyssia to die like some poor animal trapped in a snare. *Lose a life . . .*

. . . or lose a hand?

Drew stared up at the moon and let in the Wolf completely. The transformation was fast, racing through his body and giving him new life and energy. The sudden pain in his wrist demanded his attention. His lupine eyes focused, the change continuing as his arm and hand enlarged round the manacle. He could feel bones breaking inside the iron bracelet and tried to banish the pain. When the change was complete he assessed his wrist once more, expecting the hand to have come away.

It was still there, swollen, throbbing, covered in blood. But the hand remained connected to his arm, manacle in place.

The dead had reached the top step now, gathering round him and recognizing the Werewolf as a threat, even with their decaying minds. Drew roared, kicking out at them and slashing with his free arm. Some of them stumbled back but others remained standing, moaning hungrily, looking for a way to the injured Wolf.

Drew's mind was on fire. *Why was it never easy?* He snapped his jaws at the dead.

His jaws.

The Werewolf ran his tongue over his deadly teeth. Quickly his jaws clamped round his hand, biting down hard and worrying it loose. The pain was blinding, but he wouldn't be halted. Drew ripped through the bone, pulling his hand away and spitting it out. He heard the chain and manacle clatter to the ground, free at last.

The dizziness hit him like a tidal wave as his arm bled freely. He collapsed on to the floor, trying to channel his healing therianthropy and stop the blood loss. He felt fingers on him, tugging. He looked up and saw a familiar face. *Broghan? What are you doing here?* Broghan was trying to embrace him, his neck twisted, broken? His mouth was open, black liquid pooling . . .

Drew struggled to remain conscious. He rolled, allowing dead Broghan to land face down on the filthy granite as the other dead arrived. With a silent prayer to Brenn he brought his clawed right hand round and drove the dead Werelord's head into the stone. It stopped moving instantly. Drew scrambled back, tucking his severed wrist into his belly, backing into the drapes as they tumbled around him. He was shifting again, back into the man and away from the Wolf. The cool night air greeted him as he struggled on to the balcony, the dead rising about his feet. He looked to the courtyard five storeys below.

A group ran into the courtroom, Gretchen leading the way with Whitley at her side. The two girls screamed Drew's name. He couldn't find his voice as he stumbled back to the balcony. One of Whitley's companions, a tall leathery skinned fellow who carried knives, pointed up the chamber towards him. They hurried, slashing and stabbing at the dead as they came. There was Harker, longsword in his hand, fighting alongside an old man with a rapier. And there were others, transformed, therians like him and Whitley. The Horselords? They ran into the chamber, cutting down the dead, trying to get to Drew before the corpses did.

Drew staggered, desperate to embrace his friends, so near yet so far. The dead crowded round, pushing him back.

At the last, when he thought he might fall, he felt strong talons grasp him, digging into his shoulder blades like knives, lifting him off the ground. *Am I dead? Is this one of Brenn's angels, carrying me away to meet the maker?*

In seconds he was flying, the dead on the balcony grasping at thin air as he was hoisted into the star strewn sky above Cape Gala. He watched High Stable swiftly disappearing behind him as he struggled to stay awake. His head lolled, eyelids heavy, as he tried to understand what was happening. He saw great wings beating, he saw the sea rushing by, the moon reflected off its rippling surface. And he heard a woman's voice before he was swallowed by the night.

'Sleep, Wolf. You're safe . . . for now . . .'

7

The Lion Unchained

The carriage rocked, perilously close to toppling over as the crowd buffeted it. Lofty Lane was heaving, people struggling to reach the Garden of the Dead, Highcliff's ancient cemetery. Hector hung out of the window to assess the situation, quickly realizing it was impossible. Towards the cliffs the road was thick with panicked townsfolk, fighting to get through the gates to the graveyard. Men of the Thieves Guild shouted them on, urging them towards the garden and the tunnels that awaited them. Ringlin peered down at Hector, shaking his head, as Ibal cracked the whip over the heads of the crowd to no effect. They were going nowhere. Hector collapsed beside Duke Manfred, opposite Queen Amelie and Bethwyn, her lady-in-waiting.

'It's no good, Your Majesty. The streets are choked. We can go no further.'

'Then we must continue on foot,' said Amelie. The sounds of battle floated down Lofty Lane, the Tall Quarter having fallen as the army retreated. Manfred kicked the door open. He was still injured, the brown cloak he wore stained all over by the wounds beneath, but he was moving. The Staglord stepped out of the carriage into the street. The sight of the Werelord, even in human form, caused the townsfolk to pull back in awe. He might have been a shadow of his former self but there was no hiding his nobility. His greatsword strapped across his back, he held his arm up to the carriage and offered it to Amelie.

'My lady.'

Amelie slipped from the wagon to her old friend's side. She was followed by the girl, Bethwyn, carrying her case, and finally Hector. The girl looked terrified, her eyes bigger and darker than ever. Hector reached across and took the case from her, giving her a reassuring nod. He would allow no harm to come to her. The Boarlord paused to speak to his drivers.

'Grab my belongings, leave nothing, and follow us.'

Ringlin and Ibal nodded, dropping the reins and whip immediately to follow their master's orders.

See how late you've left things, brother? Fetching the old woman, so noble a deed. Look at you now – trapped in the city, stuck pig ready for slaughter! See, Hector . . . they come . . .

Hector looked up Lofty Lane over the crowd. Maybe a hundred yards away he could see the battle raging, swords, spears and scimitars clashing in the street. People screamed as the violence closed on them, a thin line of defending soldiers was all that kept the civilians safe. Duke Bergan was up there somewhere, leading the rearguard. The crowd surged on in a panic, too many people trying to get through too small a bottleneck.

They'll be here soon, Hector. Do you have your pretty dagger? You may need it before the night is through . . .

Hector checked he still had his dagger, cursing himself for listening to the vile. He noticed that the sky was brightening; dawn approached. The screaming of a nearby woman alerted everyone's attention to the harbour.

The armada had appeared, filling the southern end of the bay, thousands of ships' lanterns illuminating them on the horizon. The sheer number made Hector's head spin.

'How many ships? How many soldiers?'

Manfred shook his head, pointing up the street towards the battle.

'They don't need the ships; the Dogs are doing all the work for them!'

'This is no good. There has to be another way!'

'There is none,' said the Staglord, catching sight of a couple of Omiri warriors running down an alley. They chased a fleeing watchman, cutting him down from behind. Manfred whipped his greatsword off his back, guarding Amelie and Bethwyn.

'We make a stand here.'

You die here.

'No!' shouted Hector. 'There is another way!'

Bergan's legs pounded between the gravestones, his muscles burning as he pushed his body on. He and the remaining

Wolfguard had been the last line of defence. The civilians had disappeared into the Garden of the Dead, hopefully finding the tunnels. He hoped Carver had kept his side of the deal. Ahead and about him Greycloaks kept pace, stopping occasionally to fire their bows at their pursuers. There were maybe thirty Wolfguard remaining, the best of the best, having given everything in defending Highcliff. The only thing left to give was their lives. Two of Manfred's knights accompanied him, one on each flank, each having shaken off their platemail once the fight had moved from the walls.

A roar bellowed behind, closer now. Bergan risked glancing back, seeing shadows racing between the tombs and crypts, some of them threatening to overtake them.

'Keep going!' he shouted, veering away suddenly in a mighty bound.

The Lionguard was flattened instantly by the Werebear's axe, while his companion brought his sword up with a shriek. Both men were frail looking, the siege of the keep having starved them of their muscle and sanity, but they fought with the fervour of extremists. These were Leopold's most faithful, driven mad by imprisonment within the castle. The second man lunged at the Bear, his Lionhead blade catching Bergan in the ribs. The sword went in like a hot knife through butter, the silver burning his insides on impact. Bergan punched the man through the air, the broken body crashing into a tombstone.

He struggled for breath, catching the sword and whipping it from his torso. He tossed it, sick with pain. Every Lionguard carried silver weapons far more deadly than the

Omiri's. He saw figures moving through the morning mist of the cemetery.

'The noose tightens,' he murmured, turning to run.

Bergan could see the cliffs now, and the ancient tombs of the old Werelords. Sure enough the last of the Greycloaks stood beside the open crypt of the Dragonlords, waiting for him. The tomb of the Dragonlords had long been a holy site for a select few who followed the ancient gods that pre-dated Brenn. Flowers littered the stone steps outside the ancient place, the bouquets flattened underfoot by the fleeing thousands.

Carver stood in the open stone doorway with Captain Fry and the Stag's knights.

'My lord,' said Fry. 'There's a problem.'

'What?' blustered Bergan, breathing heavily.

'The doors,' said Carver. 'There's nothing to stop them from following us.'

'I'll stay here with the men, sire, while you go on,' said Fry. Manfred's knights made noises of approval, deciding to stay and fight as well.

'And when you're dead?' asked Carver. 'Who stops them then?'

Bergan's head ached as if he'd been struck by a hammer blow. The sword wound in his chest wouldn't stop bleeding. He'd stand and fight himself if he had to.

'Did the queen make it through?'

'Was she supposed to? I haven't seen her pass by,' said Carver.

Bergan felt sick. Amelie, Manfred, even young Hector. He'd sent them this way to escape the city. *Where were they?*

The roar of the Lion alerted them all that he was in the Garden of the Dead. The men gathered round Bergan. He'd let them down, every one. The city was lost, the future king gone, his closest friends possibly dead. He'd lost everything. He cast his gaze over the brave men around him, tears streaming from his eyes. Behind, Carver retreated as the roars drew closer.

'I have to go. You'd be right to do the same, Bergan!' he said, beckoning him with an open hand. Bergan looked round the doorway, huge pillars of stone holding up the rocky tunnel. He knew what had to be done.

Raising his huge arms he leaned out across his men to the right, sweeping them back into the tunnel with a mighty paw. Then he did the same with his left, making the soldiers retreat.

'What are you doing?' shouted Fry. Carver put a hand on the man's shoulder, but he shook it off. 'The Lion and the Omiri! They come!'

'Let them come, captain,' bellowed the Bear. 'Go!'

The men backed away as Bergan raised his axe, just as Leopold landed beyond the stone steps outside. The Lion looked ragged, emaciated, his mane matted and torn. His features were lean and angular, his ribs visible down either side of his enormous torso. His red robe trailed in the mud as he rose to his full height, his sword held aloft. Its silver runes glinted in the half light of dawn.

'Bergan!' roared the Werelion, the cry echoing down the tunnel past the Bearlord, every fleeing man, woman and child hearing the rage of Leopold. 'Thief! Take my city would you? If I can't kill the Wolf then his protector will suffice!'

The Werebear shifted his axe in his huge paws as the Lion-guard and Omiri gathered behind the king.

'You'll never get the chance,' said Duke Bergan as he swung his axe.

The huge blade bit deep into the supporting pillar on the right side of the crypt, then was ripped swiftly out again with all Bergan's might. He heaved it to the other wall, smashing the axe head into the opposite pillar, knocking the stonework away. Back again it went as the ceiling crumbled. Leopold roared, mouth foaming like a rabid beast as rocks began to tumble around Bergan. Still he swung his axe, stepping back, retreating, hitting more pillars and sections of the ceiling. Stone lintels tumbled, bouncing off him, knocking him from his feet, his lungs choking with dust.

The last thing the Lord of Brackenholme heard was the roar of the rocks as the cliffs the city took its name from collapsed around him.

Vega's feet danced along the rain-slicked cobbles, his balance his greatest weapon as eight Omiri horseman chased him down. Around him the city was sacked, flames visible in the Tall Quarter on high while the harbour ahead was beginning to fill with Bastian warships. The bay was alive with smaller vessels rowing towards the shore from the anchored armada, each boat loaded with men-at-arms.

Two spears bounced off the street at his feet, reminding the Sharklord to change direction occasionally. He'd remained in human form so as not to draw attention; a shifted therian would draw a crowd for all the wrong reasons. Regardless, the horsemen had found him and weren't giving up the chase. He left behind him a burning fishmarket in the Low Quarter. Ahead he could see the pierhead, and beyond that the *Maelstrom* anchored away out to sea, her sails unfurling, ready for the off. *Faster, you foolish old fish, faster!*

Twenty Omiri foot soldiers emerged at the bottom of Lofty Lane, the street that led directly to the long jetty that ran out to the sea. That had been the route he'd planned to take, the swiftest to his ship. A short hurling spear hit him in the shoulder, causing him to stumble and fly through the air. He skidded along the cobbles as the chasing horsemen surrounded him. He was short of the docks, so close yet so far. Instantly they were on him.

Spears thrust down, jabbing and stabbing, tormenting the Sharklord from every angle. When the spears were lost or deposited in the Werelord's body they switched to their scimitars. The swords proved equally deadly, slicing Vega as he struggled to rise. His hands came up to defend himself, and he felt steel graze bone, cutting his wrists and forearms. Was he the last man standing in Highcliff? Had everyone escaped? A scimitar slashed down his back, tearing into his scalp and sending a cloud of his dark curling locks through the air. That was too much for the Pirate Prince.

Embracing the Shark he came up fighting, lashing out with teeth and hands. Rather than transforming into fins, his arms acquired sheets of flesh connecting his elbows to his torso like bat wings, his hands taking on a clawed form. He'd lost his cutlass long ago. The horses' bellies erupted as he tore into them, their riders tumbling. As they fell he lunged, catching them, tossing them, hurling them back into the air. Bodies fell around him, broken and butchered.

Vega was up and running now, his therian form embraced. Four of the Omiri remained standing, screaming to their companions that they'd found a Werelord. The twenty at the pierhead joined them as they pursued Vega towards the docks.

The Sharklord's feet tore up the ground as he ran. The cobbles were replaced by wooden boards as he thundered along a short jetty between fishing boats and lobster pots. The approaching Bastians saw him now, firing arrows that peppered the jetty and Vega's body. He stumbled, struggling to the end of the jetty. Spears rained down as he staggered to the edge, falling with a great red splash into the cold dark water.

By the time the chasing Omiri and the boatloads of Bastians arrived at the jetty's end, Count Vega was long gone.

8

Honoured Guests

Leopold sat on the stone throne of Highcliff, his hands patting the carved serpents' heads that rode over the arms. It felt good to have his city back, to be able to walk freely out of the great doors and across his drawbridge. He picked up the roast chicken that lay in his lap, tearing the breast off and devouring it in one mouthful. He tore into a drumstick, savouring the flavour. Never had a meal been so fine. He and his men had been prisoners in their own keep for two months. His anger rose again as he choked on the chicken, thinking of the humiliation the Wolf had put him through. How they would suffer, how they would know his rage.

The Rat King gathered round the table below, fighting among one another as they gorged. Vex, the youngest, had taken a haunch of rare beef to one side, his teeth worrying the bloody meat apart. Vorhaas and Vorjavik were busy clawing at one another, their sibling bickering knowing no bounds as they fought over a dish of ribs. The plate flew through the air, ribs skittering along the floor as the Wererats dived after them, hissing at one another as they retrieved the fallen meat. The metal dish rolled round on its edge, spinning, rattling, refusing to stop, the sound grating. A boot slammed down on it, halting its momentum instantly.

'Show some class, you vermin,' spat Vanmorten, the tallest and most formidable brother towering over the others. Even Leopold flinched, his lord chancellor's wicked tongue never failing to impress him. The Rat brothers pulled away from his gaze, picking up the last ribs and standing once more by the table, their bickering ceased, for now.

Vanmorten walked up the steps of the dais towards his king, pausing at the top. Leopold still found it difficult to look at the lord chancellor, even when the Wererat wore his cowl up, as he did now. He'd been hideous enough after losing half his face to Drew, but since the flaming Spyr Oil had removed most of the skin from his body he was even more repugnant. The lord chancellor's therian healing was useless against fire and Vanmorten was stuck in this disfigured state until Brenn finally took him. Only the care of his brothers had kept him alive in the following weeks, nursing him slowly back to health. And the smell was something else. Leopold winced as Vanmorten leaned in close, turning his nose up at the odour of decay.

'Your Majesty. Our guests have arrived.'

Leopold clapped his hands and rose from the throne. The great doors to Highcliff Hall swung open as a procession of soldiers marched in. Leopold's weary Lionguard stood to attention around the chamber, eyeing the new arrivals as they filed in. The Omiri came first, seven in all, dressed in the garb of tribal leaders. The man who led them was very tall for an easterner. He had a wide face and a snub nose. A black moustache draped down his face on either side, the waxed ends braided together beneath his square jaw.

The tall Omiri noble didn't bow, instead coming to a standstill halfway across the throne room. He stopped short of walking to the throne, an act that Leopold thought odd and rather disrespectful. The man's companions gathered on either side of him, looking around the great hall as if they were considering buying the place. The tall one simply stared at Leopold.

The Dogs having taken their places, it was time for the Cats. Leopold's face lit up as he saw his cousins stride through the huge doors of the ancient throne room, flanked by twenty armed Bastian warriors. The soldiers wore a mixture of leather breastplates and chain shirts, swords, spears and shields buckled to their hips and backs. The sight of them sent Leopold back to his childhood and the warriors who had fought for his father. Bast was a truly beautiful land, jungles buttressing up against the mighty cities of the Catlords, with their towers and palaces reaching towards the sun. Its men were brave, fearless and devoted to their therian masters. This was what the Lionguard was missing: warrior men of Bast.

A young felinthrope unfamiliar to Leopold ran into the room ahead of the others. The king waved as the Werelord approached. He was a pale-skinned fellow with white hair who carried a long staff in one hand, but the Cat ignored the king. His pink eyes blinked as he stared at the three Wererats who stood by the table. He hissed suddenly, causing the older Rat twins a moment of tension. Leopold raised his hand in alarm, staying their response. The albino Catlord slunk back, tapping his staff on the flagged floor as he retreated.

Next into the chamber came the enchanting Opal. She was in deep conversation with Field Marshal Tiaz, the Tiger, high commander of the Cat armies. Their conversation didn't cease and they didn't acknowledge Leopold. They continued talking as they made their way to the opposite side of the hall from the Doglords.

Leopold could see the alarmed faces of his Lionguard. Nobody behaved in this way in the court of the king.

Last to enter the chamber was the Werepanther, followed by his own entourage of courtiers. Two tremendous black jaguars, as large as horses, prowled along on either side of him. The Pantherlord was seven feet high, a giant among his brethren. He seemed almost as wide, his purple black skin glistening as the early morning sunlight caught him from behind. Leopold squinted as his cousin approached.

The Pantherlord's arms, legs and feet were bare. The top of his broad bald head was scarred, the smooth skin scored by claw wounds from combat with other therian lords. The only clothing that graced his dark flesh was the loincloth round his groin and the golden breastplate across his chest. He carried no weapon. He'd never needed one. He was the most fearsome therianthrope in all the known worlds: Onyx, the Beast of Bast.

'Welcome to my city, cousin,' said Leopold, striding forward to meet him with his arms open wide. Onyx sidestepped him and pointed towards the throne. The white haired Catlord was sitting in it, lounging casually as he stared at the ceiling.

'Show some respect!' His voice boomed like an earthquake. Leopold's stomach reverberated. Instantly the albino was off and down the steps, standing beside Opal and Tiaz.

'It doesn't matter, Lord Onyx,' blustered Leopold, adjusting the crown on his head. 'Treat my home as your own.'

The Panther stalked by, not having spoken to the king directly yet. Leopold glanced at the Rat Kings, the five brothers watching with keen interest. Before he knew it the crown was gone from his head. Leopold turned and saw Onyx holding it, inspecting the plain iron headpiece.

'Not really your style is it?'

'The crown?' Leopold's face was red. This was outrageous. 'It's the ancient crown of Westland. He who wears it rules over the whole of Lyssia.'

Onyx arched an eyebrow.

'Interesting.' He placed it on his head, where it perched, not fitting. 'Does it suit me?'

Opal laughed where she stood nearby. The albino clapped his hands. Leopold tried to snatch the crown back, and Onyx stepped out of reach, plucking it off his own head. He waited a moment before handing it back to the Lion.

'You've been sloppy, Leopold,' said Onyx, strolling round him. 'Look at what you've done to this continent.'

'What *I've* done?' gasped Leopold. 'I've faced down a

revolution. That hound Wergar has an offspring, a boy who's laid claim to *my* throne! They all connive with him, the Bear, the Stags, the Shark!'

'You led them to that, by being a weak ruler.'

'They've never accepted me!'

Onyx turned suddenly, growing in size while Leopold seemed to shrink.

'You came here fifteen years ago and we supported you. We supplied warriors, warships and weapons. We gave our gold to your war chest. And we waited. We waited for fifteen years to see that gold return, and more. Bounty, you called it. You told us Lyssia was there for the taking. That you'd return with wealth beyond imagination. And what do we get in the end?'

Onyx pointed across the room to his entourage.

'An outrider. You send a human to us, begging for our aid. No gold, not even a single copper. So we come. We're here. Now.'

The Catlords all stared at Leopold. Their eyes were fixed on him. The Lion didn't know where to look.

'We can still have that bounty, cousin! Let us, the Catlords of Bast, crush our enemies together!'

Onyx backhanded Leopold across the face, the crack of his jaw echoing around the court. Leopold looked back, eyes wide with shock.

'Do not *dare* describe yourself as a Catlord, Lion. Look at you, a stinking, broken wretch without a friend in the world. You're a disgrace!'

'I have friends,' shouted Leopold, his fists clenching as his chest grew. He wouldn't stand for it, not in *his* court. *This self*-aggrandizing *Prince of Bast thought he could strike the King of Lyssia, did he?* 'I have the Rats of Vermire!'

The Lion gestured to his lord chancellor, surprised to see Vanmorten was no longer at his side having joined his brothers nearby. They looked away, all except Vanmorten who stared back.

'Vanmorten?' asked Leopold, his voice breaking as his body began to change.

He felt a clawed hand tear down his back, ripping the red, royal robe off his shoulders. He spun, roaring, lashing out at Onyx, but the Panther was quickfooted and beyond his reach. Turning to try to strike the Beast of Bast had left his rear and flanks open. Opal hit him from behind, crossing her claws across her brother Panther's blow. Tiaz slashed his clawed fist down Leopold's right ribs, while the albino darted in to rake at his left. They withdrew as quickly as they'd attacked, leaving Leopold on trembling legs.

The emaciated Lionguard, those most faithful to Leopold, were moving for their weapons, but they were too slow and too weary after their endeavours. The Bastian warriors poured over them, the air misting with the blood of fallen Redcloaks. Leopold watched in horror.

'Why do this? We are family!'

'Don't worry, Leopold,' said Onyx, returning to his entourage who parted for him. 'There's nothing more important than family to me.'

When he turned he revealed Prince Lucas. Scars etched the side of his face, three livid lines that spoiled his pretty looks.

Onyx placed a hand on the young Lion's shoulder and propelled him forward.

'My boy,' sobbed Leopold, opening his tired arms to embrace him. 'My beautiful boy . . .'

Lucas approached his father, his face twisted and his eyes wild with emotion; hate, anger, lust. Leopold looked up at the prince and didn't recognize him. The prince was changing, claws growing, teeth jutting from his jaws. Where was the boy he'd nursed and cherished? The child he'd spoiled and indulged? Where was his son?

'Lucas?' he whispered, as his son pounced.

The iron crown flew off the king's head with the impact, rolling along the flagged floor as the young Lion tore into the old one. The crown bounced, beginning a final clattering spin as it started to turn in on itself. A black booted foot slammed down on to it, the crown clanging against the stone as it stopped suddenly. Vanmorten bent to pick it up with a burned and blackened hand as the king screamed under the murderous onslaught.

Onyx looked at Vanmorten and the Wererat looked back. And bowed.

Epilogue: Fractured Family

Clenching and unclenching his fist, Hector pumped life back into his hand. The tingling sensation, not unlike the dead arm one felt when the blood had been cut off, slowly disappeared. Whipping his black glove off he unfurled his fingers to inspect the black mark. It filled his palm like a big black inkstain, the skin discoloured and showing no sign of returning to normal. He glanced over his shoulder as he heard footsteps approaching across the creaking floorboards, quickly tugging the glove back on.

Ashamed, brother? You should show the black as a badge of honour!

Duke Manfred appeared at his shoulder, clapping a hand on to Hector's back and banishing the vile instantly.

'What are you doing lurking down here in the dark, Hector? We could do with another head at the table, if you follow. We need to make sense of this.'

'Certainly, Your Grace,' said the magister, smiling politely.
'You can drop the title now, Hector. You're the Baron of
Redmire for Brenn's sake. We're equals now.'

Manfred set off through the hold back to the staircase, Hector
following. The two Werelords made their way through the ship
and back on the deck of the *Maelstrom*, which was cutting an
elegant line through the White Sea. Hector looked back through
the gathering dusk, catching sight of the smaller vessels that
followed: five ships, packed with refugees who hadn't made it to
the tunnels below Highcliff. The deck of the *Maelstrom* remained
relatively uncluttered, the Wolf's Council insisting that as their
only fighting ship the pirate vessel must remain free of civilians.

The cabin boy, Casper, stared at Hector as the Boarlord
strode past, his robes trailing along the dry deck. The rain had
ceased when they'd departed Highcliff days earlier, the city
flaming in their wake. Cold northern winds had replaced it,
autumn closing her grip over Lyssia. With clear skies ahead
the mood had lifted on the ship, some of the crew laughing
and even singing. It seemed to Hector that sailors needed to
sail. Casper watched him go, eyeing him intently. Hector
stared back, slightly unnerved by the boy's hard stare.

Arriving on the poop deck at the rear of the *Maelstrom* they
found Figgis at the wheel. The mate nodded as they passed.
Sitting in a fixed chair on the viewing deck was Queen Amelie,
wrapped in Duke Manfred's old grey winter cloak. The warm,
grateful smile she threw to the Staglord wasn't missed by
Hector. Bethwyn, her shy lady-in-waiting, stood at her shoulder, doe eyes watching the Werelords. Hector smiled at her,
wishing he could think of something charming to say.

'Gentlemen,' said Captain Vega, clapping his hands together. The sea marshal ran up on to the deck, a long scroll curled up under his arm. 'Glad you could make it. I'd like to hear your thoughts.'

Hector observed the Sharklord as he joined the gathered therians, watching how confident he was. Vega smiled at them all, bowing flamboyantly as was his way.

Resilient isn't he? The voice hissed in Hector's ear. *He seems remarkably happy considering the mess you're all in.*

'He's as scared as the rest of us,' whispered Hector, the wind stealing his voice from the ears of his companions.

He's a good actor then, brother. He's a shark, a monster, a killer. I don't trust him and nor should you.

Vega unfurled the scroll, revealing a sea chart to his fellow Werelords. He held it down over a raised hatch as they gathered round.

'We may be homeless, but we're still the Wolf's Council,' said Vega.

'Indeed,' nodded Manfred. 'And we need to decide where we're heading.'

They looked at the map, revealing the northernmost shores of Lyssia. Manfred's finger jabbed at the map, indicating the Sturmish port of Roof.

'Perhaps Duke Henrik of Icegarden can aid us?'

'Henrik?' Vega shrugged. 'He hardly raced to swear allegiance to Drew, did he? Who knows what the White Bear is planning for himself? It's hard to know where we'll find allies any more.'

Amelie traced her fingertip over Shadowhaven in the east, her homeland.

'We have allies out there, Vega. They just might be hard to find.'

'Enemies, on the other hand, surround us,' snarled the Sharklord, punching the map. 'We're close to Slotha's land now, and can expect her raiders to be patrolling the sea. Vermire, cityport of the Ratlords, isn't so far away either, hardly a safe port of call. And the Kraken, Ghul, is at our back all the while, setting my own pirates of the Cluster Isles against me!'

Vega stroked his throat and looked out to sea, scanning the distant horizon.

'Yes, enemies surround us.'

Hector stepped away as they reviewed the map. He looked on to the deck and caught sight of Ringlin and Ibal, the fat one nodding at him as he whittled away at a length of wood with his wickedly curved dagger. Hector looked back at Vega as the captain of the *Maelstrom* held court.

Keep an eye on him, Hector. He can't be trusted.

'No,' muttered the magister to himself, clenching his gloved fist. 'I'm not sure he can.'

The camp was quiet but for the gentle sounds of Romari harps and lutes. The weather was clement enough, but it was on the turn, autumn now mistress of the Longridings. The grasslands were faded, the green bleached to yellow as the life drained from the plains. Three hundred tents dotted the slopes of the east ridings, home to the refugees from Cape Gala. Stragglers were joining all the time as word of the camp spread to those who had escaped the city of the Horselords. The folk who'd fled had joined forces with those of the shanty town and the Romari, sharing what they had with their fellow men as they left the city port in search of a new home. A safe home.

The surviving Lords of the Longridings had set up their tents at the heart of the encampment. Lorimer and many of the senior Horselords had been slain in High Stable, and as Viscount Colt had wickedly sided with the Catlords, all eyes were on the young Lord Conrad. He was grateful for the presence of Baron Ewan, the old Ramlord providing guidance at this difficult time for him. Expectation weighed heavy on the blond Horselord's shoulders.

'It makes no sense,' said Conrad. 'He can't have simply disappeared. There was only one way off that balcony, and that would have been a fatal fall to the courtyard below.'

'No body was found in the courtyard,' repeated Ewan, not for the first time. 'He didn't fall.'

'Then what are we to believe?' asked Gretchen. 'Drew sprouted wings and flew away?'

Conrad looked to Ewan who shrugged, tugging at his short, stubby beard. Whitley put her hand on Gretchen's shoulder to calm her.

'There's no point us arguing about this,' said the Bearlord's daughter. 'What's done is done. Drew is gone, and we don't know where. We can only hope we find him before the Catlords do.'

Gretchen placed her hand over Whitley's and gave it a squeeze. The two young Wercladies had become closer, the Fox of Hedgemoor helping Whitley grieve for Broghan. They had been close before, but the loss of a loved one brought them closer still. Both of them feared for the well-being of Drew.

'So where to?' asked Gretchen, struggling to stay calm while the young man who'd chased after her across Lyssia remained missing.

'The Horselords will head to Calico,' said Conrad on behalf of his brethren. 'Duke Brand, the Bull-lord, will provide shelter and arms, I don't doubt that for a minute. We'll regroup and ready ourselves for the Bastians' next move.'

They all nodded approvingly at this. Gretchen met his gaze, smiling grimly. It was refreshing to hear Conrad's decisive words after the inaction of the Horselords in Cape Gala. He knew he was in a fight, and he was stepping up to be counted. Ewan clapped him on the back.

'I shall stay with this young Stallion as long as I'm needed, before heading back to Haggard. My city is insignificant to the Catlords, but I'd rather get home and prepare for whatever comes. War approaches and I want my people to be ready.'

Whitley spoke on behalf of herself and Gretchen. The two girls had discussed their next steps and had been in total agreement.

'Lady Gretchen and I shall head to Brackenholme. The perils of the Dymling Road and the danger of Wylderman attack should dissuade anyone from assaulting the city. The Woodland Realm is my home, a fortress that nobody would dare wage war upon. It's the safest place for us. Hopefully my father will be there upon our return. He'll know what to do.'

'And I'll escort you there.'

The group turned to see Stirga, the Romari sword-swallower, stepping out from the shadows of the tents. The old man had taken on the role of spokesperson for the Romari, an act that was met with hearty approval after his heroism in Cape Gala. Gretchen and Whitley both smiled up at him.

'That's very kind of you, Stirga, but we'll be fine,' said Whitley.

'I'll hear none of it,' said the Romari, settling down beside them, cross-legged in front of the fire. 'There are predators out there. We've only been in the grasslands for four nights and there've been three youngsters gone missing already.'

'Another child is gone?' gasped Gretchen. Three children missing in four nights, taken from their beds while they slept; she shivered at the thought. Conrad sighed.

'There are beasts that roam the Longridings that might have done such a thing. Not to offend but there are wolves, bears and even big cats; it could be any one of those creatures. Stirga, I'll make sure there are more bodies on watch at night. See if we can halt these attacks.'

The Romari nodded.

'So I'll be accompanying you to Brackenholme, m'ladies. Let's not forget, nobody knows the roads like the Romari.'

Before Gretchen and Whitley could reply, a commotion in the camp caused them all to rise from where they sat, as Captain Harker and Quist made their way towards the fire. A crowd of people followed, speaking animatedly, the two Greencloaks escorting a young boy between them. As they approached the Werelords the boy looked between them, eyes wide and fearful.

'Who's this?' asked Conrad, trying not to intimidate the lad any further.

'Just arrived from Cape Gala, a merchant's son,' said Harker, his hand on the boy's shoulder. 'He lived in one of the big town houses outside High Stable. Tell his lordship what you told me, boy. Don't be afraid.'

The boy was dumbstruck, unable to find words.

Whitley stepped forward and knelt before him, taking his hands in her own. She smiled and nodded, encouraging the boy to speak. He cleared his throat.

'The Wolf,' he said. 'The one they had imprisoned in the citadel. I saw how he flew out of there.'

'Flew?' said Whitley, her big brown eyes wide with astonishment.

Harker nodded beside the boy before leaning in.

'You're not going to believe this, my lady.'

A bucket of icy water over his head woke Drew abruptly from his slumber, the young Wolf shouting with shock at the rude awakening. He lay on the floor inside the belly of a pitching ship, a lantern swinging over his head and sending nightmarish shadows around the room. The walls were bare, no portholes, no furniture, the only creature comfort the bucket for him to use as needed. He wore his tattered breeches, pitted with dirt, sweat and blood. His ribs were proud above his stomach, hunger gnawing within. *How long has it been since I've eaten?*

As the lantern continued its pendulous motion, he noticed a woman standing against the wall. She wore a leather coat tied about her waist by a large red sash. Her long black hair was braided and piled on top of her head. She cocked her head as he looked at her, appraising him with cold, grey unblinking eyes. He was about to ask her a question when a fist from behind caught him on his temple. He hit the deck, splashing into the icy water, head spinning.

'Is there any need for that?' asked the woman.

'Every need,' replied a familiar voice. 'He's an animal.'

Drew blinked, eyes focusing on the woman as she sneered at his assailant.

'Where am I? What happened?'

'Don't you *dare*!' said the woman, stepping away from the wall and raising her hand past Drew. By the sound of her voice she could back up her threat. 'He's still a Werelord, Djogo, prisoner or not!'

Djogo; Kesslar's captain. Drew looked back at the towering man as he was lit up briefly by the swinging lantern. He filled the open doorway behind, glaring down at Drew with his one good eye. The Wolf had taken the other. Beyond the slave-master, Drew could see a wooden staircase up into the ship. Drew turned back to the woman.

'It was you in the dream, carrying me.'

'It was no dream, Wolf. I brought you here, to this ship.'

Drew recalled being carried through the air, talons in his shoulders and wings beating overhead. What kind of therian-thrope was she?

'How did you get me out of there? Why bring me to him?' said Drew, his voice thick with anger.

'Excellent, our guest awakes at last!'

The voice was Kesslar's, the Goatlord walking down the wooden staircase into the room.

'I feared you were dead, lad,' said the Goat. 'Five days asleep! Can you imagine that? You must feel like a king now after all that rest.'

Drew didn't answer, his eyes locked on the woman.

'Why do you work for him?

'We all have our reasons.'

'We all work for somebody, Drew,' said Kesslar, crouching on his haunches in front of him, looking him up and down. He reached a hand out and took hold of Drew's ear, turning his face one way and the other as if examining a bull at the market.

'Will he be well enough to perform?'

'He should be,' said Djogo. 'Once you've fed him.'

'Excellent.'

'You murdered those people,' said Drew. 'In Haggard. You killed Lord Dorn, the young Bull!'

'He had to be made an example of. I shall not tolerate disobedience among my stock. You, however, having nothing to fear, you're worth *infinitely* more to me than some common Bull.'

Drew retraced his steps in his mind. The events in the city of the Horselords. He remembered being held by Vankaskan, the walking dead, the fight . . . He looked down at his hands. The left was now gone, a bandaged stump in its place. He nodded slowly to himself.

'Is this the point where you lose your mind, boy?' laughed the Goat, standing and pointing at the stump Drew cradled in his right arm. 'That was your own doing. Amazing what you're prepared to do when your life depends upon it, isn't it?'

'Be grateful I was able to see to the wound,' whispered the woman as she walked past towards the door. Drew was instantly intrigued; though hard, the woman had shown kindness to him. Was she also a prisoner of the Goatlord?

'No screaming? No wailing? You disappoint me, Drew,' said Kesslar.

Drew looked up at the Goatlord, and calmly smiled, steely eyed. Kesslar arched his brow, unnerved, a smile the last thing he'd expected from the young Wolf.

For the first time since the murder of Tilly Ferran, the woman who'd raised him as her own, Drew saw everything clearly. He felt as if everything had led to this moment of clarity, locked away in the belly of a filthy slave ship. He'd gnawed off his hand because he was a survivor. He wouldn't be beaten by the Rat. He wouldn't be beaten by the Lion. And if he could face such wicked adversaries he could certainly take anything the Goatlord might throw at him. A determination within told him that he could face anything and defeat it.

He was Drew of the Dyrewood, son of Wergar the Wolf, Lord of Lyssia and rightful king of Westland, and he would run no more. His people needed him, and he would be there for them. He was no longer afraid of his destiny. He now embraced it, and he felt stronger, more powerful and more resolute than ever.

Kesslar nervously reached past Drew to take something from Djogo, while the young man still stared confidently at him. He threw a huge piece of raw meat on the floor in front of him, the blood instantly pooling round it. Kesslar then followed his lieutenant from the room, Djogo locking the door behind his master.

'Eat up, boy. You'll need your energy where we're going. We'll need you fighting fit for the Furnace.'

The Furnace: Dorn, the slain Bull, had mentioned the arena to Drew. So Kesslar wanted the Wolf to be his gladiator? Drew nodded grimly to himself. The Goatlord was going to get so much more. Nothing would stand in the way of Drew and his return home to his friends and family.

A return to Lyssia.

Sorin's mouth was dry. He risked a quick look at the men behind him, their faces displaying a similar look of fear. He turned back to stare at the vast frame of Onyx in front of him, as the Pantherlord inspected the sacked courtroom of High Stable. The white haired Catlord wandered nearby, stepping gracefully between the corpses. They moved in a way that was unlike the Werelords of Lyssia. They were more bestial. Two dozen of Sorin's fellow soldiers stood in the open doorway, afraid to enter. All of them watched the Beast of Bast, waiting for him to react.

The chamber was littered with decapitated and hacked-up bodies, the air thick with the buzzing of flies. Crows had gathered on the circular steps, fresh from feasting on the dead. They hopped out of the way as Onyx advanced towards the balcony, the albino hissing at them with annoyance.

Finally Onyx turned. In his hand he held the stripped skull

of Lord Vankaskan, the features of the Rat not quite obliter-
ated in death. He tossed it down to the albino and stared at
Sorin. His voice made the sergeant's head thrum.

'The Wolf did this?'

'He . . . and his friends,' said Sorin, his voice cracking. 'The
Horselords, Your Highness. The Ram as well, he was with
them and the Romari. All conspirators.'

'And Vankaskan? My sister left him in command. How did
he let it come to this?'

'I served him for many years alongside Prince Lucas. I fear
his fascination with necromancy was his downfall, your highness. He was gripped by dark magicks.'

'There are worse things one could be gripped by,' said the
albino Catlord, shaking the skull as if trying to coax a word
from it. Sorin shivered.

Onyx bent down and pushed a corpse to one side, having
found something in the carnage. He pulled it out, brushing
the flies from it, before showing it to the others. He held the
severed transformed, clawed hand of a lycanthrope that bore
a white metal ring on its index finger. He pulled the ring off
and rolled it in his palm.

'The mark of Wergar,' he smiled, revealing the Wolfshead
to his men.

'If that's the Wolf's paw, I'll take it,' said the albino, gratefully receiving it from the Pantherlord.

'I need to find this Wolf,' growled Onyx as he stared at the
ring. 'Leopold was weak and deserved what came his way, but
the weakness ends now. There can be no opposition to King
Lucas. No alternative to a Catlord on the throne. Wergar was

a monster and the time of the Wolves is over. So long as this one lives he mocks the Lords of Bast.'

There was a noise from the soldiers in the doorway, as they parted and one broke ranks. He wasn't a Bastian warrior, and he wore the red cloak of the Lionguard. He walked up to the Beast and bowed low. Sorin recognized him immediately.

'Up,' said Onyx, looking to the others for an answer. 'Who's this?'

'The outrider, my lord,' said Sorin, seeking the Catlord's pleasure. He hadn't seen the young scout since they'd parted ways in Highcliff many moons ago. The outrider looked older, stronger, tougher. 'Prince Lucas sent him to you on behalf of his father.'

'Ahhh,' said the Werepanther, smiling at the man. 'I do remember; the messenger. You braved the enemy lines, the wilderness and the ocean to seek our aid for your king, didn't you? You have the heart of a panther, human. What do you want?'

'I can help you find the Wolf. I can kill him for you.'

The albino laughed, and even Sorin grinned nervously. What was this fool doing making such a brave boast? Was he mad? He was still mulling this when the young soldier reached forward and snatched the Wolfshead blade from the sheath at Sorin's hip.

'Not so fast,' shouted the captain, his decorum lost. 'That's mine!'

'I don't think so,' replied the outrider, staring at him coldly.

'Silence!' snapped Onyx at Sorin, and the captain went mute. 'How do you expect to find him? Why should he let you close to him?'

'I know him, Your Highness,' said the outrider, removing his own sword from his sheath and throwing it at Sorin's feet. 'He'll trust me.'

'How do you know him?' sneered Onyx, his eyes narrowing at the young human.

'My name is Trent Ferran,' said the outrider, slamming the Wolfshead blade home into his scabbard.

'He's my brother.'